SUMMER AT THE CORNISH CAFE

Phillipa Ashley writes warm, funny romantic fiction for a variety of world-famous international publishers.

After studying English at Oxford, she worked as a copywriter and journalist. Her first novel, *Decent Exposure*, won the RNA New Writers Award and was made into a TV movie called *12 Men of Christmas* starring Kristin Chenoweth and Josh Hopkins. As Pippa Croft, she also wrote the Oxford Blue series – *The First Time We Met*, *The Second Time I Saw You* and *Third Time Lucky*.

Phillipa lives in a Staffordshire village and has an engineer husband and scientist daughter who indulge her arty whims. She runs a holiday-let business in the Lake District, but a big part of her heart belongs to Cornwall. She visits the county several times a year for 'research purposes', an arduous task that involves sampling cream teas, swimming in wild Cornish coves and following actors around film shoots in a camper van. Her hobbies include watching *Poldark*, Earl Grey tea, Prosecco-tasting and falling off surf boards in front of RNLI lifeguards.

PHILLIPA ASHLEY

Summer at the Cornish Cafe

avon.

Avon
A division of HarperCollins*Publishers*
1 London Bridge Street
London SE1 9GF
www.harpercollins.co.uk

A Paperback Original 2017
6
Copyright © Phillipa Ashley 2016

Phillipa Ashley asserts the moral right to
be identified as the author of this work.

A catalogue record for this book is
available from the British Library

ISBN 978-0-00-824830-7

Set in Minion by Palimpsest Book Production Limited, Falkirk, Stirlingshire

Printed and bound by
CPI Group (UK) Ltd, Croydon, CR0 4YY

For Rowena Kincaid,
One of a kind

Never give up, for that is just the place and time that the tide will turn.

Harriet Beecher Stowe

PROLOGUE

'Good morning, good people of Kernow! This is your favourite local DJ, Greg Stennack, coming to you live and kicking from The Breakfast Show *on Radio St Trenyan. So wakey wakey all you lazy folk still snoring under your duvets! The sun's shining, the surf's up and it's a fabulous start to the Easter weekend. Whether you're a local or a visitor to our bee-yoo-tiful corner of West Cornwall, remember to stay tuned to the county's brightest and best independent radio station for the coolest sounds, the hottest news and the tastiest commercials from our station sponsors: Hayleigh's Pasty Shack. Now, let's kick off the show with 'Happy' by Pharrell. Take it away, Pha—'*

After emerging from a nightmare in which a giant pasty was attacking me, I find the 'off' button on the radio alarm and cut Greg off in his prime. It's actually a shame to cut off Pharrell too, but I need to get up, have a shower and get ready for work. I can already hear my boss, Sheila, singing along to the radio in the kitchen of the cafe, two floors below my attic room, even though it's only six a.m.

Did I say *six*? With a groan, I pull the duvet over my head again but a wet nose nudges its way under the bottom edge and a warm tongue licks my big toe. It's not only Greg who wants me to wakey wakey.

1

'OK, boy. I hadn't forgotten about you,' I mumble through the cover.

My dog, Mitch, clearly doesn't believe me and I let out an 'oof' as four paws land on the middle of my stomach.

I throw off the duvet to find a hairy muzzle in my face and a waft of early-morning doggy breath in my nostrils.

'Eww, Mitch. What did you eat last night? OK. OK. I am getting up!'

After gently pushing Mitch off me, I drag myself out of bed, and cross to the skylight in the roof of the attic. Standing on tiptoes, I tug back the blue gingham curtain, push the skylight open a crack and peep outside. My eyes blink at the dazzling brightness. Although it's still early, the sky above the little seaside village of St Trenyan is already postcard blue and I can almost taste the salt on the air. A tractor chugs up and down the beach opposite the cafe where I started work a few weeks ago, raking the sand ready for the deckchairs to be laid out.

The masts of boats bob up and down in the harbour at the far side of the beach. A few people are already up, jogging along the flat sand or flinging balls into the sea for their dogs. As the breeze carries the rattle of the tractor and snatches of distant barks through the window, Mitch yips excitedly. I take a deep gulp of the air and close the window. It's Easter: the turn of the tide, a fresh day and the start of a new summer.

I wonder what this one will bring.

CHAPTER ONE

You can always spot the customers who are going to be trouble, no matter how hard you try to please them, but as I grab my notebook ready to take his order, I know that the man at table sixteen won't be one of them.

Crammed in a corner under the kitchen extractor fan, that table has a wonky leg and most people only take it as a last resort, but I saw the guy head straight for it, even though there were other seats with better views at the time.

Sheila's Beach Hut has the best spot of any cafe in St Trenyan, but he might as well be back in some trendy London espresso bar. He pores over an article in *The Times*, oblivious to the clotted-cream sand or the turquoise sea with its frilly wavelets or the holidaymakers, of all shapes, ages and sizes, sunbathing and playing cricket on the beach in front of the cafe. The water's too cold even for a paddle this early in the year, but there are some hardy surfers at the far end of the beach, catching the bigger breakers. The Surf School has pushed out its racks of wetsuits and yellow foam boards, and set up its sign, promising to teach anyone to ride a wave in a two-hour lesson. Like, yeah. I've lived in Cornwall all my life and I've never managed it so far.

I flip over my notebook, pen poised. 'Can I take your order, sir?'

'Hmm . . .'

'May I get you something, sir?'

'Double espresso,' he mutters, without even glancing up from the article in the newspaper. It's in the features section and there's a picture of a glamorous blonde standing behind a camera on a film set. Perhaps he's not so highbrow after all?

'Anything else with that? Toastie? Cake? We also have some homemade blueberry muffins.'

'Just the coffee,' he growls and suddenly flips over the page to the book review section.

OK, fine. If you don't want one of the *delicious* muffins that I baked this morning, I think. 'Coming up, sir.'

'There's no need to call me sir,' he says, then adds a gruff, 'Thanks.'

I could tell him that he's nothing special and that I say the same to all the male customers, from twenty-five to ninety-five and anyway, I've seen his type before. Though I can't see his face properly, his arms and hands are deeply tanned, even after the winter. His khaki sweatshirt hangs off his lean body and his black beanie hat is pulled over his ears, though the sun is beating down. Typical surfing wannabe, probably on a gap yah from his job in the City. Probably flew straight to Cornwall from Bondi Beach or a French alpine resort. Probably has his skis and surf board in the boot of his 4x4 on the drive of his parents' holiday home in Rock. Not that I'm judgemental, much.

Feeling as hot as the pasties in my white shirt and black trousers, I weave my way onto the terrace. Every table, inside and out, is now taken, and people are even perched on the wall overlooking St Trenyan beach. As well as its fantastic views and Sheila's famous pasties, the Beach Hut has an easygoing atmosphere that makes it a popular spot for surfers, families and dog owners alike.

'Hey, you there!'

A customer barks at me from table twelve. She can only be in her twenties but has the air of an older, more harassed woman. Judging by the likeness, she's obviously with her father and a younger sister who looks as if she's in her late teens – a few years younger than me. Unlike beanie man, the older daughter definitely wants to be noticed. With her fitted black business suit, high heels and heavy make-up, she stands out like a sore thumb from the tourists. None of her party seem happy to be at the cafe, however. The father has a permanent scowl and the teenage daughter is a goth, so maybe she'd look miserable anyway.

The woman in the suit glances at her diamante watch and purses her lips.

'*Excuse* me. Did you hear? We've been waiting for *hours*. When are you going to actually take *our* order?'

Actually, she's only been here five minutes but I give her my shiniest smile. The customer is always right and I can't afford to upset any of them because Mitch and I need this job more than you would ever believe.

'I'm sorry about that, madam.'

'You obviously haven't planned your staffing levels accordingly.'

I could tell her the staff consists of me, Sheila, her niece (who turns up as long as there's no decent surf) and Henry (who called in sick with an infected nipple ring this morning) but I don't think it would help.

'Apologies. I'll pass on your feedback to the manager. Now, may I take your order, please, so we can get you served as soon as possible?'

'We haven't decided yet, have we?' She throws out the challenge to her family. Her goth sister keeps her eyes fixed on her phone while their middle-aged father frowns at the menu and lets out a bored sigh. Fixing on a smile, I answer a long list of queries about the menu and wait for them to make up their minds.

Twenty minutes later, having delivered the beanie man's espresso, served several other tables and taken a load of orders, Sheila shouts to me over the top of the serving counter in the kitchen. Her face is red as she slides steaming pasties and a slice of quiche onto three plates. 'There you go. One steak, a cheese and bacon and a spinach and ricotta quiche for table twelve. You said they're awkward customers, so I've given them extra garnish.'

'Thanks, Sheila. I'm on it now.'

'And can you clear some tables before you come back, please? It's mayhem out there but we need to get as many customers as we can over the holiday weekend. I can't believe the weather we're having this early in the year. This is the warmest Easter I've ever known. If this is global warming, bring it on.'

'No problem, boss.'

Sheila doesn't stand for any nonsense but she's very fair and while the money is only minimum wage, it comes with something far more important to me. She lets me and my beloved dog, Mitch, sleep in the tiny loft conversion above the cafe free of charge. Despite the long hours and the difficult customers, I'm beyond grateful to have a job and a warm place to stay after months of uncertainty, sleeping on couches, in hostels and occasionally even roughing it in the caves along the bay. I don't mind admitting that it's been a tough time but Sheila's kindness had proved there were people willing to help in the world.

Blowing a strand of hair that's escaped from its scrunchie out of my eyes, I dump my tray of dirty crockery beside the dishwasher. Sheila carefully heaps fresh salad and homemade coleslaw next to the pasty and the quiche. The spicy aromas waft under my nostrils and make my stomach rumble almost as loudly as the extractor fan, but there's no time for us to eat yet.

'Demi, wait!' Sheila calls as I'm half in and half out of the door to the cafe.

'What?'

'Can you possibly do something about Mitch's barking? I don't mind him staying in the flat while you're at work but some of the customers have been asking if he's OK.'

My heart sinks but I nod. 'I'll try to get him to settle down in my break. I'm sorry but it's new for him here and he misses me.'

'I know but do your best,' says Sheila with a brief smile. Then she's gone, already preparing the next order.

From the flat above, Mitch whines again. I really hope I can settle him down but he gets so excited, with so many interesting canine smells and noises drifting up from the cafe. We already went for a jog together on the beach before dawn and I'll take him for another walk when I eventually get my break.

Back on table twelve, the younger daughter of the family brightens a little as I smile at her and hand over the spinach quiche but her sister and father are stony faced as I serve them.

'Here's your lunch, madam, sir. I'm very sorry for the delay.'

'About time, too. I could have made the pasties myself.' Her tone is icy. Her eyebrows are also weird, so weird that it's hard not to stare.

Gritting my teeth, I offer them cutlery wrapped in serviettes. 'Once again, I apologise for the wait, madam, and I'll certainly pass on your feedback to the owner.'

'Make sure you do and you can also inform her we're not paying for my meal.'

'You tell her, Mawgan,' says the father to his older daughter, while the young goth sister glances down at the ground, embarrassed. I feel sorry for her.

'I'll have to ask the owner about your bill.' I feel faintly sick. I can't just give away Sheila's food. She's only the tenant at the cafe and her profit margins are wafer thin as it is.

'I don't care . . . and what's this? Coleslaw? I specifically asked for *no* coleslaw.' Mawgan wrinkles her nose at the pasties.

'I'll have it removed immediately and bring a fresh plate, madam.'

Mawgan snatches the plate back. 'If you do that I'll be waiting until Christmas.'

'Whatever you wish, madam.'

Gritting my teeth, I take the tray, desperate to move on to new customers but dreading what Sheila will say about their refusal to pay the bill. It was my fault that the coleslaw ended up on the plate; I must have taken down the order wrong in the rush.

'Would you like anything else?' I ask in desperation. 'Condiments? A jug of water?'

'Some mayonnaise,' Mawgan grunts, leaving me wondering what the objection was to coleslaw anyway.

Wondering how I'll break the news to Sheila about the discount, I head for the condiments alcove at the side of the kitchen, and scoop some mayo from the catering jar in the fridge into an individual pot. Maybe Mawgan will change her mind when she tastes the homemade pasties that Sheila and I slaved over this morning? While I carefully place the pot on a tray, I can hear the odd yip from above but I have to harden my heart.

I reckon no one will hear Mitch anyway above the squawking of seagulls and head back outside. A large group of them has already gathered on the beach wall opposite the cafe, eyeing the lunchtime chips and pasties with their beady eyes and sharp beaks. They're a menace all over St Trenyan, but the tourists will keep feeding them. The gulls must think Sheila's is a drive thru.

Make that a *dive* thru. I'm almost at Mawgan's table with the bowl of mayo, when I spot three of the big birds circling low over a young family at the edge of the terrace. The mother is trying to manoeuvre a buggy with a baby down the steps to the beach while a little girl clambers down beside her. She can't be more than four and she has a bright pink ice-cream cone clutched in one hand. Her tongue sticks out in concentration as she negotiates the stone steps onto the sand. I'm in two minds whether to leave the mayo and give the mother a hand when there's a deafening screech.

Wings beating like pterodactyls, two large gulls launch a double-pronged attack on the little girl. The birds are probably only after the food, but they could do some serious damage by accident.

'Look out!'

Too late. The mother looks up from the bottom of the steps, there's a flapping of wings and screeching like nails over a blackboard. The toddler lets out a wail as the gulls attack her ice cream. Dashing forward to try and chase them off, my shin connects with someone's beach bag, I stagger forward and the pot of mayo flies through the air. It lands, smack onto the back of Mawgan's jacket, just as if I'd aimed right for it.

Ignoring Mawgan's shriek and my throbbing foot, I run over to the mum. The toddler stares at her empty hand which thankfully is still in one piece. Pink gloop trickles down her chubby arm, while the seagulls tear the cone to pieces on the sand.

'Are you all OK? Is the little one hurt?' I ask.

Her mum crouches down and hugs her. 'She's fine. You scared them off just in time. I was so busy with the buggy I hadn't realised what was happening.'

'I'm glad she's OK.'

'Thanks to you. Nasty things. Don't cry, Tasha! I'll get you another ice cream, darling.'

'You! Waitress! Have you seen my suit?'

'Sorry,' I mouth to the mum. 'Have to go.'

On the terrace, Mawgan holds up her jacket, her mouth set in a fuchsia line. It's spattered with mayo, just like a seagull pooped on it.

'I'm *so* sorry, madam, you can see it was an accident.'

She thrusts her jacket under my nose. Mayonnaise dribbles down it. Her gaze scythes through me. 'Maybe it was, but my suit's still ruined.'

'I – I'll pay for it to be cleaned,' I say, though every word kills me to say it and it will take most of my savings.

'*Cleaned*? It's ruined. This suit cost over three hundred pounds. I expect you to pay for a new one. You or your boss.'

The words leave my lips before I can stop them. 'Three hundred quid? You're kidding?'

She gasps. 'What did you say?'

The hipster lowers his *Times* and stares at us. His dark eyes glint in the sunlight. He frowns, seems about to speak but then raises the newspaper again. A woman nearby giggles nervously and faces look up from their lattes and pasties at the unexpected free entertainment.

'I . . . didn't mean to be rude, madam.'

'Oh, really?' She lowers her voice so that only I and her family can hear her. 'You do know I can make sure you get the sack and never get another job in this town? I don't let anyone speak to me like that.'

I hesitate, anger bubbling up in me like the fizz in a bottle of pop. Then my cork blows. Just as quietly I say: 'Neither do I. *Madam.*'

I'm on the point of fetching Sheila when loud barks ring out from the side alley of the cafe. They sound exactly like Mitch's barks but he's supposed to be safe inside the flat. He *can't* have escaped, but seconds later a hairy ball of energy hurtles from the rear of the cafe and onto the terrace. Two Pugs and a Cockerpoo start yapping and before I can blink, Mitch leaps at me, barking joyfully. Mawgan's eyes flick from Mitch to the back door of the cafe and back at me.

'I take it that's your dog?' There's ice in her voice.

'Yes.'

'And it lives here?'

'Um. Not as such. He's just staying in the attic temporarily while I'm at work but he wasn't supposed to get out.'

'So, you live here too?'

My stomach swirls with unease but I don't want to let Mawgan see that she's rattled me and I'm getting annoyed now. The customer may be always right but she also has no right to interrogate me about my private life. 'Yes, but I really don't see what it has to do with you.'

She smirks. 'Rather a lot, actually. I own this building. Your

10

boss is my tenant so she shouldn't be subletting the place, for a start, and there are no pets allowed, especially not a great big dirty thing like that one.'

'Mitch isn't dirty!'

Mitch glances up innocently then resumes his pursuit of a seagull. Squawks fill the air. My heart sinks to my boots. If I've got Sheila into bother I'll never forgive myself. Even as I think the words, I know I must already have got Sheila into deep trouble. Mawgan raises herself up. 'In fact, I'm going to see your boss right now.'

'Mawgan . . .' the goth sister murmurs.

'Keep out of this, Andi!'

Andi caves in like a sunken sponge cake but their father beams proudly and folds his arms.

'OK,' I say. 'You do that, but no one treats me like this and if I'm going to lose my job, I may as well go out with a bang.' I reach for the nearest cold drink, which just happens to be an abandoned raspberry frappuccino and throw it over Mawgan's skirt.

Her jaw drops and then she shrieks. 'You little cow! You did that on purpose.'

'My daughter could sue you for assault,' says her father as Mitch skitters back to lick up the bright pink slush from the terrace. I glance over at the hipster but can't see him any more and despite my bravado, I'm shaking inside.

I rip off my apron. 'Be my guest. My legal team will be in touch.'

I glance around me defiantly and everyone turns their faces away. No one backs up Mawgan but somehow, I don't think this is going to help Sheila's Trip Advisor rating either. Oh shit, what the hell have I just done?

Pink slush drips from Mawgan's skirt onto her shiny stilettos and her voice is barely more than a hiss. 'You'll live to regret this.'

Trembling inwardly, I shrug. 'Actually, *madam*, I think I'll look back on it as one of my finest moments.'

CHAPTER TWO

I thought about the waitress all the way out of St Trenyan, knowing I probably should have said something – that I could have stuck up for her – although I'm not sure what good it would have done or if she'd have thanked me for it. My shining armour turned rusty a long time ago and I've stopped trying to solve everyone's woes. No good comes of crashing in on other people's lives, no matter how well intentioned.

Besides, she didn't seem to need my help. In fact, I really admired the way she stood up to the Cades . . . unlike me. The real truth is I wasn't ready to face *them* or, at least, risk being plunged headlong into a confrontation with them.

They're a local family of businesspeople who are well known in St Trenyan and the surrounding area. Mawgan was at my school, albeit she was a couple of years below me. She'd joined the Cade family empire before I went away and it seems as if she's relishing her role at the helm. Her father, Clive Cade, is obviously proud of her although his younger daughter, Andi, doesn't look cut out to be a business mogul. You never know with people, however. Before I left St Trenyan for the Middle East, I wouldn't have thought Mawgan would become as spiteful and petty as she was towards the waitress.

Ignoring my aching knee, not to mention my niggling conscience, I stride out along the path which lurches its way over every tiny cove and sliver of beach. I've already had to change my route a few times where parts of the cliff have dropped into the sea. Judging by the rock falls on the beach, there must have been some almighty storms while I've been away.

At the top of one of the cliffs, I duck inside an old whitewashed huer's hut for a break from the sun. Tankers and a cruise ship are tiny specks on the horizon as they head out into the Atlantic and I can taste salt on my lips again so I know I'm almost home. I shrug the pack off my back and stretch my spine.

The desert boots I had to borrow are caked in Cornish mud now, although I still feel self-conscious in the combats and khaki T-shirt. On the upside, the beanie hat and beard meant that I wasn't recognised in St Trenyan. If I'd stepped into the row with the infamous Cades, they definitely would have.

Squashing down another pang of guilt, I shoulder my bag again. The path hugs the edge of the cliff, the worst of the climbs are over and I can see the black and white lighthouse on the headland in the far distance. The afternoon sun is mellowing, yet the sweat trickles down my spine. A few yards further on, I reach the milestone, which is just a lump of grey granite spattered with orange lichen. The words weathered away long before I was born but I know what it used to say, all the same.

One way lies Kilhallon Park, my home: the other leads to Bosinney House, my uncle's house – and possibly to Isla Channing. The report in *The Times* said she was scouting out the locations for a new drama series and that she'd won an award for her last production. I always knew in my heart that she'd make it big, that she was too good to stay in one small place; with the likes of me. Perhaps that's why I left in the first place, perhaps not – I've had too much time to reflect over the past few months.

On the other side of the valley, a group of ruined engine houses cling to the cliffs and on the moor the tower of the church looms above the trees. Some of them are almost bent double trying to escape the gales from the Atlantic.

For a second, I hesitate in the middle of the narrow path, wondering if I ought to go home to Kilhallon Park or to Bosinney House. Uncle Rory will know if Isla's back. Luke might even be around too as it's Good Friday. He's an old buddy of mine and he works as an advisor for my uncle's finance company, or rather he did when I last heard from him which was months ago now.

A young guy and his girlfriend shake their heads at me, eager to get past on the coast path which has become very narrow here due to a fresh growth of gorse.

'Thinking of moving, mate, or will you be here all day?' the guy says with a grunt.

'Sorry.' I press against the scratchy gorse and they squeeze past me, muttering something about 'losers'.

A moment later, I've decided – and turning away from home, I head for Bosinney.

Oblivious to the trouble he's caused at the cafe, Mitch trots after me along the cobbles of Fore Street. The houses and shops of St Trenyan tumble down the steep cobbled streets to the sea, their roofs and windows shimmering in the afternoon sun. A few marshmallow clouds float across the sapphire blue sky and white-caps sparkle on the sea. Tourists 'oh' and 'ah' at the shops full of Easter eggs and gifts, hand-crafted chocolate and trendy china, and posh tea towels that cost as much as a morning's wages. The tang of fish and chips and rich scent of coffee follow me along the street but I need to save every penny now, even more than before.

I was crimson with shame and fighting back tears as Sheila paid me the rest of the week's wages which I know was more than I deserved. She was almost crying too which made me feel even worse, but she said there was no way she could keep me on. It turns out Mawgan Cade and her family *do* own the Beach Hut:

they bought it when the previous owner, an old lady who'd lived in St Trenyan for eighty years, had to sell up and go into a nursing home. Mawgan hiked the rent up, which is why Sheila's margins are now so thin.

'Someone should do something about people like that!' I said to Sheila, after Mawgan had left.

'No one dares stand up to the Cades. They have their fingers in too many pies.'

Sheila offered to make excuses for me but I stopped her. In the end I knew the best thing for everyone was for me to leave the cafe as soon as possible before she was forced to sack me. But leaving my job also meant leaving the temporary shelter I'd found too.

'Come on, boy,' I say as Mitch sniffs around the bins by the harbourmaster's office. I find a vacant bench with room for me and my worldly goods. The tourists tend to avoid the working end of the harbour: it's too far from the souvenir shops and car parks and always smells of fish, but I need time to think. My stomach growls while Mitch curls up at my feet, full of pasty and sighing contentedly. At least he's happy and, whatever happens, I'll make sure he's looked after. I'd let him go to a good home, rather than see him want for anything.

Rubbing my wet face with the back of my hand, I squeeze back the tears and think of happier times, hoping an idea will come. When I was a little girl, Mum used to take us for tea with my Nana Jones every Sunday afternoon. A proper Cornish tea with a brown pot under a woolly tea cosy, flowery china loaded with goodies you don't see any more, figgy 'obbin, spicy parkin, fairings, and 'fly pastry' with currants. She even made a stargazy pie once but I burst into tears when I saw the little fish peeping out of the crust so she never made it again.

Talking of fish, a few yards away from me, a boat has just landed its catch. The gulls circle overhead, fighting and screaming over scraps. The tang of fresh fish fills the air.

'Maybe they'd take me on as crew?' I tell Mitch, who drops his muzzle onto his paws. He looks as confident about the plan as I feel.

'Well, if we're not going to sea, we need to find a new job and somewhere to stay. Come on,' I say as much for my benefit as his. Mitch's ears perk up ready for a new adventure which cheers me up a little too. 'We've done it before and we can do it again,' I say with a new determination. 'We'll just have to make the best of things.'

CHAPTER THREE

By the time I reach Bosinney House, my knee aches like crazy and a young woman I don't recognise bars the doorway. The frilly white apron round her waist looks odd with the spray-on jeans and pink T-shirt.

'Can I help you, sir?' she asks, reminding me of the waitress, apart from the accent, which is definitely not Cornish but from a lot further east. Krakow? Bucharest? For some reason, she also looks scared of me. Maybe I should have had a shave.

Feeling guilty, I summon up a smile for her. 'Hi. Is Uncle Rory at home?'

'Uncle Rory? I do not know who you mean . . .' She eyes me suspiciously and I don't blame her. What with the attitude, the borrowed combats and the beard, she must think I've come to tie up and terrorise the household.

'I mean my uncle, Mr Rory Penwith.'

She bites her lip nervously before replying. 'Mr Penwith is here but he has guests with him.'

I should have realised that from the row of vehicles parked outside: a Range Rover, an Audi, and a couple of Mercs. Then, it dawns on me that today must be his birthday.

'I can see that but I think he'll find room for one more. Tell him it's his nephew, Cal Penwith.'

She looks me up and down. 'You are family?'

'It may be hard to believe but I am. Can I come in? I won't steal the silver.'

She tightens her grip on the door frame. 'They are in the big glass room, having drinks.'

'The orangery?'

Finally, she nods and stands aside to let me in. 'Yes. I will take you.'

'There's no need. I know my way.'

Leaving my pack on the floorboards, I march past her, across the great hall and down the corridor that leads to the orangery, with the girl's heels click-clacking behind me. The great hall smells faintly of ashes and wood smoke as it does for three seasons of the year. That's the only part of Bosinney House that hasn't changed: the rest has been built on over the years. It's many times bigger than the house on Kilhallon Park and a hundred times grander. Uncle Rory inherited it from my granddad, who left Kilhallon Park to his younger son, my father. Dad never quite got over being treated as second best but I love Kilhallon, even in the state I left it when I went abroad. I'd never swap it for all Bosinney's grandeur.

The girl catches up with me. 'I will tell them you are here.'

I stop and turn. '*Don't* do that.'

Seeing the genuine fear in her eyes, I feel ashamed and soften my tone. 'I'd like to surprise them. *Please?*'

With another nod she scuttles off, muttering. 'I'll be in kitchen. I'll fetch more champagne.'

Champagne, eh? Uncle Rory's idea of extravagance used to be opening an extra bottle of Rattler . . . maybe they do know I'm coming after all.

The sound of laughter and the pop of corks drift along the corridor. Are they expecting me? It's not possible or I'd have known about it by now and besides a handful of people, no one knows I'm back in Cornwall.

There's applause, a few gentle cheers. I didn't know Rory made a big thing of his birthdays, but maybe this is a landmark one or perhaps he's made his first million from his financial advisor business. It was doing well when I left, despite the recession.

It occurs to me that I should, perhaps, have warned them first, not just turn up like this . . . but the truth is that a small part of me was afraid – *is* afraid – that no one would actually *want* me back.

The voices become more distinct, glasses chink and I hear a deep laugh – Uncle Rory – and a giggle – my cousin Robyn and my ears strain for the one voice I really want to hear. I walk towards the orangery and pause at the door, observing, assessing . . . the scene plays out like a surreal movie. These people I once cared for and loved are like actors in a play.

There must be around a dozen people in here, most of whom I recognise. Uncle Rory is downing a whisky – as I thought he would be; my old mate Luke is laughing nervously at something Isla's mother is telling him. Robyn is handing round a tray of canapés, her face flushed. This is obviously a celebration.

There's also someone else, whose honeyed hair brushes her bare shoulders, whose dress shimmers in the early evening sunlight and clings to her bottom. Whose slender legs are accentuated in silver heels higher than any I've ever seen her in before.

My body tautens like a wire. She hasn't seen me yet, no one has seen me yet . . .

'Jesus Christ Almighty!'

Uncle Rory's face is purple. He's lost a bit more hair since I last saw him. Luke's mouth is open like a goldfish gasping for air. Isla's mum looks shocked to see me. Robyn freezes, still holding the tray of canapés.

And Isla, she stares at me and her champagne glass trembles in her hand.

'Cal? Is it really you?'

'Isla . . .' Her name squeezes out from my throat, almost inaudible. I never thought it would be like this. Every ounce of strength has gone.

'Cal? Bloody hell, I thought you were a ghost!' Luke suddenly rushes over and gathers me up in a man hug, slapping me on the back so hard I wince.

'Are you OK, man?'

'I'm fine. Looking good, Luke.' And he does. Bigger, beefier, the extra weight suits him and he looks happy. It's great to see him; I never expected to feel so emotional so I must be going soft. Luke gives me a man hug again, but this time I suppress the wince.

He stares at me. 'Man, you look thin . . . I can't believe this . . . I just . . . I don't know what to say.'

He lets me go and rubs his hand over his face, shaking his head in shock. I don't blame him. I've changed a lot while I've been away.

'Cal! Cal!' My cousin Robyn launches herself at me, tears streaming down her face, along with the kohl around her eyes. Robyn's every bit as good a mate as any of the lads – more even. 'Where have you been? Why didn't you tell us you were coming?' Her fingers dig into my forearm but I don't mind. It's wonderful to see her again.

'I don't know. Admin problems? Leaves on the line? Happy birthday, by the way.'

Uncle Rory downs the rest of his whisky and dumps the glass on a table. 'It's not a matter for levity, boy. We haven't heard from you for months. For all we knew, you might have been dead.'

'As you can see, I'm not.'

'Don't joke! You know damn well what I mean. We thought you'd decided to stay in the Middle East for good.'

'I almost did,' I say, with half an eye on Isla, watching me from a few feet away, still dumbstruck and even more beautiful than she looked in that newspaper article. She's let her blonde hair grow and it's been cut in a style that manages to be both classy and damn sexy.

'How long have you known you were coming home?' Rory asks.

'A few days.'

His face is almost purple. 'Then why didn't you call us? We've hardly heard from you in the past two years.'

Isla has abandoned her glass and is hugging herself as if she's freezing cold. Under the light tan, which I presume she picked up on her last shoot in Cannes, she's pale as the moon on the sea.

'I'm sorry,' I say more to Isla than my uncle. 'I've been . . . tied up and I couldn't get away from work that easily.' I swallow hard. 'It's been . . . complicated.'

'Too tied up or complicated to phone us or email?' Luke asks, an edge creeping into his voice. I can't blame him.

'Why didn't you phone or text, if only to say you were on your way home?' Isla's voice cuts through the air, more London than in my imagination, yet still with the Cornish lilt. Everyone else may as well be on Mars.

'It's complicated,' I repeat, knowing I can never un-complicate it or tell anyone the real truth. 'I've only been in the UK for a few hours and I did call *you*.' With a smile, I switch the focus back to Isla. 'I tried to call you on the train here but your phone was dead.'

She smiles back, apologetically. 'Oh . . . I'm sorry. I've changed my phone and my number while you've been away. I had to; a fan got hold of it and started stalking me.'

'A *fan*?'

'Isla's a celebrity now.' Her mother glares at me like Medusa, obviously hoping to turn me to stone while her dad takes refuge in his champagne glass. He always was a man of few words and he's lost for them now. 'She's an award-winning TV and film producer, you know,' Mrs Channing adds.

21

'I know that. I read about the last one in the newspaper. Congratulations.'

'So you had time to read the papers?' Isla remarks. She wrinkles her nose like she used to when she was trying not to cry. Like she did when I left her at the station the night I left Cornwall.

'Actually I did email you on my way down on the train,' I go on, refusing to let Isla off the hook.

'Oh, Cal. I haven't even looked at my emails since yesterday. We've all been completely tied up here all day, organising the party . . . and Luke forbade me to do any work this weekend, didn't you?'

'*Forbade* you?'

'I forbade myself.'

She puts her glass down on the table but it's my hands shaking now as I walk towards her. A huge wave of memories thunders towards me and I pull her into my arms. I'm swept away by the sight and smell and feel of her. She is fragile, delicate, a porcelain figure, always way out of my league. Instinct stirs responses I can't stop and don't want to, even in the middle of company. I press her against me and her hands seek my spine through my shirt as if she wants to double check I'm real, not a phantom. I inhale her perfume. It's a new one, sharper and more sophisticated than the scents she used to wear, or is that my imagination?

'You don't know how much I've wanted this.' I breathe the words into her hair, which smells even better than I remember it.

'Cal . . .'

Her whisper pushes me away, then I realise that her hands are also pushing me away from her too. No. I won't let her go yet. I could lift her off her feet if I wanted to, and carry her out of here in a second but she is controlling this moment; this moment I've hungered and thirsted for so long. There's deep pain in her eyes and the realisation smacks me in the chest. 'Isla?'

'I'm sorry but things have *changed.*' Her voice cracks with emotion and it's all I can do to hold it together.

Changed? Yeah, I guess. You look even hotter than ever, if that's possible. You smell wonderful too. I want to say the words out loud but something stops me. Instead I lift my hand to her cheek and feel the soft skin under my fingertips.

She smiles and then flinches away from my hand. '*Please.* Not here. Not *now.*'

Everyone is looking at us; we're the dancers in the middle of a circle that no one dares to join.

'Aren't you going to congratulate the happy couple?' Mrs Channing, Isla's mother, speaks.

'What happy couple? I thought this was a birthday party? Is there something I'm missing here?' I make my tone light but my stomach churns with foreboding.

'It is a birthday party but we've just heard some more good news. Isla and Luke have announced they're getting engaged. Isn't that wonderful news?' her mother trills.

'Engaged?' Shock constricts my throat muscles. 'You mean engaged to be married?'

Isla laughs lightly. 'Well, there isn't going to be a wedding yet. Not for a while.'

'But probably this year. Definitely early next year,' Luke cuts in, with an expression on his face I don't recognise.

'We haven't set a date yet, these things take a lot of organising and I'm so busy with work.' Isla glances at Luke for confirmation.

Robyn links her arm with mine. 'They told us just before you came in, Cal. Isn't it an amazing day? Dad's birthday, the engagement and you coming home . . .'

Robyn beams. I don't think she or anyone realises how much I felt for Isla. Before I went away, we didn't really have a formal relationship. It was definitely on–off and no one considered it serious. Isla obviously didn't. But the past few months have made me realise that I *did*. I've been in denial about how much I felt for her and I'd resolved to tell her when I came home, *if* I came home.

My uncle pats Luke on the back. He seems as proud as if Luke were his own flesh and blood, not the son of his former business partner. Rory always had a soft spot for Luke but now there's clearly a bond between them that wasn't there when I went away. It's as if Luke *is* Rory's son now.

'Aren't you thrilled for them?' Mrs Channing's voice cuts through me and she gives me a calculating glance.

'Oh yes. Thrilled.' I echo her because I can't formulate my own thoughts any more. I can't even think straight.

'Cal, darling, I'll fetch you a whisky.' Robyn scuttles off.

I glance to Isla, clutching her glass so tightly it could shatter any second but Luke's arm is around my back.

He clears his throat nervously. He knows I fancied Isla, and that we dated for a while before I left but not how much I really felt for her. 'Hey, mate, it's great to have you home. Joking apart, I was worried that you might have decided to stay out there.'

'I thought the same myself, a few times.' My smile hides an instinct to lash out like a wounded animal. Anyone will tell you my social veneer was never thick, but now it's paper thin and rubbed to nothing in places. My time in the Middle East has shown me the worst of human nature, including my own. It was a mistake to turn up like this, an even bigger one to come home and expect to find everything as I left it.

'Cal?' Isla's voice is soft, reminding me that these are the people I love and miss, whose company I longed for, but now I'm here, now I know how much things have changed, I'd rather face the warzone I came from.

Ignoring Isla temporarily, I search Luke's face, interrogate him. 'How long have you two been together?'

'A good few months now.' His tone is overly casual, his smile over bright. 'Come through to the sitting room. Have a drink. We'll talk.'

'No. No, I . . . thanks for the offer, mate, but I need to get

24

home to Kilhallon Park.'

'Wait, Cal! Surely you're going to tell us where you've been and what you've been doing lately?'

The answer to Isla's question is so complicated, and yet so simple, that my brain literally hurts. The blood pulses in my temple, a tight band seems to crush my skull.

'Not now, I'm tired . . . and I don't want to spoil your party with my boring stories. Plus, I really should go and see how Polly is. I left a message on her phone but I haven't heard back from her yet. I hope she's been OK while I've been out of contact.'

Luke flashes me a sympathetic smile. 'Polly's fine but you obviously wouldn't expect her to cope with managing the whole place on her own, with no money coming in since just before you left, after your father passed away. Rory and I did what we could to keep things from falling into complete rack and ruin but we didn't want to take over.'

I smile at Luke and his arm tightens around Isla's waist. The sight of him with her is like a jagged knife sawing through my guts.

'I can see that. Congratulations,' I say and walk out.

CHAPTER FOUR

'Demi!'

I wake to find someone shaking me, gently but firmly. Mitch barks but in a way that says 'friend' not 'foe'. Warm fingers grip my shoulder.

Sheila's plump face comes into focus. 'You're bloody freezing, love! What are you doing here?'

'Umm . . .' I cringe inwardly, embarrassed at being found sleeping in the doorway of a chip shop.

'I'd been hoping to see you again but not like this. I wouldn't have known you were here but one of the fishermen mentioned he'd seen a girl and her dog sleeping rough when he brought some prawns round first thing. You silly girl, how long have you been sleeping out here for? I thought you told me you could stay at your friend's parents' while they were on holiday?'

'Oh, I've only been here since last night. My mate's mum and dad came home early so I had to leave.'

'Then you should have come to me. You can stay in the loft room again until you're sorted and I don't care what Mawgan Cade says. She can throw us all out, if she wants,' Sheila declares with a defiant look.

'That's lovely of you but there's no way I'm going to make any more trouble for you.'

'Well, I don't care. Someone should do something about the Cades. I'm going to find a new cafe, away from them, the money-grabbing buggers . . .' Her tone softens. 'Oh my lovely, I'm so sorry you've ended up here. Can't the council find you somewhere to stay?'

'It takes time and there are families who need homes a lot more than me. Besides, there aren't many places that would take Mitch. I haven't made things easy for myself.'

'You've had a rough start to life, that's for sure. What about jobs?'

'I tried the Job Centre and applied for a couple of catering jobs but it's early days yet.'

Slowly, the feeling returns to my limbs. The early morning sea mist has seeped through my clothes and I'm sure someone used the doorway as a toilet during the night. I hope that's not why my sleeping bag is so damp.

'Well, you bloody well can't stay here. I daren't have you back to work at the cafe but I've heard about something on the grape-vine that might suit you. It comes with accommodation.'

I stand up, wincing at the pins and needles in my feet. 'Really?'

'Don't get too excited. It might not come to anything and it was only a word from a friend. She works at a caravan site.'

'A caravan site? Er . . . that sounds interesting, but if there's work going?'

She grimaces. 'It's in the back of beyond, which is why I shouldn't get too excited, but you never know. Come to the cafe for a bit of breakfast before we open. I don't care if Mawgan Cade sees you. I'll throw something over her myself if she says anything.'

At the mention of breakfast, Mitch jumps to his paws. I gather up my sleeping bag and my rucksack and follow Sheila. I lied to her. There is no friend or parents' house. There never was. I've been sleeping rough for the past three days since the run-in with Mawgan. Since I left home after a falling out with my dad and his new partner, and had to leave my previous job, I've never been in one place long enough – not even a shop doorway – to make long-term friends, and definitely not ones with room to put me and Mitch up. As for the housing office, I want to try and find my own live-in job first. There are hundreds of people who need council accommodation a lot more than I do.

Sheila slaps a plate of bacon and eggs in front of me and refills my mug of coffee. 'Here you are. Get that down you.'

Mitch has already demolished a bowl of Chum and is snoring in a patch of early morning sun.

The smell of crispy bacon fills my nostrils. 'You've got to open in an hour. I should go when I've had this.'

'Not until I know you won't be on the streets.'

'Have you got the number of this friend with the caravan site?'

She scribbles on an order slip. 'Here it is. It's called Kilhallon Holiday Park.'

'Never heard of it? Where is it?'

Sheila grins as I lick a trail of egg yolk from the corner of my mouth.

'Around five miles out of town on the coast road. Like I said, I'm not sure the job will suit you but any port in a storm, as they say, and I've heard they're looking for a live-in worker.'

'What about Mitch?'

'It's in the country, so they might be more accommodating of him. Polly's lived there for years and I expect she'll tell you more. All I know so far is that the owner of the place has decided to re-launch the park and needs someone to help out fast so I guess that means they want someone cheap too. So don't let them exploit you.' Sheila wipes her hands on some kitchen paper.

'I won't. Can I use your laptop and do a bit of research on it? Then I can call this Polly woman when they open. If the job's not advertised yet, I want to get in there first before anyone else.'

'Course you can but don't get your hopes up. Kilhallon Park may not be what it was.' She smiles.

'They haven't seen me yet, have they? I could be exactly what they need.'

She shakes her head and laughs. 'Good luck. You and Mitch . . . and by the way, don't take this the wrong way, but do you want to have a shower and freshen up, first?'

With my damp hair wrapped in one of Sheila's fluffy towels, I put down the phone. Mr Penwith must be really keen for staff because Polly Tregothnan said he'd meet me this afternoon in St Trenyan. She asked for some details so I gave my address as the Beach Hut and said that Sheila had to let me go for 'financial reasons' but was happy to give me a reference.

Not that Polly listened much, she was too busy barking at me and telling me 'not to be late as Mr Penwith was a busy man' and 'had I written down the name of the chain coffee bar he'd meet me at because young people these days never listened to anything in her experience.' She claimed to be his PA but she sounded more like his mother, to be honest.

Sheila says Polly can be a 'bit of a Tartar', whatever the hell that is, but also reckons Polly has a 'heart of gold' which probably means she's even scarier than she sounded on the phone. I also decided not to mention Mitch at this stage of our conversation.

After I left the cafe, with an extra bacon butty wrapped in foil and some pouches of food for Mitch, I hung around town looking for waitressing job ads in the cafe windows but in all honesty I liked the sound of working at a holiday park far more. There ought to be more opportunities, despite what Sheila said about not getting my hopes up.

The meeting is scheduled for twelve-thirty so by twelve-fifteen, I've already bagged a table outside a big name coffee bar, and I'm pretending to read the newspaper. However, I don't think I've taken in a single word my stomach is churning so much. Half-past twelve comes and goes, and my hands are smudged with the newsprint. It's now almost quarter to one and I push the paper away, nerves taking over my brain completely. I glance up the street for the umpteenth time, my heart banging away every time any lone bloke approaches the cafe. I don't even know how old Mr Penwith is. He could be anything from thirty to seventy.

The woman who's clearing the tables comes over to me. 'Are you going to buy anything?'

'Yeah but I'm just waiting for a . . . colleague.'

She raises an eyebrow.

'He should be here soon,' I say firmly.

'Course he will be.' She shrugs and goes to clear the neighbouring tables.

It's ten to one now, and there's still no sign of Mr Penwith. Has he changed his mind? Has he already got someone else? Has word of the frappuccino incident already spread beyond St Trenyan? Do Mawgan Cade's tentacles reach as far as Kilhallon park?

I laugh out loud, but it's only nerves and my heart sinks again.

'He isn't coming,' I say to Mitch, who dozes in a pool of sunlight.

Wait. A man has caught my eye. He's hanging about outside the Shell Shop on the opposite side of the street but he's watching the cafe and frowning. He wears jeans and a white shirt and a jacket: smart casual. He's not seventy, that's for sure. He checks his watch, seems to make a decision and weaves between the queuing cars to my side of the street.

Slowing his pace, he walks up to the outside tables and glances around him. Oh my God, surely *he* can't be Mr Penwith?

Yet by the way he scans the customers, it has to be.

I jump up. 'Mr Penwith?'

He looks at me, his tanned forehead creases and his eyes flicker to Mitch. 'Don't I know you?' he says.

'Oh God, yes. . . and I've seen you. You were at the cafe when I . . . That was a one-off, of course. I don't usually chuck stuff

30

over customers . . . I mean, that's not how I usually behave when I'm working . . .'

His expression doesn't change which is not a great sign. 'So you're Ms Jones?'

I squirm with embarrassment. 'Yes.'

'Hmm. I see. You're not what I was expecting.'

'What were you expecting?'

'Someone . . .' His voice trails off.

'Older?' My heart sinks.

He nods. 'I guess so. More experienced.'

'I told your PA I had extensive catering experience. She mentioned you wanted someone who could turn their hand to a multitude of tasks.'

'My PA?' He frowns. I don't think he's over thirty but he already has fine lines in his face.

'Mrs Tregothnan?'

'Ah, you must mean Polly. I was thinking of someone with admin skills and previous experience of running a business like a holiday park.'

'I've had plenty of experience of dealing with tourists and the public and I can definitely multitask.' He raises his eyebrows, probably recalling my ability to chase off seagulls, throw a frappuccino over a customer and get the sack, all within five minutes, but I press on. 'Look, Mr Penwith, You've come into town and we've both made time from our schedules so you may as well interview me now.'

'My schedule?' He smiles and immediately I revise my original opinion of him as being a surf hipster. He doesn't look how he sounds. His face is tanned, his hair is dark brown with a hint of natural highlights from the sun. It's also wild without the beanie to tame it and suddenly I realise that he reminds me a little bit of a hot vampire from a TV show that I used to watch when I lived at home. That seems a very long time ago now.

'Shall we have a coffee and discuss the role in more detail?' I ask, more in hope than expectation, while trying to banish the words Hot Vampire from my mind in case they slip out by accident.

He sighs and his mouth curves into that smile-that-isn't-really-a-smile thing again. 'As we've both cleared a spot in our busy *schedules*, I suppose it won't do any harm.'

He drops a set of car keys on the table. The key fob is a bit of polished wood tied to them with an old piece of string. 'So, Ms Demi Jones,' he says, turning the words over like they're treasure. My name sounds almost sexy in his accent. 'What's that short for?'

'Demelza,' I mutter, cringing at having to reveal it. 'It was my nan's name and I loved my nan but I've always hated it myself. No one else at school was called anything so weird,' I say, trying to get a grip. How did I not notice how gorgeous he was at the cafe? 'Just Demi will do.'

He smiles. 'Fine. I'm Cal. Short for Calvin, also an old family name that I could have done without.' He holds out his hand. I take it, feeling self-conscious even though the contact is firm but brief. His skin is warm but his palms are rough like he's been working a lot with them recently.

His bushy eyebrows knit together. 'What's the matter?'

Feeling my face heat up, I glance away. 'Nothing.'

I shrug because there's no way I'm going to tell my potential new employer that he looks like a hot vampire, even if he *does*. He runs his hand through his thick hair. 'Want a coffee and we can talk?' he offers, still sounding unsure if it's a good idea to interview me.

'Yes. I'll get them.' I dig in my purse and hold out one of the precious notes.

'Don't worry, I'll get these,' he says and disappears into the dark of the cafe. My stomach gurgles and Mitch's wet nose pokes at the threadbare patch on the knee of my jeans.

He sets down coffees and cake on the table and I try not to

devour them like a ravenous beast. After we've finished, he examines me like I'm some weird creature he discovered in the jungle. I swallow the last of my cake as he sips his espresso. The silence is killing me.

'Sheila's Beach Hut wasn't my first job, you know. I've a lot more experience than that.'

'Really? Where?'

'I worked in a cafe in Truro for a couple of years. I started off by clearing the tables and washing-up then they trained me as cook.'

'I bet you were a good cook.'

'Not bad. What makes you say that?'

He smiles. 'You obviously like cake.'

'Thanks! I didn't only make cakes. I made wicked pasties, lovely quiches and pies and I already had some training and my hygiene certificate which is why Sheila took me on. She was going to send me to catering college to do some more courses.'

He checks his watch. I feel as if I'm about to lose something important.

'Are you in a hurry?'

'A bit. I need to go to the bank to sort out my account.'

'Does it have lots of money in it?' I meant this comment as a joke but I blush the moment the words are out of my mouth. Cal laughs, but not like what I said was funny. 'I doubt it, unless someone dumped a load of extra cash in it that I don't know about while I was away.'

A penny drops in my mind. 'Away? Was that while you were in the army?'

'No, I wasn't in the army. Why would you think that?'

'When I saw you at the cafe you were in combat gear with one of those big bags soldiers carry.'

He smiles. 'Anyone can get that stuff at an army surplus store. I used to work for a medical aid charity.'

'I don't need aid,' I say quickly.

He smiles. 'I'm sure you don't. On the contrary, the way you handled Mawgan Cade, I doubt you need any help at all.'

'You know her?'

'Yes.' He reaches for his car keys from the table. 'Look, thanks for meeting me but I'm not sure you're quite what I'm looking for.'

I panic. 'Wait! You don't really know what you're looking for, do you?'

He stares at me, as if I just said the cleverest thing in the world. 'Maybe not but I do need someone who can do *everything*. It's a – um – fledgling business and it's going to take a lot of energy and enthusiasm to get it off the ground. There's a lot to learn. For both of us,' he adds.

'Then I'd be perfect. I want to develop my career in leisure and tourism too.' I fold my arms in what I hope is a confident gesture.

He hesitates. 'Even if you *did* work for me, I can't afford to pay you much.'

I sense he's weakening so I move in for the kill. 'We can negotiate on the terms. I've never been afraid of hard work.'

'I'm sure you haven't.'

'And I won't throw stuff over the customers. It was only Mawgan who got my back up.'

He smiles, properly this time, and my stomach does a funny little flip but it's only the excitement and adrenaline of being so very close to getting this job and a new home.

'Believe me, you can throw a whole bucket of anything over Mawgan. However, on a serious note, in addition to dealing with customers, there'd be a lot of fetching and carrying and cooking and cleaning and boring admin. We all have to muck in at Kilhallon.'

'I can do all that.'

'What about building work?' He eyes my skinny arms as if they're twigs. 'Any experience in gardening? Plastering?

Roofing? Carpentry?'

'I can learn,' I say defiantly.

He stares at me, biting his lip briefly. He is wavering. 'Yes, I'm sure you could but you won't have to, that was a joke.'

I try to laugh but I'm too wound up, waiting for a definite offer.

'I'm afraid the accommodation is a bit poky. It's only a little cottage.'

'A *cottage*?' I try not to get too excited.

'A *tiny* cottage that needs refurbishing. I'm sure you'd want something bigger and smarter,' he adds.

'No way. I mean . . . I'm sure I could manage if I *had* to and I could refurbish it myself. Look, everyone deserves a second chance, don't they? And let's face it, you look like someone who needs the help fast; or why would you have come straight down here today to interview me? Give me a trial period – we can both see how we like each other and if you change your mind or I do, there are no hard feelings. Go on, take the risk, live dangerously.'

He leans back in his chair, his eyes wide. Even before I finish speaking, I realise I've probably gone too far, ruined my chances again with my big mouth and my attitude.

'I must be mad,' he mutters.

Well, I think that's an offer. I try not to punch the air in triumph.

'I can't offer you much money – not much more than the living wage – until I get the place back on its feet, which could be a while, if any time,' he says, jangling his keys.

I point to Mitch who pricks up his ears at the mention of his name. 'What about Mitch? He'd need accommodating too,' I say, fizzing with triumph, knowing I have the upper hand now.

'Right. Well, of course, I suppose Mitch can come too. I need a dog that can pull his weight.'

'He doesn't work.'

'OK, then I need a dog who can look appealing and pathetic.'

'You won't regret this,' I say, wanting to run round the cafe terrace shouting 'yessss!'.

A smile tugs at the corner of his mouth. 'No . . . but you might.'

CHAPTER FIVE

'*This* is your car?'

Demi wrinkles her nose as I kick the brick from under the front wheel of the Land Rover. I don't trust the hand brake on the sloping car park perched above St Trenyan harbour, until I can get the car serviced.

'Yeah. Why?'

'You should lock it. There are thieves around.'

'One, the door lock's busted and two, do you really think anyone would want to steal this?'

She takes a longer look at the rusting paintwork, the dented side panel and bumper hanging off and curls her lip. 'For scrap, maybe.'

I'd like to smile at Demi – she has a habit of making me want to smile – but my facial muscles seem to have seized up after my trip to the bank. Demi took Mitch for a run on the beach while I saw the manager. The probate from my father's estate was sorted out before I left, and I've transferred most of his legacy from my savings to a business account. There wasn't a huge amount but I own Kilhallon Park and with careful management and some extra investment, I should be able to make the changes I need to re-develop the site. I open the rear door. 'Mitch can travel in style.'

'In you go,' she says, as Mitch hangs back. 'Come on, get in, you daft dog.'

'Maybe he's worried about getting into a strange man's car,' I say.

'He's probably got more sense than I have.'

Demi hesitates too, her arms folded, her chestnut hair flying in the wind, like the flames of a bonfire.

'I'm not desperate, you know.'

'I know you're not desperate.' Actually, I think she may be more desperate than she'd ever let on but I can't take advantage of that: she deserves better, and I don't want to exploit her. There's enough of that going on round here from what I can see.

She laughs at me. 'It's too late to back out now, Cal Penwith.'

'Don't you believe it. Now, get in. We've got a lot to do,' I say, more gruffly than I mean to.

The Land Rover groans up the steep hill from the harbour and onto the moor road. The tax has run out, though Polly told me I can do it online now, and its last MOT was before I went off on my last aid project. I'll sort it all out soon, for now I have more pressing concerns. I glance at Demi but she's staring out of the window.

'How long had you been sleeping rough before you started working for Sheila?'

She turns sharply. 'How do you know I was sleeping rough?'

'I can tell someone who has had a tough time. I worked for a charity, remember?'

She shrugs. 'I do but I told you, I'm not a charity project.'

'I know that.'

A glance tells me she's staring out of the window again but then she finally answers. 'I slept rough for a couple of months.'

'In St Trenyan?'

'Truro too. Penzance for a week or two but here mostly.'

Maybe I shouldn't have pushed her but I'd like to know more

about the new employee who's going to be sharing my home. 'Any particular reason?'

She waits before replying. 'I fancied a change, I suppose.'

I leave it, figuring she'll tell me more when she's ready. I'm hardly in a sharing mood myself and more importantly, Kilhallon is around the next corner. The road dips, curves sharply and the Land Rover shudders its way around the bend, then I press the gas pedal to the floor to make it up the other side of the hill. I turn the wheel sharply and we rattle over a cattle grid through two stone pillars that frame a narrow gap in the wall. The sign lies on the ground by the pillars but half the letters have weathered away so it now reads Kil l Park.

'Oh my God,' Demi mutters.

'What's up?'

'Sheila said this was the back of beyond and now I know what she means.'

'That's how I like it.'

'You must do . . . I mean, it's, er, very peaceful and wild out here.'

While steering the Land Rover between the larger potholes, I try to keep a straight face while taking a sneaky glance at her. She holds her rucksack tightly in her lap while Mitch starts snuffling and whimpering in the back. When I put out the feelers for a new assistant, I never bargained on someone like Demi, let alone a great shaggy hound. I've no idea what variety he is.

She lets out a squeal as the Land Rover bounces over a particularly deep rut and into a pool of water. 'There's no need to look so terrified,' I say.

'I wasn't until you said that.'

'Thanks.' I turn the engine back on and coax the Land Rover out of the puddle. 'Soon be there.'

She wrinkles her nose. It's a very pretty nose, I have to admit, even though it's turned up at the moment. Freckles dot her face; she's so vulnerable and yet fierce too. An image flashes into my mind out of nowhere of a painting my mother hung at Kilhallon of a beautiful girl floating in a river, surrounded by willow trees.

I stop the car in the middle of the yard that was once our car park. Demi stares at the dandelions and grass sprouting between the gravel.

'Is that it?'

'Yup.' I jump down onto the yard, wondering if she's ever going to get out of the car. Finally I open the door and she slides down reluctantly from the passenger seat, her rucksack in her arms. She looks around her, at the old office block on one side of the yard, and the peeling wooden veranda that served as our reception and the moss-coated 1970s touring caravan blocking the entrance to the barn.

'You said it was a holiday park . . .' she says, her eyes widening as she takes it all in.

'It was. It is. There's a lot more to the place than this.'

She glances at me, agonised.

Still clutching her rucksack, she wanders up to the barn, eyes wide at the decaying, tumbledown wreck that confronts her. I wouldn't blame her if she turned right round and ran back to St Trenyan.

'I can see we have a lot of work to do,' she says.

'You did say you weren't afraid of it.'

As she walks towards the reception, Mitch scoots past her to a pile of rusting signage that once read 'Welcome to Kilhallon Park. Your holiday starts here.'

Then he cocks his leg and proudly pisses all over the signs.

I don't blame Demi for being less than impressed by Kilhallon but when someone who's been sleeping in a shop doorway is shocked by the state your place is in, well, there's something seriously wrong. I was a bit taken aback myself when I walked home from Bosinney after crashing Uncle Rory's birthday party. Though I have to say that the state of my house was somewhat dwarfed by the state of my mind on finding out that I'd lost my girl to my best mate, and it was all my own fault.

Now I'm seeing the place through fresh eyes – Demi's – and the scale of the task that lies ahead of me comes painfully into focus. Resurrecting Kilhallon is going to be a huge challenge. Why would anyone want to come here on holiday when it's in this state? After my meeting at the bank I've also decided I'll need to drum up some extra money to refurbish the place in the way I want to.

I know Polly thinks I've gone mad but I need to focus on something or I really will go nuts. I can't do anything about Isla for now but that doesn't mean I've given up on her. She's not married yet; there's still time for her to change her mind, although I'm sure Luke would have something to say if he knew how I felt. I keep trying – and failing – to feel guilty about my resentment of him. I ought to wish him well, but the pain is still too raw and I can't see our relationship healing any time soon.

But first, Demi.

'There's Polly,' I say as our housekeeper bustles out of the front door. She looks younger since she dyed her hair an ash blonde while I've been away. The neat bob has taken years off her, not that I'd dare risk such a personal remark to her. However, judging by the glare on her face, she doesn't look ready to roll out the red carpet for our new employee. But Mitch seems to have taken to Polly and races forward and leaps up at her.

'Get that dog off me!' Polly's from hardy Cornish farming stock. She's a formidable woman, even though she's now in her mid-fifties. She pushes Mitch away, not roughly but firmly enough to startle him.

Demi dashes forward and grabs Mitch's lead. 'Don't worry. He won't hurt you.'

'I don't care. I don't like dogs and neither does Cal. You never mentioned an animal on the phone.'

'I've decided to make an exception for this one, and he can act as a guard dog,' I say as Mitch cowers under one of Polly's withering looks. 'This is Demi, she's going to be working for us.'

Polly plants her hands on her hips, sizing up our new employee. 'I know her name. You don't look like you sounded on the phone.'

'How did I sound?' Demi replies, so smoothly I can *feel* the danger.

'Polly, *if* you don't mind,' I cut in before there's a wrestling match right here in the farmyard, 'I'd like Demi added to the payroll, and a contract and all the proper paperwork done as soon as possible.'

Polly narrows her eyes at me. 'There's no need to be so high handed.'

'I'm sorry. Before you do that, can you find some clean bed linen and towels for Stables Cottage? I'll help Demi get it into some sort of habitable state.'

'Of course, *boss*. I'll get onto it right away.'

Polly flounces off, muttering to herself. I grit my teeth. Polly's been used to running the place without me while I was away and I'm out of practice with the social niceties these days. I know things have been tough on her but it's time we both got used to having other people around again.

Demi pulls a face behind her back. 'Polly doesn't look very happy to see me.'

'She'll get over it. Come on, I'll show you around the place.'

Cal leads me towards a wood and glass porch that looks modern, if you count the 1970s as modern, and is tacked onto the front of the old stone farmhouse itself.

'This is – was – the reception area. Sorry. This sticks in the damp,' he says, giving the peeling door into the reception a heavy shove.

There's still a counter in there and the type of dial phone you'd find in a retro shop, with dusty ring binders piled all around it and a faint whiff of damp and food. The metal racks by the window still have leaflets and brochures on them, faded to monochrome by the sun. I'm sure one of them says *Escape to Kilhallon Park, 1985* on it. Escape to Kilhallon? They'd be trying to escape *from* it these days.

There's a button on the desk with a sticker next to it, on which I can just make out 'Please ring for attention'.

'This way,' says Cal, pushing open a white-painted door that reads *Private* on a once-gold plastic plaque. We fight our way past old fleeces and wax jackets and Cal curses. 'Who left that bloody boot scraper there?' he grumbles. 'Be careful.'

Sidestepping over the scraper, I glimpse a chink of light as Cal pushes open a heavy oak door.

When I was little, my mum read *The Lion, the Witch and the Wardrobe* to me. As the coats part, and my eyes adjust, I feel I just stepped into another version of Narnia. Except this Narnia smells of curry and is like a *skip* – and that's from someone who's actually rummaged in a few.

'This is the sitting room. Obviously.'

He stands awkwardly but I'm fascinated. The windows are tiny with bottle-shaped panes, like an old harbour-side pub, but they'd probably let in more light if someone had cleaned them. Dead ashes powder the air when Cal shuts the door to reception behind him.

He tosses his phone on a huge carved dresser. 'You'll have to take us as you find us, as my dad used to say.'

'My mum said it too but she always tidied up anyway.' I cast my eyes around the sitting room while Mitch twitches at my feet, itching to give the place a proper sniff.

'Does your mother know where you are now?' Cal asks me.

'I doubt it. She's dead.'

'I'm sorry.' He pulls a face as if I've upset him, not the other way round.

'It's OK. She died eight years ago.'

He winces. 'Really? You must have been young to lose your mum.'

'Thirteen.'

'When did you leave home?' he asks.

'A couple of years ago.' I shrug as if it doesn't matter but actually I can remember it to the day and hour. I was eighteen, it was raining and *EastEnders* was on.

'Do you have any other family?'

Cal's voice interrupts my memories and I'm grateful for it. No one wants to be reminded of bad times, especially when there's guilt attached. 'A brother but I haven't seen him for years and I don't want to see my dad again.'

'Life throws some crap at us, doesn't it? I know what it's like to lose your parents when you're young,' he says.

'Do you?'

'Yes. My mum passed away when I was a teenager and I lost Dad just before I went away on my last overseas project.'

'God. I'm sorry. Really.'

'It happens, doesn't it?' he says. 'Make yourself comfortable if you can find a spare patch of sofa.'

I perch on the edge of an old settee between a pile of old garden magazines and for a while Cal remains standing in front of the hearth. He doesn't seem to know what to say to me; perhaps he's wondering what to do with me now I'm here. I'm beginning to wonder what I'm doing here myself. Mitch finally settles at my feet: he'd make himself at home anywhere. Unable to look Cal in the eye either, I focus on the room again. There's a big oak settle by the fire like you get in old pubs, paintings of horses and dogs, seascapes, boats and fishermen and dead rabbits and pheasants.

'Sorry. I'll have to have a word with Polly,' Cal mutters, gesturing at the state of the room. 'She's not used to having to share the house again but she's been here as long as I can remember. She worked for my father until her husband died and she's become part of the family.'

'When did the site last open?'

'About twelve years ago. There used to be dozens of people working here in its heyday.'

'*Dozens* of people?'

Cal hangs his jacket on the back of a dining chair. 'Hard to believe, but yes. We had a small dairy farm, and some arable land as well as the holiday park, but that was gradually sold off. It may not look much now, but thirty-odd years ago there were holiday cottages and a camping and caravan site here. There was even a swimming pool and a clubhouse and the place was packed, apparently, but the good times were over before I was born.'

'It's a shame a lovely old place like this is in this state,' I say then bite my lip, worried about offending him. I shift my bottom on the old settee to try and find a more comfortable position. I swear I can feel a spring sticking in me.

'It just gradually went downhill as people decided to holiday abroad. Then my father lost interest completely after Mum died. We haven't had guests since I went to uni and a place like this goes shabby fast, if it's not looked after. Other people have made a success of their parks and if I'd wanted to keep the business going, I shouldn't have gone off to save the world.'

'What did you do? Was it Africa or Syria? That must have been scary.'

'Like I said, I was an aid worker for a charity in the Middle East until I ended up needing aid myself. And that's all you need to know. Although I'm sure Polly will take great delight in filling you in on what she thinks she knows.' His voice tails off. 'Meanwhile, we have work to do. First, I'll show you the kitchen. I'm afraid we all have to muck in with the chores here but you're a professional so I'm sure you won't mind.'

So he doesn't want to tell me exactly where he has been. Fine. There are things I don't want him to know about me. 'Oh, did Polly make the curry? I can smell it.'

'You're joking. It was a takeout. Polly's never been a keen cook.'

'I've always loved cooking. I can make a mean biryani and

Thai curry, and a vegetable chilli with homemade guacamole. And a lovely fish pie – I used to go down to the harbour and buy the fish straight from the trawlers and I make fantastic pasties, steak, veggie – you should try my bacon and cheese ones. They're brilliant.'

He smiles and I realise I've been bigging myself up massively. 'It sounds like we might get on, after all. Shall I show you around the park so you can get your bearings and see what you've taken on?'

Excitement ripples through me. Sensing my mood change, Mitch sits up. 'Bring it on,' I say.

We walk through the farmhouse kitchen and a back porch, also packed with coats and boots, to a large cobbled yard at the rear of the house. A row of cottages faces the house, and they seem to be in better condition than the tumbledown barns and cow sheds at the front, which isn't saying much. Still, the building across the yard is standing, at least, and has curtains hanging at the windows.

'That's where you'll be staying,' Cal says, pointing to the end cottage with the curtains.

'Were those the holiday cottages?'

'No, they were for staff. The guest cottages are larger and in another part of the park but they need total refurbishment. People want holiday homes that are even better than their own houses these days.'

'I guess they do if they're paying a lot of money.'

'Yes, but I hope Kilhallon Park will have something to suit everyone's budgets. Come on, I'll show you the guest cottages and the buildings from the campsite that I plan to replace.'

With Mitch in seventh heaven at being out in the country, I walk with Cal through the rear yard and through a wooden farm gate along a short lane that's in slightly better condition than the one from the main road. Even so, I have to dodge a few ruts with dried mud in them. The lane is edged by Cornish hedges but the field on the coastal side falls away gently, giving us a wonderful view over the Atlantic Ocean. The sun glints on the sea as Cal strides off in the direction of a row of much bigger cottages a few hundred yards down the lane.

'The first thing we'll need to do is have this lane surfaced so that the builders can get access to the guest cottages,' he says, splashing through a large puddle in his wellies.

A few moments later, we stop outside the guest cottages. They are in a row of four, with stone walls and slated roofs covered in moss. I think they were once whitewashed but the walls are grey and moss-stained now. The tiny front gardens – more sitting-out areas really – of each cottage are a tangle of weeds.

Cal clicks his teeth and lets out a breath. 'As you'll see, the shells are sound but they need rewiring, and modern heating and plumbing, not to mention a decorative makeover. We're going to need to repair the slate roofs too. There's a lot to do but it'll be worth it. These old miners' cottages deserve some TLC.'

'They could be really pretty. Lots of kerb-appeal,' I say, channelling the TV property programmes Sheila used to record and watch back-to-back.

'That's what the guests are looking for. Something with character and a great view.'

'All the ingredients are here. You just need to turn them into a great dish.'

Cal laughs. 'With a lot of elbow grease, I'm sure we can.'

Mitch roots among the dandelions in the garden areas while I wander up to the front door of one cottage. A chipped slate plaque hangs lopsidedly from a nail. I push it horizontal and read the name.

'*Penvenen*? What does that mean?'

Cal gives a wry smile. 'My granny loved the Winston Graham novels and they were big when the TV series was on in the 1970s when the cottages were originally converted to holiday homes. It was her idea to name them after characters in the Poldark novels.

So that's why we have Penvenen, Warleggan, Enys – and Poldark, of course.'

'I'm sorry, I haven't read those books.'

'Nor me, and the TV series was on long before I was born, but Polly says it's popular again now so we should leave them as they are.'

'It's a nice thing to keep the names if they were your granny's idea. The tourists love that sort of thing. They were always asking how old Sheila's Beach Hut was. Sheila used to tell them it was a smuggler's haunt and then they'd order more drinks just to stay longer.'

Cal bursts out laughing. 'Sheila's was never a smuggler's haunt! Even the oldest part of the building can't be more than a hundred years old.'

'It worked, though. I think you should definitely keep the names.'

He gives me a sharp look then breaks into a smile. I must admit, he's cheered up while he's been showing me the place so I must have done something right. 'I think you're going to be very useful around here, Ms Jones. Come on, let's go and take a look at the camping area.'

As we walk around the rest of the park, an hour whizzes by but I've enjoyed every minute of it. Cal took me into the two fields that once housed the static caravans and the camping site. The vans have long gone; he told me that his father ran out of money for replacing the fleet so they were all sold off to people doing self-builds. The camping site and caravans were served by an 'amenity block' with loos, showers and washing-up area. That's in a right old state, almost derelict. There were birds nesting in the showers.

'And,' he says, nodding at a large grassy depression surrounded by broken tiles, 'that was a swimming pool.'

'I can just about tell . . .' I try to be diplomatic. Although the site is large, he wasn't kidding when he said there was work to do. 'What's that?'

I point at a crumbling stone building silhouetted against the late afternoon sun, at the far edge of the camping field.

'Just an old farm building we used to use for storage of the grass-mowing machines and equipment for the caravans in the winter. I haven't been in there for years so it's probably still got loads of random stuff in it.'

'It's a shame to leave it in that state.'

'Yes, I suppose so. It'll have to be tidied up, at least until we know what to do with it. I haven't got round to making plans for everything yet. That's why you're here. If you have any ideas, just shoot away. Now, shall I show you where you'll be staying?'

'Great.' With a whistle to Mitch, I follow Cal back across the field towards the reception area and staff cottages, but I can't resist a glance behind at the crumbling, unloved storage building. I wonder . . .

An idea has formed in my mind but I've only just met Cal and I'm definitely not ready to shoot just yet.

'Here you go.' A few minutes later, he twists the handle on the door of the end staff cottage. 'I wouldn't call this premium accommodation but this is the best of them. I told you it wasn't much and it's a bit damp because no one's been living here for a few years but it should do, if you're prepared to put in a bit of elbow grease. I'm sure Polly will bring over some cleaning stuff and bed linen, or I will when I get a chance.'

The door opens straight into a little sitting room with a two-seater sofa, covered in a crazy flowery pattern. There's an empty fireplace and a few pictures on the walls, mostly of vases of roses and trees. The carpet has orange and blue swirls and the curtains are a sort of pink, with abstract tulips. At least, I think they were tulips once and are now splodges. In one corner a narrow open-backed staircase leads upstairs.

'Sorry, I don't think it's been renovated since before I was born.'

'It's . . . um . . . very *flowery*.'

'It's either this or the box room in the attic of the farmhouse and I'm sure you'd much rather have your own front door.'

'Beggars can't be choosers.'

He doesn't laugh. 'So you'll be OK in here?'

'Yeah . . .' Tears clog my throat at the thought of actually having four walls and a roof over mine and Mitch's heads, then I woman up. I am working for the guy, after all. I deserve a proper roof over my head. 'It's fine. Thank you.'

'You don't sound too sure?'

I throw him a smile. 'Honestly, it's great. Can I see the rest of it?'

'Sure.'

Mitch runs ahead into the kitchen, which is basic but has a cooker, fridge and sink. There are few dead flies on the window-sill and a whiff of damp, but it's my own space and that's what matters.

Cal opens the fridge door and sniffs. 'I might have to get you another fridge.'

'I can clean it. It'll be OK.'

'If you want to have a go, fine, but I'll get a new one if you need it. You have rights here, including a decent place to live.'

'Will you just shut up?' I say, wanting to laugh at his slapped-arse face. 'And show me the rest of the place, *boss*.'

'Please don't call me that. Polly only does it to wind me up.'

'OK, boss.'

I picture his scowl as he leads the way up the stairs while Mitch explores his new territory. It's a sexy scowl, I bet, and his bum and thighs look great in the jeans. Then I rap myself on the knuckles for thinking such thoughts. This is work and he is my employer.

Cal opens a door to one side of the tiny landing. 'Bathroom, obviously. Should be OK with a good scrub.'

I pop my head round the door and smile at the rose pink suite

50

that reminds me of my granny's. The bath has a shower over it that's seen better days.

On the opposite side of the landing, sunlight casts a yellow window pattern on the floor. The open door leads into the bedroom, with more flowers on the wall, a wardrobe, a chest of drawers and a mattress on the floor. Through the window, across the fields, whitecaps dance on the inky blue sea. I pull back the net curtain and peer through a film of salt spray and grime. The first thing I'll do is rip the nets down so I can enjoy the view every morning.

'There's a spare bed frame in the attic at the farmhouse. I'll carry it over,' Cal says. I'm not sure if he was smiling at me or not while I looked out of the window and I don't care what he thinks.

'I can do that.'

'You'd be better off taking the Land Rover up to the petrol station shop to get some food in.'

I follow him downstairs. 'Me? Drive that old thing?'

'Yes, unless you want to walk five miles across the fields,' he smiles, cunningly. 'Or you can take my horse if you like. He's a bit skittish but if you can ride, you're welcome.'

'No, thanks, I don't like horses. They're dangerous.'

'That depends on the rider. The Land Rover it is. When you've settled in, come over to the house to collect the keys and some money. You do have a licence?'

'Yes. My brother taught me before he left home to join the army.'

He seems surprised. 'OK.'

The sofa boings as I test the springs. Cal glances at my rucksack and my dirty ripped jeans. Before I even realise, I'm pushing a tangled strand of hair out of eyes, and the pink rises to my cheeks.

'I'll ask Polly to find you some work clothes for now and you'd better go into town tomorrow and get a few new things.'

'I can buy my own clothes.'

'OK, fine, but if you want an advance on your pay cheque, just shout. Right, I'll go and fetch this bed frame.'

Half an hour later, Cal struggles over the yard with part of the bed frame on his shoulders. For a lean guy, he's very strong. I help him carry it upstairs and then he's off again, dumping an old TV, the fat-backed kind, on the rickety bamboo table in the corner of the sitting room.

'You can have this if you want,' he says. 'My father used to watch it in bed.'

'Good. I can watch telly later. *Sherlock*'s on tonight.'

'Is it? I haven't had a chance to watch much TV lately.' He laughs in that 'not remotely amused' kind of way and I feel I've said something stupid but I'm not sure what.

Polly bustles in with a box of bleach and a scowl on her face. 'I've got some cleaning stuff but I'll have to bring the towels and linen later. You do know there's no bed frame up there?' she says to Cal. 'The old one had woodworm so I chucked it on the bonfire.'

He glares at her. 'Then it's a good job I've already found a new one.'

Polly shudders when Mitch sniffs at her ankles. 'You needn't think I'll be cleaning up any dog hairs either. Scraggy thing,' she says.

'I'm sure Mitch feels the same way about you.'

Polly scowls.

'Sorry,' I say, as Cal stifles a laugh. 'I didn't mean to be that rude.'

'Demi's perfectly capable of looking after the place herself,' he says.

Polly flounces off, grumbling, but I don't care how much she moans. I still can't believe that Mitch and I have a new job and a place to live.

I'm still having to pinch myself later, when I sit round the farmhouse table with Cal and Polly, soaking up the remains of a chicken curry with a piece of naan. Getting to grips with the Aga was a bit of a nightmare, especially with Polly issuing dire warnings about it.

Judging by the empty plates, they seemed to enjoy the food.

Polly stabs a piece of chicken with her fork and Cal wipes his plate round with his last piece of naan.

'Was it OK?' I say.

Cal nods.

'It wasn't bad,' Polly says and I wonder if I misheard her. Was that a *compliment*? 'Shame you let it dry out a bit,' she adds. 'Agas aren't like normal cookers.'

'I'll get the hang of it,' I protest.

Cal stands up and picks up his plate. 'Finished?'

Polly gasps. 'You're not clearing up!'

'Why not?'

'She can do that. That's why you've hired her.'

'*She* is not a bloody skivvy, Polly, and *she's* been cleaning the cottage and working all day.'

Acting innocent, I swig my beer. Cal walks round to my side of the table and stacks my plate on his. He brushes against me and smells faintly of clean sweat and beer. He's been working all day too, helping me put the bed frame together and trying to fix the door of the barn.

'Thanks.' I ignore Polly's laser stare.

'Don't get used to it,' he says. 'I don't expect you to cook for me every night and you won't want to eat in here all the time.'

'I can cook tons of stuff and I don't mind eating here.'

'You'll want your own space,' says Cal, carrying the plates towards the hall.

'Yes, you will.' Polly casts a triumphant glance at me. I wonder what her problem is, apart from worrying about the extra work of looking after me. She needn't bother.

I finish my beer at the dining table and let Mitch lick my

curryfied fingers while Polly goes back to her cottage to watch *Emmerdale*. In the kitchen, I find Cal cursing and fiddling with the settings on the dishwasher.

In frustration, he stands back. 'Jesus, you need a PhD to work it out.'

'Here. Let me have a go.'

A few presses later, I get it to start. 'We had two at the cafe,' I explain.

'Thanks. I'm going to work in the study for the rest of the evening but tomorrow I'll get your contract sorted out. Can I ask you to be patient with Polly? She's very protective of me. She is an old friend.'

'I understand. I'm the newbie. It's me that has to fit in.'

'Thanks.' He hesitates. 'Will you be OK in the cottage on your own tonight? Kilhallon is a bit out of the way. You might find it too quiet and isolated.'

'You mean, me being a city girl who can't live without a night-club and a Starbucks within spitting distance? It'll be a change not to sleep in a shop doorway, and besides, I have Mitch for company. We'll sleep like logs.'

'Well, you know where I am if you want me or Polly. I'd better get you a phone sorted too.'

While the dishwasher burbles and Cal throws the empty beer bottles in the recycling crate, I hover by the sink.

'Cal . . . thanks for the job and the cottage. I mean it.' Damn the quiver in my voice.

'You might not thank me when we get the business up and running. There's going to be a lot to do. Goodnight.'

I hate to admit it, but Cal was right. I *couldn't* sleep, not even with a brand new bed and a thick down duvet and my own bedroom with pink curtains. Not even when I got up and made a cup of tea in my own kitchen and sat and drank it while I watched the midnight news on my new old TV. The wind rustled the curtains most of the night and I thought I could hear the waves crashing against the cliffs across the fields.

I don't believe in ghosts but all sorts of weird and freaky thoughts kept filling my head. I couldn't go back to bed so in the end I had to unroll my sleeping bag on the carpet and sleep in front of the hearth, with Mitch on my feet. I dreamt I was at home with my mum before everything started to unravel. I thought I'd be happy when I got a job and my own place: if someone would only give me a chance. But no matter what we have, we always want a little bit more.

I woke up early, wondering where I was at first. Mitch was already pawing at the cottage door to be let out so I put on his lead and took him out for a walk. No one else was around so I walked down the valley towards Kilhallon Cove and watched Mitch play 'tag' with the waves. On the other side of the cliffs, there was an old engine house. It's a ruin now, the roof has long collapsed but half the chimney stack still stands.

I walked back to the cottage, fed Mitch and made myself some toast in my kitchen. The cottage still needs work but I'd better go over to the farmhouse and find out what Cal wants me to do. Last night, he said he wanted me to discuss my contract and terms and conditions and I want to get off on the right foot with him. After settling Mitch in the kitchen with a dog chew, I have a bath – oh, the luxury – put on my freshly washed jeans and top and set off.

Polly meets me halfway across the farmyard. 'You're out of bed then?' She raises her eyebrows as if she's surprised.

'I've been up for hours,' I say, determined not to rise to the bait.

'Hmmph.'

'Is Cal around?'

'Yes, but you'd better keep out of his way.'

'Why?'

'You'll find out. He's in his office, last I saw of him. If you dare.'

This is not encouraging news on my first morning but I'm not going to be put off by her.

Greasy breakfast plates are piled on the worktops in the kitchen, and someone's left the bacon and milk out in the sun. One of the plates has half a sausage left on it and despite the toast I ate earlier, I can't see good food go to waste so I eat it, enjoying the luxury of not having to share it with Mitch. Sidestepping a piece of tomato squashed on the tiles, I walk down the gloomy hallway and knock on the study door. There's no answer but I can hear someone tapping away on a laptop.

'Cal. Are you in there?'

There's a pause then he grunts. 'Go away, whoever you are.'

'It's Demi.'

'Go away.'

'OK.' I turn away, thinking I may as well clear up the kitchen; that's what he hired me for. Just as I reach the door, there's a shout behind me.

'Come back.'

Cal pokes his head out of the study door.

'It'll wait until later,' I say.

'No. We'll get it over with now.'

'Are you sure?'

'I'm not at my best,' he growls.

To be honest, I haven't noticed loads of difference but I keep that to myself.

'Sit down,' he says gruffly, sweeping papers off an old wheeled chair in front of his desk.

I sit; suddenly worried that he might have changed his mind about having me at Kilhallon.

'I have to finish this email first,' he mutters, eyes fixed on the screen again. He hasn't had a shave, again, and he has dark circles under his eyes. He looks awful but drop dead gorgeous all the same.

He glances up briefly, obviously having caught me perving

over him. 'What's up?'

'Nothing.' Heat rises to my cheeks again. 'I really can come back later. Polly said you were busy.'

'She's right but I'll be even busier later. Wait a minute and I'll be done.'

Frowning at the screen, he taps away with two fingers while I try to focus on the study and not on him. It's like a junk shop – antique shop, if I'm being generous – and bigger than I expected, despite being crammed with stuff just like the sitting room. Two of the walls are lined with bookcases from floor to ceiling; proper old-fashioned leather-bound books as well as paperbacks. The desk must be centuries old and among all the letters and paper-work, Cal's laptop whirrs softly. If it was me, I'd put the light on because even though it's a bright April morning, not much sunshine penetrates the dimness.

'OK. I'm done. Let's talk about your role here.'

My role? I try to stay serious, while longing to dance around the study, shouting 'yes!', listening to Cal outlining what he wants me to do: generally helping around the place and supporting him to get the holiday park back on its feet. He also asks me if I want to go to college in September to do some tourism and catering courses.

'We need stationery from the office supplies store and I'd like you to get some costs for refitting the reception. You'd better get some new clothes too.'

I glance down at my only pair of jeans and T-shirt, wondering why he's brought up the subject again. 'I don't need a handout.'

'Fine. In that case, will you accept an advance on your salary? You can pay me back if you like but you may as well get some work clothes and safety boots on the business. The agricultural store on the road to St Ives should have what you need.'

'Thanks,' I say, wishing I hadn't been quite so dismissive.

He pulls out his wallet. 'Here's my card so you can get some cash, though we've still got an account at the agricultural and office stores.'

'I could run off with this,' I joke.

'Not without Mitch. He's my hostage.'

I snort. 'He'd never stay with you.'

'Want to bet?' He grins in such a sexy way, I get the funny fizzing feeling low in my stomach. I half-wish he was fat and old and picked his teeth or something, rather than this hot. It would make life so much easier.

The door opens and Polly stands in the doorway blocking out the light. 'Cal? I thought you'd like to know you've had a letter.'

'Leave it on the desk, please.'

Ignoring him, Polly holds an envelope under his nose. It's the kind you see in costume dramas, with elaborate, old-fashioned handwriting on the front.

'I thought I should bring this one over personally.' She waggles the envelope, a sly gleam in her eye.

Cal looks at it but doesn't take it. 'I said, leave it on the desk. *Please*.' The please is added with sarcasm, almost menace.

Polly lays it on top of a pile of other papers but makes no attempt to leave.

'You can go now.' Cal's voice is quieter, and his finger taps the table. 'And you.'

It's a second before I realise he means me.

'See you later,' says Polly, smirking.

I push myself up from the chair. 'So, do you want any lunch?'

'Just leave me.' His head snaps up. God, he looks angry – but that's nothing to the pain I see in his eyes. I don't say any more, just do as he asks. He was moody before I walked in here. I don't know what's in that letter, but it looks as if it's almost destroyed him before he's even opened it.

CHAPTER SIX

I knew it had to happen. I knew it was coming but that doesn't lessen the pain or make it any easier to take. I brush my fingers over the embossed script, and the handwritten insertion of my name. It sounds so formal and so final. Did Isla write it herself – or her mother? I can't believe it was Luke's idea but maybe I don't know him any more.

WE'RE ENGAGED!
Isla and Luke
invite
Mr Calvin Penwith
to celebrate their engagement with them
On Saturday June 25th
from 7 p.m.
At Bosinney House, St Trenyan
RSVP to Isla Channing

The date is more than two months away, which makes me feel that Mrs Channing has had a hand in the invites. She obviously wants to send a signal out to the world that Isla and Luke are officially together. She never liked me and perhaps I don't blame her if she thought I was making Isla unhappy by trekking off abroad all the time.

Perhaps Luke wants to send me a signal and formalise the engagement. Last night, all I could think about was Luke lying in bed with Isla and contrasting it with the times I lay with her in the barn here at Kilhallon, and in the warm dunes and the cool cave on the beach.

I'd been with her on that last night before I went to the Tinner's Arms for a farewell drink with my mates. Luke had warned me that evening to tell Isla how I felt but I'd held back. I thought she already did know without me saying it and as for marrying her, I thought we were too young, that we had years to do all that stuff when I'd got back from the Middle East. I could never have married her *then*, I told myself, until I'd at least tried to help the people I saw on the news and the internet. How could I sit here at Kilhallon, in my comfortable home, doing nothing, when I had the skills to help those people? What kind of a man would I be? What kind of a husband and father . . .

Two years is a long time to wait; when you've hardly heard a word and when you think all hope is lost. But the irony is that it was the thought of Isla that kept me going through the long, dark days and months. A few times, I'd have topped myself if it hadn't been for her, when things got too terrible to bear.

I can't tell her the truth, of course, the reason why I was away so long and why I couldn't contact her for the past few months. When I first went on my trips abroad I used to send her 'vintage' postcards – my retro joke – but on my last assignment, there were no cards to buy or even shops still standing in most places. It was a miracle if I could get a decent signal or Wi-Fi or even access to a computer and, if I'm honest, I'd been so wrapped up with my work I sometimes didn't have a moment to even think about home. When you're dealing with people in a life or death situation, your priorities tend to change but I should have made more effort. Perhaps I can't blame Isla for thinking I wasn't interested any more. Then, when I finally wanted to speak to her, and had time on my hands at last, it was impossible.

I slam the lid of the laptop shut and throw the invitation on the floor.

Is it really too late? Maybe I should ride over to Bosinney now and speak to Isla on her own? If I see her face to face, I can let her know how I feel and change her mind. The study door slams behind me as I hurry out to the yard.

'Cal, can you come and look at this tractor?' The mechanic from the garage calls over to me.

'Not now, mate.'

'But it needs a new clutch. It can't wait any longer.'

'Not now!'

'OK but it's your funeral.' He folds his arms. 'And without a working tractor, you won't be able to do a lot of the work you've planned here.'

'OK. Good point.' After I've heard Baz tell me how much work the tractor needs and how much it will cost, I seek solace in the stables with the one creature that doesn't seem to have changed, and who is waiting patiently for me. At least Polly made sure my horse, Dexter, was taken care of while I was away, even if the park fell down around her ears.

Dexter snickers softly and stamps impatiently as I tack him up. I mount him and catch sight of Demi with a clipboard, in front of the admin block. I asked her to do some research on other resorts and give her opinion on what facilities she thought we needed and how the park should look. She's no expert but that's what I wanted: a fresh pair of eyes to view this place as if she might love to come on holiday here herself.

Have I done the right thing in bringing her here? She's a bright girl and she'll probably be out of here in a year, maybe less. She'll want more than I can offer her.

Demi glances up from her clipboard and waves at me. She looks really happy and I'm glad but I don't wave back. I act like

I haven't been watching her, and I don't really know why. Perhaps I still haven't got used to people reading my emotions. I've had to suppress them for so long, just to survive.

With a kick on Dexter's flanks, I urge him to a gallop along the coastal path. If I ride until the land ends, maybe I can ride Isla out of my system.

At the milestone, I spot a dark hunter galloping over the moor towards me. I'd know Robyn's horse anywhere, and the rider's style. I urge Dexter on and our horses both meet by a ruined engine house.

Both of us are breathless and laughing. 'Hi, Robyn,' I say when I've got my breath back. 'I could tell it was you from miles away.'

She pushes a lock of purply black hair back under her helmet. Her face is pink with the sea air and the effort. 'Have I improved?' she asks.

'You've got worse, if anything.'

She leans over her horse and hits my arm. 'That's harsh and anyway I can tell you're way out of practice . . . ouch, sorry, great big foot in even bigger mouth.'

'There's no need to tiptoe around it.'

'I know but it must have been tough helping people out there and then you come back and found out about Luke and Isla. They'd only just told us.'

So Robyn notices more than she lets on. 'It's fine. Well, not fine . . .' It's hopeless lying to my cousin; she knows me too well. 'Maybe it wasn't the best idea to turn up like that though I did try to warn Isla. I'm sorry I shocked you and Uncle Rory though by crashing his birthday do.' I pat Dexter's silky mane, avoiding Robyn's eyes. 'How was Isla after I'd left the party?'

'What do you think? Relieved you're home safe. She was out of her mind with worry when we hadn't heard from you for a while.'

'Yeah. It looked like it. I had her engagement party invitation this morning.'

'Oh Cal. Don't be like that. Isla was gutted, she couldn't eat or sleep properly for the weeks after you left, and when you never replied to our latest emails . . .'

A lump sticks in my throat. Does hearing that Isla suffered make me feel better or worse? Is it real love, wanting her to have suffered?

'She seems to have got over it.'

'She even emailed the charity but they said you were working in a remote location and couldn't be contacted. Luke was worried as well.'

'I'll bet he was.'

'This must be so hard for you.' Choosing to ignore my sarcasm, which is probably a good thing for both of us, Robyn stops the horse, reaches over and touches me. Her fingers linger on my forearm, soothing, gentle. Once this act of kindness would have touched me deeply but that was before I learned that the only way to survive is to kill every feeling and become stone. I can't answer her, and she takes her hand away from mine.

'Are you sure you're OK? You look so thin. Did something terrible happen to you out there?'

I pause, weighing up how much I can tell her and how much of that can be the truth. 'I'm fine. I was just wrapped up in helping people.'

'Oh Cal, I can't even imagine how awful it was.'

'Then don't. Thousands of people have died or lost their families and homes in the wars. I'm here in one piece and I have all this.' I scrape up a smile and wave in the direction of the tumbledown cottages. 'Now, for God's sake, tell me how *you* are and what you've been doing. I've a lot of catching up to do.'

While we walked the horses along the cliffs, she fills me in on her latest escapades. It's comforting listening to her chatter about her jewellery design course and the fact she's working part time in the Tinner's to annoy Uncle Rory and earn some money of her own. She's twenty-two now, and she ought to have her independence but she's drifted from one thing to another since she left uni and I think it suits my uncle to keep her at home. She deserves a break: stability, love, excitement and happiness – whatever it is she's looking for.

We urge the horses over the stream and onto the sand of Kilhallon Cove. At high tide, the beach is a sliver of pebbles but at low tide, like now, it's a long strip of flat sand. The tang of seaweed and salt hangs in the air, reminding me of the times I rode here and made love to Isla.

Clouds gather over the sea but the weather front is on its way north of us. It's going to be a bright day and the longer hours of sunlight have brought out the primroses in the hedgerows around the park. I'd forgotten how seductive this place could be, even in the state it is now. 'It's gorgeous here, isn't it?' Robyn says.

'Yes. I was going to ride over to Bosinney.'

'To see me?' Robyn says, mischievously.

'Of course, and my uncle.'

'He and Luke are back in the office in Truro today. Were you coming to see Isla too? She's visiting Bosinney; she's thinking of using it in her new series.'

'Is she?'

Robyn isn't stupid; the opposite, in fact, and I feel ashamed.

'Dad can do with the money even though he doesn't want the disruption. Isla's asked her director of photography to come down and take a look. She's meant to be on holiday but I think she'll spend most of the time scouting locations.'

'I read about her success in the paper on my way here.' I don't add that I've since wasted way too much time googling Isla on the new laptop.

'She's amazing. Did you know one of her productions was nominated for a BAFTA? She's a joint director of her own production company now.'

'I bet her mother and Luke love that.'

'Isla's mother can't talk of anything else but Luke's more interested in making money these days since he became a director of Dad's company. They're playing the stock market, and making some high-risk investments – you see, they offer business and financial planning to the clients now, as well as doing the books.'

'Luke didn't used to be so money-oriented. Are things OK with the business?'

Robyn pulls a face. 'I don't know but I worry about them both. Luke's young and I suppose he can take a few hits but Dad isn't getting any younger. He had treatment for an ulcer last year and stress isn't good for him, even though he's on the mend. I'm not sure he really knows what Luke gets up to, but they've become like father and son since Luke's dad died last year. I think my dad feels he owes it to Luke's father's memory to support him.'

'I'm sorry Uncle Rory's been ill. Do you mind Luke getting so close to him?'

Robyn reins in the horse and shrugs. 'It wouldn't make any difference if I did. I've grown up with Luke, just like you have, and I suppose he was already like a brother to me, just like you are, Cal.'

Her comment makes me feel emotional. Did I say I had no capacity for feeling left? I must be going soft again. 'How does Isla feel about all this?' I ask.

'I'm not sure how much time she has to get involved. Her work normally takes her away from Luke and Cornwall a lot.'

'Funny. She used to hate it when I went away.'

'I guess she had to get used to it when she started running her own company and you were off the scene.' Robyn sighs and stares out to sea. 'That was harsh. I'm so sorry, Cal. I wish I could turn back the clock.'

'Not harsh. True and no one can turn back time.'

We ride up the path and walk the horses past an old engine house back towards Kilhallon. Crows caw and wheel around the broken chimney stack. There's probably a bird of prey around somewhere, judging by the noise they're making.

'Polly told me you've taken on some new staff,' she says as we guide our horses through the derelict cottages towards the amenity complex.

'News travels fast.'

'Is that the new girl I saw walking her dog into the complex when I rode past yesterday morning? Skinny with long chestnut hair?'

'Probably.'

'She looks about sixteen.'

'She's twenty-one, almost the same age as you.'

'Polly says she was homeless.'

'How does she know that?'

'I don't know. Village grapevine?'

I soften my tone but St Trenyan gossip never changes. God knows what they've made up about me, though it can't be any more outlandish than the truth I suppose.

'Not exactly. Demi was working at Sheila's Beach Hut but was looking for a fresh start with accommodation. She's had catering and um . . . other hospitality experience. She needed a break and I needed staff. End of.'

We ride along the edge of the cliff now and a gull swoops low, startling Robyn's horse but she soon regains control and carries on as if nothing had happened. She's far more confident than before I went away, with the horse at least. I'm not sure she's happy, though, and I don't quite know why.

'We were a bit surprised that you'd moved that quickly. Are you really planning to re-open the park again soon?'

'It's either that or let the whole place rot, and we could do with some jobs round here from what I saw in St Trenyan. It could just be me, but it looks more run-down than before I went away. I can't sit on my arse letting the park go downhill even further when I could do some good with it.'

'I'm not criticising, Cal. I'm right behind you and if there's anything I can do to help, just ask.'

66

'Thanks.'

'I didn't only come over to share the gossip. I also wanted to ask you to a party.'

I burst out laughing. 'I'm not in much of a party mood.'

'I know that but this is important. It's a charity ball at the Dolphin Country Club in aid of a homeless charity.'

I laugh at the irony. 'Thanks, but I'm too busy trying to get the business back on its feet. You know what they say: charity begins at home.'

'You don't believe that!'

I urge the horse to a trot and the ocean grows closer, the waves like the hooves of a thousand horses galloping to meet us.

'I haven't said when this ball is yet,' Robyn shouts to me.

'Whenever it is, I'm too busy.'

She catches up with me easily. 'This event will be good for your business. My friend says all the local "great and good" will be there.'

'There you are then: I don't count as either.'

'Argh, Cal, you drive me nuts. Say you'll come? You can take me with you, as there's no one else worth going with.'

My jaw aches from trying not to smile. 'Won't that be like going with your brother?'

She wrinkles her nose. 'No, this would be more like going with my gay best friend.'

'Thanks.'

'Go on, you know you're tempted. You love to shock people.'

I laugh, wondering if she has any idea what I might have done while I've been 'away'.

'I haven't upset you, have I? Dad says I never think before I speak and I talk too much . . . Luke definitely thinks so. He told me.'

'Then they're both talking out of their arses and Luke should shut up.'

'Maybe they're right.' She laughs but I feel angry with my

uncle and Luke.

'Be yourself, and screw anyone who doesn't like it.'

'That's not always so simple. I haven't got a proper job apart from working in the Tinner's and I can't afford my own place yet.'

I think of the cottages on the estate and the fact I let Demi have one, but I can't afford to give away any more of them and besides, I can't interfere in Robyn's life; she needs to stand up to my uncle and make her own way.

'So, you'll come to this charity do? You'd be doing me a massive favour.'

Her voice is light but holds an edge of desperation. I get the feeling there's something she's not telling me.

'I'll think about it.'

CHAPTER SEVEN

When Cal said there was work to do here, he wasn't joking. Over the past few weeks, he's been to Truro and St Trenyan, meeting with his old contacts to try to raise extra investment in the new resort. Polly has been moaning even more than usual about the 'bloody strangers' poking around in the derelict farm buildings and cottages and tramping in and out of the farmhouse in muddy boots.

I think it's exciting, and at least Cal seems wrapped up in the business, rather than getting slowly pissed in his study all evening. I was researching more competitor parks, but Polly asked me to take the empty beer and whisky bottles to the recycling bins in the morning. I don't want to judge people but I don't think the booze helps his mood much.

Talking of which, I finally found out why he acted like the world has ended when he received The Letter. Polly told me that it was an invitation to his ex's engagement party. Turns out this Isla and Cal were crazy about each other but when he came back to Cornwall, he found out she'd got engaged to his mate. Polly says Isla thought Cal wasn't interested any more because he'd stopped all contact with her. Polly thinks Isla should have waited until Cal came home and I agree with her on this one, not that it matters to me. There's no way I am going to rely on some bloke for my future, however much I owe him and however hot he is.

'Demi?'

Cal meets me by the waste bins. There are dark circles under his eyes, and I think he was working on a business plan until the small hours.

'I need to go to Truro to see the architect and try to shave some costs from the plans. Can you spare the time to visit the builders' merchant and get some costs and ideas for the bathrooms and kitchens in the cottages? We need to make a start.'

This sounds like an interesting job so I jump at the chance. 'Yes, if you want me to.'

'Good. Be ready in ten minutes.'

Cal dropped me off at the builders' merchants and I checked out the bathrooms and kitchens, and arranged for the designers to come and see the old cottages. He didn't ask me to do that so I hope it's OK. The staff told me it can take weeks to get the fixtures and fittings and we need to compare the estimates. My visit took over an hour so I walked over to Lemon Quay to meet him, wondering if I had time to grab a takeout coffee while I was there.

The city is busier than last time I was here because there's a food fair taking place, with stalls and vans selling everything from local chocolates and sea salt to fresh fish and even Cornish tea. The rich scents and spicy aromas compete for my attention as I browse the stores, trying to resist buying things that aren't strictly necessary. Sheila tried to use local suppliers but I had no idea you could get all of this stuff right on the doorstep.

Cal still hasn't called me yet and I've had a decent signal on the work mobile he's supplied me with and I don't mind hanging around for a while. I'm enjoying myself far too much and a new idea is brewing in my mind. It first occurred to me when Cal showed me the old storage building on the edge of the campsite, and visiting the fair has cemented the idea in my brain. With a lot of hard work, that building could make a great cafe, especially if it served the kind of delicious local goodies I've seen and tasted today. However, I need to do a lot more thinking about how a cafe would work as part of the park, before I share the plan with Cal.

After buying some sardines, fresh herbs and locally grown salad for dinner, I pop into a tiny coffee shop huddled in between a jewellers and a bridal boutique near the cathedral. These little places need all the custom they can get. I treat myself to a flat white and I decide I ought to wander back to Lemon Quay again. The architect's office is nearby and Cal *must* be finished soon.

'Demi?'

A girl about my age, in dark clothes and goth make-up, walks up to me. I've no idea who she is although for a split second I wonder if it's Andi Cade, Mawgan's timid sister.

'That's me. But how do you know my name?'

'I'm Cal's cousin, Robyn. You haven't met me but I've seen you walking your dog across Kilhallon Park. Cal told me you were working there now.'

'Yes.'

'How's it going at Kilhallon?' she asks.

'Fine. OK.'

'Good. Cal can be a bit grumpy but we're all so glad he's back and he decided to make a go of Kilhallon again. I'm so happy he took on someone to help him.'

'Me too.' Robyn seems nice but it's odd to be having a conversation about Cal, when I hardly know him and I don't know her at all.

'He told me you'd got lots of experience in the hospitality business. I'm impressed,' she says.

'Um. Did he? Well, I've worked in catering and er . . . leisure.'

'He needs help. I'd do it but I'm at college, doing a degree in jewellery design.'

'That explains the pendant. It looks amazing.'

Robyn touches the jewelled silver moon around her neck. 'Thanks. I love my course but it's harder than it sounds. Some of the tutors, you know . . .'

I nod, recalling my experience with some of the ones on my hygiene and health and safety courses. As we're blocking the entrance of the coffee shop, we move to the relative quiet of the bridal-shop window, which has amazing gowns with no price tags in it.

'Cal's here in Truro. I was supposed to meet him almost an hour ago,' I tell Robyn. 'He had a meeting with the architect but there's no sign of him at the moment.'

She frowns. 'Oh, really? I'm waiting for someone and she's really late too. I missed a lecture for this but she wants me to help her choose something for her engagement party, though God knows why. I mean, she likes full-on glamour and look at me.'

I do. Her long purple skirt brushes her DMs and she wears a dark-green velvet top with flowing sleeves. It's all a bit Guinevere and King Arthur for me but it suits her. Her choppy, cool haircut gleams like a raven's wing with layers of dark purple, indigo and green.

'You look fine to me. I shouldn't change for anyone else.'

'That's not always easy, is it?' She sighs. 'I think Isla just wanted some company, as well as my opinion. She and her fiancé are wondering whether to commission some Celtic bands from the jeweller.'

At the mention of Isla, I realise that the 'friend' is Cal's ex.

'I think I should be getting back to Lemon Quay in case Cal's waiting and hasn't got a signal or something.'

'I'll walk over there with you. Isla can text or call me.'

Robyn chats to me about her course and Kilhallon Park while we walk back to the food fair. Although she's only met me today, she chats away like I'm an old friend which is nice but I'm wary that she's Cal's cousin and he's my boss.

'I hope Cal's paying you well and not working you too hard,' she says.

I laugh. 'He pays me the living wage and I get the cottage and my meals free.'

'Hmm.'

I smile. 'Cal does his best and there might be new opportunities when the park gets off the ground.' My cafe idea pops up in my mind again. Could it really be viable?

'I hope so,' says Robyn. 'At least you have your independence. I hate having to live with Dad but I'm just a skint student.'

The smell of hot food makes my stomach rumble when we reach the stalls. After tossing my empty cup in a bin, I check my phone and Robyn does the same. There are still no messages or missed calls and it's now over two hours since Cal had his appointment.

'I hope he comes back soon or the ticket will run out on the car park,' I say.

'Oh, look. Isn't that Cal now?'

Robyn waves to a couple outside a shop, on the far side of the food fair. It's obvious Cal is talking – or rather arguing – with a tall, slim girl with long blonde hair.

'He's with Isla,' Robyn says, then groans. 'Oh, I think I have to go.'

Polly's gossip and The Letter race into my mind. That's *her*, then, the ex, the woman who broke his heart. I try to get a better look but people keep obscuring my view.

'Good to meet you. I'll ask Cal for your number and text you. It'd be cool to meet up again. Byeeee.'

Robyn dashes across the square, almost tripping over her skirt but Cal is already striding towards her. She reaches him and says something, I assume, then tries to hug him but he shakes his head and walks faster in my direction. By his thunderous expression, I wonder if I and the sardines will get home in one piece. I take a deep breath and prepare myself for a very awkward journey.

CHAPTER EIGHT

I never meant to argue with Isla. I tried so hard but it was a shock, seeing her come out of the jewellers with Luke. I'd just finished with the architect when I spotted them. I watched him kiss her goodbye and walk back towards his office and fully intended to walk away in the opposite direction.

That's what I should have done. What a sensible man would have done.

Instead I found myself crossing the street, and almost jogging through the crowds of shoppers to catch her up. Was it a wise decision? Her face told me the answer. She was shocked, dismayed, a little afraid of me, even. Oh, she changed her expression fast enough: she hid her real feelings very well; anyone would think she was an actress not a producer. But it was too late.

A nice guy would have said a quick hello, made his excuses and said he couldn't stay long because he had work to do and a holiday park to rebuild and his car park ticket was expiring. But I'm not a nice guy: not where Isla Channing's concerned and Cornwall County Council can fine me a hundred quid and it still won't make any difference to how I feel.

After a brief chat, she kissed me goodbye; I think she wanted it to be a friendly peck on the cheek but somehow, our lips met.

She didn't pull away and it was only quick but afterwards she said, 'That was for old times' sake. It can't happen again.'

'Why did it happen at all, then?' I asked.

'Cal. I want to stay friends.'

'So do I. Did you find anything you liked in the jewellers, then?' I hated myself even as the words left my mouth.

'Not yet, but I know I will soon.'

'Are you going to the ball?'

'Of course I am. Luke and his dad have bought a table. Goodbye, Cal. Take care.'

'Wait! Isla!'

'I waited for you long enough, Cal.'

I reached for her arm but she slipped away. It was probably a good job that Robyn saw us. I phoned her this morning and apologised and said I'd go to the ball with her. I owe it to her. Now all I have to do is make it up to Demi for the way I behaved on the drive home.

Bloody Cal! I could have strangled him on the way home from Truro. We just made it to the car before the warden stuck a ticket on the Land Rover but he was still in a foul mood. He hardly spoke a word and wasn't interested that I'd scoped out some locally made kitchens and bathrooms, and arranged for the designers to visit and give us a quote.

His driving is rubbish too and I seriously wondered if we'd get back in one piece, especially when we were held up in a holiday jam on the A30. When we finally got home, he thumped off back to his office and slammed the door.

I was almost ready to quit until he called me over to the house the next afternoon, handed me a new tablet and said he 'was sorry for being a bit short with me the other day'. I was grateful for the tablet as it means I can research my cafe idea more easily, but I'm certainly not ready to mention the plan yet. Still, I think I might wander down to the building with Mitch later and have a scout around to see how the layout might work . . .

Robyn came round later and asked me to go into Truro on her evening off from the Tinner's. We're going out with a gang of her mates from the college. I think she has a boy she wants to impress. She also persuaded Cal to go along to the charity ball this coming weekend, much to Polly's amazement – and mine.

Leaning against the kitchen worktop the next day, sipping my coffee, I watch Polly press Cal's tux 'as a special favour and because he'd do a crap job'.

I think it's because he bought her a bunch of roses for her birthday the other day and drove her and her mate all the way to St Austell to see Il Divo. She seemed even more astonished when I made her a cake and iced her name on top. She said 'Oh, go on with you' or something but I heard her telling her daughter all about it on the phone, that it was 'light as a feather' and that she'd save some until she went over at the weekend.

I hide a smile as she slaps a damp tea towel over the leg of his tux trousers. The black slim-line jacket hangs over the back of a chair, the Boss label visible through the chair rail. He can't be that skint, then.

'Is he really going to wear *that*?' I ask, through a mouthful of Hobnob. I still can't get used to having a full biscuit barrel at my disposal – come to think of it, I could make my own biscuits if I have time. Nana taught me how to make Cornish fairings.

Steam clouds the air as Polly presses the iron to the tea towel. 'I wouldn't be ironing the thing if he wasn't, would I? Why he couldn't have bought a new one, I don't know, but he said it was a waste of money which is why I've spent all morning trying to work miracles on a second-hand one from bloody Oxfam. God knows who wore it before.'

The suit looks good as new to me but I'm not going to give Polly the satisfaction of telling her. She's been slightly less frosty to me lately now she can see I'm ready to put in the work, but that's not saying much.

'I can't imagine Cal dressed up like that,' I say, pulling another Hobnob from the open packet on the worktop.

'He scrubs up all right,' she says, moving the tea towel higher up the crease of the trousers. 'As you'll notice.' She gives me a sly look and my cheeks suddenly feel warmer.

'I don't notice. I'm too busy.'

'Which is why you're watching me iron his trousers?' Steam rises into the air as she bangs the iron down on top of the tea towel. For a moment, I think she might be smiling.

'*Actually*, I was on my way to ask if I could use his laptop. I've got to print off some info on catering and business-studies courses.'

She rolls her eyes. 'I can't see his daft eco plans ever happening. No one's going to lend him the extra money to do this place up.'

'They might. Don't you want the park to get back on its feet?'

She dumps the iron on the board and lifts up the trousers. 'Of course I do. No one wants to see the business doing well and Cal happy more than I do. It would finish Cal off for good, if his plans don't work out.'

'He's stronger than that. He'd survive,' I say, surprised at Polly's burst of emotion.

'And you know him, do you? Having been here five minutes?'

'I know him well enough. So do you. You're just worried he'll end up like his father, aren't you?'

She drapes the trousers over the ironing board. 'I don't want to lose this place completely. I like living here for now and yes, I do worry he'll end up like his father. Something happened to him while he was away that he's not telling us. It bothers me. It'll come out one day soon, mark my words.'

'I still think that we're going to make a big success of the new park, as long as we all think positive and work together,' I say, suspecting I sound like some of the business gurus I've come across on Twitter.

'Maybe . . . don't you laugh at me, Demi. I may speak my mind but I'm not a total ogre. I know you work very hard here and you want to do well, and you care about Cal, but take my advice: don't you get too caught up in him and his plans. You'll only end up hurt. Cal draws people to him; they'd walk over hot coals for him but he knows his own mind and if you want my opinion, it's still fixated on Isla Channing. He'll never let go of her.'

'And this has what to do with me? I have no idea what you're talking about. I want to make the new resort a success and build a career.' I sound arrogant but I'm troubled that Polly thinks she needs to warn me off.

She softens her voice. 'Then you'll have to excuse my interference. It was kindly meant.' She holds out the trousers. 'Here, I've better things to do than act as Cal's valet. If you're not too busy, can you take them up to his bedroom and save me the trouble? The jacket's hanging off the back of that chair but make sure you don't get crumbs all over it. I'm not doing it all again.'

'No problem,' I say, torn between annoyance and amazement that Polly thinks A – I'm after Cal, and B – that she actually cares that I might be hurt.

'Won't he need a shirt?'

'He can iron one himself if he does.'

She flicks off the switch and pulls the plug out of the wall. While she puts the kettle on, muttering about how much work she has to do before she goes to her daughter's for the weekend, I drape the trousers over one arm, pick up the jacket between my fingertips and take them upstairs. I've been up here a few times over the past few weeks, to collect fresh towels and bed linen from the airing cupboard, but I've never seen Cal's bedroom.

Floorboards creak and I walk to the far end of the landing and up a wooden step. His room is almost in another wing of the farmhouse, overlooking the back of the house. I have to transfer the jacket to my arm to lift the latch. The door swings inwards over the uneven floor, and sunlight spills out into the landing.

Wow. I stand in awe at the four-poster bed. The other rooms have modern beds in them but this must be centuries old. The duvet and cover aren't, because I helped Polly haul them back from Marks and Spencer in Truro in the week. Polly said that Cal's father had died in the bed so they'd chucked out the mattress and duvet. A shudder runs down my spine. I'm not sure I could sleep in a room where someone had died.

There's a great big wardrobe on the opposite side to the bed so I lay the suit on the duvet and carefully open the doors. One side has several suits and tweed jackets and smells a bit musty. Judging by the size of the suits, and the pairs of well-worn brogues underneath they must have belonged to Cal's father. I wonder why they haven't been thrown out yet. Perhaps Cal's been too busy and Polly didn't like to do it.

The other half of the wardrobe is almost empty apart from a couple of shirts and a pair of jeans on a wire hanger. It's as if Cal hasn't quite decided to move in here permanently yet.

I don't really think it will do the tux any good to be hung in the musty wardrobe so I pick an empty hanger, slot the trousers over the bar and slip the jacket over the top. I hook the suit over the back of the door.

A thought occurs to me. All of the top holiday cottages are big on the local materials they use and the way they 'channel influences from heritage and environment and vernacular architecture'. OK, Kilhallon house itself is a bit of a mess but there are some fantastic antiques and quirky bits and pieces we could use in the new cottages. Plus the general look and ambience of the place could be our unique selling point for the premium holiday cottages that are going to bring in the most money. I grin to myself, enjoying 'channelling' all the buzz words I've been picking up from luxury letting sites. Though I must admit I had to look up 'vernacular'.

On the dresser, there're a gorgeous silver-plated hairbrush and mirror set, although it's tarnished now, and a pretty carved wooden box with an inlaid lid that looks like it came from India or Malaysia. I look in the silver mirror and frown at my reflection and then pick up the box. It's much heavier than I thought and instead of rattling as if full of trinkets, it feels full and solid.

'Damn.'

The lid and box part company and the base tumbles with a thud onto the bare floorboards, along with the contents: dozens of faded postcards. In a panic and feeling guilty for letting my curiosity get the better of me, I scramble on the boards, trying to gather them all up. They must have been from Cal's parents to each other or from friends of theirs, although I can't see why they'd have saved them and oh . . .

The cards are all addressed to Ms Isla Channing. It would be wrong to read them but as I gather them up and stack them neatly in a pile, my eyes can't help lingering on some of the words. It's Cal's writing, of course, spidery in different colours of biro, one in pencil and a couple in purple felt pen, probably the only thing he could get hold of in these remote places while he was busy working. They date from a few years ago, some are seven or eight years old.

Hi Isla,

Guess where I've ended up this time? Yeah, the ruins on the front are a bit of a giveaway. Like the retro card? Think it dates back to the seventies. I found it at the back of some dingy shop. The place has changed a bit now and sadly not for the better. Man, it's hot here. Hotter than you could ever <u>believe</u> *and I won't bore you with the stuff I've seen and heard and smelt but I swear, if you were here and saw the people and children, you'd forgive me for trekking off for three months to come out here.*

Sorry, have to go. My boss is after me and I'd better not

piss her off again. Good luck with the BBC interview, though
I know you'll ace it.

   See you soon,
   All my Love,
   Forever,
   C x

Why would Cal have postcards he sent to Isla? Did she give them back to him before he went away or more recently?

'Demi? What are you doing in my wardrobe?'

I almost jump out of my skin. Cal stands in the doorway, his curly hair brushing the lintel. His face is stony and my heart thumps. He steps into the room and I think I've made a big mistake. *Huge.*

CHAPTER NINE

'Oh, I . . . I'm sorry. I was going to hang up your tux in the wardrobe and I knocked over a box of cards. I didn't mean to be nosy.'

'Really?' He stares at me and the cards for a second then at the tux hanging on the picture rail. 'Forget it.'

Hardly able to believe I may have got away with my indiscretion, I hold the box up to him. 'I'll put them all back.'

'No, I'll do it later.'

I lay the box on the bed, wishing the floor would swallow me up.

'Thanks for pressing my suit,' he says gruffly.

'Don't thank me. Polly did it.'

He gives me a sharp look. 'Really?'

'She's not so bad. I'd better get on with my work,' I say, edging towards the doorway. 'I need to use the laptop to check out some college courses.'

'Yes. Of course.'

He doesn't seem to register that I'm here or doesn't care. He looks so lost that I want to throw my arms around him and kiss him. What would he do? Would he push me off him? Say I've got to leave? Kiss me back? Push me onto that big bed . . .

I redden at the thought. He's my employer, and though I'd rather die than admit it, Polly was right to warn me off him. As I walk along the landing, the bedroom door closes softly and the lock clicks behind me.

Mitch woke me the next morning, his sharp barks punctuated by knocks on the cottage door. Pulling on a hoodie over my pyjamas, I scoot downstairs to find Cal peering through the kitchen window. In his cracked waxed jacket and dark-green Hunters, he could be a country squire although the two-day stubble and the scowl ruin the image. The glare of the morning sun makes me blink when I open the front door.

'Cal? Is everything OK?'

'Yes. Why wouldn't it be?'

'You don't usually come to get me out of bed.'

'I've come to take you out.' He checks his watch impatiently.

My stomach rumbles. 'But I haven't had my breakfast, yet.'

'You can have it when we get back.'

'Get back from where? Mitch hasn't had his food and he needs a wee.'

'Then he can come with us,' he says firmly.

Shivering in my PJs, I nod at the grey clouds billowing over the sea 'I'd better get dressed properly first.'

'OK. I'll wait here.'

The moment I shut the front door behind me, after I've got dressed, Cal sets off. 'Hang on; I haven't even got my laces tied up yet!'

He stops, rolls his eyes, walks back to me and grabs my hand. 'I haven't got time to hang about.' He pulls me across the farm-yard towards the house with Mitch running ahead, nose to the ground. Obviously a walk is even more tempting to him than breakfast. I try to protest as Cal hauls me over the yard, though not very hard, and he takes no notice of me anyway.

The truth is, I can't believe how good it feels to have his hand in mine, even though he's doing it to wind me up, but then I feel embarrassed so I pull away from him. Polly glowers at me through the kitchen window.

He pulls a waxed jacket from a peg in the porch. The navy blue fabric is streaked by rain and salt. Mitch sniffs at it. 'Here, it's blowing a gale out on the cliffs. It was Robyn's.'

'Doesn't she want it?'

'She left it here years ago so obviously not.'

Although the arms are a little short, the coat fits pretty well and I'm glad of it as we battle the wind gusting off the sea in the lower field. Huge white clouds race across the sky like some invisible demon is chasing them. Mitch sniffs every post and tree like a coke addict as we stomp down the field.

Cal shakes his head. 'Does that dog have a bottomless bladder?'

'I said he needed a pee. Where are we going?'

'You'll see.'

Bent almost double against the wind, we walk along the path in the opposite direction to the cove. Now I know why the trees around here are so bowed down and twisted. Cal strides on, obviously a man on a mission. At the far end of the field, we pass the holiday cottages, now with scaffolding around them and walk through a gate into another field full of grass where I can see the ruins of the pool and amenities block.

'It's hard to imagine this in its heyday, isn't it?' he says gloomily.

'I suppose the market began to change and families wanted to travel to Spain and Greece for their hols,' I say.

'Yes, but it was doing OK, apparently, until my father took over the business. I think he had other distractions . . .'

Cal grimaces at the ruined mess. I wonder if the distractions he's talking about were his dad's affairs with various women. Polly may moan but she also loves to have someone to gossip to, not that I believe all of what she says.

'Dad didn't put enough time and money into keeping the place smart and we started to get lots of complaints. Now, I want to make the whole park self-sufficient and eco-friendly, install a ground source heat pump and use local materials from local craftspeople. I don't want an ocean of static vans, or a club with bingo or karaoke or any of that crap. I want people to be able to have campfires and I thought of having yurts in the wood down there.'

The field slopes away gently towards the sea past a small thicket of trees. Mitch skirts the hedges and marks his territory on a stile in the corner. Cal pushes the arrow-shaped gate open and I follow him, pulling up the zip of the jacket as the wind gusts in from the sea. We're into the second half of May now but today, it feels like March.

'I've been looking at yurts too,' I say.

He cheers up at last. 'Great minds think alike. So you think they would work too?'

'Yes. I think we should try half a dozen to start with and I agree about the wood as a good site for them. You don't want too many. The type of people who rent them are looking for individuality and tranquility. The back to nature thing. But they want to do it in comfort and style, with running water, loos and proper beds.'

He smiles. 'You have been doing your research.'

I shrug, but feel very happy that he agrees with me. 'I also thought we could use bric-a-brac from the house for some of the cottages and the yurts but make sure people had iPod docks and super-fast broadband too.'

'Great idea . . . but do you really think we could re-use stuff from the house? Some of it's been there for donkey's years.'

'Oh, I think we could find enough. If it has a clean and polish, it'd look great.'

'You really believe in this project, don't you?' Cal sounds amazed.

'Why wouldn't I?'

He shrugs. 'I don't know. Maybe because no one else seems

to. Luke and Uncle Rory told me they think it will be a "huge challenge" and Polly just thinks I'm mad.'

'No, she just worries about you.'

By his expression, I can see he's surprised to hear me defending Polly. 'She's not such an ogre when you get to know her,' I qualify.

'No . . . but I'm still glad someone is with me on this. I want you to believe in it like I do; I want you to believe that we can transform it and change it. Not like Polly who thinks I'm off my rocker or soon will be: you're young, you've not been destroyed by life yet. I want you to believe in it in case I stop believing and I want you to scream at me and tell me when I get cynical and moody.'

'You? Moody and cynical? Never . . . Besides, even you can change.'

I meant the comment as a joke but Cal takes it seriously. 'Maybe you have too much faith in me,' he murmurs.

'I'm willing to take the risk.'

So many emotions pass over his face at once, as fast as clouds racing over the sea. Pleasure, confusion, pain. I don't think I'll ever fathom him out.

Cal made me breakfast when we came back to the farmhouse kitchen. We sit at the table, discussing his plans for the business while eating bacon sandwiches. Polly keeps rolling her eyes when she thinks Cal isn't listening as he shows me the yurts he plans to order, which do look very cool even if I've already tasted the 'charms of sleeping under a canopy of stars'.

The ground source heat pump holds about as much interest for me as watching Polly gutting a fish, but I could listen to Cal's voice all day. Sharing his plans and being asked for my opinion feels good, even if I don't totally buy his comments about me stopping him from being cynical. I'm not sure anyone could do that.

Polly bustles off, muttering about having 'real work to do', while Cal surfs the internet. While finishing my breakfast, I pretend to be interested in one of his *Green Living* magazines but I risk a sneaky look at him when I dare. I like the way his eyebrows meet together when he frowns – and incidentally, they could do with a trim at the barber's – and the way his eyes crinkle at the corners when he manages a smile. In fact he has more lines on his face than you'd expect for someone who's only nine years older than I am. I suppose that grooming and sun care weren't top of his list of priorities recently.

I lick a trail of brown sauce from my fingers, while Cal tucks into his bacon bap. His eyes are the same colour as the sauce, I think, and wish I hadn't because I can't help giggling.

'What's so funny?' he asks.

'Nutthin.'

'Yes there is. You're laughing at me? Is there some way I eat a sandwich that you find hilarious?'

'I wouldn't dare.'

'You were. Come on, tell me.'

'I can't.'

He leans forward with his chin on his hand, his gaze fixed on me until I have to look away. 'Come on, tell me what you're thinking.'

'You so do not want to know.'

'I do.'

He sits back and folds his arms.

'OK. You asked for it. I was thinking about the way you sound,' I say.

'How *do* I sound, Demi?'

'I don't know? Posh. A bit like Prince Harry.'

He gasps in horror. 'I hope not!'

'Well, maybe not that posh. Maybe more like the BBC presenters when they're trying to sound less posh than they really are.

He folds his arms. 'So you're a linguistic expert, are you?'

'I told you, I've had a lot of time to um . . . *observe* people.'

'Do you spend a lot of time observing me?'

Instantly, my face is on fire, a blush that creeps down my neck. Anyone would think he was flirting with me and I'm not sure I like it. It's confusing, because Cal can't possibly have feelings for me while he's still in love with Princess Isla. He must be taking the piss. 'Of course I don't,' I say, getting up from the table. 'Get a life.'

'Hello, Cal.' A voice interrupts our conversation.

Cal's face lights up at the sight of Robyn who's just walked into the kitchen.

'Hi, Demi.' Robyn smiles at me from under her slanting fringe and plonks herself down on a kitchen chair. 'I hope Cal isn't working you too hard.'

He tuts. 'As you can see, I was bullying Demi into eating some breakfast; breakfast which I cooked, I might add.'

'You let Cal cook the breakfast?' She winces, ignoring him.

'It was OK for a beginner. I've plenty of other things to get on with if you want to chat.'

'Oh, there's no need to go. In fact, I was hoping to see you,' says Robyn, clasping her hands nervously so that I wonder what's coming. 'I hope you don't mind and please say "no" if you don't want to but . . . Cal might have told you that my friend Emma is organising a charity ball at the country club on Saturday night. It's in aid of homeless people – oh, I've put my foot in it again, haven't I? Luke says I could win an Olympic medal for tactlessness.' She fires an imaginary gun at her head.

I have to smile. 'No, you haven't upset me and I've heard about the ball from Cal and Polly. He's even got his outfit ready,' I say risking a reference to the tux.

Cal wrinkles his nose, to show how happy he is about attending. 'I still haven't decided if I'm going or not.'

'You'd better do!' Robyn squeals.

Cal smiles at her.

'I hate you sometimes,' she says then turns to me. 'He's

impossible, isn't he?'

'You can say that again.'

She laughs. 'Well, the thing is . . . my friend, Emma, sent me a panicky email this morning because half of the serving staff at the club have gone down with a horrible stomach bug, you know the full works, throwing up and the other thing.'

'Eww.'

Cal has returned to his laptop, or at least is pretending to.

'We-ell,' Robyn goes on, drumming the toes of her boots nervously on the kitchen tiles. 'It can be a nightmare trying to get waiting staff down here at the best of times especially at short notice like this and you're very experienced at catering and I told Emma all about you and she was really excited and so I thought . . .'

Cal closes the lid of his laptop. 'I hope you're not trying to poach Demi from me?'

'Only if she wants the extra work. The club is willing to pay extra if she can help out because it is very short notice.' She looks at me, pleadingly. 'Cal is coming to the ball anyway and I thought he could give you a lift?'

'Demi has enough to do. She'll want the night off,' he says shortly, beginning to annoy me.

'I don't mind. I'm not tired and I could do with the extra cash.'

Cal is stunned into silence.

Robyn grins. 'Great! You'd be doing the club and the charity a massive favour. If they can't get enough staff, they might even have to call the event off.'

'As a favour for you and Emma, of course I'll do it.'

'Thanks sooo much.'

She hugs me. I'm not used to people invading my personal space apart from Mitch. It's been so long since anyone hugged me. Nana Jones must have been the last one.

Cal stays silent. He's not a huggy person either, though I think Robyn could get away with it.

'I think Cal is pissed off with me,' she says, not sounding the least bit bothered.

He gets up from the table. 'No, I'm not. Demi can do what she wants. I'm not her keeper.'

'Oh, tetchy.' Robyn laughs and turns her attention to me. 'I'll call you with more details or I can ping you an email. Thanks, I won't forget it. Cal, would you like to look at my horse, Roxy? I think she's picked up a stone or something on the way here.'

So they leave me, because no matter what Robyn said, she and Cal do want to talk without me being around. I'm cool with that; I'm a stranger to them and I really do have a lot of work to get on with. I may have a new home but I don't belong here, not yet and not for a long time.

That was hours ago. The afternoon sun burns the back of my neck as I help Cal clear out some of the rubbish from the other staff cottages. Now I know what he meant about having to turn my hand to anything, but I like working out in the fresh air for a change. He carries a roll of carpet on his shoulders and hoists it into the skip, breathing heavily. When I sling a broken pine chair on top of the carpet, dust flies into the air, making me cough. Cal stands back. His faded navy T-shirt has a damp upturned triangle on his back and holes under the arms. His knackered old jeans show off a pair of muscular thighs and calves that end in a pair of battered desert boots.

'You look hot.' The words pop out before I realise how they sound.

He slants a look at me and does the raised-eyebrow thing.

'I didn't mean it like that!' I insist, heat rising to my cheeks. 'I meant that it's baking out here, isn't it? Shall we have a Coke?'

His gaze lingers on me until my whole body sizzles. Then he lets me off the hook. 'Actually, I'd much rather have a beer.'

The deep shade of the kitchen does nothing to cool me down, in fact the shadows only seem to make Cal look even more smouldering. He leans his bottom against the worktop while I pull two cans from the fridge, and hand the beer to him. His hands are dirty; he hasn't shaved – again – and to be honest, he needs a shower, but I find my body doing tingly things that make me want to squirm. Unable to meet his look, I keep my eyes on the kitchen floor. Little clods of earth dot the tiles from his muddy builders' boots. I've never noticed how big his feet are before.

'Sorry, I've ruined your clean floor.'

I shrug and risk a quick glance at him. He must think I'm pissed off about the floor, when really I'm only pissed off at how turned on I am. 'I'll forgive you.'

'No. It's my mess. I'll clean it up.'

'S'alright,' I say, desperately trying to get a grip of myself. 'How do you think the work's going?'

'Well, I'm glad we've nearly finished clearing out the cottages, which is a rubbish job but it needed doing. Some of that stuff dates from way before I was born and the fact that the crows have clearly had a party in one of the houses hasn't helped. I've asked Tom Fallon to give me a hand. He needs the work and you have enough to do, planning out my business empire.'

'Sounds like a plan.' I'm finding it impossible not to focus on the dark springy hair in the open 'V' of his T-shirt or the tantalising glimpses of nut-brown skin under the frayed knee of his Levis. I pour myself a glass of water and feign an interest in the farmyard for a few seconds.

'Demi? Are you OK? You're not really annoyed about the floor, are you?'

'Yeah, I'm furious. You should lick it clean for me.'

A smile tugs at the edge of his mouth. 'I'm not sure my tongue could cope.'

'I'm sure it can.' Worrying I might leap on him at any moment and even more furious with myself, I gulp down the water and change the subject.

'Um. When do the builders start work properly?'

'Next week, I hope, now the scaffolding's up. They'd better do.

I want the work finished at least in time for the tail-end of the holiday season. The property agency wants to start advertising the cottages.'

'Already?'

'The sooner the better. This place needs to start earning its money.'

He wipes his mouth with the back of his hand and his knuckles glisten. 'You don't have to help out at this bloody charity do on Saturday night if you don't want to, you know.'

I'm surprised but happy at his concern for me. 'I don't mind. It'll make a change.'

'If you need the extra money, I can sort something out for you.'

'I don't need a hand out and you said yourself, the estate needs to pay its way. You're not made of money.'

'I don't want you to feel obliged to Robyn.'

'I want to do it. It could be a laugh.'

He blows out a breath. 'I doubt it, the country club people will keep you busy all night. I'm not sure they deserve you waiting on them.'

'And you do?'

He finishes the beer and puts the can on the table. 'Point taken.'

'I can handle a few old fogies and snobs if that's what you mean, and I used to enjoy serving the customers in the cafe. This won't be much different.'

'Well, I recommend you don't chuck the drinks over them,' he says with a grin.

'I don't do that normally!'

He pretends to reel in a fish.

'Robyn's right. You *are* impossible.'

'I try, but seriously, be careful people round here don't walk all over you, Demi.'

I'm grateful for his help and the job and place of my own but I want to try and make my own way if I can. The fact that Cal has so much financial power over my life, however well intended it is, makes me feel as if that's all I ever can be: his employee, even though I've no intention of ever becoming anything else.

'How did you end up sleeping on the streets?' he asks out of the blue.

When I turn back from the bin, he's watching me intently from those lovely saucy eyes. I dump a dirty cup and plate left from Polly's coffee break into the washing-up bowl. I could use the dishwasher but I need something to occupy me.

'I haven't asked the details until now and you don't have to tell me anything.'

I turn to him with soapy hands. Drips slash onto the tiles, in tiny little pools.

He hands me the tea towel. 'I'm sorry for poking my big nose into your private business.'

'It's not that big.'

He frowns. 'What?'

'Your nose. It's kind of average, as noses go.' Unlike the rest of him, which is so far above the average of all the men I've known, that it's almost a joke.

He rubs the nose in question, leaving a dirty mark on the end. 'I should keep it out from where it's not wanted.'

'If you really want to know, my dad and I never really got on that well. I don't know why. He didn't hit me or anything but he always seemed disappointed in me somehow. Then, when Mum died, he lost interest in me completely. My nan said he was suffering from depression but he'd certainly never have admitted it. He made sure I had money for school stuff but he took no interest in what I did.'

'I'm sorry.'

I shrug. 'Not your problem. Not your fault. Probably mine, in fact. My nan passed away when I was sixteen and that coincided with Dad finding a girlfriend.'

'Ah. You didn't hit it off?'

'You could say that. She was way younger than him, not loads older than me, and there wasn't room for us both in the same house, so I left.'

'Have you seen your dad since? Does he have any idea where you are now?'

'I don't want to see him or her again, so don't try and persuade me to.'

'I won't . . . but does he even know you're OK? He'd want to know that much, take it from me. I never noticed how ill my dad was, I was so focused on my work with other people. Luckily I was here when he passed away.'

'Dad knows I'm OK, or at least he did. I called him from Sheila's because she nagged me too, but we ended up having another row. There's no way I'm going back to him. He has his own life now with his new partner.'

'You can't blame him for needing someone.'

'I don't but I don't have to like her, do I?'

'No.'

I sigh. 'You're right. I can't blame Dad for everything. I wasn't easy to live with and I got into trouble at school after Mum died. I was doing GNVQs in tourism and food tech . . . I told you I could cook.'

He smiles encouragement.

'After I left home, I started working in the Truro tea shop and sleeping on friends' sofas but I couldn't stay with them forever. My brother had joined the army by then and we never heard from him. I tried a few more mates but eventually I ran out of sofas.'

'How did you come to leave the tea shop?'

'They built a big supermarket out of town, the market had to close and the town centre went downhill, taking the tea shop with it and by then I was already sleeping rough. I tried to get some more work, odd bits of washing-up and stuff. I don't want to moan, there are people a lot worse off than me. I managed to

94

hold down the job at Sheila's Beach Hut before the Mawgan Cade incident and now I'm here and hey, everything is hunky dory.'

He looks at me again, the way he did before Robyn walked in and not the same way he looked at her. Not in a friendly, happy way but almost as if he's confused about exactly *how* to look at me or how he sees me. I'm not sure I like it, it doesn't make me happy or sad, only uncomfortable, but not in an unpleasant way. Polly talks a lot of crap but she did say that Cal's father left a trail of broken hearts all over Cornwall and that Cal will do the same.

CHAPTER TEN

So Cinderella went to the ball. But I bet she didn't look like something from the scullery at Downton Abbey. I knew I'd probably have to wear some sort of uniform and Robyn lent me a black skirt and a pair of smart heels, but I feel a total dork in the frilly white apron the catering manager has insisted all the staff wear. In contrast, the guests are all dressed to kill, including Cal.

He called at the cottage for me in his second-hand tux and his dark-green Hunters because it had rained and the yard was muddy. Instead of a bow tie, he's wearing a slim black tie and he looks gorgeous. To cover my embarrassment, I made a joke about his wellies and then spent the whole five-mile journey to the country club pretending to stare at the scenery while checking out his reflection in the window.

He smiles when I walk past him through the bar with a tray of drinks for the 'champagne' reception.

'What's so funny?' I say.

'Nothing. I like the outfit.'

'No, you don't. I look stupid and these shoes are a bit high for waitressing, really.'

'I can see you wobbling but you look fine, although I don't

like you waiting on us. You could have come as a guest if you'd really wanted.'

'Thanks, but A – I can't afford the tickets and B – having to make small talk to a bunch of overdressed, probably pissed people I don't know would drive me nuts. This way I can get paid for being nice to them.'

I'm not sure he believes me but I know he feels guilty about me waiting on him so I'm going to wind him up some more. I bob a curtsey, which isn't easy in the shoes. The glasses wobble more than me and almost spill onto the tray.

'Would you care for a glass of champagne, sir?' I ask sarcastically then lower my voice. 'It's cheap cava really. They're trying to cut costs.'

'Well, it is for charity.'

'Waitress! Can we have some drinks over here?' Gritting my teeth, I head in the direction of a braying voice, aware of Cal following behind me. I'm acutely conscious of my bum wiggling in Robyn's slightly-too-small skirt. I hope Cal is not looking at me; or perhaps I hope he *is*.

'Hey, you! Can we get a drink here?'

I turn round.

'*You…*'

My heart plunges into my ridiculously uncomfortable shoes. Mawgan Cade stares at me as if I'm an alien. I didn't recognise her at first, with the extensions and the extra layer of fake bake. She's so orange, I need sunglasses to look at her. There's only one course of action.

'Can I help you, madam?' I say sweetly.

She purses her lips at the drinks and then asks me in a butter-smooth voice. 'So you managed to get a job here, did you? I hope you haven't brought your dog.'

I have murder in my heart but there's no way I'm losing *this* job. She must want to provoke me and I refuse to give her the satisfaction. 'Not tonight, *madam*.'

She curls her lip. 'Good. So, can you tell me, as I'm sure you're an expert if you're working the bar, is this Moet or Lanson?'

'I'm not sure, madam. I can ask if you like.'

She swipes a glass, sniffs at it and wrinkles her nose. 'Don't bother. It'll have to do but I'd have expected something better than this, with the price of the tickets. I've bought a whole table.'

Without thanking me, she turns away and resumes her conversation with her mates. My eyes shoot daggers at her but I keep a serene smile on my face.

Cal walks over to me on my way back to the bar.

'You could have told me *she'd* be here!' I say when he's closer.

He grimaces. 'I wasn't sure if she would be and you were determined to come. I did warn you. You shouldn't waste your time on some of these people.'

'Well, thanks for nothing!'

Not trusting myself not to do something stupid, I persuade one of the other waiters to serve Mawgan and collect some empty glasses from the tables and window ledges. On my way back to the tables with a new drinks order, I swear some sweaty perv brushed my bum with his hand but I restrain myself from tipping the tray of fizz over him. It would be a waste of alcohol, even cheap alcohol, and I want my fee for tonight. It matters to me that I earn some money that hasn't come from Cal, so I can be more independent.

I try to focus on my job, gathering up empty glasses and half-eaten canapés, until Robyn hurries over to me. She looks amazing in a man's tux with pointy PVC boots. 'Demi! Thanks for doing this. Have you got a minute? There's someone I'd like you to meet.'

'I'd love to but I'm supposed to be working.'

'Oh, you can spare a minute or two. If anyone gives you any bother, I'll get Emma to sort them out.'

I smile weakly. All I really want is to get on with my job but she's determined. 'Come and meet Isla.'

Robyn points at the back of a girl standing by the vodka fountain in the centre of the bar. It's Isla. I recognise her even though my previous sighting was merely across a crowded marketplace from a distance and even from the back. I know my theory was right. She *is* a shimmery girl. Her dress is a column of oyster silk ripples in the light of the chandeliers, accentuating her slender waist and perfect peach of a bum.

Abandoning the tray temporarily on a table, I follow Robyn. Isla flicks back her hair and she must be smiling or saying something witty or sexy or both because Cal is enthralled by her. He laughs, and his eyes are lit with an intense pleasure I've never seen before.

I can't help thinking he should have stayed away tonight.

'Come on. Don't be shy!' Robyn tugs at my elbow.

'I'm not. I just don't know these people.'

'Don't worry. They'll love you and Isla is a sweetheart.'

Yards away now, feet away and finally I come face to face with Isla for the first time and the shock hits me.

She isn't pretty after all. She's beautiful.

Beautiful in a way that makes me want to glance away, hoping that when I look again, she won't be as perfect as the last time. But she is.

'Demi, isn't it?' she says as I reach her. 'I've been dying to meet you.'

'Have you?' I try to sound witty and sophisticated but end up sounding sarcastic and I really didn't mean to.

'Yes. Robyn told me how kind you were to help out here tonight. The organisers are really grateful and you must be knackered after working for Cal all day. I hope he isn't working you too hard?'

Cal rolls his eyes. 'Of course I'm not. You know me better than that, Isla. Or you used to.'

'I'll bet you're more than a match for Cal,' Robyn says hastily.

Isla lifts her glass to her lips, her engagement ring sparkling in the light of the chandelier. It's an intricate Celtic love-knot with a band dotted with sapphires. Cal is totally magnetised by her but if I had a knife from the kitchen, I'd be able to slice the tension between them. I really wish I hadn't come over. 'Sorry but I have to carry on working. Good to meet you, Isla.'

'You too. Maybe we can meet up for coffee sometime with Robyn while I'm down here. If you want to, that is?'

'That would be great,' Robyn beams, obviously delighted to have spread sisterly affection all around.

'Will Cal let you have any time off?' Isla asks.

Cal is stony faced. I'm not sure he likes the idea of the three of us cosying up together.

'Oh, I don't know about that. He's a hard taskmaster.'

'No, I'm not. Of course, Demi's entitled to time off like any other employee.'

'I think she's winding you up.' Robyn giggles and Isla smiles.

'She knows you too well already, Cal.'

'You all do, obviously,' he says wearily but with a hint of a smile.

I really don't know what to say other than, 'I have to get back to work before I get into trouble.'

Out of the corner of my eye, I spot Mawgan Cade heading straight for us. Or should I say, shuffling, because that's about all she can do in the emerald silk fantail dress she's wearing. She actually has a good figure and the dress looks super expensive but it's also sprayed on and has a sort of a train that makes it hard for her to walk. It reminds me of a green penguin and I have no idea how the top half is staying on. She air kisses Isla on both cheeks. Cal's lips are pressed tightly together.

'Isla! I've been looking for you everywhere.' She turns to me long enough to rap out an order. 'Fetch me a large gin and tonic. Not too much ice and absolutely *no* lemon.'

Cal's face is thunderous but Isla gets in first. 'This is Demi, Mawgan, she's working for Cal and helping out tonight.'

Mawgan's eyebrows make another attempt to shoot up her forehead. 'What? Oh, *you're* the girl he picked up in St Trenyan, then? I'll bet you can't believe your luck after you were sacked from the cafe.'

'Not at this precise moment, no,' I say, reining in the urge to tell her where to stick her lemon. God, those eyebrows really are something else. They should have their own Twitter account.

She purses her lips. 'You're staring at me, is there anything wrong?'

'Nothing, madam.'

'It's Ms, actually. Ms Cade.'

'Actually, I always thought you always were a right little madam, Mawgan,' Cal says before knocking back his whisky.

'And you'd know all about that, wouldn't you?' Mawgan shoots back.

'We mustn't get Demi into trouble,' Robyn says with a nervy laugh.

'No we mustn't,' Cal says dangerously, 'and I'll get your drink from the bar myself, Mawgan.'

Mawgan's eyebrows bob up again. It's hard not to become obsessed with them. She smiles at Cal. 'Well, I can't say no to a Penwith offering to buy me something.'

CHAPTER ELEVEN

I should have known Mawgan Cade would never change and yes, maybe I should ignore her petty snobbishness but I won't stand by and see Demi treated like a servant. I wish Robyn hadn't asked her to work here tonight. I feel responsible for her and that only complicates things. I already knew this event was going to be a trial as my first public 'outing' with the great and not-so-good of the area.

Where the hell has Luke got to? Isla said he was busy 'networking', but we've been here almost an hour and there's still no sign of him. Why would he leave Isla here alone in this room full of men who'd give their right arms, most of them, to take her to bed? Why would he leave her alone with me, who feels like killing any of them who tried? And why have I put myself through the torture of standing so close to her, hearing her voice, drinking in her perfume, longing to undress her and feel her body next to mine one more time . . .

If Luke knew what I was thinking, he'd probably kill me himself.

'Cal. Are you OK?'

'What?'

Isla is right at my side, with Mawgan opposite, watching me like a hawk. 'You seemed miles away.'

Her lip gloss glistens in the lights and it would be so easy to lean in and taste it.

'Did I? I'm fine.'

'I was telling Mawgan about your plans for Kilhallon Park. Luke says you're planning on turning the old caravan site into a sustainable eco-resort?'

'An eco-resort? You make it sound much grander than it is, Isla.'

I *know* Isla is trying to please me, out of guilt or pity or both, and my answer is rougher than I meant it to be. Or maybe I *did* mean it.

'You're putting yourself down, Cal.'

I knock back the rest of my whisky. 'I doubt it.'

There's silk in Mawgan's reply as she joins in the discussion. 'That sounds very expensive to set up, not that I'm an expert on the leisure industry, *of course*, but do you really think people with money will want to come all the way down here? Kilhallon's very out of the way and from the last time I saw it, there is a lot of work to do.'

'I'm not afraid of hard work.'

She sniggers. 'I can't imagine Kilhallon attracting the *right* sort of people.'

'I'm not only looking for 'the right sort of people'.'

'But you will need families with plenty of disposable income. I assume you'll be charging the market rate?'

'For those who can pay, yes, but there'll be a campsite too, which anyone can afford and I plan to open the site to school and community groups at a discount in the off-season. I want to make Kilhallon accessible to the widest possible range of people.'

'How very noble, Cal, but you also need to make it viable or you'll end up bankrupt.' Mawgan sips her drink carefully. 'Like your father would have ended up if he hadn't, very sadly, passed away, of course.'

Isla must have seen my expression because I find her hand on my arm. I can hardly bear to be touched by her, I want her so much.

'It sounds like a great idea to me,' she says, with the kind of smile I thought of every day in the desert. 'I know lots of people who'd love to get away to somewhere as wild and lovely as Kilhallon. As long as there's a Waitrose within shouting distance, of course,' she jokes.

'If the profit margins are big, it might be worth all the investment, I suppose,' Mawgan says grudgingly.

'All I want is to run a sustainable business and make a reasonable living so I don't have to depend on other people.'

Isla tightens her grip on my arm. 'Go for it. I'll tell all my friends and colleagues about the resort.'

She's trying too hard, and I can't bring myself to hurt her. 'Thanks for the offer,' I say carefully. 'But I need to get it up and running first. Mawgan's right about one thing; there's a lot to do before I can advertise it, but the work's already underway.'

'So. How are you financing it?' Mawgan asks.

'It's all planned out,' I say firmly.

'I'm sure it is. A word of advice, Cal, whatever you do, don't resort to mortgaging Kilhallon to the hilt as your father did. I know his life insurance paid off the loan but it was never a wise strategy.'

'I know what I'm doing.' God, the woman is like a bird of prey spotting a rabbit but I won't be intimidated. Thank God she doesn't know I've already looked into re-mortgaging the house.

'I still think you'd be better off selling Kilhallon Park for re-development. I know you could get planning permission for a couple of premium properties on there. You could make a killing and never have to work again.'

'I don't want to make a killing. I've told you, I want to work on my own land and build something sustainable that helps the community.' The Cades would get their hands on the place over my dead body.

'So you want to protect the environment? I never had you down as a romantic, Cal.'

Mawgan winks at me but Isla looks puzzled. I might have known Mawgan would never let me forget what happened that night but I don't regret refusing to have sex with her. It happened when I was home from uni in the vacation before my exams and Mawgan had just finished a business course at the local college. We were young, she was drunk, and it would have been a mistake for both of us if we'd slept together. I tried to explain that to her but I know she was hurt and angry. I hadn't realised quite *how* angry . . . damn, I seem to make a mess of everything I touch, which is why I'm determined not to make a mess of Kilhallon – or Demi. Thankfully *she* doesn't look at me as anything but a grumpy boss. I'd die rather than mess up her life.

'I'm not going to sell,' I say.

'Well, if you do change your mind, Cade Developments is waiting and if you don't mind me offering some more advice, if you're going to reinvent yourself as a business tycoon, you'd better toughen up. Business-wise, that is.'

I try not to snort at the mention of Cade Developments, which is the property arm of the Cade's 'empire' in West Cornwall. 'You mean buy up places for a pittance from people who are desperate and throw up mansions that no local can afford? Hire a London lawyer so I can avoid my tax?'

Mawgan laughs. 'You're so naïve, Cal, but you know I'd make you a fair offer for Kilhallon. Enough for you to retire on and leave Cornwall.'

Luke bounds up.

'What's this about Cal leaving Cornwall?' he asks, slapping me on the back like he didn't steal the woman I love.

'I'm not going anywhere, Luke. Where've you been?'

His arm snakes around Isla's back. 'Meeting some business contacts.'

'We'd started to think you'd decided to escape while you had the chance,' Isla says lightly.

'Escape from you? Why would any man ever do that? I love you.' He plants a kiss on her lips.

I down the whisky and dump the glass on the table. 'Does anyone want a beer?'

'I'll have one, thanks, mate,' says Luke.

Isla shakes her head. 'I'm driving.'

Mawgan holds her hand over her glass. 'Thank you but I have to go and mingle with other people. We've received the go-ahead to convert the old Headland Hotel into apartments and some of my investors are here tonight. You know where I am, Cal, if you want to talk.'

She leaves us with a finger wave.

Somehow I make it through the starter and mains, sandwiched between Robyn and Isla, though I can't remember what we ate. It was physically painful to be so close to Isla but Luke seems oblivious to what's in my mind, either that or he's deluding himself. After the main course, it's my turn to get another round at the bar.

On the other side of the room, Demi dishes out more drinks, smiling at the guests and, by her forced smile, probably putting up with the men's jokes and sexist comments. Some bloke paws at her arse, and I want to punch him in the face. No man should treat a woman like that. Demi says something back to him and his wife gives him a death look. She's right: she can take care of herself but she's way too good to be putting up with tossers like him – or me. I don't think she'll stay at Kilhallon long when she's found her feet.

I twist round as someone brushes my arm.

A pretty girl, a good foot shorter than me, grins up at me. 'My, don't you scrub up, Mr Penwith?'

I can't help smiling. 'Tamsin Penrose. How are you?'

'Fine, thanks. It's great to see you back in Cornwall. You're looking good, Cal, considering what you've been through.'

'Ah but you don't know what I've been through, Tamsin.'

'Something must have happened to keep you away from us all for so long, especially Isla.'

Admiring her directness, while determined to give nothing away, I smile. 'I think you know that's ancient history. I'm focusing on developing Kilhallon into an eco-resort now.'

'I heard on the grapevine. If you want to add a spa at any time, you know where to come. Here, have my card.'

She goes to open her handbag but I stop her. 'Great idea but my assistant is dealing with that aspect of the business.'

Tamsin giggles. She's a great girl and I can see her attraction for half the guys in the area but we were always just friends, which suits me. I don't want any more complications in my life.

'Your assistant?'

'Yes. Actually, she's here tonight. Robyn begged her to do the charity a favour by helping out on tables and she wanted the extra money. That's her, over there.'

I point out Demi, who's expertly negotiating her way across the floor with a tray of drinks.

'Oh, I see. She seems young to be your assistant and I thought Polly was in charge at Kilhallon.'

'I needed an extra pair of hands and Demi's very enthusiastic. If you want to give her your card, I'll take it, but you'd be better off dropping us an email. Address it to me or Polly and I'll forward it to Demi.'

'OK. Will do. I'm really pleased you're back and restoring Kilhallon. I always thought it was a lovely spot.' She touches my hand. 'Isla and Luke must have come as a shock though? You two were close, once?'

'Once, but these things happen. I'll get over it.'

She takes a longer look at Demi. 'Demi's a very pretty girl too. You know people might jump to conclusions.'

'Yes, she is,' I say, fuming inside, not with Tamsin but the local gossip mill. 'She is very pretty but she also has plenty of options. She's smart, spiky, and ambitious and she won't hang around Kilhallon long.'

Tamsin raises an eyebrow at my passionate defence of Demi. I don't blame her: I've surprised myself. 'There's nothing going on between us. I'm her employer. That's it.'

At that moment Demi approaches us.

'Excuse me, sir; can I collect those empty glasses, please?'

'Of course.' I smile at her cheeky comment. 'Demi, this is Tamsin who runs a local beauty spa. She wanted to contact you about offering treatments to the guests and I told her you're in charge of that aspect of the business.'

'That's a brilliant idea, when we're up and running. Can you ping me an email about it?' Demi asks, looking pleased.

'Of course. I'll send you all the details and when you're closer to opening, maybe we can have a meeting and I'll show you what we have to offer. I can even give you a free treatment.'

'I'd love to.'

'I could even offer Cal a freebie too. You know a chest wax or a facial.'

I cringe but the girls burst out laughing, then I find myself smiling too. If they want to make me the butt of their jokes, fine. 'No chance, it sounds like torture,' I say and they both laugh.

The glasses chink loudly as Demi gathers them up. 'Well, I have to get on. We'll be serving dessert in a moment,' she says.

Tamsin has amusement in her eyes. 'See you later and I'll be in touch, Demi. Great to meet you.'

CHAPTER TWELVE

Pots and crockery clash, people yell over the rattle of the dish-washers and the extractor fan sounds like an aeroplane taking off. When Robyn said the caterers were short of staff, she meant it, not that I'd ever complain to her.

No sooner have I dumped my latest tray of dirty bowls next to the dishwashing area than Abby, the manager, calls to me. 'Demi. Table ten still haven't had their desserts and Gill's too busy cleaning up after someone threw up in the bar area. Can you take them, please?'

That's Cal's table – and Mawgan's. So far I've avoided waiting on them.

'Um . . .'

'Demi?'

'Sure. I'm on it.'

Weaving between tables of half-cut diners, in Robyn's heels, with an armful of mini strawberry Pavlovas should be an Olympic sport. I knew I should have worn my trainers. Cal's seat is empty; he's probably gone for a pee or to the bar again.

As I reach the table, I stumble slightly and the plates wobble. For a split second I have a vision of a Pavlova landing smack in Mawgan Cade's lap but luckily I recover. She ignores me as I serve the dessert and with a sigh of relief, I hurry back to the kitchens for another lot.

After I've served the tea and coffee, there's just some clearing up to do, and then I'll be able to leave. A few of the waitressing girls want to get a cab into St Trenyan tomorrow night to go clubbing and I might just join them.

Abby, the catering manager, throws me a smile as I pass by her, tray in hand. 'Thanks for all your hard work, I really appreciate it.'

'No problem,' I say and carry my tray back to the function room, gathering glasses as I go. The lights are low now, and the DJ has just started up. People have taken to the dance floor, throwing some shapes that make me smile. I put the tray on a table and collect some glasses from behind the curtains on the window ledge. People love to hide them there for some reason. I turn round and bump into something – or someone.

'You!'

'*You.*'

Mawgan glares at me and I mumble my apologies and pull away, only to hear a rip, even above the disco music.

It could only be her penguin dress.

'Get off me!' Mawgan screeches.

'Keep still or it'll be worse!' Isla is suddenly there, on her knees, extricating the heel of my shoe from Mawgan's fantail but it's too late. There's a six-inch tear in the fabric. All my – genuine – apologies are drowned by a tirade of shrieks.

'I'm *so* sorry. It was an accident. I didn't know you were right behind me.'

'You expect me to believe that? You did it deliberately.'

'It was an accident, *really.*'

'I don't care. Do you have *any* idea how much this dress cost?'

'Probably a lot more than it looks.' Oh no, did I really say that?

'What did you say?' Her voice is a hiss.

'I said it looks a lot worse than it probably is. I'm terribly sorry.'

'Mawgan, that's enough! It was an accident.' I'm amazed to hear Isla jump to my rescue but I can look after myself.

'No it isn't. I want her fired. She's done this kind of thing before.'

That's it. 'I can't be fired. I'm only doing this job to help out Robyn's mate.'

Mawgan snorts. 'That doesn't surprise me. You're incompetent. I can't believe Cal lets you in his house, but then he always has enjoyed rescuing waifs and strays.'

'You're not wrong, but didn't he even refuse to go out with you once?'

Mawgan jumps up, spitting venom. 'Who told you that, you cheeky little cow!'

'Just a guess,' I say, already wishing I hadn't revealed what I'd heard in the kitchens earlier.

Isla's face is pale but it's clear the revelation is new to her. Me and my great big mouth.

She tries to calm Mawgan. 'Come on, you two. It was a genuine accident.'

People are staring: we're the highlight of the evening and the charity auction hasn't even started yet.

Cal strides over, followed by Robyn and Abby, the catering manager. 'What's going on here?' Abby asks.

Mawgan points at me. 'I want this stupid girl sacked and I want my dress replacing.'

'Why? What has she done?' Cal demands.

'Ruined my dress, the useless little cow!'

'There's no need to speak like that, Miss Cade,' Abby says calmly. 'And the catering company's insurance will cover your dress as it was obviously an accident.'

'Don't make a big thing of it, Mawgan,' Cal intervenes. 'Calm down. Demi didn't do it on purpose.'

She laughs at him. 'Oh, shut up. Everyone knows why you're sticking up for her.'

That's it! 'Leave him alone!'

Mawgan rounds on me, her eyes narrowed like a cornered cat. 'So you're defending him now, are you? That makes sense. Everyone knows you only got the job because you're shagging him. I never thought he'd resort to the gutter. Literally.'

'Mawgan . . .'

'Yes? What are you going to do? Ride in on your white charger and challenge me to a duel? You think you can play the lord of the manor but you're just a washed-up loser now. You and your cheap tart should crawl off back to that dump you call Kilhallon.'

Cal bursts out laughing but my anger and humiliation bubbles over. *Cheap tart?* I've tried to act the lady, I really have, but my fingers twitch. I'm going to have to slap Mawgan . . .

Cal's hand closes around mine. 'Demi. Come on. This is pathetic. She truly isn't worth it.'

His grip tightens and I try to pull my hand away. 'I can fight my own battles!'

'That's what I'm worried about.'

Mawgan folds her arms in triumph. 'What did I say? I knew there was more to him taking her on than philately.'

'I think you mean philanthropy,' says Isla coolly. 'Philately is stamp collecting and I really think everyone needs to calm down.'

'Isla's right,' says Cal exchanging glances with Isla. 'Come on.' Cal half drags me across the dance floor.

'Let me go.'

'No. I'm trying to save you from getting arrested for assault.'

He lets go of my hand and propels me out of the function room and outside. Frost glitters on the driveway and the wind whistles across the car park. I realise I'm shivering.

'Are you OK?' he asks, his breath misting the air.

'Fine,' I mutter, still fuming. 'It's just a bit cold out here after working in the kitchens.'

He takes off his jacket.

'I don't need it, thanks,' I snap.

He shrugs it back on. 'OK. Have it your way.'

'I can look after myself.' I wrap my arms around my chest.

'That's the problem. If you'd smacked Mawgan, and yes, I know most of the people in the room wanted you to, you'd have been arrested and ended up with a police record. That's exactly what she'd have loved.'

Deep down I know he's right but I'm too angry to say it. Ripping off the stupid frilly apron, I throw it into a puddle and stomp off.

Cal runs after me and grabs my arm but I shake it off.

'How the hell are you going to get home?'

'Not your problem.' I march off. Who cares if I get paid? I took some crap when I worked in the cafe, but *no one s*peaks to me like that and I agree with that cow, Mawgan, on one thing: I don't need Cal doing a knight in shining armour act.

At the gates of the country club, I finally stop and risk a glance round but he's not following me. The damp air clings to me and seems to seep into my bones.

Of course, I already regret storming off and letting Mawgan wind me up, and being angry with Cal for dragging me away from doing something silly. I felt I was being treated like a child, but maybe that's because I was behaving childishly.

Will I ever learn?

I've spent many nights out in the cold but without shelter, without a coat or Mitch, I've never felt more alone. For the first time since I saw Cal, I wish I was back on the streets in the shop doorway. I wish I'd never met him or Mawgan or Isla. Especially Isla, because that one glance between them told me everything: they're still in love with each other.

CHAPTER THIRTEEN

I could have run after Demi again but I can hardly force her to go back to the club and I don't blame her for being angry with Mawgan, who really has grown more bitter and volatile since I went away. The past two years have definitely magnified all her worst aspects, not mellowed them.

A quick jog down the club's driveway shows no sign of Demi sneaking back to the club. If she really *does* plan to walk back to Kilhallon, it's a five-mile hike and she can't walk all that way on unlit roads in that outfit and shoes.

What if she decides to hitch a lift? I doubt if any harm would come to her round here but I'm not prepared to take any chances.

A couple of minutes later, while I'm still debating whether to walk home myself or go back into the club, Isla comes up to me. She's shivering in the cool night air and it is all I can do not to pull her into my arms.

'Cal? Are you OK? Where's Demi?'

'She went off.'

'On her own?' Isla looks horrified.

'She said she wanted to walk home but I've called Sandra Tremayne at the taxi firm and told her where Demi's heading. She should be with her in five minutes.'

'I'm glad to hear it. I'm sorry Mawgan kicked off.'

He sighs. 'Yes . . .'

'I didn't know you and Mawgan had history.'

'We don't and that's partly why I'm not Mawgan's favourite person.'

'Oh I thought . . .'

'I would never have screwed Mawgan or anyone while you and I were together. I swear it.'

'I believe you,' she says softly.

'Good. At least one thing is straight between us. I'm going now.'

'So soon? The disco's started.'

'I'm not in the mood for dancing.'

She touches me on the arm. 'Not even with me?'

'Is that a threat or a promise?' I ask, wondering if she knows how she tortures me every time she touches me.

'Whatever you want it to be. What about one dance for old times' sake?'

'Won't Luke mind?' I try not to sound bitter.

'He's in the casino and he's pissed. He won't even notice and anyway, I want to talk to you.'

She's so close; I can smell her perfume, and the sensuality beneath it. My body reacts painfully to the thought of that smooth, warm skin beneath my fingertips and the tight heat of her body inviting mine inside.

'Cal . . .' Her voice curls around me, seductive, delicious, tempting.

I snap to my senses. I don't know what Isla's playing at but it's a game I daren't join in. 'You can talk to me out here,' I say.

'It's freezing and I don't think that would be a good idea.'

'Why? Are you worried about people seeing us out here and getting the wrong idea?'

'No!'

I can't help myself and I don't care if my demand gives her

pain. I have to hear the answer, however much it hurts. 'For God's sake, Isla, why are you marrying Luke?'

She stares at me, as if I've asked her why the tides have to come in twice a day. 'Because I gave up hope,' she says. 'Because . . . I was lonely. Because he makes me laugh. Because you never asked me to marry you. Because you never even told me you loved me. Do you want any more reasons?'

I find I'm holding the tops of her arms, my fingers resting on her perfect flesh. She doesn't push me away. This moment is so dangerous, I only have to press the button, step off the path and everything could explode in our faces and destroy us.

'Will saying "I love you" now change your mind?'

She shakes her head. 'Would you *really* mean it? Ask yourself. We're different people now. I want different things and I think you do too.'

'I don't.'

She pulls away from me. 'You *have* changed. You didn't care about Kilhallon before you left; nothing here meant enough to you. You were hell-bent on proving to your father – and everyone – how little you needed him or us. Now Kilhallon means everything to you suddenly? You want to turn back the clock and have all that you threw away? It can't happen.'

'So I'm a good guy now and I'm here to stay.'

She shakes her head, tears shining in her eyes. 'I hope you're not doing all this work at the farm to prove a point to me because I forgot to say the number one reason I'm marrying Luke. I love him.' She moves further away from me. 'Move on, Cal, or the regrets will destroy you and I never want to see that.'

Long after she's left me, my body aches for her with a pain that's almost worse than I endured in prison.

'*I love him.*'

I don't believe her, I don't want to. Why did she ask me to dance with her if she really loves Luke? Why tempt me?

'*Move on, Cal.*'

How can I?

The need for oblivion overwhelms me and I may as well find it at the bottom of my own whisky bottle as one of the club's. I'll save myself a fortune too. Turning up the collar of my jacket, I start walking down the drive and away from the lights of the club, hoping I don't sober up too much on the way back. I don't want to think about Isla's words or the way she looked at me; pleading for me to leave her alone.

CHAPTER FOURTEEN

This morning, I was going to try out the fairings recipe on Cal but instead I've been wallowing on the sofa, eating cornflakes out of a mug because the dishes are all dirty, flicking between cookery shows, house programmes and *Judge Judy*.

I'd arranged to meet up with Nina, Shami and Holly later, some of the waiting and kitchen staff I worked with last night. Nina helps her mum run an animal shelter and she said we could take Mitch and some of the rescue dogs for a walk this afternoon. I was going to ask Cal if I could borrow the Land Rover and drive into Penzance to see a film tonight with her and the other girls.

I doubt Cal will want to lend me the car anyway after last night. I really kicked off and now I'm regretting it. I let Robyn and her friend down, and worse, I let Cal see I was upset, even if he doesn't know exactly why.

Mitch nudges me with his damp nose.

'He didn't give a toss, did he?' I say to Mitch, inviting him onto the sofa, much to his bemusement. 'He didn't come after me. I didn't even have my phone or a coat and he could see my feet were killing me but he didn't care.'

Mitch lies across my lap and drools on my bare legs.

How could I slink back to the club after making a scene like that? I knew I'd have to hitch and frankly I didn't fancy it much. Fortunately, I got my first lucky break of the evening: an empty minicab passed me on the edge of the village and I flagged it down. The driver was a friendly woman called Sandra who reminded me of my mum and she agreed to take me home and offered to charge it to Cal: apparently his business has an account with them. She even offered to call the country club and they asked Robyn to collect my bag and coat.

'What have I done?' I ask Mitch, who rightly ignores me. I've embarrassed Robyn and her friend and Cal must be furious. What if he sacks me? I'm still on a trial period. How stupid was I to rise to Mawgan's bait?

'Oi! Demi, Are you in there?'

Polly bangs on the window. I think about drawing the curtains and ignoring her but instead, I push Mitch off my lap and answer the door.

She looms in the doorway. 'There's a phone call for you, your ladyship.'

'For me?'

'Well, there's only one of you round here, thank the Lord.'

'Who is it?' It must be the catering manager, Abby, threatening to sue me for ruining the reputation of her business.

'I'm not your social secretary, madam.'

'Well, I'm sorry to have made you get up off the sofa but I left my phone at the do last night.'

Polly tuts. 'So I heard. It's Robyn. I told her you'd call her back.'

'Right.'

'Don't be on long. That's Cal's phone bill.'

'I wouldn't dream of abusing his phone bill.'

'Hmmph.'

She trudges off. Just when I think she's warming to me, she turns into an ogress again. Anyone would think she'd got it into her head she was Cal's mum and I was after him or something.

Squashing down a sigh, I walk after Polly to return the call from Robyn.

After I put down the phone, I feel even worse, if it's possible. Robyn was nice, much nicer than I deserved. She asked me if I was OK and kept apologising for Mawgan kicking off, as if it was her fault. She said she'd got my stuff and would ride over with it later, 'if it was convenient'. She's so bloody nice and I really like her but I think she lets people walk over her – people like her dad and even Cal, sometimes.

'Where's Cal?' Polly has crept up behind me, which is no mean feat, I can tell you.

'How should I know? I got a cab home. I've no idea how he got back.'

'He didn't come home. His bed hasn't been slept in.'

'Hasn't it?'

'No.' She eyes me suspiciously as if I might know where he is. 'Well, I suppose he decided to stay over. Maybe he went back to Bosinney with Luke, Robyn and Isla.'

This is news to me. 'I don't really care what he does.'

'No, I don't suppose you do.' Polly smiles as if she knows me better than I do, which makes me even pricklier.

'I'm going back to my place now. Robyn's coming over later,' I tell her, refusing to rise to the bait, but on the way back to the cottage my stomach churns though I don't know why. Cal probably did stay over at Bosinney House. They are his family, after all . . . but I know Luke and Isla were staying over too.

Mitch sits in the doorway, giving me evils, which must mean he wants to be let out.

I puff my way up the path that leads from Kilhallon Cove to the ruined tin mine, hoping the faster I walk, the more I can blot out last night's disaster, but it's not my lucky day. Cal is walking along the coast path, swishing an old stick at the gorse bushes at either side of the path. There's no way of hiding from him, and why should I? The truth is that I feel embarrassed about my behaviour last night and stinging at the realisation that he still loves Isla, even though that's perfectly understandable.

Yet my heart still sinks when Mitch races off ahead of me and leaps around Cal's feet, barking, like he's a rock star. Cal bends down and fusses him and Mitch rolls over and presents his belly for a rub. That dog is as much of a man whore as Cal is and no matter how slowly I walk, I've got to reach him sometime.

We end up almost face to face at a part of the path that ducks between a large piece of rock and a gorse bush.

'Morning,' he says.

'Is it?' I'd like to push past him but there's no room and that would mean I'd have to touch him.

Mitch squeezes through our legs to investigate a rabbit hole.

'Polly was looking for you,' I say, shoving my hands in my jeans.

'Was she?'

'Yeah.'

'Did you get home OK?' he asks, chopping the grass with his stick.

'Course I did.' Close up, his eyes look a bit bloodshot and there are dark smudges under them.

'It's a long walk,' Cal mutters.

I shrug. 'So?'

'And dark.'

'I got a minicab.'

'Oh. Good. I'd hoped you might.'

'I was lucky to find one,' I say. 'Actually, the driver knows you. Sandra something, she said she'd charge it to the business. I do hope that's acceptable to you.'

He grunts. 'It'll have to be, I suppose.'

We stand in silence. I don't know why every bone seems to tingle with hurt. I hate it and I can't explain it.

'I'd better get back home. I've got loads to do then Robyn is coming round with my stuff. Didn't she say anything about it at

121

Bosinney last night?'

He examines his boots. 'Bosinney?'

'Yeah, I thought you must have stayed over. Polly said you might have . . .'

'No. I didn't stay at Bosinney. I walked home. Sort of.'

'What do you mean, sort of?'

'I may have called in at Tinner's on the way. There was a late lock-in.'

I snort. 'No wonder you look like death this morning if you spent all night at the Tinner's.'

'Thanks! It wasn't *all* night.'

'You should watch how much you're drinking.'

'Now you sound like bloody Polly!'

'It's only because she cares about you. We both—' I stop myself just in time. 'Do what you want, I don't care.'

'Demi, are you *still* pissed off with me for dragging you away from Mawgan?'

'Mad at you? Look, Cal, I couldn't care less. Honestly. *Mitch!*' I run towards him and grab his collar, more sharply than I mean. He yelps but I snap, 'Come on, you stupid bloody dog!'

'Demi! Wait!'

Cal's voice is a scrap of paper snatched away by the wind, whirling round my head. I push past him and dart into a turning in the gorse, stumbling over the tussocks, brambles scratching at my bare legs, my chest tight as a ball of twine. Mitch keeps stopping and turning and looking at me, confused. I'm *not* confused: I've never been so sure about anything in my life: Cal Penwith isn't worth shedding a single tear over.

CHAPTER FIFTEEN

It's been over a fortnight since the ball and Demi *still* hasn't forgiven me. I don't know if it was me dragging her away from Mawgan or spending half the night in the Tinner's or what but we've hardly spoken a word that wasn't to do with work and she hasn't been over to the farmhouse for dinner.

I've never known anyone work so hard – or work so hard at ignoring me – but that's Demi: she doesn't do anything by halves.

I've just got back from the bank to find her taking pictures of the progress on the cottages with her new iPad. She's intent on her work but every now and again she smiles, as if she's pleased with something. Eventually she catches sight of me, and walks in the opposite direction. She carries herself so proudly and that slender body has more strength in it than I'd realised; she reminds me of the young women in the desert, farming and building homes while their men were away fighting – or dead. Her hair seems thicker than when I first met her and more lustrous, and there's an air of confidence about her that I hadn't noticed. You could almost say she'd blossomed here, despite our recent spats.

'Cal!' Polly's face is bright red as she shouts to me. She's lugging two bulging bags between the kitchen and the recycling bins by the barn. My warning shout about the bottom of the bag is too late and suddenly it bursts. Bottles cascade out and one drops onto her foot.

'Ow.' She abandons the bags and rubs her toes, which are peeping out of her sandals. Bottles roll down the cobbles as she hops about, cursing.

'Here. Give me the bags. You shouldn't be carting this stuff about.' I'm angry at myself, not her.

Crouching down to massage her red foot, Polly snorts. 'It needs doing. Did you know the loo's blocked again in the office? I need to call the plumber to unblock it.'

'I'll sort this mess out while you call the plumber,' I say as she mutters about broken bones. 'Why don't you go and bathe your foot and rest it?'

Polly gives a humph and straightens up. 'You do know that all of these empties came out of your study? My God, you look rough. You'll end up like your father.'

My guilt lessens at being hectored by her. 'Would that be so bad?'

She plants her hands on her hips. 'Not if you don't plan on seeing sixty.'

'I know what I'm doing.'

She pokes the bag of empties. 'There are more of them rolling round the study floor and you might like to know you're out of whisky. Demi's already been out to the Co-op and she didn't add it to the list.'

'I'll live.'

'Maybe you will and maybe you won't, if you carry on like this. Staying up all night drinking, working all the hours God sends on those run-down old buildings. Chasing a dream.'

Polly's brand of tough love is stretching my patience. 'If I do keel over, you'll have the major advantage of not having to wait on me, but for your information I don't want anyone to buy any more whisky. Does that make you happy?'

'Hmmph.'

'I'll take that as a "yes". Have you contacted the builders about the green roof yet?'

'No, I asked Demi to do it. She needs keeping occupied. Better to have her working than her daydreaming and moping about like she has been lately.'

'Moping about? Is she ill?'

Polly snorts. 'Of course not! She's as fit as a fiddle but like most of us, she needs to be busy or she has too much time to dwell on things that won't do her any good.'

'Dwell on what things?'

'Sometimes, I wonder why your father ever wasted all that money on your education, Cal Penwith.'

With this cryptic comment, Polly blusters off back to the house, leaving me wondering what she means. Is Demi worrying about her family and if she should contact them? Is she feeling the pressure of her new job here? Has she *really* been so down? I've neglected her while I've been working and on my bender. I've seen her every day. She's either stayed in with Mitch or borrowed the Land Rover to go out with Robyn or the girls from the catering firm. Which is great, of course, she has her own life and it's great to see her making new friends, but I have missed her, especially her banter, and Mitch drooling on my thigh . . .

The kitchen smells of baking as I walk in. There's a jar of flowers on the middle of the scrubbed oak surface and an open tin of biscuits which must account for the delicious aroma. Sunlight fills the room, catching the coppery highlights in Demi's hair as she bends over her iPad. Radio Four plays softly in the background which must be Polly's doing, surely, because Demi is a Pirate FM addict. A familiar warmth fills me and my chest tightens unaccountably. The sights, the scents and sounds remind me of when my mum was alive so much so that I half expect her to walk through the door, wiping her hands on a cloth and telling me to take my muddy boots off.

'Hello.'

'Mmm.' Demi scrolls through the pictures on her tablet, while munching on a biscuit.

Well, I think that was 'hi' but it could have been a growl. Any visions of my mother evaporate, and I'm grateful for that. I don't want to dwell on how much I miss her.

'How are you?'

She crunches down her biscuit before replying. 'Fine. Why, shouldn't I be?'

'No reason, except Polly says you've been a bit quiet.'

She snorts crumbs and glances up. 'Polly's concerned for my welfare?'

'In a roundabout way, I think she is.'

A smile flickers across her face then she re-focuses on the screen, as if embarrassed that I caught her caring what Polly thinks – and happy that Polly cares about her.

My chair scrapes the tiles as I pull it out to sit on. 'Are those biscuits homemade?'

'Yeah.'

'They look familiar. The smell reminded me of when my mum was here.'

A pause then. 'They're fairings. Made to my nan's recipe.'

'May I?'

She shrugs. 'If you like. Polly's already had three so you'd better grab one while you can.'

The fairing is gingery and melts in my mouth. Demi is trying to see what I think about it but I don't want to jeopardise this delicate early stage of the peace process by saying the wrong thing.

After I've finished it, I help myself to another which I hope will answer her question. 'Do you want to know how I got on at the bank?'

She glances up. 'If you want to tell me.'

'The bank manager agreed to my loan extension. Added to my father's legacy, we should be able to carry on with the work on the new buildings.'

She beams. 'That's brilliant news!'

I feel touched by her enthusiasm and relieved to see her happy again. I've missed that cheeky smile so much. 'It is. Come on, let's go and check out the state of our empire.'

With Demi by my side, we go outside to survey the park from our vantage point at the top of the yard, from where we can see the part-restored cottages, and half-built campsite amenity building. We've achieved so much already, against my expectations, frankly, but there is so much more to be done.

'It's really underway,' she says. 'I can't believe it.'

'Nor me but we have to push on. We need to get the glamping business going while we renovate the farm cottages. With luck we could catch the tail-end of the camping season and have the cottages ready for October half-term. I'm going to put Kilhallon back on its feet, if it's the last thing I do.'

Standing here with Cal, I'm reminded of what Polly told me the other day in one of her gloomier moments. She says that developing Kilhallon *will* be the last thing Cal does. She says he's a shadow of the man who went away but I think he looks much better than when I first met him in St Trenyan. He's stronger and fitter and he doesn't wince so much when he's working. He tries to hide how much pain he's been in but I still notice.

I'd promised myself I wouldn't show any more enthusiasm about his plans but the problem is that they feel like *my* plans now too.

Cal was out last Thursday night again and didn't come back till three a.m.: his taxi woke me up and started Mitch barking. Polly reckons he's been drinking too much at the Tinner's.

Yet my heart still started pitter-pattering from the moment I heard the Land Rover struggling up the lane after his visit to St Trenyan this morning. Although I hate to admit it, it's not only the job and cottage that I've invested in. I've come to feel that Cal, Robyn, even Polly – and me, well, we're one big dysfunctional family together.

Sometimes, I feel we share more than Kilhallon. I know a little of what it's like to be an outsider too; to be outside people's lives, a non-person.

Mitch trots up and nudges a wet nose in Cal's crotch.

'Demi . . .'

'Yeah?'

He turns to me. 'Would you give me a hand loading some of this scrap from the old cottages into the skip, please? I'll shift the window frames and heavy stuff, if you can help with some of the lighter stuff.'

'I won't break. I'm stronger than I look.'

'The frames are heavier than they seem and I don't want you to sue me for breaching health and safety.'

'And here was me thinking you actually cared about me.'

He smiles. 'I do. Let's get changed into our work clothes and get on with it.'

Back outside, both of us in work gear, ready to move the frames, Cal asks me to fetch his toolkit from the workshop.

'It should be at the back next to the timber offcuts. And please be careful,' he warns.

I've no idea how anyone gets any work done in the 'workshop' because it's almost as crowded with stuff as the barn was. You can barely see the lathe and other tools for discarded bits of equipment, an old sewing machine like my lovely nan had and a broken food mixer and a set of heavy iron pots and pans. There's an ancient Aga that's being used as storage for even more stuff and a new dishwasher, still in its cardboard packing case, that no one has had time to plumb in.

The one thing there's no sign of is the toolbox but some of the junk is actually quite interesting; like the old stone cider flagons and pottery bowls and a rusting AA road sign that reads 'Kilhallon 1, Lands' End 7.' I've seen stuff like this in the antique shops in St Trenyan and Truro, on sale for silly money to the tourists.

Cal could sell the decent pieces or, even better, we could restore them and use them in the cottages. I pick up one of the pottery mixing bowls and rub the grime off with my finger. The sea-green glaze shines like a jewel in the gloom and it feels cool and smooth in my sticky hands. With a good scrub, it would look really pretty. Holding the pottery up to the light that filters through the grimy panes, a thought stirs in my mind. These pieces would be great in the cottages – and to decorate my 'cafe'. When we looked over the site earlier, I saw the storage building and almost said something to Cal about it, then. I have to find the nerve to tell him my plans. If I don't, the cafe will always stay a fantasy.

A dull crash from the farmyard makes me almost drop the bowl.

I run back to the yard to find Cal breathing heavily in the middle of a cloud of dust next to the skip. Damn him, while I was daydreaming in the workshop, he's moved most of the heaviest pieces of wood. He wafts away the dust, coughs and steps out into the sunlight. His T-shirt is damp with sweat and he can't hide the wince as he picks up a piece of broken window frame.

'I looked everywhere for the toolkit but I couldn't find it,' I say, feeling guilty that I lingered so long in the workshop.

He doesn't seem bothered, however. After tossing the wood into the skip, he wipes his forehead with the back of his hand. 'Really? I . . . could have sworn it was in there.'

'You look wrecked.'

'Thanks.'

'You should have waited for me to come back.'

'I needed to get the job done,' he says gruffly.

'Well, I'll help with the rest of the stuff.'

I hurry into the barn, try to lift a piece of frame and almost topple over with the strain. Cal curses but I drag the frame through the dust and out onto the yard. He joins me, and together we lift the thing over the rim of the skip. Before he can stop me, I march straight back into the barn and pick up a cardboard box of door knobs and window catches.

Cal taps my arm as I'm about to tip them in the skip. 'Not those. We can reclaim them.'

The brass and iron metal gleams dully in the box. Perspiration trickles into my eye and stings, making me blink. 'I guess you're right. They're too nice to waste.'

'They'll save us a lot of money and they'll look authentic in the cottages. I'll store them in the workshop,' he says, softening his voice.

'Maybe you'll find the toolbox in there.'

'Maybe . . .'

I wait for him in the shade of the barn, glad to be out of the sun. My arms ache, my knuckles are skinned and my nails are crusted with dirt. I think of Isla's French manicure, Tamsin's perfect nails and Mawgan's glittery talons. I had an email from Tamsin about her treatments yesterday. She's invited me to her mini spa in the village for a trial manicure and facial when I can find the time, not that spending a day shifting window frames with Cal is a bad way to spend my time.

'Found it!' Cal lifts the toolbox as he walks back to me.

'How? I looked everywhere.'

'It was in the tractor cab where I left it. I must have forgotten.'

A thought occurs to me. Did Cal send me on a wild goose chase to hunt for the toolbox so he could move the heavier pieces of scrap? I don't know whether to be annoyed or pleased about that. Pleased, on balance . . . and the idea I had in the workshop is nagging at me though I don't know if I dare share it with him.

'Fancy a drink? I think we've earned it.' He smiles at me, looks happy again.

'Yes. Why not?'

In the farmhouse kitchen, he hands me a bottle of chilled cider. 'Enjoy.'

We drink the cider along with a pack of tortilla chips and the remains of a salsa dip that I made to go with last night's chilli.

Cal wipes his hand over his mouth and dumps the empty bottle on the worktop. 'Wow, I needed that.'

'Me too.' I hand him the packet. 'Last one?'

'Go on then, then I'd better carry on clearing the yard.'

'I'll get back to the barn. Cal, while we were moving all that stuff, I was thinking . . .'

He scoops up the last of the salsa with the final tortilla. 'Always dangerous, in my opinion.'

'I know this may be a pie-in-the-sky idea but I've had an idea for the old storage building on the far side of the camp field. You know it's adjacent to the coastal path?'

'Yes?' He stops, tortilla chip halfway to his mouth. I can tell I've piqued his interest.

I take a deep breath. 'Well, have you thought of converting that building into a cafe rather than using it for storage? Once the barn up here is cleared out, that could be used for equipment and spares. Which means the storage building is vacant. It's got so much character and once it's repaired and fitted out, it would make a brilliant cafe.

'In fact, I've been taking a closer look at it while I've been out walking Mitch. I think it's the perfect size; there's room for the catering kitchen, plenty of tables inside and we could have a terrace to one side that overlooks the sea and a big glass area where the doorway is now. Everyone would love it, walkers on the coast path, families visiting Kilhallon Cove as well as our own guests.'

A smile tugs at his lips.

'Are you laughing at me?' I ask suspiciously.

'I wouldn't dream of it.'

'Because if you're taking the piss out of me, I won't tell you any more.'

He holds up his hands. 'Demi! I am not taking the piss. If I'm laughing, it's only at myself for not thinking of it before.'

'I've done a sort of business plan thing, if that helps,' I mutter.

'A business plan for the cafe? Already?' He blows out a breath. 'Don't sound so surprised.'

'I'm not, I'm impressed you've got this far so fast. Do you want to bring it over to the office this evening?'

He must notice my disappointment. 'Or I can come round and look at it now?'

After the 'meeting' in my cottage, Cal has been considering my initial ideas for the cafe and has taken them seriously. Which means, deep breath, that I have to take them seriously too – and that scares me almost as much as it excites me.

Since I first mentioned it this afternoon, I've spent all my spare time compiling some more detailed proposals and I took them over to his study earlier this evening. Cal has asked me so many questions my head has started to spin. He can be very brusque and sometimes I wonder what kind of charity he actually worked for: Polly told me he was in charge of the logistics, delivering medical and food supplies to refugees. She mentioned the name of it, but I couldn't find a website so she must have got the name wrong, or it was a small local affair. I don't like to ask Cal and especially not now.

'I was at the food fair in Truro when I first had the idea. Do you have any idea how many local producers there are? You can buy almost anything home grown in Cornwall, so we'd try to keep as much produce as possible sourced from within a few miles.'

I show him the leaflets I picked up at the food fair and from a successful organic place near St Ives.

'You have been busy. Go on.'

'As well as the cafe we could have a mobile bike stall or a little van next to the coast path for people passing on their way down to the cove, selling real Cornish ice creams and homemade treats. I could make the pasties, the fairings and figgy 'obbin and Cornish splits.'

He folds his arms and those glorious guns bulge. My body heats up and my stomach swirls but I won't be put off. 'Figgy 'obbin . . . I haven't heard that word since I was a lad.'

'Nan used to make it but I didn't think anyone else knew what it was.'

'My great great aunt used to make it – that's Robyn's great-grandmother – I was still at infants' school and the name was so weird I wouldn't touch it. I think I may have cried when offered a piece.'

'I can't imagine you ever bursting into tears.'

He smiles ruefully. 'Go on; tell me more about this fortune-making enterprise.'

'Are you being sarcastic?'

'No.'

'We could use produce from Polly's hens and home-grown veg and stuff. Mitch would sit by the cafe and look appealing and all the people with dogs would stop. These doggy-mad people are a soft touch . . .'

'This is all brilliant, but Demi, there's only one of you.'

'I thought of that and we will need some staff but I *know* I can make it work. I'm not afraid of working hard and at busy times we could have someone to help in the shop. Nina and the girls could do with the extra cash and I'm sure Robyn would enjoy having some money of her own. I'd probably need at least a couple of extra people in the season, possibly more if it takes off . . .'

His dark brown eyes are intent on me and I feel I might burn up. My hands shake as I stack the leaflets together. He smiles, very softly, and his lips part as if he wants to say something.

'Cal, why are you looking at me like that?'

'Like what? Don't be silly, I'm just thinking.' His smile fades and his tone is serious. 'Now, let's take a closer look at the costings you've prepared. If this is ever going to work, we need to have everything planned to the last detail.'

He glances up from his notebook and looks at me. It's hard to read his expression, impossible to know how he feels.

'I've thought about this morning and night, every day, for the past few weeks and if you can find the finance, I'll do anything to make it work.'

It's then I realise that our fingertips are almost touching and it's like an electric current has jumped between us.

For a second I think our fingers might meet, and that he might lean forward and kiss me, or that I might lean forward and kiss *him*, but we stay as we are, our skin still millimetres apart.

'Cal, I've never felt so passionate about anything in my life before.'

'I can see that, Demi.' He sits up straight, and the connection is lost. 'In that case, I'd better find the money from somewhere.'

CHAPTER SIXTEEN

Spring is turning into summer at Kilhallon. When I walked Mitch this morning, the little copse behind the house was carpeted in bluebells and hundreds of sea pinks were out in the dunes above the cove, nodding their delicate heads in the breeze.

I'd hardly noticed how fast the time was flying because I've been so busy. Cal has been working on the renovations from dawn till dusk, leaving me in charge of plans for the cafe and helping Polly in the garden. When I'm not talking to builders' merchants, researching or doing admin, I'm helping Polly with her vegetable patch. She showed me how to earth the potatoes to protect them from any late frosts, not that it's likely this far south in May but she likes to be cautious. We planted some autumn rhubarb and scattered straw around the strawberry plants – which I don't mind – and did tons of weeding – which I'm not so keen on.

I doubt if we'll have enough strawberries for the jam and cream teas in the cafe. I'll have to find some suppliers ready for next spring.

Polly seems different when she's in her garden; I wouldn't say she's happy but she's way less grumpy. The vegetable patch is one of the things she kept up while Cal was away. In a funny way, I think she genuinely loves him and out of the blue this morning, she told me she always knew Cal would find his way home eventually – that Kilhallon would draw him back.

I wonder why Isla and Luke didn't have the same faith?

The sun is hot on my back as I gouge a dandelion from the carrot patch but the ring of hooves attracts my attention. Robyn rides into the yard off the moor which is ablaze with red and purple heather.

I haven't seen her for a few days, since we went shopping in St Trenyan. I bought a lush new skirt and top in the Primark sale with money I'd saved from my pay packet.

I walk to meet her.

'You're becoming a real domestic goddess, or is it an earth mother?' she says.

'Neither, I hope.' I wipe the soil from my hands on my work overalls.

'It suits you,' says Robyn, climbing off her horse. We hug and then walk to the stable and she tethers Roxy in the next stall to Dexter, Cal's gelding.

'If you want Cal, he went out first thing to see the architects in Truro.' Cal has gone to discuss the costs and feasibility of building a shop and cafe on the site. The hard work involved doesn't scare me but the thought that my ideas will cost real money is terrifying.

'I wasn't looking for Cal particularly. I just wondered if you wanted a coffee but you look busy.'

'I'm not too busy for a chat. I've been slaving away in the garden all morning and I need a drink. Are you OK? Is anything the matter?'

She kicks at the hay. 'Not really but I'm getting stressy over this engagement party.'

'Why?' I ask on the way to the farmhouse.

'Oh, I don't know. Dad's been getting on at me about one thing and another, I think he's worried about the business, and

Isla asked me to be a bridesmaid.'

'That doesn't sound so bad, does it? And it's ages away.'

'Yeah, but I'm too old to wear a tacky dress. It's not my thing at all.'

'No, but if she asked you I suppose it's difficult to say no.'

'My dad would be upset.'

I laugh. 'Robyn, they haven't even set a date yet and there's the engagement party to get through first.'

She sighs. 'I know. Dad's freaking out about the cost of the party. He insisted on holding it at the house because he says Luke's like a son to him but I also think he's picking up a lot of the bill. Isla keeps asking if he can afford it and offering to contribute more, but he won't let her.'

'It sounds very posh.'

'It will be. They've got professional caterers in.'

'Wow. I was a bridesmaid to my auntie when I was fourteen,' I say. 'I had to wear a horrible tight, shiny dress and I drank four glasses of cava and was sick in front of everyone. Dad hit the roof and we all had to leave early. The dress had to be chucked out and my auntie was mad because she'd wanted to sell it on eBay. They never spoke to us after that.'

'What did your mum say?'

'She wasn't around by then. It was the year after she died.'

'I'm sorry, and I know this isn't the same but I miss my mum too.'

'What happened to her?'

Robyn sighs. 'She lives in Sydney.'

'Oh . . . I thought that . . .'

'She was dead? She may as well be, as far as my dad's concerned. He goes mad if we talk about her in front of him. She ran off with a surf instructor from Newquay who wasn't that much older than I am now. They split up but Mum runs a recruitment company over there now and has a new partner.'

'Do you see her?'

'I've been twice since she left us five years ago. I'd like to go again at Christmas – I've saved enough and Mum says I can stay but Dad will hit the roof.'

'Your dad can't keep you away from your mother.'

'I know but it's not that simple.' She plonks herself down at the farmhouse table. I've a feeling this may take some time. After I've got the worst of the dirt out of my nails I find two cans of Coke. Robyn flips the top.

'I'd love to move out of Bosinney but I can't afford a flat on my own.'

'Could you share one with your friends?'

'Most of my friends are loved-up and the ones that aren't, I don't want to share a bag of popcorn with, let alone a flat. They're not even house trained. Actually, there is someone but I don't think Dad would be too pleased.'

'What is he? A serial killer?'

She hesitates. 'No. Not that bad . . . but Dad definitely wouldn't approve. I depend on him for my college fees and I don't want to upset him. That might sound crazy and I don't expect you to understand.'

'I do understand. I totally do.'

'Really?'

'Yes. I haven't seen my dad for ages. He had drink problems and they got worse after my mum died. He wasn't that nice to her while she was alive but I think he felt guilty after she died and I reminded him of how much he'd lost and the things he hadn't done to show her he loved her. When he found a new partner, it was the last straw for me so I walked out.'

Robyn hugs me. 'Maybe your dad was just an arse,' she says fiercely then sighs. 'I suppose my dad wants me to get married or take over Bosinney, not that we'll have it for long the way my dad's business is going, but I want my own life, not the one he had planned out for him and Mum.'

'You're right. It's your life not anyone else's!'

'So when I tell Dad that I want to move in with a girl, he'll have a fit.'

It takes a second for the G word to register. 'Ah. So the boy you love is a girl.'

'You mean you didn't know I was gay?'

'No. I didn't. I hadn't even thought about it.'

'It's fine. I'm bi, actually, not that my dad would understand or care,' she says gloomily. She prods a loose tile with the toe of her riding boot.

'Are you sure he hasn't guessed already? I had a gay mate at the cafe; he was terrified of coming out and when he finally did, his mum and his brother were just like "and you have news for us?" They'd known for a long time and were just waiting for him to tell them in his own time.'

She shakes her head. 'No way. Dad has no idea and it definitely won't be cool with him, trust me. Even if he wasn't so old-fashioned. Andi isn't just any girl.'

'Come on. She's not a serial killer, is she? Or a Cade?'

Robyn stares at the broken tile and swallows hard. When she does look at me, her pale face has turned a shade whiter.

'Oh wait . . .'

'She's Mawgan Cade's younger sister.'

Ah. The goth girl at Sheila's cafe with the Cades. Oh. Dear. 'That doesn't mean she's like Mawgan or her father.'

'Oh, she isn't!' Robyn springs back into life, leaning forward, her eyes sparkling. 'Andi is the exact opposite to *them*. She's kind, funny, talented . . . she's amazing.'

I struggle to square the gloomy goth at the cafe with this description but you know, love and all that. 'Your dad and Luke get on with the Cades, do they? It's only Cal and Mawgan who can't stand each other.'

Robyn slumps back into the chair. 'I think Luke likes Mawgan though I've no idea why: she's an evil cow and Isla isn't that keen on her . . . my dad tolerates the Cades but he has no choice because Mawgan and her father own the building where his office is. If my dad's Victorian in his attitudes, the Cades are stuck in the Stone Age. They'd probably chuck Andi out and disinherit her if they found out she was gay and wanted to move in with me. I can't do that to her.'

'Do you think it would make a difference if your father liked Andi and she wasn't a Cade?'

'No. Maybe. I don't know.' She sighs heavily. 'I can't take the risk. What if Mawgan and her father decided to make trouble for my dad and Luke because of me and Andi?'

'Surely they wouldn't do that?' Even I don't believe what I'm saying.

'Get real, Demi.'

'There has to be something you can do, a way round it. Two people in love should be together. No one should have to live a lie.'

'This is the real world.' She pauses. 'It will kill me that she's at Isla's engagement party and I'll have to pretend we're just friends . . .' Her voice trails off and she changes the subject. 'Hey, a really great indie band is playing at the college next weekend and Andi and I are staying over at a friend's place afterwards. Would you like to come to the gig and meet her?'

I want to help. I know what it's like to feel like an outsider and she's been so nice to me. On the other hand, I don't feel totally happy keeping such an important secret from her family or Cal, even if it is Robyn's business.

'Have you thought of telling Cal about this?' I say, feeling desperate. 'He knows you all way better than me and he might be able to help.'

'He's got enough on his plate with the building work and dealing with Isla's engagement and he still misses his dad badly. He doesn't need to take on my problems too.'

'Do you think he'll ever get over it?'

'His dad or Isla? I don't know. He's always been obsessive and gone to extremes. If he likes you, he'd cut off his arm for you but if you hurt him, he never forgets.'

My stomach churns but Robyn seems unaware of how much her words have affected me.

'Oh, come on, say you'll go to the gig and meet Andi. You'll love her; she's nothing like the rest of the Cades.'

With a plea like that, how could I refuse? It would be nice to get away from here and make new friends and this is Robyn's secret to tell, not mine.

'I'd love to. I'll ask Cal if I can borrow the Land Rover.'

CHAPTER SEVENTEEN

Since Robyn's visit, I've spent the past couple of days clearing out the old park workshop, sorting the stuff into boxes for the tip, the charity shop and recycling. Mitch 'helped' by wriggling under the workbench, knocking things over and cocking his leg up against Cal's mowing machine, which has been brought out of the 'cafe' building and up to the workshop. A lot of the old caravan spares and fittings have already gone to the tip but the farmhouse bric-a-brac is a different ball game. I took some of the crockery and tins to my cottage, and sealed up the rest of the pieces in cardboard boxes ready for 'dressing' the cottages, when they're restored.

'Is this the same place or have I been beamed up to a new workshop?' Cal asks when he comes in for the lawn mower at the end of my long day of clearing up. Fortunately, I wiped it down before he got here. 'I hardly recognise it. I never knew we had all this stuff.'

'Polly says your father couldn't stand to chuck anything out.'

'She's right, but I didn't see it as a problem when I was young. I liked messing about in here.'

'Polly asked me to take anything we can't re-use to the charity shop in St Trenyan but I thought I might list some of it on eBay.'

Cal surveys the workshop. 'Good idea. I can actually work in here now you've tidied up and it seems brighter.'

'I cleaned the windows.'

'You've done a great job. Do you fancy a takeaway and a beer later?'

'Um . . . Thanks but I'm going out tonight.'

'Oh. OK. That's fine.'

He seems genuinely disappointed which makes me feel good, even though it probably means nothing. 'Robyn asked me to go to a gig. It's Friday night.'

'Did she? Cool. I'm sure you'll have a much better time than hanging round here with me and a takeaway.'

Debating this statement, I carry the last box of 'keeper' china over to my cottage. I have this idea of using the best stuff for the cafe. I think the mismatched cups and saucers and plates will add a look of retro chic to the place. My ideas have been fermenting since I talked over the cafe proposals with Cal. In fact, I have so many thoughts about it that I can hardly sleep some nights, while I'm planning and researching.

Cal has asked me to do detailed costings for the cafe, and more research into the market. Since that's involved driving round the best ones, trying out the cream teas and carrot cake on expenses, I don't mind. Neither has Mitch, I've taken him to some of the places with outdoor space and decided to have a dog menu. Now all I need to do is try out some recipes on a willing victim.

I didn't get in from the gig until two o'clock last night because afterwards we all went over to Nina's house until really late. Her mum gave us a lift home because she'd been up late with some new born pups. The band weren't bad considering they're only a college outfit and I had a much better time than I'd expected. Andi seemed wary of me at first but then she confessed she was embarrassed by Mawgan's bitchiness at the cafe. She kept apologising for her sister having me sacked but I told her that I was glad, in the end, as I'm much happier now. Andi and Robyn were totally loved-up together. I hardly recognised the pale, downtrodden girl I saw with Mawgan and her father at Sheila's cafe. I thought about persuading them to come out to their families but now I'm not so sure it's a good idea, however unfair that seems.

Ignoring my throbbing head, I dragged myself out of bed at half-past seven to practise the dog menu recipes. I could have used the farmhouse kitchen but don't want to put up with Polly's snide comments: she thinks I'm barking mad without cooking cakes for dogs. Hey, there you go: *A Barking Mad Menu*. I can call it that!

'Have I gone completely nuts since I met Cal Penwith?'

Mitch glances at me briefly and then returns to inspecting his bits. I bet Mary Berry never has to put up with this behaviour from Paul Hollywood. A long time later, every surface of the tiny kitchen is covered in flour, bacon rind, broken egg shells and dirty bowls and pots. I retrieve a tin that smells way better than it looks from the dodgy oven in the cottage.

'Ow!' I drop the tin on the worktop and blow at my burned fingers. Now I know why Polly had chucked out these oven gloves for the recycling bank. Mitch drifts into the kitchen and sniffs the meat-scented air.

'Bacon and chicken layer cake, sir?' I bob a curtsey but Mitch is unimpressed.

With the help of two tea towels, I turn the cake onto a plate and cut a piece off, blowing on it to cool it. Mitch nudges my leg. He sniffs at the still warm chunk of sticky 'cake' I've placed in his bowl. I hope it goes down better than the meat dog cake he turned up his nose at.

He licks the slice of layer cake, then wolfs it down and lifts his head, as if to say 'and the rest?' I think it's a hit so I get started on the gluten and dairy free carrot dog muffins.

By five o' clock, with the sun shining through the window and the oven having been on almost all day, it's roasting in the kitchen.

A bee buzzes past the open doorway and the sky is the same sapphire blue as Isla's engagement ring. I changed into my new Primark cut-offs and a tank top before starting the carrot muffins but even so, perspiration trickles down the small of my back. My hair is gathered up in a messy bun – appropriate considering the state of my latest creation – and I know I must be pink from the heat.

'OK, Mitch, you've been very patient today testing all these recipes. Do you fancy a walk? I don't want you to end up on a fat pets show.'

Mitch peers up from his cool spot on the quarry tiles as if to say. 'In these temperatures? Are you out of your freakin' mind?'

'I've got to get out of here, whether you're coming or not. Come on, let's walk to the cove and go in the sea. You like that.'

I rattle his collar and lead and wearily he scoops himself up and follows me out of the door. The sun is still high above the inky sea. I love the park at this time of the day; not quite afternoon but not really evening. Mitch runs ahead, cocking his leg against the stiles on our route to the cove. The wash block in the yurt field is coming along, and has plastic sheets covering the roof.

A few walkers amble along the coast path but most have gone back to their cottages and guest houses now. It feels as if Mitch and I are the only ones left at the ends of the earth. From the top of the stile, the view over the Atlantic towards the Far West is to die for. Beyond that, there's nothing until you reach America and suddenly I feel very small.

I decide to take a closer look at the building I'd like to use for the cafe, turn a corner and spot Cal. He swings a sledgehammer and aims it at the decaying wall of the clubhouse. It's a sixties building and we're not keeping it, but I'm amazed he thinks he can demolish it by hand.

Crash. Birds take off, screeching from the roof and even Mitch stops sniffing and looks over to see what the noise is. I walk towards him, wincing every time he wallops the wall. The bricks crumble and pieces fly into the air. Cal is almost obscured by dust but I'm close enough to see the sweat glistening on his bare thighs exposed by his denim cut-offs. He already had a tan from his 'desert holiday' as he likes to call it but working outside over the past few months has deepened it. I don't want to perv over him but I can't take my eyes off his biceps and his sinewy forearms. The good food, fresh air and hard labour of the past few months have added muscle to his skinny frame, making it lean and mean and sexy.

A crow flaps out of the hedge, croaking, and Mitch barks.

Cal looks straight at me through a haze of dust. My cheeks burn like fire at being caught but I wave at him cheerily. It's a good job he's wearing safety goggles so he can't see just how red I am.

'Sun's out, guns out,' I shout.

He pushes the goggles over his forehead.

'Wouldn't it be better to let the builders do this? You look like you were trying to kill someone with that sledgehammer.'

'Yeah, I feel like it this afternoon.' The dust settles slowly, sticking to his guns. I feel almost faint with lust but he drops the hammer onto the ground.

'Why? What's up?'

He wipes the sweat from his brow with the back of his hand. 'Hasn't Polly told you? The planners have turned down the application to develop Kilhallon Park. We're finished.'

CHAPTER EIGHTEEN

'What? They can't do that!'

'They can and they have.'

Anger bubbles up inside me. 'Why? I don't understand. I thought you said that gaining permission would be a foregone conclusion.'

'Apparently, there were "a number of objections raised pertaining to noise, increased traffic and the development was injurious to the maintenance of a tranquil, natural environment".' He snorts in derision.

'That sounds like bullshit to me.'

'It *is* bullshit.'

'But there was a bigger, noisier site here years ago and that's exactly what you don't want now. You're trying to create a peaceful place that will bring money and jobs to the area. How can anyone object to you wanting to make things better for everyone locally? What's wrong with people?'

'I don't know but I'm going to find out.'

'You have to. We can't give up. You're not going to, are you?' I see Cal's dreams sinking like water into sand. My dreams too. I want Kilhallon to succeed as much as he does.

'I won't give up but the problem is that I've been clearing the land and getting some foundations done without planning permission but I thought that part would be straightforward. The man I know at the planning office said he couldn't envisage any major problems and that the outline plans looked like exactly the type of development the area needed.'

'Then I don't understand why they were turned down.'

'There *is* no reason,' he mutters.

'Then *why*?'

He gives a bitter smile. 'I have my theories.'

I think – actually, I *know* – that he means that the delay may have something to do with the Cades, but I'm not sure I want to add fuel to the fire by mentioning their names at this particular moment. He looks pissed off enough without me encouraging him to rant about Mawgan and her father. If it is their doing, though, surely Cal won't simply give in?

'What will you do next?'

'I'll appeal it, of course, but worst case? I'd have to stop the development and they could make me demolish all or part of the building. Plus it will cost more money to put a case together and present it.'

He picks up the sledgehammer again, winces and stares at his palm. His fingers and hands have white blisters, a couple of them oozing blood.

'That looks sore.'

'It's only a few blisters.'

'What happened to the builders' gloves?'

'I forgot to put them on.'

It's more than my life's worth to ask if he might be a bit distracted and not thinking straight. 'Do you want me to strap them up for you?'

'No. Thanks, but I want to get this wall down tonight.'

I follow his gaze. One side of the wall is rubble but there's no way he's going to take the lot down before dark. The gap has revealed a new view of the sea, however, which is the same blue of the new jeans I bought with my wages. I feel like I'm seeing it through new eyes; the eyes of the families who will come and stay here.

'Watch out!'

He swings the hammer again and the wall cracks but doesn't fall.

'Damn.'

He drops the hammer. Blood streaks his palms. 'Maybe I had better sort these hands out so I can carry on.'

'Come over to the farm. I'll get the first-aid kit.'

Mitch lies on the kitchen tiles, chewing an old nylon bone while Cal sits silently at the kitchen table. I keep my eyes down, concentrating on dabbing the blisters with antiseptic cream. I'd be lying if I said that being inches from him wasn't doing some crazy things to various bits of me.

I cut some gauze up and find a bandage. 'It'd be much better to let these have some fresh air and rest them for a few days rather than carrying on.'

'No chance. I've got to finish the job tonight.'

He doesn't even wince as I wrap some microfibre tape around the blisters and tape it securely. 'That should help but I still think you're going to have to rest your hands or they'll be ripped to shreds.'

He smiles. 'I've had worse.'

I make the mistake of looking up and his dark eyes catch mine. I press my finger into the bandage. He winces.

'I told you. You can try and carry on but if you do, you won't be able to drive or take a pee, let alone demolish a wall. Let me take a turn or get the builders in.'

'I can't afford to get anyone else in and there's no way I'm letting you do it.'

'You don't think I can?'

'I think you can do anything but you'll end up with hands like mine in five minutes.'

'I can get a lot done before that happens.'

So I lasted an hour before my arms felt as if they were on fire and my back was screaming at me to stop. Even with a pair of gardening gloves, my hands are blistered, though they're nothing to the state of Cal's. By the time we'd finished, the bandages were a deep pink between the grime. I left my blisters open to the air but his needed redressing.

'I need a shower. We both do.' My mouth has run away with my brain. I drop his hand like a blazing coal. 'That'll do.'

Cal watches me intently. 'I'll take your advice and have a shower. Would you like to stay for dinner?' he asks.

'OK. If you're cooking.'

He waggles his bandaged hands. 'Sort of.'

'Don't get your bandages wet,' I say.

He glances down and groans.

Later, in my clean shorts and a T-shirt, with my freshly washed mane tamed by a scrunchie, I walk back into the farmhouse.

The smell of onions, chilli and garlic meets my nose before I reach the door.

'Wow, that is amazing. I totally can't wait for this. Oh . . .'

Cal strolls into the kitchen, a white towel knotted low around his hips, hanging perilously low on one side. His happy trail arrows from his navel towards his pelvis, and I'm not sure if I'm imagining the faint shadow of hair at the crease of his thigh or not. But if that towel slips one millimetre lower I'll be able to see everything. Heat races from my chest to the roots of my hair. I must be as red as a traffic light. My throat is dry, my voice crackly.

'Um. Sorry. I thought you'd be dressed by now. I mean, I thought you'd be ready. For dinner, that is . . . shall I come back later?'

'Why would you want to do that?' Frowning at my obvious stupidity, he pads over to the table where onion skins and chilli seeds lie on the chopping board. The bandages are gone, and I'm not redoing them. He'll have to suffer, and I do hope the chilli hasn't got into his sore hands.

Not that I am focusing on the chilli or his blisters. I have absolutely *no* idea how that towel is staying up.

As he turns his back to gather the scraps onto the board, the thin towel stretches across his bum, outlining his muscles. My hormones leap about like popcorn, my body sizzles and I don't know where to look next. He flips the pedal of the bin with his foot and bends over to scrape the vegetable scraps off the board. The towel tautens over his bottom. I almost have to bite my knuckles in frustration. What's wrong with me? I've turned to complete mush.

He swings round to face me. Miraculously, the towel stays up. 'Demi, what's the matter with you? You look like you're going to have a heart attack?'

'Nothing. It's hot in here. With the oven on and whatnot and I must have had the shower up too high.'

He nods. 'The thermostat's on its way out. It is a warm night so I thought we'd eat outside. There's some cold cider in the fridge. Why don't you take one out while I put some clothes on?'

Either he genuinely has no idea what he does to me, or he has every idea and doesn't care – or he is deliberately trying to fry my brain and hormones at the same time. But I can't believe he'd lead me on like that. In which case he *really* has no idea which means he can't possibly think I could ever be any kind of threat to him in that way. I'm just an employee, a friend at best: part of the fixtures and fittings like the table or the chickens.

I skip outside, gulping in the fresh air, although it's so still and dusty it hardly helps but at least I don't have to look at him any more.

But, what's this?

Beside the back door, Cal has laid two places on the old iron patio table and carried two of the farmhouse chairs into the yard. In the centre of the table, some wildflowers from the meadow are stuck in an old Doom Bar bottle.

With a chilled cider swilling through my veins and a lot of concentration on a green roof leaflet I found in the recycling bin, I manage to cool myself down a little. Sounds of the Aga door opening and plates clinking let me know he's back but I don't offer to help him.

Shortly after, he carries two plates of curry outside. To my relief, he's put jeans and a T-shirt on, though the sight of him with hair still damp, and skin smelling of pine shower gel, is raising the temperature again.

'Wow, this is posh.'

He grins. 'I'm a man of many talents. Now, would madam care to be seated?'

The curry was delicious and over the last couple of hours, we demolished a few ciders. OK, make that three for me and four for him – I think – and suddenly I realise it's barely light enough to read the labels and that my thighs are covered in goosebumps.

'You wouldn't think it could be so cold after such a hot day,' I say.

'It was freezing in the desert at night.'

This is one of the first times I've ever heard him refer to his time in the Middle East and I hesitate before responding. I want to hear more about his life before he went away, and what happened while he was away, even though I'm almost afraid to hear it.

'Was it?'

'It's the radiation loss under the clear skies. It literally can drop to freezing.'

'I hadn't realised. You must be glad to be home.'

In reply, he tips the cider bottle to his mouth.

'What made you leave home for such a dangerous place when you could have stayed at Kilhallon?' *With Isla*, I think.

'Sometimes I wish I hadn't.'

'Then why did you?'

'My mother died when I was a teenager and even before that my father was too busy having affairs and mismanaging the park to see that I was going off the rails. One night, not long after Dad had brought home another new woman, I got pissed, took a tractor for an unscheduled tour of the village and ended up in a police cell.' He laughs bitterly but I sense that this is something he wants to tell me; or has to.

With another swig of his cider, he carries on. 'Anyway, I was lucky not to end up in jail but it was my last chance. Isla persuaded me to knuckle down at college, retake my A levels and somehow I scraped the grades to get into university.'

'Polly told me you were training to be a doctor.'

'Yes, but I never qualified. I started a medical degree but I dropped out after two years.'

'Why did you drop out?'

'I don't think I really wanted to do be a doctor in the first place but my dad wanted me to have a profession, as I wasn't going to help run Kilhallon, and Isla encouraged me. But I couldn't handle the pressure of the exams; I started taking some stuff to cope with it all. In the end, I did scrape through the second year exams but I quit anyway. That's what Dad found hardest: that I'd quit while I was ahead. Anyway, I came home in disgrace and bummed around for a few months, with my mates.'

'And Luke?'

'Yeah, we hung out, but by that stage he was moving on; he was doing his finance exams, turning into a grown-up. Unlike me,' he adds. 'Isla was still here and I was just happy to be able to see her. She was doing a TV production course in Falmouth. Eventually I got bored and a friend persuaded me to do some volunteering with a charity that sends out shelter kits. I never expected to care about it as much as I did.'

'It was just a way to pass the time but the work sucked me in gradually until I couldn't imagine doing anything else. I finally felt that a loser like me could actually make a difference in the world. Over the next few years, I worked for them, going abroad for a few weeks or even months at a time when they needed me to. Eventually, they asked me to do a year-long stint.'

'Is that the group who you were working for recently?'

He hesitates. 'No. It was another organisation. One based out there.' Stopping abruptly, he picks up the dirty plates. 'I saw some scones and cream in the fridge. Do you want some?'

'If you do. I made them this morning.'

'How could I resist?' He shoots me a smile that makes me shiver. 'Stay there.'

There is no elegant way to eat a scone full with jam and cream. You just have to go for it and embrace the fact that the filling will squidge out and cover your fingers with sticky, creamy bliss. And that you will have to lick the mess from your fingers. I still haven't overcome my delight in being able to eat when and what I like and even Cal, sitting next to me in all his annoying sexiness, isn't going to stop me.

He leans over the table and stares at my face.

Automatically, I touch my nose. 'What's the matter? Do I have a burned nose? I forgot the sun cream while we cut the field. I bet I'm smothered in freckles too.'

'Your nose is rather red but the freckles are cute.' *Cute*? Is he *flirting* with me again? Is it to distract me from more questions about his life in the Middle East? Or am I reading too much into that?

I stick out my tongue. 'Yuk. I don't want to be cute.'

'Suit yourself. Actually if I was being honest, I'd have described you as annoying.'

'Thanks,' I mutter, thinking the 'cute' wasn't so bad after all.

'And gobby,' he adds with a smug grin.

I gasp. 'You can talk, Mr Moody.'

His eyebrows rise and then join together. 'Me? Moody?'

'Yes. And arsey too.'

He snorts. 'When am I ever arsey?'

'All the time, and cranky too, not to mention unpredictable . . .'

'Well, you're bolshie, Ms Jones, not to mention chippy and your nose is like Rudolph's.'

'You are so horrible, Cal— hey!'

Lightning fast, he dips a finger into the clotted cream and flicks it at my nose. Cream spatters my cheeks and my eyes focus on a yellow splodge on the tip of my nose. I curl my tongue upwards trying to reach it. Cal rests his chin on his hand and leans across the table. That handsome, sexy, annoying face is far too close for comfort. My body glows inwardly and I hardly dare breathe. 'That's a very impressive tongue.'

His voice, husky and slightly slurred, curls around me and I refocus on him. He holds half a scone piled high with jam and cream, inches from my lips.

'Go on, you may as well eat the rest now. May as well be hung for a sheep as a lamb,' as Polly would say.'

'This is a scone not a . . . mmmmm.'

He slides the crumbly scone between my lips. It's hard to laugh, eat a scone and try not to melt with lust all at the same time. The fact I'm not supposed to be interested in him seems irrelevant and the biggest lie I've ever told myself. Surely Cal must know I have a massive crush on him.

'Good?' he asks, that smile playing on his lips. He *must* know how I feel about him.

Through closed eyes, I mumble. 'Mmm. Delicious.'

'Cal? Are you there?'

I open my eyes in time to see Cal jump up from the table, wiping his mouth with his hand, smearing jam and cream on his face, like a little boy caught with his hand in the cookie jar.

CHAPTER NINETEEN

Isla stands in the kitchen doorway. She wears a simple red shift dress with her glossy straw-coloured hair caught up in a casual pony tail that must have taken ages to look so stylish. She smiles at us, like she's caught two children misbehaving but is prepared to let us off.

'I couldn't get an answer when I knocked and the front door was open so I walked in. I hope it was OK?' She steps down into the yard. I've no idea how long she's been there or what she's seen or heard of our scone fight.

'If I'm disturbing your dinner, I can come back. I wanted to ask if you've decided to come to the party. I haven't had your RSVP and I have to give the caterers the final numbers ready for the day after tomorrow. Or has it been lost in the post?'

'I've been too busy.' Cal gathers up the empty bottles with his hands. One slips from his fingers and smashes, spraying glass across the cobbles and he curses.

'Oh dear, I knew I should have phoned first but I managed to snatch a quick break from my latest shoot to fly down here.'

'It's fine. We'd finished,' he says briskly.

Had we? Had we even started? We were pissed. Nothing happened. Nothing will happen now she's here. Isla. So beautiful, so bloody *nice*.

Realising I've been a spectator for the past minute, I get up, wiping my jammy hands on my shorts. 'I'd better clear up the glass.'

Cal bends down. 'No. It's my mess. I'll clear it up in a minute.'

Isla joins him on the cobbles. 'What happened to your hands? They look sore.'

'I was demolishing a wall.'

'With a sledgehammer,' I add.

She shakes her head. 'God, Cal.'

'I'll get some old newspaper to wrap the glass in,' I say, but no one hears, which suits me. It was a good job Isla arrived or something might have happened that I'd have regretted. That Cal might have regretted. *Would* we have regretted it? While I find the newspaper from the recycling bag, I turn the possibilities over in my mind and end up tying myself in knots. When I come back, Isla has gathered the largest pieces of glass and together we wrap up the pieces in the newspaper while Cal looks on moodily. Isla's face is tense and strained.

'Thanks. I'll throw this lot in the bin on my way home.'

'Please, don't go because of me. You two seemed to be having a good time.'

I force a smile because I'm not sure what she means, exactly. She's probably just being nice. I think.

'We were only mucking about and I was getting cold. Anyway, I'd better take Mitch for a walk.'

Hearing his name, Mitch lifts his head off his paws. I pick up the newspaper bundle.

'There's no need to go,' says Isla firmly. 'I'm sure Cal can find you a jumper or something to keep you warm.'

'Demi's perfectly capable of fetching a sweatshirt from her place,' Cal says.

'I'm sure she is but I wanted to talk to Demi too. I want to ask her a favour.' She throws me a smile, a warm and friendly smile that confuses the hell out of me.

'Me?'

'This is rather short notice but I was wondering if you could spare the time to help out with the catering for the engagement party at Bosinney. There's a big event at the country club the same evening so the catering company is short-handed.' She smiles. 'Again.'

'I . . . um . . . are you sure after the . . . er . . . last time?'

'That wasn't your fault.' She looks embarrassed. My God, I think she really *is* that nice. 'Abby said you worked incredibly hard before Mawgan was such a cow to you. I promise I'll keep her well away from you.'

'You've asked *Mawgan*?'

'Of course I have, Cal.' Isla sounds weary, as if she was expecting her visit to turn into a battle. 'You know very well that the Cades are business associates of Dad's, and Robyn is very friendly with Andi, not to mention Luke's involvement with some of Mawgan's projects.'

Cal shakes his head. 'It all sounds very cosy.'

'It's done now and that's that. I can't change the guest list to suit you, Cal.' Isla sounds frustrated.

'I don't expect you to,' he growls. 'But after the way Mawgan treated Demi at the ball you can't expect her to wait on your guests.'

'It's OK. I'm over it.' I edge towards the door with the newspaper bundle. I don't want to be a spectator at a lovers' tiff. Because this *is* a lovers' tiff, whether Isla's engaged to Luke or not.

'So you'll do it? We'll pay you double what you got at the ball,' Isla says brightly.

Before I can answer, Cal leaps in with both feet. 'You won't pay her anything because Demi is already coming to the party.'

My jaw drops.

'The invitation said Cal Penwith and guest, didn't it?'

'Well . . . erm . . .' Isla's perfect brows meet in a frown. I edge closer to the door, dying of embarrassment.

'Demi is my guest so she can't wait on tables,' Cal declares.

I'm too shocked to speak and Isla seems to be the same way. The one person who doesn't have a say in this argument seems to be me but I'm not sure what to say anyway, or even how I feel about being a pawn in their game.

'Of c-course it did, and Demi is welcome, naturally, but I'd assumed . . .'

'That I would be alone?' Cal smiles triumphantly.

'You haven't replied yet. How was I to know?' says Isla, coolly.

'Then I apologise but thanks, yes, we're both delighted to accept the invitation.'

'Well, good. I look forward to seeing you. Both of you, of course, and I'm *so* sorry I made a mistake with the invitation.' She directs this at Cal, an edge creeping into her voice.

'Demi has been looking forward to it, haven't you?' he says to me. I could kill him for putting me on the spot but I'm also secretly dancing a little jig.

'Thanks for asking me,' I mutter. 'Now I have to take Mitch out. He's plaiting his legs.'

Why do I feel so angry with Isla when she's so polite? Is it because she walked in and stopped me – and Cal – from doing something stupid? Because of the way he looks at her now? Because for a crazy moment I thought he might kiss me, and that the kiss might turn into something else?

I scuttle past her, the newspaper packet clutched tightly against my body.

'Demi. Wait . . .' She smiles at me as if I'm a little girl again. She pulls a tissue from her bag and holds it out. 'You have jam on your nose.'

CHAPTER TWENTY

Isla didn't stay long after Demi left us. I walked with her to the stables because she said she wanted to see Dexter. I pretended I believed her. It's warm in the loose box and the earthy scent of hay and horse is soothing.

Dexter snickers in pleasure as we walk into his stall.

'He recognises you,' I say.

She pats his mane. 'He should do. I rode him often enough while you were away.'

'Did you?'

'Every time I was at home or at Bosinney, I took him for a hack, either with Robyn or on my own. He needed riding, Cal, and it gave me some comfort to be on his back. Argh. Did I really say that?'

'I'm afraid so.'

She lifts her face to me. With her cheeks tinged with the pink of embarrassment, she looks more beautiful than ever but there's a brittle edge to her too. She's lost more weight; and she's made-up more heavily than I've seen her. Or is that wishful thinking? Do I want Isla to be unhappy with Luke? If I'm honest, yes. Does that mean I'm a bastard or that I can't truly love her? Yet love isn't benign and altruistic, not my kind of love.

'Is everything OK? Did you really come to ask Demi to work at the party? I should have replied to the invite sooner but I've had things to sort out.'

I can tell she doesn't believe me. 'I'm happy for Demi to come,' she says. 'And I wondered about inviting you at all. I didn't want to hurt you but Luke wants you to come. *I* want you to come. Is that selfish of me?'

I let this remark pass without an answer. 'How's Luke? I haven't seen him much since I got back. I've been busy and Robyn tells me Luke's not been around much.'

'No, he's been away on business and, to be honest, I've hardly seen him. What with me being up in London and the business for him. And other stuff.'

'What other stuff could possibly keep him away from you?'

She laughs bitterly. 'You'd be surprised. There are the Cades, for a start. He spends a lot of time with Mawgan and Clive.'

'Why would he do that?'

'They're big clients of the firm. Luke and his father want to keep them sweet. I'm probably overreacting. Hell, I have to spend weeks away when I'm in the middle of a shoot. Now,' – she smiles and takes my arm – 'never mind me, how are things with you? Luke told me your planning application was turned down. You must appeal.'

'Of course I will! How long are you down here for?'

'The engagement party, obviously, then we're having a few days on Scilly before I have to go back to London. But I'll be up and down while we're preparing for the shoot and during it.'

'So you haven't run off with an actor? When I was away, I always thought that might happen.'

'Did you?'

'Not really. I imagined all kinds of things.' *But none of them involved you marrying my best mate.*

'I imagined far worse. Why didn't you keep in touch?'

My jaw tightens. 'I meant to. I tried but it was difficult at times.

We were in remote places and time flew by, you know, there were so many people who needed me.' The lie saws through my guts but I cannot tell her the truth. No matter how much it hurts her and me, I can never tell her the whole truth.

'OK. I understand you don't want to talk about it but if things were that painful, you should maybe think about getting some counselling.' Her voice is soothing, which irks me more.

'It's not that! It's not what you think.'

'You don't know what I think and if you won't or can't talk to me about what happened out there, then it's pointless me pushing you. Let's leave it.'

'That's probably for the best.' My fist balls, every bone and sinew screaming to tell her how much I wanted to speak to her, how the thought of her was all that kept me alive and how much I regret leaving her.

'I must go. I should get an early night. This party and planning the shoot have kept me up a lot. I haven't had my beauty sleep.'

'You still look beautiful to me.'

'Balls. You know I look knackered. Even Luke tells me. And Demi – she's much prettier than I am. She's fresh and original. You did a good thing, taking her on.'

'I needed an assistant. She needed a job. I could see she was bright and capable and needed a break and she earns her salary. I can't afford to be a charity . . .'

With a knowing smile, she gives Dexter a final pat. 'You'll always go out of your way to help people. You'll always sacrifice those closest to you for others.'

'I'm not a saint, Isla.'

'I know that.'

My fingers close over hers on Dexter's neck. She lets them rest there until the horse whinnies, shakes his flank and we lose contact.

'I don't expect I'll see you before the party, but for what it's worth I'm glad you're coming. Demi too.'

'I'll see you there,' I say, brushing my lips quickly over hers, putting my hand into the fire again to see if I can stand the heat.

Her eyes widen in surprise, darken with pleasure too, perhaps, but I walk out of the stable as fast as I can, for her sake and mine.

'Cal,' she calls after me but I keep on walking, giving my answer to the sea and sky.

I want to take her by the shoulders and ask her '*Why?*' Why would she be glad I was there to see her tell everyone how much she's in love with *him*? Does she want me to prove I've moved on, that I'm happy to see her with him? Does she want me to prove to Luke and our friends and relatives that I'm over her? Does she want to convince herself so she can go off into the sunset with him, guilt free? Is that to be my engagement gift to her – letting her go?

'I'm giving you fair warning that you'll have to look after yourself over the weekend, *boss*.' Polly declares a couple of days after Isla's visit. Her voice penetrates my ears while I'm stacking another load of slates recycled from the roof of one of the cottages. They'll be needed again when the new roof carcass is in place.

Polly's shadow has its hands on its hips. I concentrate on making sure the slate stack is square and stable before I look up at her.

'I'm having the weekend off. I'm going to visit my new grandson in Plymouth, in case you'd forgotten.'

'Fine by me,' I say, straightening up and taking a swig from a bottle of water.

'Well, I thought I'd remind you so you know you've to look after yourself. Though you'll doubtless be all right on your own, with Demi for company,' she adds, innocently. As Polly has never done anything innocent in her life, my suspicions are immediately roused.

'Yes, I will. She's coming to the party with me.'

'What?'

'Demi's coming with me.'

She gasps. '*She's* been invited?'

'Didn't she tell you?'

'No, I didn't even think you'd decided to go.'

'Why wouldn't I?'

Polly tuts loudly. 'You know *why* but each to their own. I suppose it's all right for some to swan off.'

'Yes, it is. I know you didn't like it when I brought Demi here. Perhaps you felt she was undermining your authority. But she's bright and hard working – which I think you know full well – and I expect her to be treated with respect. Dad relied on you when he was alive, and I appreciate that you stayed on here while I was away, even if you never thought I'd come back.'

Polly sniffs. 'I never gave up on you, unlike some around here, and I don't think you should be giving Demi ideas.'

'What? Above her station?'

Polly shakes her head. 'You really have no idea, Cal Penwith. Well, if you don't want to listen to my advice . . .'

'If it concerns Demi, I don't. I'm grateful for your help and support, more than you can ever realise, in fact, but now Demi's here things have changed. I want her treated properly. Do I make myself clear?'

'Treated properly? By me? I'm the one looking out for the girl. You watch out,' she says.

'For me or her?'

'Her. You can go to the devil in your own way. People will talk if you turn up at the do with her,' she says.

'I don't care. Have a good weekend,' I say sarcastically.

Polly frowns and then I think I've genuinely hurt her.

'Look, Polly, I didn't mean to be sharp with you.'

'I don't care what you do. I'm going. I need to catch my train.'

'I'll drive you to the station.'

She sniffs. 'No, you won't, I've got a friend picking me up.'

'Are you sure?'

'Yes, I do have a life outside this place.' She turns her back on me and I die inside. Blast and damn!

'Polly, wait!'

But she's gone, bustling over the yard to reception. Why do I always put my size ten in things? I was only trying to defend Demi, and protect her. I should have known that Polly's all bluster. Have I become so inept at reading people's motives and intentions? Which reminds me of Demi's face when I told Isla I was bringing her. I don't know who was more stunned out of the two of them.

Without waiting for a reply, I bump the wheelbarrow over the track towards the guest cottages to collect the remaining slates. Anything I can do myself will save money on labour costs and I need to save as much money as I can to help fund Demi's cafe. However, if the planning appeal fails, I'm stuffed, along with Polly, Demi and all the people I plan to employ and some of those I already owe money to. Kilhallon will sink into ruin or be sold to the bank and then Mawgan Cade really will get her hands on it.

Sweat stings my eyes and my shoulder aches. Ignoring it, I cart the barrow of slate back to the yard and return again and again, until I can hardly see straight and every muscle screams at me to rest. Battling the pain and fatigue helps me blot out the reality that if – when – Isla marries Luke, she would be out of reach forever.

CHAPTER TWENTY-ONE

It takes a minute for my eyes to adjust to the dark of Cal's study. This is the first time I've had the chance to sneak in here alone since Isla dropped in last night, but now Cal is busy taking the final slates off the cottage roof. Although I have every right to be in here, and an excuse ready if required, I still feel guilty, but I have to *know*.

The desk is covered with the usual mishmash of letters, bills, spreadsheet printouts, and flyers about heat pumps and solar panels. Polly is meant to file it away but half the time Cal won't let her move anything. I sift through the latest bunch of crap before spotting the corner of a cream envelope under a self-build magazine.

The grubby fingerprints on the envelope tell me he's looked at it many times. After slipping the invitation out, I run my fingers over stiff card that's almost as thick as my T-shirt. I can even feel the printed letters as minuscule bumps under my fingertips. Isla's handwriting – it must be hers? – is curvaceous and beautiful and, here and there, the ink from her pen has bled into the card. It's all very tasteful and classy but there is absolutely no mention of a *guest*. Not even when I read it all again and whisper the words out loud to the still air of the study:

WE'RE ENGAGED!
Isla and Luke
invite
Mr Calvin Penwith
to celebrate their engagement with them
On Saturday June 25th
from 7 p.m.
At Bosinney House, St Trenyan
RSVP to Isla Channing

So I was right.

Cal *was* lying to Isla the other evening and she *knows* he lied. She hadn't forgotten; how could she? Because why would she invite a 'guest'? She knows there was no one else but her in his life, but I'd been fooled for a while. I thought she might have added someone else to console him while he had to celebrate his ex declaring her love for his ex-best friend.

I also don't know whether I'm disappointed or happy that he asked me. Was it to make Isla jealous? To annoy her? Because he felt sorry for me and he's trying to make us both feel better? It had better not be for any of those reasons. I deserve to go as much as anyone.

'*Demi?*'

Cal stands in the doorway drying his hands on a tea towel. I hold the invitation behind my back, heart thumping. He's shirtless – did I mention that? – and he steps inside, all golden and glistening. My body zings with lust and my pulse skyrockets.

'You almost gave me a heart attack!'

He smiles. 'Guilty conscience?'

'Yeah, I was thinking of breaking into your bank account and emptying it.'

'You'd have to put something in it first.'

'Ha ha. Actually I was about to print off some of the figures for the cafe, while it's quiet and Polly can't keep interrupting me.'

He drops the towel onto the chair. 'I don't mind what you do, I said you could use the printer whenever you want.'

'Thanks.' Slate dusts his chest and dirt smears his biceps. Any moment now and I might ooze through the floorboards in a pool of lust, if I don't pass out from guilt first. The envelope is still in my hand. Surely my fingerprints will be all over it.

'How's the roof going?' I ask.

'I've stacked all the slates in the yard and covered them with a tarpaulin. The builders covered the cottage roof before they left but I ought to go and check it's secure. The forecast isn't looking good for tomorrow. I think we might have a storm.'

'Oh, that's a shame for the party. Robyn told me they wanted to have drinks outside in the gardens.'

He shrugs. 'I hadn't thought of that but Bosinney's big enough to cope with a crowd if the weather's bad.'

He picks up a letter from the boards and frowns at it. I take the chance to drop the envelope on the desk behind me, hoping I can put it back in place when he leaves.

With a grimace he throws the letter on the chair.

'Cal, are you sure you want me to go with you to this party?' I say.

He frowns. 'Why wouldn't I? Don't you want to go?'

'I don't really mind but I don't know these people, apart from Robyn, and if Mawgan's going to be there, there might be an atmosphere between us.'

He drops the tea towel on the wooden chest. 'Do you care about her?' He says it in the deep, serious voice that bugs the hell out of me, mainly because it's so sexy.

'No, I couldn't give a toss.'

'Then what are you on about?'

I shrug. 'Nothing, I s'pose. I'm just not really sure why you asked me.'

He pulls a face, as if I'm some kind of lunatic. 'Because I wanted you to come with me. Do I need any other reason?'

Because I wanted you to come with me.

I tried to hold that thought for the rest of the day while I tested some new recipes for the cafe. I also decided to plant out the basil and coriander plants I'd been growing in one of the old lean-tos in the kitchen garden. I'd already found some mint and rosemary running wild in a neglected corner of the garden and once I've cleared the nettles and weeds away from it, it should be useful for roast lamb. I used some of it to make a lamb and mint pasty the other day which even Polly said was 'quite tasty'.

Cal stands at the end of the border, with a look of amusement on his face. 'I never thought you'd have green fingers.'

'My mum liked gardening though I didn't show much of an interest. Polly's been giving me some tips.'

I pat the earth around the last basil plant and stand up, brushing the soil from my hands. Cal unscrews the cap from a bottle of water.

'You've done a good job here.'

'I wasn't sure whether to bother planting them with the gales forecast.'

'If they can't cope with a bit of wind and rain, they'll never survive at Kilhallon,' he says, watching me chase the empty plastic pots rolling around among the herb seedlings. We both make a grab for a flyaway pot and end up face to face.

Cal hands me the pot. 'Do you want some dinner? I picked up some sea bass in St Trenyan and thought I'd roast it in the oven. Some of your rosemary would be good on it.'

I take the pot. 'You're offering to cook again?'

'Don't sound so amazed. I'd make the most of it.' His eyes glint in the sunlight and then he frowns at me. I wipe my dusty palms on my bare thighs, wondering what he must be thinking. My hair is a wild bramble tangle, my hands are filthy and my shorts are held together with a safety pin because the zip has broken.

'Anything wrong?'

He smiles briefly. 'No. I *will* see you later, then?'

Cal would rather die than beg anyone for anything but there's something in his voice: an edge that tugs at me. The party is bound to be difficult for him. He must feel the engagement party is a final nail in the coffin of his relationship. He'll probably only drink too much if I don't go round so I suppose it's my duty to spend the evening with him.

'OK. I'll finish planting out the marjoram, get changed and come over.'

He doesn't thank me, or say 'great' or even smile; he nods and walks off but I think he's pleased.

Ten minutes later, I chuck the pots in the recycling and wonder how I'm going to get all the dirt out of my nails for the party which starts early tomorrow evening. It sounds very smart. Apparently, Luke and Rory Penwith have hired a marquee because Isla had invited so many locals and TV people from London.

Should I give myself a manicure? I've got varnish I bought from the bargain bin at Superdrug. I could do my toes too. I could paint them now, when I come out of the bath, before I go over to the farmhouse because I tell myself, while I wash my hair, I won't have time tomorrow. I've an early start because of the food fair.

It has nothing to do, of course, with the fact that I want to look less like I was dragged through a hedge backwards and more like a normal person for the party. Nothing at all to do with the fact I want to look good for Cal – even though he'll only be looking at one person.

A pink face with an even pinker nose stares back at me from the mirror but there's nothing I can do about it now. With my damp mane tied back, I pull on a clean T-shirt and jeans but before I skip downstairs, I decide to get my party outfit out of the wardrobe. The pale-blue summer T-shirt dress cost a fiver in the Next sale and needed a mark washing out. I've worn it out to the pub a couple of times with Robyn and it will have to do for tomorrow. Robyn let me keep the heels she lent me for the waitress job, she lives in DMs and customised Vans anyway. I can walk to the party in my trainers and change into them there and hope I don't trip over. Not that anyone would notice if I did. Tomorrow is Isla and Luke's day and that's as it ought to be.

'Going to be a rough one.' Cal parts the faded brocade curtains and peers out of the farmhouse window. It's already almost dark outside, even though it's barely nine o'clock. His weather report is also one of his longest statements all evening.

'I spent a couple of nights like this on the streets, but it was cold too.'

Cal drops the curtain. 'That must have been tough.'

'I survived.'

He pokes the embers of the fire he lit before dinner. Iron grey clouds rolled in from the sea and the temperature plunged, turning summer into autumn within half an hour.

He sinks back into the armchair, and all I can see from the sofa is a hand cradling a glass. Sometimes he seems a lot older than he is. I imagine his father sitting there, a wrinkled, gruffer Cal, waiting and wondering when he'd see his son again while Cal was on one of his humanitarian trips. 'When I was in the desert I dreamt of nights like this. The rain, the gales . . .' Cal says quietly.

A gust of wind makes the flames dance wildly in the hearth. Mitch lifts his head and whimpers.

'Well, maybe not *quite* this wild,' I answer, hugging the cushion, grateful for Mitch lying across my bare feet.

The wind howls even louder around the farmhouse, rattling the latched doors. Every now and then, a squall of rain patters against the panes as if someone is outside throwing gravel at the windows. The dirty plates, with the remains of the sea bass, have given the room a fishy scent and an empty wine bottle rolls back and forth over the quarry tiles with every gust of wind under the door. Cal can't be bothered to clear away, and I'm too tired. I was happy he asked me to come over but I'm not sure he's been that aware of my presence. He's been drinking steadily all evening and I've had more wine and beer than I meant to. Perhaps I should leave. I don't want to oversleep and miss the food fair in the morning.

'D'you want a nightcap? I've got a fresh bottle of whisky somewhere.' Cal's voice, coming from the depths of the winged armchair by the fire, startles me.

'I thought you gave orders there was to be no more whisky in the house?'

'This one is for emergencies.'

I could tell him he's had enough; I could say 'goodnight' and leave him on his own but something keeps me here, unwilling or unable to leave him. 'I'd rather have a beer,' I say.

'Fine.'

He hands me a beer and I curl up on the sofa, Mitch acting as my duvet as he has so many times. Cal takes his father's chair, cradling another glass of whisky. The wind is a dull roar that I've almost ceased to notice, but every now and then, the old house lets out a groan and a flurry of hail hurls itself against the windows. Isla must be wetting herself, worrying about the party marquee at Bosinney, and I don't blame her. It's me that's here with Cal now. I wonder if she'd swap places with me?

'What are you smiling at?' His voice cuts into my alcohol-fuelled memories of my first 'interview' with him and how he reminded me of a sexy TV vampire.

Instantly I'm not smiling any more but blushing instead.

'Nothing.'

'Yes, you are. You have that look on your face.'

'What look?' I look at him, smiling again now, because I have a secret he doesn't know, which makes a change from the other way around.

'There's something you're not telling me.' He puts his glass on the table and leans forward a little.

'No, there's not . . . not really.'

If he had ears like Mitch's, they'd definitely prick up, and instantly I regret what I said.

'Not *really*?'

'It was just something silly. A stupid name I had for you once.'

'A silly *name*? Come on, out with it.'

'No. It wasn't really a nickname, just a silly idea.'

He wags his finger at me. 'You can't say that and not tell me.'

I wink at him, enjoying the banter but vowing to die rather than tell him. 'I'll never talk, no matter what you do to me.'

He puts his glass down on the table and leans forward. 'Oh, *really*? You'd be lucky to last ten seconds.'

My bones are tingly and shivery. The words somehow pop out of my mouth.

'*Try me.*'

He watches me, his expression dark and smoulderingly sexy, then shrugs and picks up his whisky glass again. He might as well have chucked a bucket of icy water over me but I'd rather die than show him how disappointed I am so I reach for my beer, to hide my embarrassment and frustration. As soon as I've finished my drink, I'm off to bed; things are becoming dangerous in here, in every way.

The bottle slips out of my fingers. Two hands haul me along the sofa and off it. My bottom thumps onto the rug.

'Ow! What d'you think you're doing?'

Cal says nothing but his expression is steely, determined. What have I started? I wriggle and try to scramble away from him but it's useless.

'Stop!'

My heart races wildly and my bottom throbs from hitting the carpet. Cal pins me down on the rug, sits on top of my thighs facing away from me and tickles my feet mercilessly.

'Argh! No. No!' I try to push myself up on my elbows, collapse back to the carpet. His fingers dance along my bare soles.

I shriek and writhe. 'No, stop!'

'Not until you tell me this name.'

'No, I can't. I cannnnn't!'

His fingertips dance over my soles. It's absolute agony. I batter his back with my fists but he ignores me, running his finger from my toes to my heels until I scream for mercy.

Mitch starts barking.

'Mitch will bite you!'

'Down, boy!' Cal orders. 'Demi and I are only playing.'

'We're not! We're so not. Mitch! Help!'

Mitch, the traitor, sniffs at my feet and starts licking them.

'OK! I'll tell. I'll tell!'

Cal holds my toes in his fingers. 'Go on.'

'It was the Hot Vampire,' I mumble, my face burning with shame.

Cal keeps hold of my foot. 'The *what*?'

'The Hot Vampire. OK, Satisfied? Now let me go!'

His hands circle my ankles. Cal releases me and stands up.

I turn over and bury my face in the carpet.

'*Hot Vampire*?' he repeats.

'Go away, Cal,' I murmur to the rug.

'Get up.'

'No.'

'Don't be silly. Get up.'

Turning over, I open my eyes. He is six feet above me, holding out his hand. I grasp it and he pulls me to my feet. His eyebrows meet over a deep frown.

'I can understand the hot part . . .' he says.

I gasp. 'You arrogant . . .'

He smirks. 'But a *vampire*? Where the hell did that come from?'

'It was a *joke*, just some stupid thing on the TV.' I rescue my flip-flops from the sofa. The gale rumbles around the house and the rain sounds like the house is under a waterfall.

'I'd better get back to the cottage; see if the roof's still on.'

'No way. You'll drown in this rain and anyway I don't think I can let you go . . . *now, I've got you in my lair . . .*' he adds in a horror film voice.

I stare at him. 'You're pissed.'

'No, I'm thirsty . . . thirsty for *you.*' He holds up his arms and zombies towards me. Shaking my head at him, I back away from him towards the door to the hall. Mitch watches, cocking his head from side to side.

'You're nuts.'

'I'm coming to get you,' Cal booms, a metre away from me now. On cue, a crack of thunder seems to shake the rafters and Mitch whimpers faintly.

'You won't get me,' I whisper and make a dash for the hallway. Cal follows me. I laugh at him. 'Rubbish vampire you make. *Rubb-ish.*'

I'm giggling helplessly but my heart's pounding as I run towards the stairs.

'There's no escape,' he says in his voice of doom, advancing on me. 'I'm coming . . .'

I scamper up the stairs, with a vague plan to lock myself in the bathroom, out of harm's way, not that there's any real harm but you know, just in case, because my breath's short and my pulse is racing and I may actually have a heart attack before the vampire even gets me. The stairs creak madly and I stumble up the top step, stubbing my toe on the wooden riser.

'Ow!' The vampire's hand clamps around my ankle. 'Argh!'

At my shriek, Mitch barks from the bottom of the stairs. He doesn't know this is only a stupid game between two drunken idiots.

'Get off me!' I twist my foot out of Cal's grip and scramble onto the landing but I've only managed a few feet before he catches up with me. He grabs my arm, pulls me against him and bares his teeth, showing me his canines.

'Don't you know there's no escape from the Hot Vampire?'

I try to look unimpressed. 'Will you please stop saying that? I told you it was a *joke.*'

He shakes his head. 'I'm not joking, Demi.' He kicks the bedroom door open and it bangs against the plaster wall. He pulls me through into his room and grabs my upper arms.

'Come into my lair.'

'You're completely mad. And completely pissed.'

'I'm stone cold sober. And *thirsty.*'

With a Hannibal Lecter hiss, he bares his white teeth again. I giggle but my stomach swirls like mad. We tumble onto the bed and Cal looms above me in the half-light that spills up from the hall below. We're face to face, inches from each other. His eyes burn, not with blood lust but a desire for something else, for someone else: me. My body is alive, glowing, and my heart beats thick and fast.

'This is a joke, right?' I whisper.

'No, I'm deadly serious.' He touches my cheek and every cell and nerve ending fires into life.

There's a sharp tug in the pit of my stomach, so hard it hurts.

'If you're hoping for a virgin, you're going to be disappointed.'

He smiles. 'Good. I couldn't handle the responsibility.'

We both look up at a whimper from the doorway. Mitch watches us, cocking his head on one side.

Cal climbs off me, and ruffles Mitch's ears. 'Sorry, boy, but I don't need an audience for this.'

Then he shuts the door and drops the latch.

With roughened fingertips, he traces the line of my jaw from below my ear lobe and under my chin. He tilts my chin up with his fingers and holds it while he kisses me, so deeply, I wonder if I might drown in pleasure. This can't be real . . .

My limbs feel liquid. I have no bones left so I give in, crushing every rational reason why having drunken sex with my boss is the worst idea in the world. My body tells me it's the best idea, and the only thing I want to do. My body, tingling, hot, and zinging with lust, only wants one thing: Cal Penwith, as deep inside me as possible.

He is a shadowy figure in the darkness, lit up in a brief shaft of moonlight before the room is plunged into darkness again. Perhaps he is a vampire, a fantasy man.

His body feels real. Solid and lean under my hands as I push up his T-shirt and press my fingers into his back. His tongue is hot and probing in my mouth, seeking out my secrets, demanding a response. He tastes of whisky, bitter and sweet at the same time. Before I met him, I always thought food was better than sex but now I'd starve if I could have sex with Cal for the rest of my life.

'Oh . . .'

I'm ashamed of my moan of pleasure as his palm closes around my breast but I can't hold it back. I hear the rasp of a zip as he undoes my jeans. The gale howls like a banshee and rattles the panes. It feels as if the storm is squeezing the life out of Kilhallon and the whole house seems to shudder.

Cal slips his hand inside my knickers and touches me. I groan and whimper. He rolls his fingertip over me. This is too much, I can't cope, but I want him so much.

I grab his wrist and stop his hand. 'Cal . . .'

His face is clear in a brief shaft of moonlight; puzzled, edgy. 'What's the matter? You *do* want to do this?'

'Yes, I want it. I *really* want it but I know I said I wasn't a virgin but it's been a long time for me.'

His features relax. 'Demi, I don't care. Just enjoy it.'

He flicks the buttons on his jeans. Lightning flashes, showing him above me, shoving his jeans and boxers down his legs. A huge crash of thunder sends tremors through the house. Mitch starts barking from the landing. The house creaks and groans, glass shatters and I scream.

'What the hell . . .' Cal's mouth gapes, a black hole in the moonlight.

I look up in time to see a great black mass crashing down on top of us.

CHAPTER TWENTY-TWO

Can't move. Can't see. Don't think I breathe. The storm roars in my ears and chest, ten times louder than a moment ago. My face is wet, but I don't know if it's rain or tears or blood, mine or Cal's. Layers of darkness press down on me: Cal, the bed canopy and something spiky and sharp. I try to lift him off me but I can't even move my arms.

'Cal. You. Have. To. Get. Up.'

In the darkness, he groans and stirs. Lightning flashes and shows a huge, black mass of branches filling the room like an evil giant.

The pressure eases. 'Cal! I think a tree came through the window. The bed canopy's on top of us. I can't move.'

'Hold on,' he says, easing himself off me. I let out a big breath. Cal manages to lift a tangle of broken wood, branches and curtains from us and the lightning flashes again. Branches, twigs and broken glass litter the floor and leaves race round the room. Above the roar of the wind, I hear barking.

'Mitch!'

'He'll be OK. Good job I locked him out of the room.'

'I must go to him. He'll be terrified.'

We wriggle out of the jumble of bed and tree. My leg hurts

but I'm more worried about Mitch. Cal helps me off the bed and pulls his jeans up, and we duck under the branches and force open the door.

A furry ball leaps on me, licking me madly. 'I'm here, you silly dog. It's OK. Stay out of here. I need to help Cal.' Reluctantly, I close the door. The clouds have parted and the moonlight filters through the branches, showing Cal with his hands on his head in despair.

I flick a switch but know it's useless. 'The electric's off.'

'That strike will have knocked out the power for miles. Is Mitch OK?' he asks.

'Yes. What can we do?'

'Not much tonight. The window frame's gone and will need replacing along with some of the masonry. Best see if I can board the hole up but we may have to wait until morning. You'd better stay inside.'

My leg throbs. I think I've cut it. 'I'll help.'

'No.'

'You'll need all the help you can get to shift that tree.'

Downstairs, Cal pulls on his Barbour and boots and heads outside with the torch while I find an old lantern with a stub of candle in it. The flickering light reveals a gash on my shin, not long enough for stitches but bleeding and sore. Before I put my jeans back on, I quickly wash it and stick a plaster on it before finishing getting dressed and going down to find an old coat and Polly's wellies from the porch. The wind takes my breath away and blows my hood off. Rain lashes my face, and whirling debris stings my skin.

Cal has rigged up an arc light linked to the generator. His head is visible among the branches of the tree. 'This oak's been there for centuries. I knew it needed felling but I was putting it off because of the cost.'

'Should we call someone to help?'

'No point. The fire service will have enough to do and it's too rough to start clearing the mess. It'll have to stay like this until morning.'

'It's the last thing we need.'

'It could have been worse. It could have brought the whole house down.'

Cal shakes his head at the spiky bulk of the tree propping up the wall of the farmhouse. 'The structure of the house could be damaged. I'll have to get the builders to look at it tomorrow. What happened to your leg?'

Despite the plaster, blood oozes down my leg. 'It's nothing.'

'As long as you're sure. Come on, we can't do anything here and the old house has stood for four hundred years. It'll last 'til morning. I need to check the new building. I hope the roof tarpaulin has held.'

We battle across the field, almost blown horizontal by the wind. Twigs and leaves fly through the air and I can feel the tang of salt carried from the sea. The tarpaulin on the amenities block is still in place but one end is flapping wildly against the stones.

'We need to lash that down!' Cal picks the metal ladder from the ground.

'Be careful!'

A few minutes ago, we were in bed and now we're both stone cold sober and neither of us has time to talk about what happened while we work to secure the roof tarpaulin. My hair whips around my face, catching my eyes. Cal is up the ladder, balanced precariously. I hold the bottom while the tarpaulin flaps like a huge winged monster but eventually, we get it fixed over the gaping hole. God knows how much it will cost to fix the roof; it's money Cal doesn't have but I suppose it could have been worse.

And we're all alive; me, Cal and Mitch. I suppose there's a lot to be said for that.

CHAPTER TWENTY-THREE

'Demi!'

I wake to Cal shouting and banging on the door. Dragging my hand over my eyes, I push myself up off the sofa and twist the lock. My leg is sore and my arms ache. Cal points to the chunky watch on his wrist.

'I fell asleep. I've not even showered.'

'We need to get going to the food fair and I have to be back to meet the builder about repairing the window. You have ten minutes to get ready. I'll see you at the house,' he says gruffly and stalks off again.

Instantly I know that the spark between us has evaporated. We were both drunk, and it's probably a good thing we didn't go all the way. Cal looks like he wants to forget what happened. Rubbing my hair with a towel after dunking myself in the bath, I walk into the bedroom and my heart sinks further.

'Oh, no . . .'

My 'party' outfit lies on the carpet in a pool of water under a dark brown patch on the ceiling. There's nothing I can do but pull on my least scuzzy T-shirt and an old pair of jeans. I hug Mitch goodbye, tell him again that Nina will be over to feed and walk him while we're at the food fair. He doesn't know he's also being 'dog sat' while we go to the party.

We got back from the fair in Helston in the early afternoon. Cal and I spent the rest of the afternoon trying to make running repairs until the builders can fit us in, because there were many people in a far worse state than us after the storm. Nina said that some of the dog runs at the animal sanctuary were damaged and Robyn posted an Instagram picture of a gazebo at Bosinney that had been blown down in the gale.

Far from being cancelled, as we'd feared it might have been, the food fair was packed. Luckily the south coast missed the worst of the gales. Cal and I toured the food market, earmarking potential suppliers and setting up meetings. The sun broke out of the clouds, the winds eased and hordes of people descended.

There was a fringe market too, with stalls selling bric-a-brac and vintage clothing – and a dress. While rummaging around the stall, congratulating myself on rescuing pieces from the barn that would have cost hundreds, I spotted The Dress. I think it's a 1950s cocktail dress and it is in decent condition apart from a tear in the hem and missing fastener. I tried not to show too much interest and I managed to walk away from it, telling myself I couldn't afford twenty pounds but I kept imagining myself in it at Isla's engagement party.

It's the kind of dress you slither on over your silk thong and bra, being careful not to smudge your make-up. The kind of dress you wear with silver heels that you can't walk in, but it doesn't matter because you're going to arrive at the film premiere in a limo, and spend the evening drinking champagne and eating canapés that wouldn't keep a flea alive.

While Cal went to the architectural salvage yard to look at some pieces for the cottages, I went back to the vintage clothes stall and bargained the stallholder down to fifteen quid for the dress. I really didn't have time and I really can't afford it but with my other outfit ruined, I need something new. All those TV people will be there and when the cafe opens – *if* it opens – I'll need something glam, although I can't think at this precise moment whether that event will ever happen. We've no planning permission and no staff.

Never mind. The engagement party could be a great networking opportunity if Cal stays sober enough and is nice to all the local businesspeople that might turn up. Hopefully they won't remember me from the charity ball. Another reason to buy the dress, then.

There was no time to spare when we got home to Kilhallon. Cal and I have spent the past couple of hours covering the shattered pane with hardboard and cutting up the branches. It's a good job we were busy as neither of us said much all day. I know I've been snappy, at the end of my tether after my broken, soaking night and at his lack of sympathy/being back to square one after all that happened between us last night.

Finally, we were done. Cal went to shower and I came back to the cottage. Using Polly's sewing kit, I just had time to stitch up the tear in the hem and put a new hook fastener on it. Unless you were looking for it, I don't think you'd notice.

The fabric slithers through my fingers, almost liquid. Oh God, it's gorgeous. Please, please, let it fit. A shake and the silky material cascades onto the floorboards like a waterfall. In the sunlight other colours ripple through it, sea greens, purples, blues and soft pinks. With its spaghetti straps and plunging neckline, it reminds me of the stars in the gossip magazines, not that I'm aiming to compete, but I do *love* it. A quick freshen up and I'm shimmying into the dress but before I can zip it up, my phone beeps.

DEMI. ARE YOU READY WE HAVE TO GO NOW.

Caps lock on. Not a good sign.

No point texting Cal back.

To my great relief, I manage to get the zip up. It's a bit snug round my bum and boobs. I turn towards the window, and the dress glistens like the inside of an oyster shell. My damp hair tickles the bare flesh in the deep back 'V' but there's no time to dry it or put it up and as for make-up: no chance. Goosebumps pop out on my bare arms. Although the wind has died down, the residue of the storm will leave a cool evening. I'll probably freeze outside but there is *no* way I'm not wearing this dress.

I lace up my trainers, grab the clutch I found for 50p in a charity shop, a lip gloss and Robyn's heels. Walking into the kitchen a minute later, I find Cal pacing the tiles and jingling the car keys in his hand.

'About time too. One more second and I'd have gone without you.' My phone beeps and he stares at me hard.

My phone beeps again. Another text.

DEMI I'M LEAVING WITHOUT YOU. WHAT R U DOING?!

'I was getting changed,' I say.

'I can see that. I like the trainers.'

'I thought they completed the outfit.'

A smile tugs at his lips but I'm at a loss to know what it means or what anything Cal Penwith says or does means any more. Last night he saw me half-naked, touched my breasts . . .

'Is this OK? My other dress was wet so I decided to get this in Helston.'

He bites his lip and can't seem to work out what to say next. I shiver, unable to forget last night and lusting after him more than ever. The white shirt, the black jeans, the damp hair. I've got it bad, no matter how much I try to deny it. 'I think you'll pass muster. Have you got a jacket or something? It might be cool later out of doors after the storm,' he adds gruffly.

'In the cottage, probably, but I forgot. You said we're in a hurry.'

'Yeah, I did, wait.'

He plucks his tux jacket from the hook in the porch. It's been there since the ball, where he must have hung it when he came home that morning.

'Is this any good?'

'I s'pose so. Thanks.'

He drapes the jacket over my shoulders. 'Better?' He should move away now. We're in a hurry, as he said, but he lingers behind me, his hands resting on my shoulders. He smells of crisp, clean shirt, shower gel and the sharp citrusy aftershave I've seen in the bathroom.

'It's perfect.'

'Good. You look lovely, by the way. The dress suits you.'

His breath is warm on the nape of my neck and I catch mine. He hasn't forgotten last night; how could he? What if he kisses the back of my neck? The tiny hairs prickle in anticipation. If he touches me, I know we'll carry on from where we left off last night. Instead, his hands fall from my shoulders. The pressure was only light and it makes me feel empty.

'Come on,' he says, picking up his keys again. 'Let's go and get this bloody thing over with.'

CHAPTER TWENTY-FOUR

'That's it, then.' Uncle Rory finds me standing on the terrace at Bosinney overlooking the formal gardens. He pats me on the shoulder. 'Bad luck, Cal, my boy. I'm sorry.'

'Why are you sorry? Luke got Isla. Isn't that what you wanted?'

'You've got me wrong. Luke's been like a son to me since his father died – just as you are and of course I'm happy for him but I know today must be hard on you.'

'Not as hard as you think.' If I keep saying that, it will be true. The manicured grounds stretch out below me and a smart gazebo has been set up on the rear lawn to cover the temporary bar area. Apart from a few stray leaves and twigs in the gravelled walkways, you'd never know that nature unleashed hell here last night. This party must have cost him and Luke – and Isla – a lot of money but they move in glamorous circles these days so I guess they want to put on a show.

Rory beckons to a waiter and waves away the champagne. 'Can you find me a pint from somewhere?'

'Of course, sir.' The waiter nods.

Rory loosens his collar. 'I feel trussed up in this suit and tie. You're looking better, by the way, my boy.'

'Thanks.'

He pats my arm. 'No one planned any of this, you know, and if you hadn't gone away . . .'

'But I did and maybe that was for the best.' If I say it often enough, I might start to believe it. Last night with Demi and this morning in the kitchen showed me I can at least feel something again for another woman, even if I don't know what that something is yet.

'We can't change the past. I'm happy to hear you've thrown yourself into reviving the park. Your father would be proud,' Rory tells me. His face is red, he should ditch the tie, in my opinion.

'He'd be bloody astonished. He'd given up on the place years ago.'

'Hmm. I tried to tell him and I offered to help but he was having none of it. Is that your new girl?' He squints at Demi, who's standing on her own, my jacket draped around her shoulders like a cape.

'Demi *works* for me,' I qualify.

'Of course. For a moment, I could have sworn . . .' he says, patting his trouser pocket. 'Where are my glasses? She looks like Hannah, Cal.'

'Nah! My mother's hair was much darker.'

'It's not the hair. It's the way the girl carries herself. She looks half-wild but still a real looker like your mother was and . . .'

'What?'

His eyes disappear into the folds of skin and his brow puckers as he squints at Demi. 'There's something else about the girl. I can't quite put my finger on it.'

I laugh. 'I never thought you were a romantic and I definitely don't see any resemblance to my mother,' I say.

He frowns as if he's deciding whether to continue the argument then grunts. 'Maybe you're right. Well, I suppose I'd better bloody circulate. Where's that waiter chap with my pint?'

I walk down the steps to the lawns towards the gazebo, past women whose heels sink into the lawns and men knocking back champagne like it's lemonade while dying for a pint. There's the occasional sympathetic look at me from the odd local who knows my history with Isla although they're all too polite to mention it tonight, of course. The ones I don't know, especially the beautiful ones, must be from Isla's work.

Rory told me the events team were up half the night battening everything down and clearing up the gardens and re-pitching the gazebo. I try not to think of the mess that has to be sorted out at the park too. The cost of it all, and I don't mean the repairs. Demi and I haven't spoken about what, almost, happened. Maybe that's for the best. The image of her last night, below me on the bed, flashes into my mind, and today, in that dress. She's a cracker too, my father would have said, a little belter. He'd have probably tried to seduce her. Despite all his 'distractions', I know he adored my mother. Putting her on a pedestal was perhaps his weird way of justifying his affairs: Mum was in a league of her own.

Feeling guilty about my encounter with Demi, especially as I was enjoying it so much, I swipe another glass of fizz from a passing waiter. If Uncle Rory's paying, I may as well make the most of getting legless at his expense. I decided after my first drink that we wouldn't be driving home.

Isla floats into my field of vision: or a version of her. She's a little stiff and formal, in a black silk cocktail dress and flawless make-up. Stunning, of course, but also untouchable in her own way.

'Hello, Cal.'

We exchange a brief brush of the lips and it's like kissing an image on a screen; either that or one of us isn't really here at all. Sometimes I wonder if I'm back in that hellhole, hearing the gunfire again and the cries of the children, dreaming of home.

'Are you OK?' She pulls away from me, gently. Colour dots her cheeks and I don't think it's the blusher.

'I'm fine. Congratulations. 'Will you be Mrs Wilton after you get married?'

188

'No. I'm keeping my name for professional reasons. It's simpler and anyway, we live in the twenty-first century now, don't we?'

'Yes. Does Luke mind you not taking his name?'

She lifts her chin proudly. 'Luke wants me to be happy, Cal.'

'So do I. So *did* I.'

'Don't do this today, *please*.'

'What? Tell you I still love you? Tell you I regret going away?'

'It's too late . . .'

'It's never too late. I know that better than anyone.'

'You seem to have found solace pretty quickly.' She glances at Demi, who is at the centre of a group of men. They swarm around her like bees to a honey pot. 'Demi looks very pretty. Isn't that your tux?'

My tux slides off her creamy shoulders onto the floor. She does look *very* pretty. More than pretty, as beautiful as Isla, but in a different way. Like comparing a perfect rose with a perfect cornflower.

'Don't take this the wrong way but I hope you know what you're doing, in that direction . . .' she says.

I sip my champagne and keep my eyes on Demi. She laughs as a man – Jack Kincaid – slips my jacket back around her shoulders. His wife shoots daggers at him.

'I hope *you* know what you've done,' I say, turning back to Isla.

'Cal!' Luke bounds up like an over-enthusiastic Golden Retriever and puts his arm around Isla's shoulders. 'How are you? We've hardly seen you since you came home.'

'I've been busy with the work at Kilhallon. Congratulations, by the way.'

'Thanks and as for the busy part, tell me about it. With the business and the party – and last night's chaos – I've not had a moment, either. We must meet up for a pint. It's been too long since we had a night in the Tinner's.'

'It has,' I say, feeling a little guilty about the lock-ins I enjoyed earlier this summer.

'Mind you, the Tinner's isn't what it was. Robyn's definitely worth more than working behind the bar of a scuzzy pub.'

I frown at him. Since when did he think he could dictate Robyn's life choices? 'Maybe she enjoys it.'

'She only does it to annoy her dad and me.'

'Oh, I'm sure she doesn't,' Isla interrupts.

Luke tightens his arm around her back. 'Come on, you can't monopolise one guest, even if it is Cal.'

I give Isla a little bow, she shoots me a puzzled look and her new fiancé, my old friend, sweeps her off.

With her chestnut hair and that amazing dress, Demi is easy to find. She's standing a little apart and, for the first time this evening, she's alone. Her wild curls are now tamed with a glittery clip that really suits her.

'Who gave you that?' I ask.

'Robyn made it for me. It's not OTT, is it?'

'You're asking the wrong man. I'm no fashion expert.' Damn, why can't I even bring myself to give her another compliment? I must be afraid of reviving last night's events.

Her smile fades and I could kick myself. 'You look great to me and Robyn's a talented artist,' I say, trying to soothe her and because she does look great.

'Thanks, but I don't really care what you think.'

'Then why ask me?'

'Maybe I thought for a little while that you weren't a moody, grumpy arse.'

'Then you were obviously wrong.' I knock back the rest of the champagne. 'I'm going to find a proper drink.'

I shouldn't have come today. This party – this life – has made me toxic. Kilhallon is falling apart as fast as I try to build it up. Isla destroys me with a look, even when I thought I was moving on. Now I've crushed Demi. She of all people I never wanted to hurt. Last night, in bed . . . I thought . . . her body was so inviting,

I wanted her and she wanted me.

We were drunk.

Not *that* drunk.

I was deluding myself. No woman I care about should come within a hundred miles of me.

'Can you get me a whisky?' A passing waiter takes the outstretched tenner from my hand. The drinks are on Uncle Rory but I don't expect to be waited on for nothing.

'Of course, *sir*. Anything else with it?'

'No, thanks.'

'Well, you know where I am, *sir*.'

I shake my head, a smile on my face. Make that no woman *or* man should come within a hundred miles of me. 'I'm flattered by the offer but I'm only interested in a drink.'

'Shame,' says the waiter, leaving me amused and impressed at his nerve in trying to pick me up at a party.

The whisky has banked down my fire to dull embers as the sun slides behind Bosinney's handsome façade. Fairy lights twinkle in the trees and the string quartet has been replaced by a jazz band. More people have arrived, 'oh-ing' and 'ah-ing' at the splendour of Bosinney and its softly lit gardens, which are at their best now. Uncle Rory must employ a full-time gardener to keep those rose beds looking so perfect. More friends of Isla's mill about, some of whom I recognise from schooldays, plus actors, crew, business acquaintances of Luke's, a few relatives too. Demi must be inside the house.

'Cal. Glad to see you back in the land of the living.' Dave Patterson claps me on the back while he mashes my bones with his paw. He's a prop forward with the St Trenyan rugby club and our fathers were mates at school.

'Thanks, Dave.' Numbed by booze, I nod. He must know I'm a bit pissed.

'Who's the hot brunette I saw you with earlier? Is she why you're looking so well? Glad to see you're not moping over Isla.'

'That's Demi.'

'She's a stunner.'

'She's my assistant.'

'Then I apologise and sympathise. You'll never make a saint, Cal, so don't start trying. If she keeps your spirits up at Kilhallon then go for it. How is the old place? I heard you're trying to resurrect it from the ashes. Big job, but admirable.'

I don't tell him how last night it almost *was* ashes. 'Hard work doesn't bother me,' I say. 'It's people throwing obstacles in my way that pisses me off.'

'Really? What obstacles? And which people?' he asks.

'The planners turned down my application.'

He raises his eyebrows. 'On what grounds? I heard that you're trying to build some kind of eco-heaven there. Should have thought it ticked every PC box of this bloody council.'

'Me too but there were objections on the grounds of noise and disruption, and increased traffic.'

He sighs. 'From who?'

'Neighbours. Interested parties.'

'Any specific ideas?'

'Possibly, but let's face it, I can't prove anything and even if I did, they're entitled to their views.'

'But you don't agree.'

I smile.

'Hmm. You'll appeal, of course.'

'Of course.'

'Good. That's the Cal I know. For what it's worth I think it's a sound plan and even more importantly, a sound investment. It could be what the area needs and I recognise when there's genuine passion and will to succeed behind a project. God knows, no one has more instinct to survive than you must have.'

'That's before I came up against the local mafia.'

He laughs loudly. 'If you need an ally, I could be interested. My wife is going to skin me if I don't go and circulate but here's my card. Talk to me if you want to discuss taking things further.'

With another slap on my back, he lumbers off towards a petite blonde and slaps her bottom, earning a whack on the arm in return. The lawns are dark now, dark grey-green like an angry sea. In the middle of that sea, stands a slender white ghost with chestnut brown hair. She holds out her hands to me, seems to be calling me.

The mermaid of Zennor has come to steal away her lover from the land of the living . . . I *must* have drunk more than I thought.

CHAPTER TWENTY-FIVE

Cal's drunk again. More pissed than last night or any night since I met him and that's saying something.

And, oh, deep joy. There's Mawgan.

Carrying my shoes, I pad across the damp lawn towards Cal who is heading for the shrubbery, probably for a pee. I hope it's for a pee and not to find some secret stash of whisky he's salted away.

'Demi!'

Mawgan is heading straight for me, holding down the skirt of her mini, her heels sinking deep into the grass. I try to speed up but my own dress hobbles my legs.

'Wait!'

By the time I untangle myself, Cal has vanished.

'These bloody Louboutins. Andi told me they were too high but I couldn't resist them.'

She points out her shoe so I can see the red sole then peers at my dress. 'Nice dress. Did Cal buy you that?'

'I can buy my own clothes.'

'Really? I must say I was surprised to see you here. I didn't know you were a friend of the family.'

'I'm here as Cal's guest.'

She snorts. 'His guest? Hmm. That's one way of describing it.'

'Better than being his reject.'

I was determined not to let her get to me but the words slip out before I can stop them.

'I'm sure you'll be joining the scrapheap soon,' she says, butter smooth. 'But unlike me you won't have anything left to fall back on. You may think he's a hero but Cal is a washed-out loser who hasn't a clue how to make a business a success. When he's had enough of you, you'll be out of Kilhallon so fast you won't know what's hit you and back on the streets. In every sense of the word.'

'I'd rather be on the streets than turn into someone like you.'

'If you mean a successful businesswoman, I'll take it. You see, I know what I am, unlike you. You're deluding yourself if you think Cal will carry you off on his white charger. Cal has only loved and *will* only ever love one woman: Isla Channing. And no matter what you do, you'll always be the scraggy mongrel to her pedigree. A bit of rough when he's drunk and doesn't mind slumming it.'

'You know what? It must cost you a fortune to look that cheap.'

She smirks. 'You'll see. Cal may act the man of the people but never forget he's a Penwith. He'll marry someone like Isla in the end.'

She turns her back and wobbles off, holding her skirt down.

I hate her. Not for being a cow: I'd have been disappointed if I hadn't had a scrap with her. Not for being right about Cal. I don't want to marry him; I want to make my own way in the world but I'd be lying if I said her taunts haven't found a mark. Last night – and today – has showed me that Cal might want me for a quickie but he's still crazy about Isla. So crazy, he has to get paralytic to dull the pain.

Robyn is on the other side of the garden, nodding to a couple on matching mobility scooters, decorated with ribbons. She spots me and stomps across the grass, looking amazing and quirky in a Guinevere-style dark emerald dress.

'Thanks for giving me an excuse to get away from Auntie Alison and Uncle Trevor. They keep asking me when I'm "going to find a nice chap".' She mimes sticking her fingers down her throat.

'Join the club. I've only just escaped doing something silly to Mawgan Cade.'

Robyn laughs. 'Don't talk to me about Mawgan. I'm sure she's deliberately keeping Andi away from me. She must suspect there's something going on between us.'

'Is that the dress you saw in the Boho boutique in St Just?'

'Yes. I went back and bought it in the end. You like?'

'Looks fabulous on you.'

'Thanks.' She touches my dress. 'You look incredible. Where did you get that from? Ghost?'

'No, it's vintage. From a stall at the fair in Helston. There was a leak in the cottage last night and my dress was soaked so I splurged on this.'

'You look amazing in it, especially with the tux. Is it Cal's?'

I nod. 'He let me borrow it because I didn't have time to dry my dress and everything else was dirty. We've been up most of the night because a tree came down on the house in the storm and we had to go out and secure the tarpaulin on the conversions. It's the last thing Cal needs with the planning being turned down.'

'I heard about that. Poor Cal. Does he know who objected yet?'

'Some of the neighbours from the village. When he checked the council website, some of the people who complained were old friends of his father's.'

'Ex-friends now.'

'He was mad as hell but hurt too. I don't think he can understand why they turned on him. He's threatened to go and have a word with them all individually but I told him it wasn't a good idea.'

'No. The last thing he wants is to be accused of intimidating people. What will you do now?'

'He's going to appeal though he can't afford it but we're not going to give up. No way.'

Robyn raises her eyebrows. 'Wow. I can see that. Cal's lucky to have you.'

'I'm not so sure he agrees.' I think back to the night before and our almost sex. It was drunken and silly and probably a very bad idea but it most definitely wasn't *kind* sex. He really wanted me.

My eyes seek him out among a group of glamorous people who must belong to Isla's crew and cast. Cal looks so hot he could start a grass fire. A cool gust makes me pull the tux tighter around me. I swear it still smells of Cal's aftershave, that and horse.

'Your eyes have gone all sparkly. In fact you've gone all sparkly. You're in love with him, aren't you?' Robyn has a sly look on her face.

Horrified, I shake my head. 'No. I'd never be that stupid. He still loves Isla.'

'Maybe he does. Maybe he always will, but that doesn't mean he can't love anyone else. It doesn't mean there's no room for someone else.'

'I don't want to fit into the space that's left by someone else. Even someone as amazing as Isla.'

'Then unless you find someone who's never loved before, you may always be alone, how do you know you'd be second best? Cal knows Isla is gone and now, I'm not sure he'd have her back. He may love her, yes, but he loves the Isla he knew before he went away. The one who hadn't abandoned him and fallen for Luke. Isla is tarnished for him now and I think he was always in love with the idea of her, rather than her. She's flawed now, flawed and human.'

'Flawed?' I laugh. 'Unlike me.' She hugs me.

'You don't have to pretend to be someone else, you're good enough for Cal, just the way you are. Too good.'

Robyn bites her lip as Andi joins Mawgan by the gazebo. She keeps glancing around her nervously, obviously looking for Robyn.

'How's Andi?'

'I daren't even speak to her,' Robyn says miserably. 'I'm afraid of what I might do and she won't speak to me because she's angry at our families – and me. She thinks we're both being cowardly.'

'No one should be kept apart if they love each other.'

'I know but neither of us have any money if we did decide to go public and live together. Dad would cut off my allowance and God knows what the Cades would do to Andi.'

'Maybe Cal could help you.'

'Cal? He won't want to get involved and I don't want him to. He's got enough trouble with the business and Mawgan as it is. She hates him.'

'I've worked that out. I can't stand the thought of you being unhappy because some people are stupid and ignorant. Don't give up on Andi. Why not bring her round to Kilhallon? Cal won't mind and you know, I'm sure he could find you somewhere to live, if we asked him.'

'Yeah. Maybe. But Mawgan and my dad could still make life incredibly difficult for Andi, mainly. I want to be with her so much but I'm not sure I'm that brave; not yet. I *want* to risk everything for her. That's what real love is, isn't it?'

Andi spots us and her pale face breaks into a smile.

I don't know how to reply to Robyn because I'm not sure I know what real love is and I feel completely powerless to do anything for them. 'You know where I am if you want to talk,' I say, helping the only way I can. 'At least bring her round to Kilhallon or my place for dinner. No one will find out.'

'Thanks. I'll think about it.'

Who am I, I think, urging her to be honest and brave while I won't even admit to her, or to myself, how I feel about Cal? He's talking to someone by the fountain. He catches sight of me and comes over. I think of walking off in the opposite direction but decide to stand my ground.

'Has someone upset you?' His brow creases in concern.

'There were one or two people being stupid but it takes more than snarky gossip to upset me.'

'One or two? Like who?' he asks sharply.

I shrug but he catches me glancing over at Mawgan, sharing a cocktail with some bloke from the local council.

He laughs. 'I thought you had more sense than to let Mawgan get to you.'

'She's a nasty piece of work. I can stand so much but then I lose my temper. It's allowed, isn't it? You're not exactly Mr Zen Calm yourself.'

'No, I'm absolutely fine.' He tosses back his whisky. 'More than fine, in fact.'

'Why? What's happened?'

He taps his nose. 'That'd be telling.'

'Cal Penwith. If you don't tell me what you look so smug about I will hit you right in the middle of this party and then everyone here will be delighted that I've lived up to what they think of me; that you dragged me off the streets.'

'I don't give a toss what they say but if I hear anyone talking like that, they'll have me to answer to.' He sways a little and I don't fancy his chances of fighting his way out of a paper bag in this state.

'Then tell me.'

'Patterson . . .' he whispers in my ear with a broad grin. 'Dave Patterson says he'll go into partnership with me at Kilhallon. Not a half-share, of course, but he's prepared to back me. With his support, the additional work I want to do can go ahead.'

'Providing we win the planning appeal.'

He waves his hand airily. 'We will.'

I smile but inside I'm worried. His eyes aren't focusing that well. 'Shall I ask the caterers to make you a coffee?'

'Why would I want a coffee?'

'Because if you have any more booze, I might have to roll you home like a barrel and tomorrow we've got work to do. Kilhallon needs us, remember?'

He hesitates, and then nods. 'True.'

Mawgan watches us from the terrace. She catches my eye and raises a glass to us but I get the distinct feeling she isn't wishing us well.

CHAPTER TWENTY-SIX

'Cal. It's almost dark. We'd better go *home*.'

Ignoring my plea, Cal hangs onto my arm as we say goodbye to Luke and Isla. Most people have moved inside the house now and I've been trying to persuade him to leave with me for the past half-hour. I'm not worried about going home on my own but he's in no state to make it back to Kilhallon alone.

Isla nibbles her lip anxiously. 'Shall we call you a cab?'

'Nah. WhadoIneedacab for? I can walk. Demi knosh the way home and she can carry me if she has to.'

Smiling, Luke shakes his head. 'Man, let's call you a taxi. You'll never get home in this state.'

Cal flails his arm at Luke who ducks. 'I'm fine. Yoush worry about yourshelves tonight, eh? You know what I mean.'

'I'll get one of the catering staff to phone the taxi firm,' Isla says firmly.

'No need. I'm leaving. Bye.' He blows a big kiss to Luke and Isla and calls to me. 'Come on, Demi. Time to leave the lovers to it.' He taps his nose, misses it and almost pokes himself in the eye. 'Don't want to play gooshberry.'

'Cal, wait! You can barely walk,' Isla calls but Luke pulls her back.

'Leave him. He'll be OK. It's Cal, he has nine lives, remember?'

'Yes, but he's already used up eight of them!'

'I'll take care of him,' I say as Cal steers a wobbly course between the guests and the antique furniture in the hall, slurring his goodbyes. 'I'll be back for the Land Rover tomorrow afternoon when he's sobered up.'

'Be careful on the cliffs,' says Isla.

Luke laughs softly. 'Come on, they *are* adults, Isla, and we need to say our goodbyes.'

'Luke's booked us into a hotel near Land's End before we catch the plane to Scilly tomorrow. It was a lovely surprise.'

'She works too hard and we both needed a break.' Luke kisses her. 'I can't wait to have her all to myself for a few days.'

'Sounds fab,' I say, relieved that Cal can't hear his remark.

Luke steers her away while I struggle back into my trainers and hurry out of the door after Cal, holding my dress above my ankles to avoid it dragging in the gravel. For a drunk, he's fast. By road, Kilhallon House is ten minutes from Bosinney, but by the coast path at midnight it will take four times as long and I'm not exactly wearing the ideal hiking outfit. But it's the time of year when it never gets truly dark and there's a clear sky and the full moon to light our way.

Not long after we've left Bosinney and its grounds behind, the cliff-top moorland opens up and the broken chimney stack of the tin mine comes into view. Tonight it's a sinister black stump against the dark-blue sky, and an owl hoots from somewhere inside the broken shell of the engine house. Cal meanders down the cliff path to Kilhallon Cove. It's a miracle he hasn't fallen over.

'Slow down!' I shout, my dress in one hand. I had to leave my heels in the Land Rover.

He turns. 'Come on, Demi. We'll never get home at this rate!'

'I've been trying to get you home for the past hour and you should try climbing down here in this dress.'

'I've told you that dress wouldn't suit me,' he slurs then blunders on.

The path drops us down at the top of the small strand of beach that's left at high tide. Sand and sea are silvery in the moonlight and the tang of seaweed fills the air. The surf thunders up the shingle and sand, throwing spray into the air. It's still rough after the storm, and debris washed up by the ocean litters the cove.

I pull the tux collar up and clutch the lapels together.

Cal stands on a rock, swaying slightly and staring out across the sea. Pebbles are bleached white in the moonlight and the stars prick the skies.

He pulls off a boot.

'Just what d'you think you're doing?'

'Going for a swim.'

'Don't be stupid. It's freezing.'

He holds his arms wide as if to embrace the sky and the cove. 'Come with me. Wimp.'

'No. There's a big swell running and you know there are rips when the tide's on the turn.'

'I know thish cove. I know what I'm doing.'

'Yeah. Trying to kill yourself.'

He jumps off the rock, drops his jeans and kicks them off, along with his boxers. His bottom is almost as white as the pebbles in the moonlight.

I shove my hands through my hair in despair as he wades in deeper. Then I hear a noise, sharp and echoing around the cove.

'Mitch?'

The barks grow louder and a dark shape comes hurtling down the path and leaps onto the sand.

'It's Mitch! What are you doing? You're supposed to be in the cottage with Nina!'

Cal is waist deep in the water, jumping over the waves, shouting and laughing. Mitch bounds down the beach, barking wildly.

'Stop, boy!'

He never listens to me and he races into the waves.

Cal stops swimming and shouts above the waves. 'Mitch?'

'He must have escaped from the cottage!'

Mitch swims towards Cal, ignoring me. It's all a game to him.

'Demi!' Cal shouts before being swallowed up by a wave.

'Come back! Both of you, you stupid stupid idiots!'

There's a moment, when a big wave breaks over the rocks at the side of the cove, when I think I've lost both of them, but then they pop up again. Cal spluttering and Mitch whimpering.

I make a decision. Ripping off the tux, I run towards the surf.

It took about a minute to wonder why I ever thought this was a good idea. The cold embraced me and tightened its grip, squeezing the breath from my body. When I first learned to surf as a boy, I remember the instructors telling me that the sea off Cornwall is almost as cold in June as it is in December. But there's one thing, if I drown, at least I'll be sober.

I was going to turn back, swim to the shore but then I heard barks. Loud barks and I saw that bloody stupid animal jump into the water after me. I tried to shout at him to go back but all I got was a mouth full of saltwater that burned my throat.

Demi is shouting too. I hear her just as the next wave lifts me up and tosses me forward, closer to the rocks at the side of the cove.

And Mitch is still swimming to me, frantically.

I strike out towards him but my arms feel like they're made of cotton wool. The booze, of course, and being up half the night repairing a roof. I'm weak, pathetic, this is justice. Demi didn't deserve the way I behaved at the party: the moodiness, the sarcasm, the arse that I was – am.

'Cal!'

'No! Get back!'

My shout is cut off by another mouthful of seawater. Mitch

paddles towards me but a wave slams into me from the side. I'm clawing at water, my mouth pressed shut, my eyes stinging in a maelstrom of darkness. I've wiped out many times, years ago when I surfed. I even surfed when I was high and wasted a few times but that was a long time ago.

Now I'm weak and washed out. Washed up.

'Mitch!'

When I pop up, spluttering and gasping, Demi stands waist deep screaming at me. Mitch has been carried by a wave closer to the rocks, a hairy cork bobbing up and down.

'Cal! Look out!'

A great white wall of foam hangs above me. I duck under the surface and curl up as the wave thunders down. I'm in a great giant concrete mixer. I don't know which way is up or down and the water is black and green and angry with me. Then there's fresh air again and I gulp, but only suck down stinging saltwater as another wave crashes down on me, hurling me against the rocks.

I think Demi is screaming. I think Mitch is barking. I know I am drowning.

The water is a steel trap now, crushing my chest, numbing my limbs. I thrash about, knock against something slimy and then hear Demi scream again.

'Over here!'

Demi stands on the rocks a few yards away, her white dress shining in the moonlight. She is the mermaid luring me into the sea.

'Grab this!'

She throws a red lifebelt at me. She must have found it by the RNLI hut on the beach. By the sign that warns people about the rip currents and not swimming alone or when you've had too much to drink.

'Go back. You'll slip . . .'

My words are engulfed by more water and I slam into the

rocks. Pain tears through my legs and arms.

'Take the bloody lifebelt!'

I swim like a madman towards the red belt, flailing at it, losing it, and finally catch the edge in one hand as another wall of white thunders towards me. I cling to the lifebelt and the wave lifts me up very high.

Demi is on the rocks below me. So close, I could touch her. Only the sharp black teeth are between us. Mitch is next to her, shivering, barking.

'I'll pull you in!'

The thunder of surf swallows her shout. A wave hits me again from the side and I'm flying through the water and down onto the rocks.

'Cal!'

I don't have time to register the pain of being hurled onto the rocks. All I know is I'm alive and scrambling up slime, while the sea tries to suck me back down. My feet scrabble on seaweed but Demi tugs at the rope, pulling me up the rocks. A wave breaks over her. Mitch goes berserk.

'Get away from here!'

'Take my hand. Come on, Cal. The waves – I can't stand up much longer.'

She's soaked, her dress, her hair. I can't lose her, not her and Isla. I think about what I survived in the desert and make one last effort and haul myself out on my belly, while she pulls the rope.

'Come on! Before we're both washed away.'

She pulls the lifebelt off me and drags me to my feet. Coughing and spluttering, I stumble over the rocks and onto the beach. Mitch dances around us, hoarse from barking.

'He's OK,' I mumble, as Demi helps me down onto the beach.

'He climbed out himself. What did you think you were doing?'

'Trying to save him. What did it look like?'

'Your leg.'

My shins are soaked in blood.

'I'll live. Your dress . . .'

Is pasted to her body. Every contour, every curve. There's no hiding place in the moonlight. Her small, tight breasts, her nipples as hard as pebbles, the 'V' between her thighs. She shivers and doesn't stop.

She wraps her arms around herself.

'What were you thinking of, going in the sea when you were completely wasted! Mitch only went in because of you.'

'We're both alive and I was wasted but funnily enough I'm not now. What's he doing here anyway? I thought Nina was looking after him.'

'She was – is. He m-must have g-got out. It was your fault he went in the first place, you idiot.'

'You're shivering.'

'I'm f-fine.'

'No, you're not.' I put my arms around her. Her mouth is hot and dry, tastes of salt. Earthy, I'm lost in it, deep, wanting to disappear into her. My hands seek her bottom through the wet silk of the dress. She doesn't stop me. Mitch barks. Suddenly, from misery, near death and almost certain ruin, everything is going right for me.

With no warning, I fly backwards onto the sand, with Demi towering over me, shrugging my tux over her drenched body.

'You're still pissed, Cal. Now grow up and put some clothes on.'

CHAPTER TWENTY-SEVEN

Thumps come from above me, the floorboards groan and curses rip through the house. I pop a couple of paracetamol in my mouth and wash them down with some cold black coffee. If my hangover's bad after last night, I hate to think what Cal's is like. No, actually, I hope it's the hangover to end all hangovers, because he deserves it. It was his decision to get lethally pissed, his decision to jump in the sea and almost kill Mitch.

Though I've made a piece of toast, I'm not sure I can face it and it falls from my fingers onto the counter as the kitchen door slams back on its hinges.

Cal stands in the doorway, looking like death. I have *no* sympathy.

'Have you seen my mobile?' he growls, stalking over to the sink.

'Good morning to you too, boss.'

He turns on the tap and sticks his mouth under the stream of water, then grabs a tea towel and wipes his face which is as grey as the dishcloth.

'Where's Mitch?' he asks.

'Asleep in his basket. I've already taken him for a walk. Nina said she's sooo sorry he got out. About fifty times.'

'Good,' he growls. He pulls out the kitchen drawers, rakes through the contents and curses. My head throbs as he slams each one shut.

'D'you want to tell me what's happened?' I say, eventually.

Everything has changed.

'I need Dave Patterson's number. It's in my phone but I can't find it.'

'Was it in your jeans pocket?'

'Maybe.'

'Then it probably fell out when you ripped off your clothes and decided to go for a swim.'

He rounds on me as if to shout but then hisses instead.

I toy with the toast. 'Polly might have his number in the little green phone book in the snug.'

He perks up slightly. 'I hope so.'

'Is it that urgent? He probably has a hangover after the party like most people.'

'He's gone mad, more like. He's changed his mind about going into partnership with me.'

'When?'

'Since last night.'

'But I thought he was really interested in helping us yesterday.'

Cal scatters a pile of letters and magazines over the table and mutters a curse. 'He was but he's sent me an email. He claims he's had time to think about it overnight and he's already over committed with one of his other development projects.'

'I'm sorry. He did seem keen. He even told me he thought the cafe was a good idea and that he thought I'd make a great job of it. He might have been being polite . . .'

'I doubt if he was being polite.' Cal looks at me; for the first time since last night, acknowledging what happened between us. I swallow hard, glance down at the table pretending to shuffle some envelopes in the search for Dave's number.

'What about the other people who were interested in backing

209

you?' I ask.

'Patterson was the only serious one. The others avoided me like the plague at the party, which was one reason I was so pissed. Someone must have got to them and I think I can guess who it is. Well, they can all go to hell. I won't be defeated.'

He sweeps a pile of brochures from the table, knocking a mug over. The dregs of his coffee soak the paperwork. Mitch growls from his basket.

He grabs a tea towel to soak up the coffee. 'I'm sorry, Demi.'

My heart flutters. 'What for?'

'The mess. This mess.' He waves a hand around and then shoves it through the roots of his hair.

'Am I part of the mess?'

'No . . .'

But. He doesn't say the word but I can feel it, see it in his eyes. The night of the storm was wonderful, hot – nothing has ever come close to it, maybe it never will now. I was consolation for him; I knew that and I thought it was enough for me. It was enough, the other night, me a bit drunk and Cal a lot. It was enough, but this morning, it's way too little. Which is why I was so angry with him on the beach last night. If he thinks he can simply look at me and I'll melt whenever it suits him or he needs comfort, he's so wrong.

He dumps the coffee mug and soggy tea towel in the sink.

'So what happens next?' I ask.

'I'll carry on. I won't be beaten, not by anyone. Somehow I'll find a way to save Kilhallon but first I'd better start sorting out that bloody tree.'

That's not what I meant. What I *really* meant.

Cal knows it. I know it. I think back to what Mawgan said at the party. I hate her and everything she stands for but I also think she's right: Cal will always love Isla and I'll always be a distraction and a consolation prize. The question is, can I live with that?

*

210

Since the engagement party everything has returned to 'normal' at Kilhallon Park, as far as anything is ever normal here. Polly returned from her weekend away, muttering at the extra work the storm has created. Cal has moved into the guest room at the farmhouse and has been busy helping the builders to remove the tree and repair the damaged window and wall. I've kept out of his way, there's tons to do; drying out the bedroom after the storm, working in the kitchen garden and making more plans for the cafe because I have to believe that it will happen, despite our recent setbacks.

July has finally begun, with long warm days and hordes of 'emmets', as Polly calls them, packing the beaches and cafes and blocking the narrow lanes around the park. Their accents are from the Midlands, London and further afield – Holland, France and Germany. It's all good and shows me that, in theory, there's a strong market for Kilhallon Park and the cafe, even though the main school holidays still haven't started.

Last week, I went to look at a pop-up 'bistro' where they hold sell-out barbecues on the beach once a month in the summer. Nina and Robyn came with me, and took their own vodka, cranberry and grapefruit juice to make Sea Breezes. I love them but I was driving that evening so I stuck to Coke. The restaurant which organises the barbecues cooks from a mobile van and the event was packed out. Next summer, I think, we should hold food nights like this on the cliffs overlooking Kilhallon Cove; the sunsets are amazing. We could have fresh fish and seafood curries and lamb tagines. People would bring their own chairs and plates and wine. The new park has so much potential, if we can get it up and running.

I've got so many ideas that I can hardly sleep, at least that's what I tell myself is keeping me awake during the spate of warm and humid nights we've had lately. As for Cal, he's acted as if nothing ever happened between us, yet for me nothing can ever be the same again.

He pops his head round the door while I'm finishing the washing-up after breakfast.

'So you know, I'm fixing the broken slates on the roof of your cottage today. I'll have to paint the ceiling another time.' His voice is brisk.

'I can paint it. I used to help Mum with the painting when I was little.'

'Right. There's some spare paint in the garage. Help yourself.'

There are bumps and rattles as he sets up the ladder and ties it on to the guttering. I stretch out the washing-up after another baking session so I can watch him from my window. He's wearing ripped faded jeans and the tattered grey T-shirt, a toolbelt slung around his waist and over his bum. The soap bubbles dry on my hands until a bang from the roof shakes me out of my stupid daydreaming.

I dry my hands on a cloth and walk outside, angry at him and myself but not sure exactly why.

'Can I help?'

He stops, hammer in his hand. He shakes his head. 'It's not a good idea.'

'Why not? You think I can't do it because I'm a woman?'

'I just don't want you breaking your neck.'

'But it's OK for you to break yours? I'd like to help and we can run through the new plans I've had for the park.'

He nods. 'You'll need gloves. There's a spare pair in the shed. You go and get them while I find another ladder.'

While he goes to the barn. I wipe my sweaty palms on my jeans, wondering why I'm doing this. To prove a point? What point? I just feel I've gone backwards here. Almost having sex with Cal blew away the relationship we had as friends, co-workers, business buddies. I don't know what place I ever had in Cal's world but I do know it's shifted – but where to, I've no idea.

He secures the second ladder and holds it while I climb up. I'm OK with heights. Mum was always telling me off about climbing when I was little, but this is different. Having to balance while doing heavy work is much harder than I'd expected. I stand at the top of the ladder as Cal scoots up the other one and stands alongside me.

The sun is hot and I'm grateful for the baseball cap.

He shows me how to lever out the slate with the ripper. 'Be careful, it comes out with a fair force and you could over balance.'

'Whoa!' I wobble and my heart rate goes bananas. Cal's hand is at my back, steadying me.

'You were right about the force.'

He keeps his hand there. 'You're fine. Now, I'll show you how to replace it.'

Ten minutes later, I've managed to hammer in two new slates. Sweat pours down my back and I'm red hot. The roof catches the full glare of the summer sun and there's barely a whiff of breeze. I lay the hammer down on the roof and wipe my forehead with the back of the glove.

Cal smiles. 'Not bad for a first timer.'

'I know. You see, I told you I could do it.'

'I always knew you could.' He's so close. 'You can do anything you set your mind to.'

Is it a good idea to snog a man when you're wobbling on a ladder? I don't know what to say so it all rushes out.

'Well, I did have another idea.'

'Interesting timing but go on.'

'I had another idea about the yurts. Actually, I got it while we were at Isla's engagement party.'

He frowns hard. 'The yurts?'

'Yes. That do would have cost thousands to put on. What about if we held events like landmark birthday parties, wedding receptions and corporate events in the yurt field at Kilhallon?'

'I hadn't thought of that but I like the idea if we ever get the plans passed and the money.'

'Let's be optimistic. This could be another revenue stream.

213

The cafe will be licensed for drinks and music and we could have hog roasts. Singing and dancing around the campfires, you know, people love partying in the great outdoors. We still have the cottages for the grannies and people who can't or won't do camping. We could have one of those giant tipis for the receptions.'

'Hmm. You're right. I guess not everyone wants the whole silver-service thing any more; the hotel and the etiquette.'

'It's fine if that's your thing but if I was getting married, this is the kind of party I'd want . . .' Damn, foot in mouth. I focus on the slate again. 'Anyway, it's something to think about. We'd need to hire an experienced freelance events planner, of course. That would mean we had the four larger cottages that are under restoration, plus the two small ones that we can spare from the staff accommodation, the yurt colony, camping field and the cafe plus its mobile outlets and events. We need the diversity to bring in revenue at different times of year.'

He smiles. 'Of course and it's a great idea. In fact, it seems as if all of the great ideas about Kilhallon have been yours.'

He puts his hand on mine. Glove on glove: not romantic at all yet I feel his skin burning into mine all the same.

'You know the morning after the engagement party, when I was thumping around the house, I didn't mean to be . . .'

'An arse?'

He smiles. 'Yes. An arse.'

'You do remember some of what happened, then?'

'*Some* of it? How could I forget it?'

'You could have fooled me.'

'I told you I was sober after my drenching. Thanks for pulling me out. I should never have gone in while I was pissed. I put you and Mitch at risk.'

'You did, but thanks for swimming after him even if it was completely stupid and he got out by himself. It was the thought that counted.'

'You're all heart.'

'I know. That's why you like me. Because you need someone to remind you that you're a self-righteous bastard who thinks he's always right and that the world doesn't revolve around Cal Penwith.'

'True. You do know me, you know me too well. So well it hurts. You see too much, make me see too much about myself . . . Look, give me time, Demi. I'm shit at this stuff.'

'Oh, I don't know, you seem to know what you're doing.'

'I didn't mean the roof or the business, actually. I just don't want you to think I'm taking advantage of our situation.'

'Why would I think that?' I laugh but I don't feel happy at all. 'You don't have to apologise or feel guilty. I'm a grown-up and I agree, it would be a disaster for us to get involved in that way.'

'True. I was drunk and not thinking straight. We both got carried away.'

'It was a silly game.'

'Yes. And the tree falling on us was probably the best thing that could have happened.'

'Of course,' I say.

Every word I say and he agrees with is making me even more miserable even though I know he's right. I half-wish I'd never come up here but it's too late to unsay the words.

'That didn't stop me enjoying it. A lot,' Cal says softly. He looks at me with his deep brown eyes and my stomach flips. Just when I'd given up all hope, he goes and says that. 'But it still means we shouldn't repeat it.'

'I had no intention of repeating it, Cal. Ever.'

'Hello-ooo!' Robyn has just ridden into the yard.

I'm not sure who is more relieved to see her, Cal or me. Swallowing back the stupid lump in my throat, I climb down from the roof, realising my hands are shaking. Whether that's from the adrenaline of being up high, or because I'm tired from manhandling the slates – or something else – I'm not sure.

215

Cal grunts a 'Hi' and starts hammering the final nail in the slate, in time with my thumping heart. I don't know whether to laugh or cry.

'You look busy,' says Robyn cheerily. 'Has Cal made you go up that ladder?' Robyn raises an eyebrow as I walk up to her.

'I wanted to learn how to mend my roof.'

'You wouldn't get me up there,' she says.

'And you wouldn't get me up *there*.' I'm still not that keen on horses but Robyn's horse, Roxy, is quiet and steady, so when she stops in the yard and jumps off, I don't mind giving it a quick pat on the neck.

Roxy snickers loudly, making me jump and Robyn laughs. 'You should ask Cal to teach you how to ride.'

I cringe. 'That's probably not a good idea.'

'You'd love it and Cal is a good teacher. He helped me when I was little – my mum used to go mad at the things he encouraged me to do but I loved it. I love it now.'

'What am I teaching Demi?' Cal comes up to us, wiping his hands on a rag. He nuzzles Roxy, calling her a 'darling' and a 'sweetheart' and she makes a soft whinnying noise.

'I was suggesting that you could teach Demi to ride,' says Robyn mischievously.

'There isn't a horse for me.'

'There's a pony at Bosinney that you could have. Or you could ride Dexter.'

She's trying to matchmake us. Considering the excruciating conversation we just had, I could shrivel up.

'Dexter is too big,' says Cal quietly.

'There you are. Cal knows I'd be hopeless.'

'I didn't say that and you wouldn't.'

Robyn laughs in delight. 'There! Cal thinks you can do it so I know you can. You can both come to Bosinney and see how you get on with my old pony, Harry. It can't be any scarier than being up on the roof.'

Leaving Roxy tied to an old hitching post by the water trough, Robyn follows us into the kitchen for a drink.

'I'm going to wash my hands.' Cal marches off with the embarrassment of a man asked to throw a box of Tampax in his shopping trolley.

'How are things?' I ask while we sit in the kitchen eating the fairings I made earlier.

Her face falls. 'Crap. Andi says her dad and mum are watching her like hawks. She can't even get out of the house without saying where she's going so they keep having rows.'

'I'm sorry. Andi's lovely and I can see how happy she is when she's with you.'

'Can you? Still it turned out OK here with Cal, didn't it?' she adds slyly.

'That depends on whether his planning appeal works,' I say, ignoring her hint.

'I hope so. Your ideas sound fantastic. Cal was raving about them the other day. I could see him coming back to life now he has the park to focus on and you've been such a help. You've transformed him and I really think he might be getting over Isla at last.' She reaches for another fairing from the barrel. 'Mmm, these are delicious.'

'Thanks, hun. It's great that Cal likes my ideas and I'd do everything I can to help him with the business but that's all there is between us: work. Please don't think there's anything, you know, romantic because there isn't.' And definitely not *now*.

She munches her biscuit before replying. 'OK. Whatever you say. I only want you and Cal to be as happy as me and Andi, but of course, I wouldn't dream of interfering.'

We talk more about the gig and Andi but as I wave her off on Roxy, I'm sure she hasn't taken a scrap of notice of anything I've said.

'Cal . . .' I say as he rebuilds Polly's chicken run a few days after

Robyn's visit. Cal suggested it so that she can increase the egg production and get in and out of the run more easily to feed them and collect the eggs. It's a fine evening, and the sun is a sliver of gold on the horizon in a pink coral sky.

'Hmm.' He takes a tack from his mouth ready to secure the wire to the post.

'You know Robyn was here the other day.'

'Hmm.'

I have to stop talking while he hammers the tack to fix the netting to the post.

I take a deep breath. 'There's something I need to tell you.'

Cal's face gives nothing away as I tell him about Robyn and Andi. I've been agonising over whether to share their secret for a while now and decided that I can trust Cal not to let on. I thought he might be able to help them.

'So, you now know why Robyn hasn't been totally happy,' I say, hoping for a positive reaction.

He blows out a long breath, his work abandoned. 'I guessed something was troubling her and suspected it was her love life but I'd no idea Andi Cade was involved. I thought they were just friends.' He winces. 'Nice girl, apart from her relatives, and you're right, Mawgan would *not* understand.'

'Even so, I don't think they should be kept apart and I wondered could you let her and Andi rent one of the cottages here?'

Cal shakes his head. 'I don't think that's a great idea.'

'You're not scared of what Mawgan will do to you if you encourage them? Or your uncle?'

He snorts. 'Of course I'm not scared of Mawgan and we don't know how Uncle Rory will react if Robyn tells them the truth. He may surprise her.'

'You know the Cades will go mad. Please think about it. I can't bear the thought of them being apart.'

'It's not that simple. I'm happy to have them here at a peppercorn rent even though I can't really spare the cottage but it would be better if Robyn and Andi sorted stuff out with their families and moved away to their own place. Frankly, I think they should break away and make their own lives.'

'But they're students. They have no money and Andi's terrified of what Mawgan will do when she finds out the truth. Mawgan already suspects . . .'

'Does she?' He winces. The wind ruffles his hair, softly tweaking the shorter curls he sports since he had it cut. 'Even *if* I thought it was a good idea to invite them to live here, I don't know how long I'm going to be able to give them a home. What if it all goes tits up, as it well could, and I have to sell up; then they'll be back to square one.'

'Is it that serious?'

'You know it is.' The pink glow of the setting sun softens his features.

'But that could be months away or never. You love Robyn and you want her to be happy and everyone seems to be against them. You want to help the community and people who can't stand up for themselves, then start close to home.'

He shakes his head at me. 'Demi, has anyone ever told you you can be a bloody pain in the arse?'

'Yes. You have. Frequently. So promise me you will reconsider having them live here.'

He lets out a long sigh. 'I'll *think* about it. Now let me get this run finished before it goes dark.'

CHAPTER TWENTY-EIGHT

Sometimes Cal can be full of surprises. After I told him about Robyn, he called her to offer her and Andi temporary use of one of the other staff cottages, if they're prepared to do some work on it. I know he's anxious for Robyn's sake about the possible fallout if they do move in here. Although I've had a text from Robyn, she didn't mention my intervention with him. Maybe she thinks he decided to make the gesture, all by himself.

I can hear her old Corsa pulling into the newly gravelled car park outside reception now. I was sorting out some more of the vintage junk I found in the loft above the barn but I head out to meet her and fling my arms around her.

'How are *you*, hun? I hope I did the right thing in asking Cal for his help.'

Robyn pauses before she replies quietly. 'Thanks, it was a lovely thought and I'm relieved that Cal knows, to be honest, but I've told Andi we can't move in here after all.'

'What? I'm sorry, but maybe it's for the best, for a few days anyway.'

'Not a few days. Not for a few weeks . . .' Robyn goes on. 'Luke asked me not to do it. He said that the shock could be too much for Dad.'

'What? Surely your dad wants you to be happy, and how dare Luke say that to you!'

'I think Luke's worried that Dad can't take any more stress at the moment. The party cost a lot of money because Dad insisted on having it at Bosinney and he's not that flush with spare cash anyway. Most of it is invested in the business and I think he worries about whether Isla and Luke are as happy as they make out.'

'Really?' My skin prickles.

'Dad worried Isla might not go through with the wedding, especially if she and Luke leave it too long.'

'Do you think so?'

'I think she genuinely loves Luke.' Robyn's voice trails off, as if she's changed her mind about something. 'I know I'll never stop loving Andi, no matter how far apart we are,' she goes on after a pause.

I wonder if Robyn was going to say that Cal still loves Isla, but didn't want to hurt me. Even though I know that's probably true, in my heart, and even though I know it doesn't mean Cal can't love someone else, it cuts me deeply. I realise that's a selfish thought so I refocus on Robyn.

'Have you told Cal you can't move in here yet?'

'No, I was hoping he'd be here. Do you know where he is?'

'He's in the house. Someone phoned him from the council. I'm so sorry, Robyn. There must be a way through this.'

'Andi will be upset but maybe it's better like this, until my dad's in a better frame of mind.'

'Can't you and Andi get jobs and move away after college?'

'Maybe, but that's over a year away, even if we can get jobs and afford the rent. Even if my dad and Luke were cool with that and supported us, and there's no way they will be, Mawgan and her dad will create hell if I move in with Andi. I should have realised that. They hate Cal, for some reason, and I don't really know why.'

'Why do Mawgan and her father hate him so much? It can't be because he wouldn't sleep with her. Is she really that petty?'

'I don't know but she has something on Luke and Dad. She has tentacles everywhere.'

I want to laugh at the image of Mawgan like the octo-witch in *The Little Mermaid* but I feel terrible for Robyn and helpless to do anything for her. And I'm hurting too. Cal will probably lose Kilhallon and he's lost Isla and I can never have him.

But I still have a job and a home, and Mitch and new friends like Robyn and Nina and the girls. I have skills and a future. Things are a zillion times better than a few months ago, so why am I digging my nails into my palm and trying not to cry?

For the next few days, I keep my head down and try to focus on my work while Cal goes away on a heritage building course. We have to carry on believing there is a slim chance that we can get the development moving again. I also called Robyn and asked her if she wanted to help design a new logo for the cafe signage and menus. She seemed to perk up a little when I mentioned it, but only because it would give her an excuse to meet up with Andi and work on it together. I couldn't really offer them any payment other than cake but she didn't seem to mind.

While Mitch and I are out on our evening walk, I see Cal down below in the cove. He's skimming stones on the sea. I watch him for a while from on high, wondering whether to disturb him or not but Mitch solves my dilemma by spotting – or scenting – him and tearing down the cliff path like a lunatic. Cal turns at the sound of Mitch's barking and smiles briefly. Mitch skips around his feet while I hurry to catch him up.

'Here, this is better than chasing stones,' he says, launching a twisted stick of driftwood into the edge of the waves. They're big tonight and the breeze drives the salty spray through the air. Mitch races into the water, grabs the stick and runs back.

'Hi, Mitch spotted you. How was the course?'

'OK. Interesting, I guess, if you like lime plastering.'

'You have white stuff in your hair.'

He pats his dark curls and gives a wry smile. 'Do I?'

Cal wrestles the stick from Mitch's mouth and tosses it back into the water. Mitch gallops off again.

'He'll do that all night if you let him.'

He smiles. 'Yeah, but at least one of us is happy.'

'Are you sure everything's OK?'

'What? Apart from Andi and Robyn being miserable and the fact that someone else has applied for planning permission on Kilhallon.'

My stomach twists. I *knew* something else was wrong. 'What? How can they when you own it?'

'At the moment I do, but the planning system entitles anyone to apply for permission to develop a plot of land, whoever owns it.'

'But that's mad. Who is it? I bet it's the Cades.'

He gives a bitter smile. 'Officially it's called Parson Holdings but I bumped into my bank manager on my way back from the course and she let on that Parson Holdings is a holding company of the Cades so that confirms that they're behind it.'

'You have to do something. *We* have to.'

'I can't do anything without proof. Perhaps, if I could find some hard evidence that the Cades have been involved in blocking the planning process by illegal means, then I could try and stop them.'

Mitch nudges Cal to play tug of war with the stick.

'I've been trying to keep this from you while I tried to find a solution but you deserve to know the whole truth,' he says, wrestling for the stick with Mitch. 'We're going to lose everything to Mawgan unless we win the planning appeal and the builders are demanding payment for the work they've done so far.'

'I've saved up a bit of money. A couple of hundred, but it's better than nothing.'

'No!' Abandoning the game, he looks horrified. 'Has it come

to this? You offering me your last penny?'

His dark eyes are full of sadness. 'I'm sorry I got you into this. You must regret coming here.'

'Me, regret coming here? No way. I don't regret a thing, apart from having to put up with your moods, of course.'

He smiles briefly.

'You have helped me, even if you don't think so. I have a hell of a lot more than I did a few months ago.'

'No. Everything you have is your own doing. Talent, enthusiasm, a maddening ability to see the best in everything and I don't regret bringing you here. I'll never regret it and I would cut off my right arm to change things. But I should start looking for a new job and home and so should you. Unless we can win the planning appeal next week, the resort is never going to happen and the Cades will own Kilhallon before we ever get it off the ground.'

'Fingers crossed, everything crossed. We have to keep hoping.'

He smiles. 'Yes, there's always hope.'

My footsteps echo on the floorboards. A thick layer of dust coats the carved chest that's probably been here since the days of smugglers and wreckers. The walls are yellow where the paintings of dead rabbits and pheasants once hung and the hearth is cold. There's no Polly shouting 'Demi, are you going to be in that bathroom all day?' from the kitchen. No Cal tip-tapping away in his study. No ping of email arriving. No muttered curses . . .

That's how I've always imagined it would be if – when – the Cades take over at Kilhallon. The planning appeal is due to be heard later today and the atmosphere is as gloomy as a November evening on the moors. Polly told me that Cal has been up half the night and refused to let either of us go to the appeal with him to support him.

It seems pointless to dust the china or even open the windows to let some air in. I pick up a Toby jug of a pirate and rub its blackened teeth, half-heartedly. Its eyebrows remind me of Mawgan's.

I wonder if the Cades will demolish all the buildings or just convert them into one mega pad complete with underground swimming pool and staff quarters. Even though Kilhallon is listed, Cal said that a convenient fire would destroy it in a few hours. That's what happened to the water mill in St Trenyan that the Cades converted into flats.

'Demi?' Robyn leans against the doorway of the sitting room. She looks thin and frail and tears run down her cheeks.

Leaving the jug on the window, I run to meet her. 'What's happened? Is it Cal?'

'N– no. He's OK. It's me and Andi. I think it's over between us.'

Anger fires me up. 'What? Why?'

I give her a huge hug but her hands hang limply by their sides.

'I – I decided it was better to end things cleanly for both of us.'

I stare at her face, seeing there's nothing clean about this ending. 'I'm so sorry. I'd really hoped you'd decided to come and live here and to tell your families together after all.'

'I *had* – we both had – but I told Luke first because I'd hoped he might have had a change of heart and would help me break the news to my dad. I was wrong.'

'Did he bully you? He shouldn't be allowed to do that.'

'No, he didn't shout; in fact, he went very quiet. It was weird. I actually thought he was going to cry.'

'It's your life!'

Robyn takes the tissue I offer and blows her nose. 'He told me it was my decision to move in with Andi but he warned me again that it could cause a lot of trouble.'

'It's the twenty-first century! That's disgusting and vile. You need to be honest with him, now more than ever.'

'Luke says not. He says Dad was worried that I was involved with someone, and that it might be Andi but that he couldn't believe it.'

I hold her by the shoulders, suddenly feeling like the big sister neither us of ever had, even though I'm the younger of us. 'Robyn, even if it's tough, you have to be strong enough to make your own choices, no matter who you upset and hurt. Luke's wrong to use emotional blackmail on you.'

'But it's not that easy! You're not in my position and even if we did break away from our families, what would happen to Andi? I can't do this to her; not now. It's not the right time. And there's something else. I think Luke's involved with Mawgan. I think that's why he really doesn't want me to move in with Andi, because it would make the Cades furious.'

'Luke told you that?'

'No, but I've heard him on his mobile to Mawgan. I worked it out. I'm sure Mawgan has some kind of hold over him.'

'He can't ask you to ruin your happiness for his sake. He can't.'

Tears run down Robyn's face. 'I know and I don't care about him but I do care about my father. He and Luke are partners in the firm.'

I swore not to say anything, but with my fingers crossed behind my back. I don't know what to do. Should I tell Cal about Robyn's suspicions? If I did, what could he do? And how can I add to his worries?

CHAPTER TWENTY-NINE

This morning we heard that the planning appeal had failed.

Cal hasn't come out of his study since we found out and neither Polly nor I have dared to knock on the door. The bacon sandwich and coffee we left outside are still on the floor. More out of comfort than any hope, I baked some fly pastry and took it to the house. Shortly after we'd replaced the bacon butty with a fly pastry and fresh coffee, we heard the study door open and shut. I risked a quick look and saw the cake and drink were gone, which must be a good sign.

It's afternoon now and as far as I know, Cal's still in his room. Curled up on the sofa in the cottage now, I hug Mitch and dream up scenarios in my head for saving Kilhallon, each more desperate and bonkers than the rest. I was just thinking that I could do *The Great British Bake Off*, secretly putting Cal up for *Who Dares Wins*, persuading Polly to do *Deal or No Deal* and entering Mitch into *Crufts* when a knock on the door makes me jump up. It could be Cal. Bracing myself, I open the door.

'Isla?'

In her skinnies, navy Hunters and tweed jacket, she looks like she stepped straight from a *Vogue* fashion shoot, yet also perfectly at home on a country estate. It's as if she was born to run Kilhallon, not that there's any Kilhallon to run now. 'Can I come in?' she asks in her soft voice.

'Sure but I haven't had time to tidy up. Been baking, you see.'

'I can smell it. Look, this is cheeky because I don't have an invite.'

'Cal's up at the house,' I say, puzzled.

'Not now. He's gone out. Polly just told me.'

'I didn't know.'

'I came to see how Cal is. Robyn told me about the planning appeal.'

'He's . . . we don't know how he is because he won't come out of the study. Do you want to sit down?' I usher Mitch off the sofa, hoping the dog hairs won't be too hard to get off her jacket.

'Thanks.'

I perch on the chair opposite her.

She brushes her hands down her jeans, seemingly nervous. 'It was you I wanted to see and don't worry, I'm not trying to hire you as a waitress again.' She smiles.

'Even if you were, it would be fine with me.'

'Yes, but Cal would probably kill me.'

'I'll probably need a new job soon anyway.'

'Hmm . . .' Her brief smile at my 'joke' evaporates and she glances around the cottage. It can't be my interior design that fascinates her. 'Things look very bad for Kilhallon, don't they?'

'With the failed appeal and the financial situation, this is probably the end. Someone else has already applied to develop the site.'

She catches her lip in her teeth. 'I heard. I really shouldn't be here and I definitely shouldn't be doing this but I had to. It's disloyal, it's wrong but I've been torn.'

'Torn?'

'Between two people I love. I don't know if I'm doing the right thing but because I love them both, I have to tell you. You must know by now that Robyn and Andi have been seeing each other?'

'I knew that they'd split up. Robyn's devastated,' I say, feeling angry again.

'I know and that's one reason I'm here. One of many. I'm ashamed to say I suspect their break-up *does* have something to do with us, with Luke anyway. His finances haven't been that rosy and he's been borrowing from Rory's firm. In fact, it's only because I – and someone else – have been supporting him that the business is afloat. He's lost a fortune on a risky investment and we can't afford to lose the support of our backers.'

'You mean the Cades?'

She nods, as if she daren't say their names out loud. 'Luke told me that he'd go bankrupt and we'd lose everything if Robyn takes Andi away from Mawgan and her father. He's already re-mortgaged Rory's remaining office building and the business is only clinging on with loans from the Cades.'

'Does Robyn know this?'

'She suspects but you have to swear you won't tell Cal about this.'

'I promise I won't tell him but why does Mawgan hate the idea of Robyn and Andi being together so much?'

Isla shrugs. 'I don't know exactly. Maybe it's a control thing for her, and Clive Cade goes along with everything she wants. He relies on her since Mrs Cade left them, and poor Andi lives in Mawgan's shadow.' She picks at a cushion nervously.

'Thanks for coming to see me, but I don't quite get why you've told me this?' I say, gently.

'Because I thought it might help you put things right, for Robyn and Andi. There are a lot of things that the Cades would rather people didn't know. I've no evidence, of course, but I've heard conversations between Luke and Mawgan that I can't ignore.'

'I don't see how this can help us, though?'

She stands up sharply. 'You'll work it out. You're smart, Demi, and I've said too much. I have to go.'

'Wait! I *am* grateful and I'll see what I can do.'

She looks about to cry. 'I don't mind what you do but I know that things can't stay the way they are. What Luke has done is wrong, and goes against everything I believe in. People who love each other shouldn't be kept apart to suit someone else's twisted reasons and I'm ashamed he's been a part of hurting Robyn but he's behaving out of character. I love him and I know that he'd never do this if he wasn't under such terrible pressure.'

'Thanks for telling me. It was brave of you.'

'It was the right thing to do, for Luke as well as everyone else, though he may not appreciate that. And I care about this place, the history and heritage and everyone here. Goodbye.'

After the door closes behind her, I stand in the middle of the room for ages, wondering what I can possibly do with Isla's revelations. Any ideas that spring to mind seem even madder than my daydream to put everyone on reality shows.

An hour later, I'm just about to take down Mitch's lead and head off for a walk along the cliffs when Cal knocks on the cottage door.

His eyes are red rimmed and he looks terrible. I don't think he has any idea of Isla's visit and even though I promised I wouldn't tell him, it's hard not to share her revelations.

'How are you?' he grunts.

'Been better. You?'

'Awful, actually.'

'What can we do next?'

'Not a lot. Could get an official enquiry, possibly. Could win the lottery? Set the place on fire and claim on the insurance?'

'You wouldn't do that?' I'm only half joking, because he looks so desperate. It was one of the wilder ideas that crossed my mind.

'No. I wouldn't. I've no idea what to do next but the Cades will get their hands on Kilhallon over my dead body.'

The next day, I made the first of what I hope don't prove to be disastrous decisions. I arranged to meet Robyn and Andi at the College Arts Centre, and pass on Isla's news. I thought the girls should know the truth, even if it does cause massive trouble.

'What? How could Luke do that? I knew the Cades were behind this!' Robyn is almost in tears.

Andi's face is as pale as soya smoothie as she tries to take in the news.

'So my sister and Luke have tried to break us up. I can't believe they'd do something so selfish and vile. I thought they loved us.'

I ache with shame and hurt for them both. 'I'm so sorry this is happening to you, hun.'

'I can't believe Isla told you about it but I'm glad she did. She's OK, unlike Luke. How can she stay with him after this?'

'She says she loves him. Luke's in a lot of trouble and he's desperate, Robyn, or I don't think he ever would have done this.'

'But Mawgan and my dad have no excuse. What they're doing is illegal, isn't it? It's blackmail and extortion!' says Andi.

Robyn hugs her. 'And now we're all suffering. Us, you and Cal.'

'Isla seemed to think that telling me the truth would help in some way but I'm not sure how it can, not without getting your family into trouble.'

'I don't want them to end up in jail, even though they deserve it!'

'No one will end up in jail,' I say, though I can't possibly think how that will *not* happen if the truth comes out and without the truth coming out, we can't save Kilhallon. 'We don't have any proof of what your family has done. We'd have to have concrete evidence and how could we get that? No one's going to talk.'

'I can get it.'

We both stare at Andi.

'What?' I say.

'How?' Robyn asks.

'I know where Mawgan keeps her dirty laundry. I know the

office security code and her safe pincode and where she keeps her passwords. Unlike my sister, I actually know one end of a computer from another,' Andi declares but Robyn has gone white.

'You do know that Mawgan will never ever forgive you if she finds out. Or your dad.'

'She won't find out because I have a plan . . .' I see a new determination in her face. 'You see, they've always treated me like a piece of old furniture since my mum left us. No one took any notice of me until now but I've watched *them*. I know a lot more about Mawgan than she would ever believe and now's the time to use it.'

'No. You can't do that. If Mawgan ever found out, we'd all be in the deepest, darkest trouble known to man. God knows what she'd do.'

'I don't care. I hate her at this moment.'

Robyn hugs her. 'I know you do, but Demi's right. That's such a risk. It would be theft and blackmail, and you'd get into serious trouble.'

'But I can't think of any other way!' Andi almost knocks over her drink.

'Leave it with me. I'll try to think of something else. There has to be some way of sorting out this mess.'

Bless Polly, she always comes along at the wrong moment. I stifle a groan of frustration as she spots me just as I'm about to climb into the Land Rover. Since I met with Andi and Robyn, I've been agonising day and night about what I should do about the dilemma we're in – if anything at all. Understandably, everyone's been down about the situation. Cal's hardly spoken to us and Polly's thumped around the place as if she has lead boots.

'Demi? Can you spare a minute?' she asks, bustling up to the car.

'Um, not really. I'm late for an appointment.' I jingle the keys.

'An appointment? What appointments do you need now?'

Squashing down the urge to tell her to mind her own business, I try to answer patiently.

'I was going to the market garden in St Just to see them about supplying veg to the cafe and I'm already late.'

'What's the point of going all the way out there, when there isn't going to be a cafe, nor an eco-bloody-whotsit or anything.' Just as I'm about to say something I'll regret, Polly starts crying. Not just a sniffle but big gulpy sobs.

'Oh, Polly. What's the matter?'

'Bugger. I must be going soft but I can't bear the thought of this place going down the pan. I've made no secret of the fact that I once thought Cal's ideas were pie in the sky and that we'd never make it happen but I'd started to believe in the bloody dream too. I've stuck with the Penwiths through thick and thin and Cal's like a son to me.' She wipes her eyes with a hanky. 'I don't know what happened to him when he was abroad but it was something bad. I think he had a breakdown and is too ashamed to tell us about it. He deserves something good to happen. So do you. We've worked too hard to resurrect this place for it to disappear down the toilet now.'

I hold out my arms to give Polly a hug and she lets out another huge sob. I pat her back.

After a few seconds, she pulls away and sniffs, unable to meet my eye. 'Bet you think I'm a silly old bat.'

'No, I don't. I know exactly how you feel and it might be a waste of time carrying on with my work but what else is there to do?'

She pulls a hanky from her pocket and blows her nose. 'I don't know. We need a bloody miracle.'

'You never know,' I say. 'Do you want to put your feet up and relax? Shall I make you a cup of tea?' I can't just abandon Polly in this state but I worry that if I don't leave this minute, I never will.

She shakes her head. 'I can't seem to sit still.'

'Why don't you do a bit of gardening, then? I'd help you but I really do have to go out.'

She sniffs. 'I s'pose the patch could do with a good weed. The rain's made the dandelions and chickweed shoot up.'

'Good idea. Don't work too hard. I'll help you when I get back.'

While Polly sought solace in her garden, I managed to get away and a few minutes later I wait at the exit from Kilhallon Park to the main road. To the right is the road to the market garden at St Just and to the left is St Trenyan.

Hoping Polly isn't watching, I take the left turn.

CHAPTER THIRTY

'Demi. How lovely to see you. Why don't you sit down?' Mawgan Cade smiles at me as she shows me into her study.

To be honest I'd expected her to refuse to see me when I turned up unannounced at the Cades' Georgian-style mansion. I almost didn't recognise her when she answered the front door herself. With no make-up on, and in her 'loungewear', she looks about sixteen, although the eyebrows are still a surprise.

The study is bigger than the ground floor of my cottage and has a shiny wooden floor with thick Persian rugs that must have cost a fortune. There's a framed portrait of Mawgan on one wall, dressed in dark-blue satin and diamante in a photography studio, another of her at the wheel of a Ferrari in a showroom and one of her dad in his golf gear, receiving a trophy from a local politician. I can't see any of Andi or their mother.

Mawgan motions to the chair opposite her huge mahogany desk. From the smug smile on her face, she knows what I've come for and perhaps that's what she wanted all along. She takes the padded swivel chair, leaving the considerable width of the desk between us, which is probably just as well. 'Thanks for seeing me on a Sunday morning,' I say as the chair almost swallows me up.

'How could I refuse the possibility of such an entertaining

morning? Mind you, I'd have put my money on Cal coming begging, rather than you.'

My stomach churns but surely *no one* can be afraid of anyone wearing a leopard-print onesie.

'You know Cal would never beg you for anything.'

She shrugs. 'Not *yet*, no. So he's no idea you're here?'

'No way.'

'And you don't think he'd approve?'

'I don't care what he thinks.'

Mawgan sniggers. 'That's the first lie you've told me and you've been here two minutes.'

'OK. He wouldn't like it but what I have to say is between us.'

Her eyebrows manage to almost meet. 'I can't possibly think what you've got to say to me, but as I said, I'm ready to be amused.' She leans back against her seat. 'So, how can I help?'

'You can stop your opposition to the development plans at Kilhallon,' I say, sounding way more confident than I feel. I've decided to leave Andi and Robyn out of things for now and, to be honest, even if by some miracle I persuade Mawgan to back down on the Kilhallon plans. I don't know how I can fix the girls' problems or even if I should try but I'm terrified Andi will do something silly unless I act.

'My opposition? I don't know what you're talking about.'

'Don't try to deny that you're behind the planning blocks and objections.'

She laughs. 'You make us sound like the St Trenyan mafia and you're also confusing me with someone who gives a toss what you do. Look, I was willing to be polite and hear what you had to say but I can see you've only come to insult me so let's cut to the chase.'

I force my hands to lie in my lap, calmly. 'Mawgan, did Cal or me wrong you in a previous life?'

She affects a yawn. 'Oh, here we go. The sympathy card.'

I really feel I might have to stab her with her own fountain pen but there's too much at stake. 'OK, I can see you don't like me and I'm sorry if you think I targeted you on purpose at Sheila's cafe and the ball but they were genuine accidents.'

She snorts. 'I don't care about that.'

'Then why? I can see you think there's something going on between me and Cal but I swear there isn't. I'm his friend and I work for him. End of.'

'I really couldn't care less whether you're shagging him or not but if you are, my advice to you at the party still stands: Cal acts the concerned hero but when it comes to women, he doesn't really care who he uses. It's a Penwith trait, as you'll find out.'

'A Penwith *trait*? I've heard the rumours about his dad but you surely can't believe that Cal would inherit some cheating gene?'

'It's not just nature, it's nurture.'

I hesitate. 'If he's hurt you, then I'm sorry.'

'*Hurt* me? Don't be ridiculous.' Her eyes narrow. 'Has he told you that?'

'No, and if I've heard any gossip, it wasn't from Cal. He'd never discuss what happened or didn't between you with me, and I'm sure he'd never do anything malicious or cruel to you. The opposite, in fact.'

She laughs at me but clenches her hands together nervously. 'So, you know him inside out now? You have no idea. This is a waste of time. Please leave.'

'OK. You can deny it, but I think you *are* upset. You're wrong about Cal. Don't punish him for something that happened way back; he has never intended to hurt you.'

Even as I say the words, I know I've probably already added to Cal's problems by reminding Mawgan of how much she hates him and resents the Penwiths in general. Why did I come here? 'I'd better go,' I mumble, suddenly feeling a bit sick.

'Hold on.'

I stop, halfway out of the chair.

'You think Cal is wonderful, don't you?' she says in a tight voice. 'But he's an arrogant pig and always has been. He told me he wouldn't sleep with me because I was barely eighteen and he was in love with Isla. He told me that it would be' – she brackets the words with her fingers – '"a crap idea" because my mother had just walked out, and I was "vulnerable". I remember his words. "I'd have been taking advantage if I'd taken you to bed." Instead he chose to be a self-righteous wanker.'

My bum connects with the seat again. 'Even if you do think he's treated you like a child, you surely can't still hold that against him, enough to destroy him all these years later?'

She laughs. 'You think that the way I feel about Cal, and the way my father feels about the Penwiths, is all because he wouldn't shag me?'

My pulse races. 'I can't see any another reason.'

'No, I don't expect you do because you've been sucked in by his so-called charm as well. You think that under that brooding, moody exterior there's some kind of hero when, in fact, there's just a selfish bastard. Cal is exactly like his father; he is *so* like him. His father thought he was entitled to everything and everyone who crossed his path, including my mum.' She leans forward.

My stomach clenches. 'Are you saying Cal's dad and your mum had an affair?'

'Yes, I am. Cal's father obviously thought it would be fun to take her away from my dad and from me and Andi. Oh, I didn't know why Mum left us at the time, she kept it quiet and Dad was too proud to admit he'd lost anything, let alone lost his wife to a Penwith.

'Of course, Penwith dumped her eventually but it was too late. She'd decided that it was more exciting to run away to the other side of the world with yet another man than it was to stay with us. She decided that actually, once she'd found the nerve to have an affair, she'd found the nerve to leave us.'

I can barely believe what I'm hearing. 'Does Cal have any idea about this?'

'I doubt it.' She smirks. 'So you see, I'd like to trust people and give them benefit of the doubt like you do and Cal does, but I realised long ago that you only end up hurt. No one can be relied on, because in the end, they turn on you. I trusted Mum, I loved her and she left. I gave her everything of me and she obviously didn't give a toss. Not for me, or for Dad or Andi. You do the maths.' Mawgan's mouth snaps shut, but I can hear her breathing heavily as if telling me all that has exhausted her.

'I'm truly sorry that it's led you to this and if Cal did know, I'm sure he'd be horrified.'

'There you go again, assuming you know what he'd feel,' she snaps. 'I suppose Cal may *not* know. In fact, I don't think he does, but it wouldn't make a difference. Like I said, he's just like his father. He thinks he can click his fingers and have anyone he wants. He did that before he went away and now with you, he's doing the same. Isla had a lucky escape.'

'What do you mean, Isla *escaped*?'

'If Cal had stayed with her, he'd have screwed her life up and screwed half of Cornwall before the year was out. In fact, it was me who told Luke to go after her, the moment Cal was out of the way. Luke's always been mad on her but with Cal around, he hadn't got a hope in hell.'

'You did *what*?' I feel sick and I can't help thinking that Mawgan encouraged Luke to pursue Isla to hurt Cal and leave him free for her, not that she ever had a chance. I had no idea how toxic Mawgan's hatred for Cal was but she seems delighted that she's shocked me.

'I'm only sorry he waited so long and I give credit to Isla for one thing: not running back to him the moment he turned up again, though she may change her mind, of course, because Cal will never let go completely. He considers her his rightful property.' Her smile is triumphant.

With a huge effort, I control the urge to shout and scream at her. It's what she wants, I'm sure, to unravel me. 'I can see that you want revenge, however twisted, and there's nothing I can do to change your mind about your opposition to the plans. But if you won't help us, then think of Andi and Robyn. You've made them incredibly unhappy. What would your mum think if she knew you were making your own sister so unhappy?'

Mawgan looks as if I've slapped her. 'You have no idea what my mother would think. None!' Her voices rises, just a little hysterically but she doesn't hit me or throw me out.

'Isn't she to blame as much as Cal's father? Andi told me you hardly ever see her, even though she wants to see Andi and vice versa. I know something: I'd give anything to see my mother again if I could, but she's dead.'

She pouts. 'My heart bleeds.'

'I think your heart does bleed but you don't want me or anyone to know how much. You're eaten up with misery, Mawgan. You're consumed by hate for the Penwiths, you blame your mother for leaving and you want to destroy Andi's happiness too because you just can't bear her to be liked and loved when you're not.'

Mawgan throws the pen onto the desk with a clatter. 'How dare you talk about my family like that!'

'I don't care. You need to hear it and I'm not afraid of you and I would never beg you for anything either. But listen to me: I don't speak to my dad either, because he has a new partner and that cuts me in two. I don't want to see him, I blame him for retreating into himself and ignoring me after my mum died. I hate him for finding someone else other than her. I'm not sure I ever really loved him, but you obviously worshipped your mum, or why would you be so upset that she went off?'

She jumps to her feet and advances on me, her fists balled.

This is probably the biggest mistake I'll ever make but I do it anyway. I touch her arm. She stares at my hand like I stabbed her but she doesn't move.

'You can't say this to me . . .' Her voice is high pitched.

I take my hand away. 'I'm sorry if you've had a rubbish time; really I am, and I can – just about – see why you blame the Penwiths. So do what you want to us, but leave Andi alone. I know that you love her and you don't want to lose her too but I swear that you will lose her if you try to keep her away from Robyn.'

Mawgan's fists are still clenched but there's something else. Her eyes are glistening and I swear she's turned pale under the fake tan. I think she might cry – either that or leap on me. I've said too much. I've dropped Andi and Robyn in it big time.

'Get out,' she says in a voice so small it's almost a squeak.

'I'm sorry if I've upset you.'

'I said. Get. Out.'

'OK. I'm going, but if you do this to Cal and your family, you'll destroy yourself too.'

'Just leave me alone!' she shrieks.

I escape into the hall and the door slams behind me. My legs are like jelly. My hands tremble. I stumble along the hallway towards the huge front door.

Behind me, I hear Mr Cade shouting: 'Mawgan? Are you all right? Mawgan!'

I race up the drive, between the stone pillars and back to the Land Rover in the lane. Once safely locked inside, I try to turn the key in the ignition but my hands are shaking too much.

I think I've just made everything a hundred times worse for everyone.

CHAPTER THIRTY-ONE

'Demi? Is that you?'

Polly shouts to me from the open doorway of the building that was supposed to become my cafe. All the rubbish was cleared out weeks ago and a pallet of new Cornish slates for the roof and two of breeze blocks have been delivered. Raindrops bounce off the blue plastic shrink-wrap that protects them.

After I left the Cades' house, I drove around for an hour, not caring where I was going. Then I realised I was going to run out of diesel so I parked the car on the cliffs above Godrevy Towans and watched the nutters tackling the gnarly surf on the beach below and the waves battering the rocks at the base of Godrevy lighthouse. I can picture Mawgan now, screaming at Andi or turning up at Bosinney to confront Robyn and Rory Penwith. Why did I ever think I could persuade her to back down? I drove home to Kilhallon, eventually, but ran straight to the cafe building. I don't know why. Or perhaps I do. This half-built shell reminds me that my dreams never got off the ground.

Polly picks her way past the building materials and stands over me. 'What are you doing? It's peeing down.'

I'm sitting against the wall of the barn and I lift my face to her, hoping she can't tell whether it's rain or tears on my face.

'I'm sorry, Polly. I'm so sorry.'

'What are you sorry about, my bird?' She starts to pull off her cagoule.

'No. Don't! You'll get soaked.'

'Drop of water won't harm me but you're drenched to the skin and shivering. You'll catch pneumonia, you daft thing.'

'I don't care.'

'What's up?'

'I've messed everything up.'

'What do you mean?'

I can't tell her: I'm too ashamed. I also know that my tears aren't all down to Mawgan's reaction to my rant, but also my own. I've never told anyone what I told her about my dad. Why did it have to be her?

Polly sighs. 'You look upset and I don't blame you.'

She must know something. Mawgan must have phoned Cal or something to complain about me and hammer the last nail in the coffin.

'If you're worried about being thrown out of here and losing your home, you can stop right now. I'll have you living with me before I let that happen. I've money saved up and a little cottage near my daughter's.'

'You have a cottage away from Kilhallon?'

'You don't think I rely on the Penwiths for a roof over my head, do you? I invested in it with the money I got when my husband passed away and I rent it out at the moment, but I always intended to move into it when I retired. I only stayed here for Cal's sake and to keep the place going after his dad died. Somebody had to look after him.'

'Polly, I had no idea.'

'Well, now you do and you can lodge with me until you get yourself fixed up if we're forced to move. You and that hell hound. Did you know he's been howling the cottage down while you were out? How long does it take to visit a market garden?'

'I . . . I was held up.'

'For three hours? Get up and come back to the house this minute. Cal's been looking for you.'

'Cal? Why?'

'He wants to talk to you. He's mad as hell. He thought you'd done a runner.'

With Polly's ancient cagoule draped around my shoulders, I trudge after her, towards the unexploded bomb that awaits me.

Cal jumps on me the moment I walk into the kitchen. 'Why didn't you answer your mobile? We were worried you'd had a crash and were lying at the bottom of a cliff somewhere.'

Polly tuts. 'Calm down, Cal. She's OK and she needs a few moments.'

'Why are you wet through? What have you been doing?'

'Cal, will you be quiet and give the girl a few minutes!'

At Polly's bark, Cal's mouth snaps shut. He looks amazed and I would smile if my teeth weren't chattering so much.

'I'll put the kettle on,' he growls.

'Best idea you've had all year,' says Polly, handing me a towel from the radiator. Wrapped up warm and with a mug of steaming tea in my hands, the feeling gradually returns to my fingers. Cal sits at the end of the table, watching me in between sips of his own tea. It's all very well for Polly to fuss over me but I fear it's only drawing out the agonising moment when Cal lets rip about my visit to the Cades.

I finish my drink and pull the towel tighter around my shoulders. Polly has left us to collect Mitch, so I know I'm for it from Cal.

He dumps his empty mug on the table with a thump. 'Right. First, where have you been? Second, why haven't you answered your mobile? And third, why do you look like you fell in the sea?'

I open my mouth to confess then I realise that he genuinely doesn't know. I should tell him, I really should but I can't bear to tell him what I've done, or share the personal details Mawgan told me or that I told her. It's too painful, for him and for me.

'Well?'

'I was upset,' I say. 'About losing Kilhallon and so I just drove off.'

'Where?'

'Just somewhere.'

'Using up the diesel for fun?'

'I'll pay for it.'

'I don't care about that but I do care that I – we – were out of our minds. We genuinely thought you'd had an accident and were unconscious or worse. How could you put us through this when we already have enough to worry about?'

'I – I'm sorry.'

'Stop saying you're sorry.' He slams his fist on the table, making me almost jump out of my skin. 'Damn it. I'm sorry too, for losing my temper, but I thought I'd lost you.'

'Did you? Do you care?'

He stares at me. 'Of course I care!'

Our gaze locks. Cal holds up his hands in frustration. I'm trembling again. 'Of course, I care,' he repeats, yet so softly I can barely hear him. 'You know I do.'

Polly's shouts and some wild barking herald the arrival of Mitch who races into the kitchen, claws clattering on the tiles. He leaps on me and licks my face until I can hardly breathe or see. I almost burst into tears again.

Cal shakes his head. 'See, Mitch thought something had happened to you too. Demi, if you were that upset, you only had to talk to me.' He scoops up the keys from the dresser. 'I'm going out and if anyone wants me for anything, tell them I've gone to drive off a cliff.'

'Don't you say such terrible things, Cal Penwith!' Polly calls after him.

'I was joking,' he shouts back before adding, 'Will someone shift that bloody boot scraper!'

*

That evening, after a shower and a hot meal prepared by Polly, I'm back in my cottage, wondering when and if I can break the news to Cal and if I should phone Robyn or Andi. If Mawgan hasn't said anything to Cal yet, perhaps she won't. She must be fuming and ashamed that she let down her guard as much as she did. Perhaps she'll go ahead with her plans without telling anyone about my visit. We'll still lose Kilhallon but at least I won't have made life even worse for the people and friends I care about. Mitch curls on top of me as we listen to the rain lashing the windows of the cottage.

When I wake up, it's dark. Mitch is barking and someone's hammering on the door. I see Cal's face at the window. He looks pale and drenched. I open the door and he shoves his hands through his hair.

'What's up?'

'Demi, Mawgan Cade just phoned me.'

'Oh no! I'm sorry, Cal.' My heart rate takes off like a rocket. This is it, then.

'Don't be! She's decided not to buy Kilhallon after all. The devious little madam had the nerve to call to tell me that she'd had consultants in who'd told her it was a crap location for apartments anyway. She said that I'd go bankrupt if I carried on developing the park myself, but if that was what I wanted, then she'd enjoy seeing me go down with the place.'

'What?' I'm amazed, it's the only word I can manage.

'You look as gobsmacked as I was, but who cares? As long as she does what she says. Come over to the house and I'll tell you more, and I'll open a bottle of wine. This deserves a celebration!'

'I don't believe a word of her story about the consultants,' he tells me as we share a bottle of red wine at the house. I'm too shell-shocked and knackered for celebrating it, but I had to put on a show. 'But something's put the wind up her, I know that much.'

'You think so? But it doesn't matter, in the end, we can carry on with our plans, can't we?'

'Fingers crossed that she keeps her word. I think she's worried that someone's found some evidence of her corrupt dealings. She certainly won't have had an attack of conscience, I can tell you.'

'I don't suppose she would,' I said, in turmoil over whether to tell him the truth. I'm not even sure if what I said to her is the reason, though it can hardly be a coincidence. I'm also still terrified of what's happened to Andi and Robyn. I hope I haven't sacrificed them for Kilhallon.

'I wonder if Luke or Isla have had a word with her,' Cal muses.

'Isla? Why would she have any influence on Mawgan?' I ask.

He shrugs. 'I don't know. Mawgan doesn't dislike her and Isla loves Robyn and Andi. Isla has a way with people; she's good at pouring oil on troubled waters. I just have a feeling that Mawgan's had a wake-up call from someone.'

'Perhaps you'll find out,' I say, my guts twisting. So if Cal thinks Isla had a hand in 'saving' Kilhallon, then so be it. I can live with that, even if it gnaws at me, just a little bit. OK, a *lot*.

'I'd love to know but for now I won't look a gift horse in the mouth. Just wait until I tell Polly. She won't be able to bloody believe it.'

The following morning, I go up to the house to find Cal. I didn't stay too late last night but when I got back to my cottage, Mawgan had one last surprise for me. She phoned my mobile and the conversation lasted about a minute. She said pretty much the same as she'd told Cal – that her property consultants had said Kilhallon was too isolated for residential development, that there was a risk of mining subsidence from the old workings and in the current market it would be a bad investment for her. She also told me that if I breathed a word to Cal or anyone about our 'private conversation' in her study, that she 'could have a very rapid change of heart'. I think she wanted me to know she's still a dangerous foe, but for now, we can breathe again.

When I saw Polly this morning, she was humming a song I recognise from her Il Divo CD. She's ecstatic about the news from Mawgan and told me that Cal drove off first thing and wouldn't tell her exactly where he was going, just that he had 'business to take care of'. I didn't get much sleep after Mawgan called last night and couldn't concentrate on my work this morning, so in the end, I took Mitch up onto the moors above the park to try to get my head together.

I've just reached the car park at Kilhallon again when my phone beeps with a text. Shortly after, the Land Rover pulls onto the gravel, stopping with a crunch.

When Cal climbs out of the car, he finds me grinning like an idiot at my phone.

'What are you so happy about?' he asks.

I hold up the screen to him. 'Good news. Robyn just texted to tell me that they've told your uncle they want to move in together.'

'Wow. That's brave but I'm glad for them. How did it go?'

'Robyn says he didn't turn cartwheels but he didn't hit the roof or throw her out. She said he didn't even seem that shocked.'

'To be honest it doesn't surprise me, but I am relieved. He's not perfect by a long shot, but Uncle Rory's a decent bloke at heart and he loves Robyn to bits.'

'Robyn said he went very quiet, and didn't try to interfere. He might even have been relieved that the truth had come out. I'm so happy for her and Andi. I can't believe it. Can you?'

'It happens, Demi.' His smile lights up his eyes. He looks years younger and my stomach does a little flip. No matter how much I try, I can't help the way I feel about him.

'There's more. Mawgan has agreed to let Andi and Robyn have one of the Cade's vacant flats near to the college.'

'She *must* have had a change of heart. Or a complete change of personality! I guessed someone really does have something over the Cades for them to back off from hassling us, but with

Andi and Robyn, well, she must have some shred of humanity and sense in her after all.'

'Maybe a shred.' I move the subject on. 'You know, I'm as happy for the girls' good luck as I am for us.'

'I'll call Robyn later and find out more,' he says. 'But first, can you guess where I've been?'

'No idea.'

By his grin, Cal looks as if he's about to go pop with pride. 'I went to the DIY shed in Penzance and then to the salvage yard at Helston again. I got some fantastic old settles for your cafe. They're in the Land Rover. You can help me unload the stuff from the yard. Why are you standing there like you've been struck dumb? Aren't you even a tiny bit excited that you're going to need them?'

Realisation dawns. 'What? I mean, you mean the cafe's definitely going ahead after all?'

'Dave Patterson called me while I was in Helston, and he's on board financially again, which changes everything. When we get planning permission, and I'm sure we will now that Mawgan's withdrawn her objections, you'd better start to plan a launch event. We need to get word out fast that Kilhallon Park is alive and well, and back on track.'

CHAPTER THIRTY-TWO

The council passed Cal's new planning application at their next meeting and the building work on the park has started again. With Dave Patterson's investment in the park and the planning appeal resolved, everything seemed possible.

It's not all roses. Robyn's still refusing to speak to Luke and Cal has hinted to me that there are sure to be other, possibly bigger, battles with the Cades.

'Which makes it even more important for us to make Kilhallon a success,' he told me. 'We need to start the cash flowing as soon as possible.'

I can't believe August is already almost three weeks old, but time flies by when you're as busy as we are. Cal and the builders are pulling out all the stops to get at least some of the site finished and I've thrown myself headlong into organising a promotional event to let the world know what we have to offer. It's time for us all to move on to the next stage in our lives, if we can.

I've been up at dawn and in bed not long before, on some nights, researching prospects, sending out invites, cold calling potential guests – I never thought I'd dare – and persuading them that Kilhallon is worth a visit. I've barely had time to see my friends or go out with them although they've offered to help out at the launch day.

Now there's less than forty-eight hours to go to the launch, and I'm racing around St Trenyan picking up extra bunting, plastic plates and cleaning stuff. While passing the alley behind the surf cafe, I spot Sheila taking rubbish to the bins and realise I haven't spoken to her for ages. Her hair is shorter and highlighted. It suits her.

The cafe itself is packed despite the cloudy skies and choppy sea. A young guy with blond dreadlocks and an older woman, both of whom I don't recognise, are serving on the terrace. Business must be going OK if Sheila can take on extra staff for the summer season. We're going to need more help at Kilhallon when we open too, I've realised that in the past few weeks. I'll be in charge of them, which is *scary*.

Sheila walks in through the rear door of the cafe and I follow her. She scrubs her hands with antibac soap. I notice her niece, Kayla, adding tiny pots of clotted cream and jam to plates of scones, arranging them so they look perfect.

'Hello, Sheila.'

She glances up, frowns momentarily then breaks into a huge grin. 'Demi! What a surprise!'

She wipes her hands on some paper towels.

'I don't want to stop you from working.'

She hugs me until I can barely breathe. 'You're not. It's the post-lunch lull so I can spare a few minutes. I need a break too.'

Kayla says a quick hello and calls the cream-teas order to the young waiter.

Sheila ushers me into the tiny staffroom off the kitchen.

'So, how are things at Kilhallon? I heard on the grapevine that it's all systems go up there.'

'It is now.'

'I heard you were doing well now. It's the talk of the town.'

I hug her. 'If it wasn't for you I wouldn't have met Cal and got the job.'

'Glad to help. I'm very happy for you, love, and working for him can't be all bad. I've seen him around town a couple of times and I remember him from before he went away.' She winks. 'Hot stuff.'

I shake my head and hope my blush doesn't betray me. 'Are the Cades still giving you trouble?'

'Funnily enough, they've backed off a bit recently. I was expecting a rent rise last month but it hasn't come yet.' She smiles grimly. 'I don't doubt it will, though, but until then, I'm making the most of the good weather. I've been able to take on some extra help and as long as the rent doesn't get hiked, I should be able to keep the new staff on.'

'That's great. Maybe the Cades have other things on their minds than squeezing their tenants?'

'Hmm. Pigs might fly, but rumour has it that the Cades got their fingers burned over a new development recently. A few of their tenants in town have told me that they haven't heard from them for a while either, which is a good thing, believe me. Let's hope they've had a wake-up call.'

'Mmm. I hope so too.'

'Do you want a drink? There's some quiche left over from lunch too.'

'Love to but I can't stay. We're holding a promo event the day after tomorrow to try and drum up some publicity for the new resort. We're planning to have a cafe on the site.'

'Good luck with that.' She smiles wryly but then adds, 'Ignore me. It's a brilliant idea and a great location. I'm sure it'll do very well and anything that brings more people into the area to spend their money has to be good.'

'Yes . . . I don't think we'll be competing, and actually I might need some extra help with sourcing the baked goods if it takes off. I wondered if you might like to be a supplier for the pasties and scones because we can't always make our own?'

'*Me*? Of course, I would!' She grins.

'Well, it's early days yet but I'll be in touch when we're up and running.'

'My, my, you have come on. I'm proud of you.' She looks like she's about to cry for a different reason and I feel like welling up too. She reminds me a little of my mum, who would have been about the same age. Swallowing the lump in my throat, I hug her.

'If you can get away, will you come to the launch?'

'I'd love to, but it's a busy time . . . I promise I'll do my very best and thanks for the opportunity to supply your business.'

'It's Cal's business, really, but thanks.'

After leaving Sheila, I feel ten feet tall and really happy to have seen her again. I would have loved to have stayed with Sheila but I have a hundred things to do and buy. I wonder how Polly is getting on with baking the scones and the pasties. Most of it is in the freezer but we need more. I hope the barn won't leak if it rains. In fact, hope it won't rain at *all*. I want Kilhallon to look amazing. What if Mitch attacks another dog? He isn't aggressive but it is his territory and . . .

Just as I walk out of the alley into Fore Street, I spot Tamsin, carrying two large cardboard boxes, one on top of the other. She can't see above them and weaving in and out of the tourists is almost impossible at this time of year. She almost goes over on her ankle in the cobbled gutter and the boxes wobble, but I manage to grab one before it falls onto the street.

'Hi. Do you need a hand?' I say, taking the box.

Tamsin sighs in relief. 'Thanks. I thought I was going to end up on my bum in front of the emmets for a minute! I was just on my way from my car to the spa with a new delivery of products.'

'Lucky I was here.'

'Thanks!'

Tamsin smiles. She's super pretty with English-rose skin and bouncy, jet-black hair. Bouncy everything, in fact. Her make-up is perfect, even in the middle of the day, but very subtly done. I guess it's her job to look great, but I'm still very aware of my broken nails, tatty jeans and unwashed hair that hasn't seen a brush for days.

'I'm glad I bumped into you. I was really glad to hear that the park's going ahead.'

'Me too. Sorry, I haven't taken you up on the trial treatment offer but we've been so tied up in work . . . do you want a hand to carry this lot back to the spa?'

'Good idea, thanks.'

We start to thread our way through the throng of shoppers and tourists. There are families with children everywhere now that it's high season and it's a nerve-wracking game for any of the delivery vans trying to make their way down the narrow street to reach the shops.

'How's Cal?' Tamsin asks me as we squeeze past the queue outside one of the ice-cream parlours.

'Um. He's OK. It's a busy time. I've got tons to do for the Kilhallon Park launch event.'

'Sounds like a great idea. I heard a bit about it from Robyn Penwith. I saw her in the canteen at the college. I give lectures in beauty therapy at the college as well as running the spa.'

'I didn't know that.'

'Keeps me out of trouble.' She laughs, and I realise how much I like her. 'My salon's just up this side street.'

We turn off the main drag into a lane, between rows of fisherman's cottages, that's so narrow you could almost touch the sides. There's instant calm after the bustling shopping area and you can even hear the surf breaking on the beach. Tamsin leads me into a tiny but very pretty courtyard. A smart, pale-blue door is set in the whitewashed stone walls of her building and flanked by pewter tubs filled with hot-pink geraniums the same colour as her perfect nails. She puts the box down and takes mine, then finds her door key.

'Here's the spa. Do you want to come in?'

'I shouldn't, really. I'm so busy.'

'Hmm.' She eyes me up and down. 'So the launch is on Friday?'

'Yes . . .'

'So there'll be lots of important people there? Potential clients? The press?'

'Oh, God, yes, plus travel bloggers, someone from the government and a celebrity food writer. There's so much to do to get ready and to be honest, I've no idea what I'm going to say to them.'

Tamsin looks at me intently. 'What are you going to wear?'

'I've got a new denim mini and a branded polo shirt . . . other than that, I haven't had time to even think about it.'

She tuts. 'You should. Tell you what, why don't you spend the next fifteen minutes having that trial treatment? I'll do your nails for you and give you some make-up tips and free samples.'

Glancing at my nails again, I realise she's right and that it might do me good to chill out for a short while. 'OK, thanks.' I smile. 'I'll call it an investment in myself but I don't think I should wear polish because I'll have food to prepare.'

'No problem. I can still do a shape, file and moisturise. If you're meeting VIPs, you'll be shaking hands and you'll want yours to look good. I promise you, you'll feel a lot more confident, especially if your hands are going to be in the photographs.'

Five minutes later, I'm sitting in a tasteful grey leatherette chair in one of the spa treatment rooms, while Tamsin massages orange-scented cream into my hands and arms. Delicious smelling candles burn and soft music plays.

'So, how is Cal, *really*?' Tamsin asks, pushing back my cuticles with a wooden stick. I wonder if this is partly why she's got me in here: to have a gossip about Cal.

'He's busy but doing OK, I think. Better than when he first came home.'

'I saw him in town the other day and he looked well fit. Mind you, he looked good even when he was a teenager and the other lads still had spots and bum fluff on their chins. He just isn't my type but we've always been on friendly terms.'

'Were you at school with him, then?'

'We go back, like forever. Him, Luke, Mawgan, Isla and me, all went to the same school. Cal and I were even in the same year.'

She cleans and files my nails. I cringe at the ragged edges and manky cuticles and the grazed knuckles from shifting junk in the barn. But she magics the dry skin away with the cream and some cuticle oil and starts to work a miracle.

'I'm going to buff your nails now, so they shine without you needing any polish.'

She switches on an electronic buffer and works more miracles on my nails. 'I'm glad things are going well for Cal,' she says. 'After losing his mum and dad and working in such a dangerous place for the charity, he deserves some good luck. I'm not sure what happened to him out there. Robyn told me he was in a remote place and couldn't contact her or Isla for a while but there's something he's not telling us. Any of us.'

'I have been wondering myself, but it's obvious he doesn't want to talk about it. I think he saw some horrific and painful things,' I say, wary of discussing too much personal information about Cal but also intrigued to hear someone else's perspective.

'Or *can't* talk about it.' Tamsin is intent on my last nail; I think she deliberately isn't looking at my face. 'So, that's why he seemed pretty screwed up when he got back, and then there's the Isla thing. Who can blame him? Isla Channing is so nice and classically beautiful and clever and successful . . .'

Go on, torture me some more, I think.

'She is,' I say, through gritted teeth, not feeling quite so chilled out any more.

'Yeah, but I always thought she was a bit of an ice maiden, to be honest. I never reckoned she was right for Cal. Too buttoned-up. Too perfect. He needs someone who'll stand up to him, someone to be a spark to his flame.'

'I thought she was the love of his life,' I say, wondering who the spark refers to.

'Maybe, they were into each other at school and afterwards but things were always pretty ropey between them when he went to uni, and when he quit. Then she was away from Cornwall a lot with her TV job and of course his work took him abroad. They say he should have married her before he left, though I'm not sure it would have lasted. If you ask me, Cal put Isla on a pedestal while he was away and made her into some kind of goddess. It must have been a hell of shock to find out she was human.'

'You really think that?'

She smiles. 'Well, I can't imagine her helping to run a caravan site.'

'Caravan site?' I feign horror. 'It's an eco-friendly boutique holiday destination.'

She laughs. 'That sounds more like Isla but I can't actually imagine her unblocking the loos.'

'I hope I won't be either, though I suspect we'll all have to muck in when it opens.'

'Isla is a genuinely nice person and I like Cal but I don't think he's a long-term prospect for any woman. Not that you're looking for that, or me. Way too much fun to be had first.'

'Obviously.' I laugh, guessing Tamsin's warning me off Cal, not that I need any warnings and she's so right: there is way too much fun to be had first. I'm far too young to be even thinking about getting involved with anyone and Cal's quite a bit older than me. She's not really cheering me up, though.

She applies a drop of oil to each nail as a finishing touch and peers at them with a critical frown then smiles. 'There. You're almost done. Try to avoid any more hard labour before the launch event's over and make sure you keep using that hand cream I'll give you.'

Knowing the first part might be tricky, I promise anyway. 'I will. Thanks, Tamsin.'

'Pleasure. And if any of your guests want a treatment, you know where to send them. I'll try to make the launch. It sounds like fun and maybe we could go out for a drink sometime? My brother-in-law runs a great cocktail bar by the old lifeboat station. We could give his new bar menu a trial.'

'Sounds great. I'll see you at the launch, then.'

Tamsin sends me away with some samples and says she'll bring a stack of her leaflets and business cards to the promo event. I manage to get everything I wanted in one go from the party store on Fore Street so I'm not so late after all, despite my manicure. Cal won't notice my nails, of course, and I did it for me not him – but Tamsin was right: I could use every possible boost to my confidence.

On my way back to the harbour car park, I try to take in all she said, wondering what of it is accurate and what just gossip. That's when I see *them*: walking along the harbour past the cafe where Cal first took me. He's tall and serious and hot, and she's wearing a floaty white dress and has her hair piled up on her head like a goddess.

I stop, I can't tear my eyes away.

Cal puts his arm around Isla and she lays her head on his shoulder and they look just like they've never been apart.

CHAPTER THIRTY-THREE

Bunting flaps wildly against the rafters of the barn when I hurry over after a very early breakfast the next morning. It's the day before the launch and Polly is already working, chasing paper plates and serviettes around the floor, cursing and swearing. I rescue a leaflet before it sails out of the door and off into the sky. Outside, dirty grey clouds gather on the horizon, and the sun hasn't even bothered to get out of bed. Please, don't let it rain: not for the most important day of our lives. Kilhallon needs to sparkle tomorrow; we *all* need to sparkle.

Yet my mind isn't totally on the launch, and that makes me angry with myself, even more than with Cal. This is my big chance and I'm stressing about what he may or may not have done. I have to get a grip.

By mid-morning, Andi and Robyn have arrived to lend a hand.

'How many did you say you're expecting at this thing tomorrow?' Robyn calls from the bottom of the ladder while Andi loops the extra bunting over the rafters. They both look at me with puzzled expressions.

I snap out of my daydreams. 'Around seventy have confirmed but there were more who haven't replied or couldn't say for sure.'

'Seventy? It feels like we're feeding the five thousand,' Polly mutters, covering the plates and serviettes with a table cloth weighed down with a stone. 'We should have got the proper caterers in.'

'We'll manage with the help of Robyn's mates from college.'

'The catering students?' Polly snorts. 'And why did you have to invite *dogs*?'

'We couldn't cope without them,' I say patiently. 'And as we're going to have a dog-friendly site and cafe, it seemed a good idea to invite everyone – animal and human – who'll be using it.'

Ignoring my reply – Polly rarely needs one – she casts her eyes around the bar. 'Well, I'll admit the old place has scrubbed up better than I thought it would and it's better late than never, I suppose. You've worked very hard, I will say that much.'

She gives me a smile. Slowly, I'm learning how to curate Polly's sayings and pick the ones that she really means. Half the time, her bluster is to disguise her genuine worries about Cal and me. You'd think we were her family as much as her own children sometimes.

'I'm hoping we'll open for our first guests by mid- to late-September,' I say with a lot more confidence than I feel. 'It'll be a "soft" opening to start with while we find our feet but we can do some unbeatable offers to tempt people in. Even though we'll have missed the main tourist season we'll catch the empty nesters and half-term visitors. Then there's the Hallowe'en and Bonfire Night events we have planned, the Christmas craft fair, and Christmas and New Year itself. By next spring, the whole site should be up and running properly.'

A gust of wind blows sheets of paper off the display table. Robyn dashes forward and stamps on one while Andi catches the other.

'Oh thanks, I daren't lose those. They're the guest list and schedule for tomorrow.'

Robyn scans the names on the guest list. 'Ms Eva Spero OBE, *Sir* Kit Choudry? Rt Hon Yvette McCollum? Who are all these people?'

'Eva Spero's a food guru but I don't know if she's coming as she hasn't replied, Sir Kit owns a travel business and the Rt Hon Yvette is a junior tourism minister. The rest are potential customers or people who can spread the word to guests, wedding planners, travel journalists, glamping bloggers and business people who might hold corporate events here.'

'They sound important,' says Robyn.

'And scary,' says Andi, helping herself to a mini veggie pasty from the tray on the buffet table.

Polly glares at her. 'Hey, don't go scoffing all of those. I bought them out for Cal to try. There's only one each.'

Andi swallows and grins. 'They're very nice. Do you want one, Demi?'

Polly rolls her eyes, but I can tell she's secretly delighted. She followed a recipe I showed her from Sheila's cafe. 'I suppose I could fetch a few more out of the freezer, if they're that popular.'

'Thanks, Polly, and I've already tried them. They're delicious but I'm not really hungry.'

The truth is I haven't eaten properly for days. My stomach is in knots as I think of the list of VIPs who may turn up. I'm in charge of promoting the cafe and food outlets and ethos which makes me want to laugh hysterically every time I think of it. Six months ago I didn't know what an ethos was; now I'm trying to sell it to a bunch of people who might hold the keys to my future.

'I'll get the washing in in case this storm blows in. Don't go eating all them pasties,' Polly says, bustling off.

Shoving the list into the pocket of my cut-offs, I tell myself to calm down. 'Come on, let's get the cafe display set up.'

'Oh, that reminds me! We've got the new branding designs in the car. I can't wait to show them to you,' says Robyn. 'I'm sorry they're a bit late but you know, we've been busy with college and other stuff.'

'I hope you like them,' says Andi nervously.

'I'm sure they'll be brilliant,' I say. Mentally I cross my fingers, as anxious as the girls are about seeing their final ideas. I've seen the outlines before but Cal hasn't had time. We've really cut it fine so I hope they're OK and Cal likes them.

'What about Cal?' Robyn asks.

'Oh, I'm sure he'll love them too,' I say breezily.

'I hope so. Shall I go and fetch him so we can look at them together?'

'Can you let me take a look first? Cal is busy pitching a couple of sample yurts in the field. We still need to furnish and decorate them before we go to bed. There won't be time in the morning.'

'What time do you want us to arrive tomorrow morning?'

'As early as you can. We're kicking everything off with a buffet lunch in here and people can help themselves to afternoon teas later. Then there's a hog roast in the yurt field with more people invited, suppliers and neighbours. What time do your mates from the Tinner's want to set up for the music?'

Robyn takes a pasty. 'Oh, they'll rock up some time, I'm sure. Don't worry about them.'

The idea of Robyn's Cornish folk band just 'rocking up' worries me but I keep quiet. 'Fine. Can you and Andi be in charge of showing them where to set up? The electrician's going to wire up all the sound and lighting they'll need. I just hope it doesn't rain.'

'It won't rain. Just chill,' says Robyn, sneaking another pasty.

'Am I turning into Launchzilla?'

Andi, Robyn and Mitch all look at me with the same expression.

'OK. Deep breath. Let's see these designs.'

Cal stands in front of the graphics display in the barn, resting his elbow on his hand, rubbing the other over his mouth. Andi and Robyn have made a sharp exit, too nervous to face his reaction, so it was left to me to present the designs. I can hardly keep still and my palms are sweaty. 'I know we've cut it fine, showing you them now, but it's been mayhem here, for all of us, and the girls have worked so hard. I think they've done an amazing job.'

Without replying, Cal stands back from the boards to get a better view of the designs which are pinned up in small and larger versions to suit different media. The logo is a stylised silhouette of a tin mine with a Mitch-type dog sitting in front of it all on a background of deep aqua blue with grey granite trim.

'Mmm,' he says, picking up a mock-up of a promotional leaflet the girls have produced.

'I worked with Andi and Robyn to come up with the initial design and the graphics agency tweaked it . . .' I say, aware I'm babbling. 'I also asked them to get some sample aprons made up and some marketing collateral. They based the colours on the water in Kilhallon Cove.'

Cal spends so long leafing through the samples he doesn't seem to want to look at me and when he does, he doesn't even smile.

'I can change them if you hate them. We won't be offended. We have to get this right. I can go back to the design agency and get them to come up with new concepts. I . . .'

'Demi, I approve.'

'Really?'

'Yes, really,' he says quietly. I keep wondering if he'll mention his meeting Isla the other day but he doesn't and now is definitely not the right moment to start interrogating him, even if I wanted to. I figure he'll tell me if he wants to.

'So I can tell them to get some proper quotes for the marketing collateral?' I ask.

'Yes, you can. Thanks. They're perfect.'

'Perfect,' he said. You can't get any better than perfect so why do I feel like a deflated balloon left after a party? I will never fathom out Cal Penwith. There's a clatter as the tray of pasties hits the barn floor. Mitch starts wolfing them down.

'Mitch! No! They're not for you. Polly will go mad!'

I run forward but it's too late. As I grab his collar, he hoovers up the final pasty and looks at me as if to say: 'Is that all?'

'Mitch. How could you! You stupid, stupid dog!'

Cal's voice is gentle, his hand is on my arm. 'It's only a few pasties.'

'But they were for you to try. They were samples. This is the second batch she's made today.'

He shakes his head, smiling at me. 'And I'm sure they were delicious. Mitch approves, which is fine by me.'

'No, it's not. I want everything to be perfect tomorrow. It *has* to be.'

Cal rests his hands on the tops of my arms. His skin is rough and warm around mine. Surely, there can't still be anything going on between him and Isla, beyond friendship?

'It will be as perfect as you and I can make it,' he says.

'I'm not sure that will be enough.'

He drops my arms and takes my hand. 'It will have to be. You can't do any more now. Come on, let's get you out of here. I've got something to show you.'

He leads me down the path to the far field where a soft glow lights up the twilight. Tea lights flicker in jars and tea cups placed on assorted tables outside the yurts. I recognise some of the china and the 'up-cycled' furniture. The yurt hollow is sheltered from the worst of the wind, which is why Cal chose it, and anyway, the wind has dropped since this morning. The clouds are crimson streaks across the ink of the sky. Outside the yurts, flames perform a crazy dance in the fire pit and the scent of wood smoke perfumes the evening air.

'Wow. It looks like a fairy grotto.'

'I'll take that as a compliment. It works then?'

'Yes. It's gorgeous. The fairy lights in the trees and the decorations are amazing.'

Cal beams. I can't believe how far I've come in the past few months but I also feel I've stepped onto a tightrope and I'm wobbling along it. The prize is so big and yet I've so far to fall.

'Want to take a peek inside?'

We duck under the canvas into the yurt which is much bigger than I'd expected. The futon is dressed with the patchwork quilt I bought from a boot sale and some squishy, brocade cushions Polly was throwing out of her own cottage. A large silvery storm lantern burns on the driftwood table that was made by a student friend of Robyn's, while fairy lights snake around the central pole and the smell of incense fills the air.

'I never knew you had such a creative streak, Cal.'

'You'd done most of it and I just followed your plan for the finishing touches while you were busy with the barn display.' He steps closer. I can almost feel his body heat penetrate my skin. 'And anyway, there's a lot you don't know about me.'

'That's what worries me . . .'

Our shadows flicker on the canvas and the air smells of sandal-wood.

'You do know I couldn't have done all of this without you?' he says.

'I didn't have anything to do with it,' I say, wondering how he'd react if he knew that, fundamentally, Isla has helped to save him too. I feel I'm living a half-truth.

'You know what I mean. Reviving Kilhallon, sticking at it when it seemed impossible, and putting up with my moods. Thank you.'

He smiles at me and I know he really means what he's saying but I don't want his thanks, not even if I was able to tell him about my confrontation with Mawgan. I want his lust. I want him to need me, the way he needed Isla. Still does.

'Thank me tomorrow when the place hasn't gone up in flames or blown away and Mitch hasn't eaten all the food or tried to shag any lady dogs. Ask me then . . .'

'I don't think I can wait until tomorrow.'

In a heartbeat, his mouth comes down so softly on mine. It's like kissing a dream, a fantasy. My body feels liquid and my bones thrum with lust. Despite every doubt, warmth spreads through me, and the knot shifts from my stomach to low in my belly. I want him so much it hurts.

'No.' I push him away. 'I have to go. I have a lot to do. Tomorrow's a big day for all of us.'

'Demi, Wait . . .'

I walk away from him and have the strongest feeling I should have done so that first day in St Trenyan.

My jaw already aches from practising my customer-friendly smile but it's almost midday and there's no sign of anyone yet. Mitch lies by my side in the entrance to the barn, his nose on his paws. Even he knows something is up and that he has to be on his best behaviour. Shami and Nina are on the gate to Kilhallon while Polly has insisted on 'supervising' the catering students in the kitchen, poor things.

And Cal? We've hardly seen each other all morning, we've been so busy.

He strides across the yard towards me now, rolling back the cuffs on a sexily crumpled white linen shirt. His dark curls are damp and tiny droplets of water glisten in the springy dark hair showing in the 'V' of his shirt.

'Hi. Sorry I'm a bit late. Just managed to freshen up after I finished tidying up some rubbish in the new cafe shell.' He smiles. 'You look pretty.'

'Thanks.' I blush, happy he's approved of my new denim skirt and Kilhallon polo shirt. My hair is caught back in a mother of pearl barrette that belonged to my mum – the only thing I kept of hers when I fled the house – and I've made use of Tamsin's tinted moisturiser and designer lip gloss. She was right: I do feel a *tiny* bit more confident – as long as people turn up.

'Mitch looks smart. You both do,' he adds.

Mitch has a new collar complete with the kind of cute dog

scarf I said I'd rather die than put him in.

'I know it's a bit OTT but I couldn't resist it.'

Cal ruffles his ears. 'He could be our secret weapon and we need all the help we can get. Come on, then, let's do this.'

'What if no one turns up?'

He checks his watch. 'It's not even twelve yet. They'll be here soon enough and then you'll be longing for them to go.'

'But what if I told them the wrong day?'

'You haven't.'

'I hope we've got enough food.'

'If no one comes, you'll have nothing to worry about.'

'Don't say that!'

He takes me gently by the shoulders. He smells shower fresh. 'Demi, please stop worrying and try to relax. People will come and it's all going to be fine. You've worked too bloody hard for it to go wrong.' He drops his hands. 'Listen, is that a car engine?'

'Should we go up to the gates and meet them?'

'No. Andi and Robyn are on marshalling duty for now, with a couple of volunteers from the dog rescue coming later. So many people wanted to support us.'

I listen hard but can't hear anything. Cal glances at his watch again. Secretly, I think he's as nervous as I am. Mitch jumps to his feet a moment before I hear distant barking.

'They're here.'

Cal straightens his shoulders. 'I told you so. Come on, let's do this.'

We don't get forty people, or even fifty, there are far more than that milling about the barn displays and taking tours of the yurts and checking out the work in progress on the cottages.

I've been yakking so much, my voice is husky and it's barely three o'clock. All the mini pasties have almost gone and the doggy cakes are being devoured. The hum of chatter, laughter and excited barks echoes around the barn. Nina's mum has brought a couple of the better-behaved rescue dogs along to socialise with them.

Mitch doesn't know who or what to sniff first.

'Demi? Is that you?' A very short lady with a pink bob and a little black Pug hurries up to me. 'This is a-*mazing*. I'm so impressed.' She holds out her hand. 'I'm Eva Spero, by the way, and this is Betty.'

Betty the Pug gazes up at me from huge black eyes while I offer my clammy palm. Eva shakes it warmly but I'm trembling with awe.

'I know who you are, of course. I've spent hours on your website and watching re-runs of your cookery show. I can't believe you've actually come all this way.'

Cringing inwardly, I feel my face heat up but she laughs. 'Well, I had to come down to North Cornwall to do a feature on a celebrity chef's new sea food venture and I hoped to get all the way down here but I wasn't sure so I hope you'll forgive the lack of RSVP.'

'It's fine. I'm so happy you made it.' I feel lost for words but Mitch is in the mood to make friends and sniffs Betty the Pug's bottom. My face is on fire. 'Mitch! Stop that!'

Eva laughs. 'Don't worry. Betty is a complete tart herself.' She scoops up the Pug, who turns her big black eyes on me. Mitch gazes up longingly. I think he's in love.

'She's very impressed by the doggy menu, aren't you, Betty, darling?'

I stroke Betty's head and she licks my hand. 'She's completely adorable. Mitch has been my official taster. He can behave when he wants to, can't you, boy?'

Mitch sits beside me, looking like butter wouldn't melt in his mouth. Eva puts Betty down and Mitch touches her snub nose.

'I love your idea for selling organic doggy treats. It's something I'd like to try in the new cafe I'm opening in Brighton. Your canine ice lollies sound amazing.'

'I've got a couple in the freezer if Betty would like to try one?'

Eva claps her hands together in delight. She might be in her fifties and a multi-millionaire but she's like a little girl where dogs are concerned. 'Do you mind posing with Mitch and Betty for a picture for my blog? I might be able to use the photos in my next magazine column too.'

Resisting the urge to jump and up down like a kid, I try to stay business-like. 'I'd love to. Shall we go outside and do the photos? I can show you where the new cafe's going to be and we could have the sea in the background. Then I can find Betty one of the lollies.'

'Super idea. I'd love to see what you have planned here. I already want to pack up and move. I bet you could never leave such gorgeous surroundings.'

I glance over at Cal, who is smiling and charming the Rt Hon Yvette. He looks back at me and winks.

'No you never get tired of it.' My face is heating up rapidly. 'Shall I take you down to the site of the cafe? The coast path literally runs past the door, if we get it up and running. I mean *when* we get it up and running.'

Ignoring my shaking hands, I collect two lollies from the freezer and lead Eva down to the partly restored stone building that will become the cafe. When we reach the site, Mitch makes short work of his lolly while Betty licks hers with delicate little strokes.

'They have good things in like organic fruit and veg. Mitch likes the peanut butter ones but you need to let them thaw for a while so the dogs don't get freezer burn on their tongues.'

Eva squeals in delight. Cal, busy showing a yurt to two London travel bloggers on the other side of the field, glances up at us. 'Oh, it's all simply delightful. I'm soooo impressed with what you have planned here. I can see you have a true passion for Kilhallon and what you're trying to do, especially the food. Would you be happy for me to include some recipes on my website? They'd be credited to you, of course.'

'*My* recipes? Oh wow, I'd love you to.'

'And, forgive me if this is intrusive, but would you mind if I wrote a feature about you? I'd mention Kilhallon of course and include some photos, but Cal told me that you've had a rough start in life and were homeless before you got the job here.'

'Did he?'

'Yes. I hope that was OK. You can say no, of course, but I think what you've achieved is remarkable. I hear that Cal has been helping refugees too. It's an amazing story; homeless girl and ex-aid worker start eco business.'

'I hadn't thought of us as a story. Really, I'm one of the lucky ones.'

'Oh gosh, no. Cal told me *he* was lucky to have *you*.'

'He did?'

She smiles. 'Does that surprise you?'

'I suppose so. He doesn't gush about people.'

'Well, my love, he thinks a lot of *you*. I also know what he's been through. It's a great story and I'd *love* to tell it but Cal doesn't want any of the credit. He wants you to have the limelight and it would raise Kilhallon's profile.'

'Limelight? Well, if Cal doesn't mind and it would help the business, then I'll do it.'

She hugs me enthusiastically.

'Righty-oh. I'll get my people to contact your people and we'll set it up.'

'I don't have any people, apart from Mitch.'

She laughs. 'Then we'll let Betty and Mitch sort it all out.'

CHAPTER THIRTY-FOUR

It was after midnight when we waved goodbye to Robyn and Andi and their mates from the folk band. The yurt party was a huge success, with so many people raving over the setting and the mocked-up interior of the 'show yurt'. Sheila turned up after the Beach Hut closed and gave me a beautiful bunch of flowers, and Tamsin arrived with a congrats card and a bottle of champagne. I've never been given my own flowers or champagne and I almost lost it in front of Cal and the guests. Even the Cornish weather smiled on us, delivering a sunset to die for and a clear night with milky white stars.

The one person who didn't come was Isla, who had to go up to London unexpectedly for a production meeting. She'd left us a card and an even bigger bottle of champagne for Cal 'and the team'. Sheila told me it was a magnum of Krug and would have cost hundreds of pounds. If he was disappointed Isla didn't come herself, he didn't show it. Is it wrong of me to be glad she couldn't make it?

Cal locks the gate at the end of the drive and walks back down the drive towards me. At this time of year it never really goes dark but I can still see the stars winking in the inky sky. The cloudy swirl high up is the Milky Way, according to Robyn. She has an app on her phone that shows the stars wherever you are, even when you can't actually see them. Tonight, though, they're swarming over the sky like fireflies.

'Beautiful, isn't it?' Cal stands next to me.

'Hmm. It reminds me of a dress my mum had. It was dark blue velvet. Do you think she can see us?'

'I don't know. Anything is possible.' His voice is gentle but I know he's only being kind to me because the day has gone well.

'I know it's mad, but tonight, it *does* feel like anything is possible.' I turn to him. In the starlit twilight he seems more darkly sexy than ever.

'Are you tired?'

'It's funny, I've been up since five but I feel as if I could go on and on forever. I wish tonight would never end.'

'That's adrenaline. You'll be knackered tomorrow.'

Ah, Cal, always practical. I follow his cue as we walk down the drive towards the farmyard. 'I was worried about the logos for the cafe. When I showed you them, you didn't seem very pleased.'

'How was I supposed to look? Turn cartwheels, let off fireworks.'

'Show a bit more enthusiasm. I thought you were only going along with it to keep me happy.'

I try to make out his expression in the twilight but can't quite.

'Believe me, I'd have told you straight if I didn't like them,' he says. I dread the moment when we reach the farmhouse, knowing we'll have to part and today will be over. Well, I won't sleep. I'll stay up all night pretending today can go on forever.

'Yes, yes, I suppose you would.'

'It was just you talking about marketing collateral, and business branding.'

'Why is that funny?'

'Six months ago you wouldn't have believed it. I always knew you'd be a doer and you deserved a chance but I don't think even I expected the future businesswoman of the year.'

'Some people will say I only got where I am because I slept with the boss.'

He stops me with a hand on my arm just as we reach the yard. The lights glow from the windows but he makes no attempt to leave.

'You haven't slept with the boss . . .' he leaves the sentence hanging, then smiles. 'I don't know about you but I can't possibly go to sleep yet. Shall we go and celebrate? I think we deserve it.'

The moon shimmers on the sea as we sit on the beach at Kilhallon Cove by a fire Cal made from driftwood in a ring of stones. We carried a bottle of leftover champagne down to the beach and on this fine August night the whole world seems alight and alive with possibility. We talk about the party, and our plans, and gradually, slowly, the wine and the warmth of the fire makes my limbs relax, grow liquid. The surf breaks softly on the shore, the pebbles make a sloughing sound that soothes me.

It's just me and Cal, alone. He hands me the bottle of champagne. 'Last drop? You've earned it.'

I tip up the bottle and swallow the final mouthful of fizz, the bubble popping on my tongue, going up my nose. I giggle and Cal sticks the empty bottle in the sand. Lacy waves caress the shore and the usual roar is a whisper.

'Cal?'

'Mmm.'

'There's something I have to ask you.'

'Sounds serious,' he says but he doesn't look serious. He's trying not to smile and I'm trying not to be put off by that sexy half-smile.

'I was in St Trenyan the other day, buying some last-minute stuff for the launch and I saw you and Isla at the Harbour Cafe. She seemed upset, only you didn't mention it and I wondered.'

He heaves a sigh. 'Wondered what?'

'Oh, I don't know. Nothing. I was worried that something really bad had happened.' I scrabble frantically for a reason why

I'm interrogating him, anything other than the truth. 'That the Cades had caused more trouble.'

'For Isla and Luke? Why would Isla have anything to do with them? I'd had to go into the solicitor's to sort out the probate on my dad's estate and Isla walked out of the office as I went in. She'd been to collect some documents for her parents. They're selling their house in Penzance.'

'I didn't realise, but you had your arm around her and I thought . . .' Saying the words out loud feels a bit pathetic yet my feelings are anything *but*.

'Isla's parents are splitting up – which is why her father decided not to come back from Dubai for the engagement party – and she was upset so I took her for a drink to calm her down.'

'Oh, I see. I'm sorry.'

'Yes, it's rough on her. She loves them both and she's gutted they're splitting up but maybe it's for the best.' He smiles. 'Nothing we can do about it, though.' He scrambles to his feet, holds out his hand. 'Now, do you fancy a swim?' he asks.

'After the last time?'

'It's different tonight. It's calm and I'm not drunk.'

'It will still be cold.'

'True, but we have the fire to warm us up.' He pulls me to my feet. My limbs feel liquid. It could be the champagne but I think it's relief at hearing his explanation for meeting Isla. I'm paranoid. Of course he cares for her but there's nothing more going on. She still loves Luke.

'I haven't brought my bikini. Come to think of it, I haven't brought my bra . . .'

'I haven't brought my bra, either, and if you think I'm going home in soggy boxers, you can forget it.'

He strips off his T-shirt while I unbutton my skirt. He pulls his jeans over his legs, almost overbalancing and we both laugh. In seconds, he's naked, standing with his hands on his hips, impatient for me to do the same but I can barely take off my clothes because my hands are shaking so much.

A lump settles in my throat. I've seen him naked before, in his bedroom and later, after the party, but I was too angry and hurt that time to really *look* at him. This is different. Moonlight silvers his body, casting him in a new light. He's slim, still, but has filled out in the past few months. I see the man Isla and half of Cornwall fell in love with and I know he can never be mine. Not forever, but for tonight. The smart and sensible thing would be to walk away but I'm feeling neither of those things.

'Come on, I'm getting cold,' he says.

That dark trail of hair leads downwards. *Wow.* 'You could have fooled me . . .'

He glances down with a wicked smile that shoots fire through my body, warming me instantly. 'Oh, this is nothing. What are you waiting for?'

I can forgive him the male pride, and forgive myself for setting all my worries about Isla aside. The desire that's building deep inside me is too much. I want him. So I pull my T-shirt over my head and drop it on top of his jeans, followed by my knickers.

I shriek as his palm connects, hard, with my bum.

But he's yards ahead, running for the waves, whooping. 'Last one in clears up in the morning!'

I run after him, the sand cold under my soles, the wind tugging at my hair, shrieking over sharp stones and shells and slippery jade seaweed. Into the foam and deeper, knowing I'm already lost.

'Oh my God!'

Water laps Cal's chest. 'Wuss!'

I wade in, tensing every muscle, trying not to squeak. It's a low form of torture but Cal dives forward, and under, popping up a few feet away, gulping in air. The water laps at my waist.

'It's a lot easier if you get it over with,' he says, yards away, scattering water from his hair, like Mitch does.

'I'd rather do this in my own time.'

He dives again while I step forward, wincing.

Cal pops up next to me, grabs my legs and ducks me into the water. I barely have time to close my mouth and eyes. I strike out, swimming away from him, anything to get the blood pumping and distract me from the cold sea. I thrash around, heading for the moon which hangs suspended over the horizon like a yellow Chinese lantern. I paddle back towards Cal, my heart pounding. Gradually, the water stops being torture and becomes a cool, sensual pleasure, soothing away the last remaining tensions of the day.

'Told you it was better to plunge right in,' he says, treading water alongside me.

'I had no choice!'

He laughs. 'Come on, I'll race you to back to the beach.'

'What if I don't want to race?'

'It'll keep you warm.'

We run up the wet sand to the jumble of weed and debris at the tide line and beyond. At the top of the beach, powdery sand sucks my feet down, slowing me. My lungs almost burst and I collapse onto the sand by the embers of the fire.

'Why did I ever let you persuade me to do that?'

Cal kneels by the fire, raking it into life again. 'Because you're as mad as I am.'

'Not possible.'

I look at him, naked and lit by the glow of the fire pit. 'You have sand on your bum.'

Laughing, he glances back and dusts the grains off his bottom though some still cling to his skin. There's a glow in me as fierce and hot as the fire. His eyes reflect the flames, flickering back at me. I shiver, but not with the cold. Cal holds out his hand and lowers me onto the sand, pulling me back against his chest.

He breathes in my hair. 'You smell good,' he murmurs.

'What? Of seaweed?' Nerves force a joke from me.

'Of sex,' he whispers in my ear. 'It's beautiful.'

'You can't say that.' Trembling now, I rest my hands on his thighs. They tense and the hair is softly rough. My whole body quivers like the flames of the fire.

'Can you feel me?'

'Cal, we can't do this.'

'Shhh. Just go with it.'

He grazes my shoulder with his teeth, and the brief pain is replaced by a pleasure that melts my bones. Thank God Mitch is safely snoring in the cottage. This is a moment when I don't want him to protect me from Cal, though I probably need him more now than ever before.

Cal pulls me onto my knees and we're a breath apart, my knees sinking in the sand. The surf sucks at a shingle bar, the tide is coming in and I can't hold back from Cal or myself a moment longer. It's me who kisses him, tangling my fingers in his hair, urging my tongue into his mouth. This isn't our first kiss but it's the first one when I've been fully aware of how hot and sweet and wonderful his lips and mouth are. He pulls me tight against him, and his need for me is urgent, nudging my stomach. He feathers tiny kisses on my neck, my shoulders.

Every part of me feels molten hot and his fingers close gently over my breast and his voice is a hot whisper on my bare skin. 'Demi. I want this but . . .'

'I want it too.'

His face blots out the moon as he lowers me down onto the sand.

The sun streams through the open window and the breeze brings the tang of sea and salt into the bedroom. I pull the sheets over me, realising with a blush that I'm naked. Cal's side of the bed is cool and empty. We came up to the farmhouse from the beach and had sex again – and again – until it was light. I thought I'd never fall asleep but after the excitement of the day and night, I must have drifted off. It would have been nice to wake up with him but I don't believe in perfect endings.

Going to sleep with him is enough for now; and what happened between us was so amazing, it must herald a new start for us. After last night, I have new hope that he *is* over Isla. Hugging the pillow to my face, I smile and blush at the memories of the past night.

I wonder where Cal is. Perhaps he's gone for an early ride or he's started clearing up from yesterday. Maybe, like me, he couldn't sleep. I think I'll go downstairs and find him, make breakfast or take coffees and toast into the yard. He'll be hungry after his ride. I know I could eat a horse myself.

I dozed off again and dreamt that Cal had come back into the room but thought I was asleep. I knew he thought that from the way the boards creaked softly as he moved carefully around the room and the soft jangle of his car keys as he collected them from the dresser.

In my dream, I knew he didn't want to wake me up. My eyes and body ache with the tension of pretending to be asleep. I heard him lift the latch and close the door softly behind him, and the stairs creaking as he went downstairs.

The spluttering of the Land Rover trying to start outside the window wakes me up. *Properly* wakes me.

So I *hadn't* dreamt the part about Cal going out.

The engine coughs into life, the gears grind and it rumbles out of the yard. It labours up the track to the farm gate, and dies away until there's quiet again in Cal's bedroom. My eyes focus on the freshly painted ceiling, and the new window frame. Claws clatter on the stairs, a tail thumps the panels. Cal didn't shut the bedroom door properly.

A cold wet nose nudges my leg under the sheet.

I pull it back over my head and mumble. 'Morning, Mitch.'

Kilhallon seems unnaturally quiet when I walk out of the farmhouse munching on a crust of buttered toast. The tables are still set up in the barn but one end of the bunting dangles loose

278

and the bins overflow with paper plates and empty plastic cups. The clearing-up will have to wait because there's no sign of Polly, who's having a lie-in after yesterday's efforts.

Mitch scampers off across the field, driven mad by the scents left by yesterday's doggy intruders. He hardly knows what trails to sniff first. The sun is out, though the sky's a washed-out blue compared to yesterday's deep colour, but Kilhallon is just as beautiful to me. In fact, the peace and silence are more intense and wonderful than ever.

I wonder if Cal fancies taking a picnic down to the cove? It'll be busy as it's Sunday but we know a few secret spots you can reach through the gorse. I could rustle up something from the leftovers in the fridge. We could open a bottle of fizz.

In the yurt field, the tents are still zipped up tight and the campfire is a pit of grey ash, stirred into a cloud by the wind. The sea sparkles like a tiara as families carry their buckets and spades and body boards along the coast path to the beach. Some of them linger by the stone barn that will become 'my' cafe, wondering what it will be, and I want to scream for joy.

My cafe. OK, Cal's cafe, but I'll be running it and responsible for it being a success. It's actually going to happen. I wish my mum could be here to see this. I want to tell her, and my Nana Jones. I want to remember them even if it makes me cry but Cal would understand. That's why I love him, because he understands me without me saying anything, without him saying anything back. We don't have to speak, we just *know*.

An unknown number flashes up on my phone. I'm in two minds whether to answer it but it could be Cal, I suppose. He might have broken down and had to use a public box.

'Hello?'

'Demi! Good Morning!' I hold the phone an inch from my ear.

'Hello, Eva.'

'Have you recovered from yesterday yet?'

279

'Just about. I think.' I hope I'm making sense, I'm so shocked to hear from her this soon.

'Oh, is that Mitch I can hear?'

'Yes, I'm out walking with him on the coast path.'

'How divine! I can picture you both now, strolling through the meadows with the waves crashing against the cliffs. Bliss.' She heaves a big sigh. 'How I wish I was there but alas, I'm slaving away. On a Sunday morning! Get me. Now, listen, my lovely, I've been speaking to my editor on the Sunday supplement and she practically drooled down the phone at the idea of featuring you in their lifestyle section.'

'A Sunday supplement?'

'Yes, darling. Those magazines with all the leaflets that come out with the big papers.'

'I know what one is, but . . .'

'That's not all. I've got another editor who wants to have you in her Day in the Life feature in her upmarket coastal magazine and I might – don't get your hopes up – get you onto *Country Days*. My son-in-law is a friend of the producer and when he heard me raving about you last night, he said he might send a film crew down there.'

'Me on the TV?'

'*Possibly* on the TV. You and Cal, and Mitch, of course.'

My mind reels. 'I – don't know what to say.'

'You don't have to because I've already said "yes" to everything, I thought you wouldn't mind. Now, we'll have to get cracking if we're going to hit the deadlines for the Sunday supplement and the mag so I've arranged to send a photographer and stylist down this week. I've checked out the forecast and it looks good for Tuesday afternoon so they'll be there at two. OK?'

'I ought to ask Cal first.'

'Oh, he won't mind, I'm sure.' Eva breezes on. 'I'll cc him in on the email but I'm sure he's got enough on his rugged hands as it is, with the build. He won't have to worry about a thing because we'll take care of everything. We'll bring the clothes and the props.'

'Clothes and props?' I realise I'm starting to sound like a parrot but Eva is sweeping me along like a tornado.

'Of course, sweetheart. My editor friend thought we'd combine the shoot with a fashion feature. The mag has a big advertiser who rocks the coastal/country vibe so I thought: why not kill two birds with one stone? You'll get to dress up in some gorgeous things, darling, and I know with your figure and that amazing hair, you'll look stunning. Not to mention Cal – do you think he'll mind us styling him a little? He's magnificent raw material, of course, but with a little more tweaking, we'll have the yummy mummies of the Home Counties fighting each other to have him light their campfires for them.'

I blank out the part about Cal being tweaked and styled. It's the pace that's scaring me. 'But we're not ready for glamping until September and the first few cottages won't be ready until later in September either.'

'Heavens! September will be here before you can blink. Viola and Sean will see you on Tuesday. I'll email you their numbers. I'm not sure Viola has ever been beyond the M25 so do be gentle with her, won't you?' Sharp yaps almost deafen me.

'Betty! Betty, take that out of your mouth at once, you little horror! Sorry, I have to go, Demi, Betty's trying to eat a frog. Woofs to Mitch! Toodleoo.'

Mitch flops down at my feet. I think even he's exhausted after that conversation and he didn't hear it. Now all I have to do is let Cal know he's got to be styled and groomed. I hope he's in a good mood after his early morning trip.

My mood sinks when I see Cal's expression as I walk into the farmyard. He slams the door of the Land Rover and I decide that now isn't the time to tell him about the fashion shoot. Mitch gives him a friendly nudge in the crotch and he manages a smile which fades as I grow nearer.

'I didn't think you'd be up yet,' he says.

'It's almost eleven and Mitch needed walking. You must have gone out early?'

'Yeah, you were asleep and I thought you needed a rest after yesterday.'

'That's very thoughtful of you. Where did you go?'

'I had some stuff to do in St Trenyan.'

'In St Trenyan? On a Sunday morning?'

'Yeah. I went to the tip with some rubbish from yesterday.' He sounds a bit down although he's probably just knackered.

'OK,' I say as Mitch sniffs around the barn. 'Are you all right?' I ask.

'Why wouldn't I be?'

'You don't seem yourself.'

He laughs. 'What? Arsey? Insulting? I can be, if you like.'

'You look like you have something on your mind. You're not regretting last night, are you?'

'No. Why would I do that?'

'Because . . . I don't know.' He pulls me into his arms and kisses me again. My body fizzes with a mix of delight and misery that makes me want to throw up. I've longed for him to do the things that boyfriends and girlfriends do. Longed for him to hold me like it's a normal thing between us. But it's not normal and I'm reminded again that Cal can probably never be my 'boyfriend'. The word makes me cringe. I could never tie Cal Penwith down with a name. The thing is I don't know what will happen to us, which is exciting and terrifying.

When he stops kissing me, I decide to take my chance.

'As a matter of fact, I do have something to tell you,' I say, seizing the moment. 'While you were out, Eva Spero phoned. She wants to send a photographer and his um . . . assistant down on Tuesday to do a feature on Kilhallon for one of the big Sunday magazines. Apparently they have a deadline.'

'That sounds high powered. Well, we're too busy, of course,

but we can't pass up a chance like that.'

'That's what I thought. They want to put us in another women's mag too and there might even be a chance of getting on the TV. I hope it was OK to accept?'

He blows out a breath. 'Sure. Wow. You really did make an impression on Eva. I heard she's a tough customer under all the fluffy charm.'

'She can be a bit overwhelming but she seems OK to me.' We walk back to the farmhouse and it occurs to me that sooner or later, Polly will know something has changed between us. Should I tell Robyn? Will Cal tell Isla?

'So you'll be around on Tuesday for the shoot then?'

'I'm doing some lime plastering on the cottages but I'll be here if you need me. I'm sure you can handle it all on your own.'

'Well, I think they were hoping you'd be in the photos too. You are the owner of Kilhallon, after all.'

He bursts out laughing. 'Me? No way. No one will want me breaking the camera, I can promise you that.'

CHAPTER THIRTY-FIVE

'You want me to wear *what*?' Cal's jaw drops as Viola, the stylist, holds out a dark black waistcoat and a pair of maroon jeans in front of his body.

She arrived this morning on the overnight train from Paddington together with Sean, the photographer. I picked them and their gear up in the Land Rover so I've had some time to get used to them. Cal, however, is shell-shocked that he's expected to star in the shoot.

'We're going for the retro artisan look. Like a fusion of coastal hobo and horny handed son of toil?' Viola trills, a little hysterically. I think she's a little afraid of Cal, though I can't think why.

Cal looks completely blank.

Sean, the photographer, grins. 'She means she wants you to look like a workman, only a Shoreditch version of a workman.'

His jaw tightens and he wipes his dusty hands on his work overalls.

Viola unfurls a roll of brushes and make-up. 'And of course, you wouldn't mind if I did a teeny bit of work on you, just for the camera? I promise you won't be able to tell on the pictures. Just a trim of the stubble, a little tinted moisturiser, some styling wax on the ends of your curls. We can Photoshop anything else but we want max natural if poss.'

Viola quivers like a sea lily as Cal glowers at her. 'Tinted *moisturiser*?'

'Of course, you're *very* handsome, but in the pictures, every little flaw shows up. It would, like, only be an enhancement of your natural good looks?'

'It's for Kilhallon,' I say, desperate to laugh but worried he might bolt.

'Jesus,' he mutters. 'I should be plastering a wall.'

'It will all be worth it when you see the pictures, I promise,' trills Viola.

'I've managed to give Mitch a bath,' I say. 'And I thought he'd look good in his cafe scarf.'

Frowning, Viola fiddles experimentally with Cal's hair while Mitch lays his head on his paws with a sigh.

'At least someone agrees with me. Now we both look bloody ridiculous,' says Cal.

Viola stares at him as if an amazing idea has struck her. 'Cal, has anyone ever told you that you look like Aidan Turner?' she says, in awe.

Cal frowns. 'Never heard of the bloke. Now can we *please* get on with this?'

Two hours later, Cal is showered, styled and ready to explode. My jaw aches from smiling and Mitch has peed up Sean's tripod and been banished from the shoot. Viola has changed our outfits four times.

'Right. I think that's enough. I have to get back to the walls,' Cal pleads.

'I know. Almost done. I promise . . . What is *that*?' Viola points to the chimney of the ruined engine house.

'It's the old engine house that belonged to the tin mine.'

'And you like, actually, *own* it?'

'It's part of Kilhallon land, yes,' says Cal, unable to avoid a smile.

'It's incredible. So rugged, ruined, decadent and so tragic. We *have* to shoot some pics there. Sean, come on.'

Sometime later, I'm draped over the granite engine platform in a floaty dress, while Cal stands a few feet away – fuming but also sexy as hell in a pair of dark tweed trousers and a leather waistcoat.

'OK. Look out to sea, Demi, like you're waiting for your lover to return. Anxious but hopeful. Cal, you stand apart, as if you are secretly in love with her but you know she's been taken by someone else. We're going for pensive, forlorn yet manly and resigned.'

I hear a hiss from Cal but maintain my innocent hopeful gaze.

Viola purrs encouragement while Sean takes different shots. 'Yes, that's great. You look gorgeous. Like a real child of nature.'

'He's right, you could model. You've got the height and figure and those looks. Like a brunette Lily Cole.'

'Me? Lily Cole?'

Sean smiles. 'Sure. Can you cross one leg over the other, please, and flick your hair back.' He walks up to me and arranges my hair over my bare shoulder. 'Like this.'

'She's stunning, isn't she, Cal? I keep trying to convince her to let me do a portfolio for her.'

'Why not?' Cal says, sounding bored. 'Look, is this going to take much longer?'

'I'm not interested in modelling. I've got enough to do here,' I say firmly. Could Cal be jealous? The thought makes me want to break into a grin but I'm supposed to be longing.

Sean glances up from the camera. 'OK, I think we're almost done but we need a couple more to be sure. I'll move the tripod.'

Viola scampers over, waving a comb and aerosol can. 'Cal, can I touch up your hair a teensy bit, please? A quick spritz of lacquer?'

While Cal coughs and splutters in a cloud of noxious spray, I spot Robyn riding towards us along the coast path. She turns her horse through the gate in the field and trots over.

'Great. Now Robyn can see me,' Cal mutters.

'OK. Ready!' Sean shouts.

Viola skips back to Sean who looks into the camera and frowns. 'Cal. Could you manage to look a bit more engaged, please. Imagine that Demi has spotted her lover sailing into the harbour, safe and sound, and you know now all is lost.'

'I think he means he'd like you to look brooding,' says Viola.

'Like a hen, you mean?' Cal cuts in.

'Not quite. Mean and moody. You lost out on the hottest babe for miles to a rugged fisherman,' says Sean, obviously enjoying himself. Robyn waits by the gate on her horse, shaking with laughter.

Viola calls to Cal. 'You know, Cal, I think a little touch of eyeliner would really help the look.'

Cal folds his arms and scowls at Sean and Viola. 'Over my dead body,' he growls.

'Hell yes! Hold that look!' Sean shouts, and the motor drive whirrs. 'Yes, that's a wrap. Brilliant. Eva is going to *love* this.'

'Right. That's it. I have work to do.'

Cal stomps off over the field.

Robyn, who has spent the past ten minutes, trying not to wet herself laughing, finally leads her horse over to us and bursts into giggles again.

'Oh dear. Have we pushed him too far?' Viola asks, packing up her make-up kit.

'I think the eyeliner tipped him over the edge.'

'Cal has *eyeliner* on?' Robyn asks, astonished..

'Sadly he said that was going too far,' Viola says with a sigh. 'It's a shame but the photo editor can probably add it. He'll look amazing in the pictures. You too, Demi.'

It's all getting too much for me now. 'Um, thanks. I'm going to get changed at the house.'

'OK. I'll finish up here with Sean.' Viola scampers off, happy with her day's work.

Robyn leads her horse back to the house with me. 'You look fantastic,' she says.

'Thanks.'

'And Cal was so funny. He hated having to pose.'

'I suppose he'd better get used to it. I don't think he'd thought about the marketing of Kilhallon at all. I think he thought he could do all the building work and people would just turn up. Thanks for the graphics you did. They're awesome.'

'Glad to help. Andi loved designing them.'

'How are things going for you?'

'Mawgan hasn't caused any trouble but she still isn't speaking to us. She let us have the flat but she won't come round and avoids us. Andi's upset, of course, but hopes she'll get over it. Their dad is speaking to her again so I guess that's a good start.'

'Does she know that you and Andi designed the logos for Kilhallon and helped us at the launch?'

Robyn shrugs. 'I don't know. Possibly. Mawgan finds out everything somehow.'

'How's it going with your families?'

'Andi's dad and Mawgan seem to have accepted us living together though they're hardly putting out the bunting when we visit. My dad seems OK with us being together, and he asked me and Andi round for Sunday lunch the day after the launch. Shame Cal couldn't stay, of course; he was too busy here.'

'Cal visited Bosinney on Sunday morning?' I ask, puzzled.

'Yes but he'd left before Andi and I got there. Dad told me that he was surprised to see Cal after how manic things had been on Saturday at the launch. Cal brought over some old photos and personal items that belonged to his dad that he'd found when he was clearing out his wardrobe. He thought my dad might like to have some of them as mementos. Then Dad went to play golf but Cal stayed to chat to Isla, apparently.'

'Oh, yes, I did notice he'd finally sorted out his dad's stuff,' I say then kick myself, hoping Robyn doesn't realise how intimately acquainted I am with Cal's bedroom.

'Isla got back from London late last night and she stayed over to keep my dad company. He misses me, which is kind of nice.'

I smile. 'I bet he does.'

'Luke was meant to stay too but I heard he didn't come back until it was light.' Robyn grimaces. 'He was drinking at the country club, though he'd promised Isla he was only popping out to have a half with a friend who was getting married but in the end, he'd had too much to drink to drive or walk home. Poor Isla, she was furious.'

'I'll bet . . .' My voice trails off because my mind is working overtime.

'Didn't Cal tell you he'd been over to Bosinney?' Robyn adds after a pause.

'No, I mean, yes, he said he'd been out on Sunday morning. I had a lie-in . . .' My face flushes, but Robyn watches me keenly. I'm no good at hiding my feelings and my confusion must show on my face.

'Are you and Cal, you know . . . dating now?'

'No.'

'Some people think you are. After the party and the launch, you sort of look as if you could be a couple. Come on, Demi, you can tell me. Has Cal said anything?'

'*Said* anything. Like what? You mean declare undying love?' I laugh. 'Why do people have to assume we're together when all we do is work together?'

Robyn carries on talking, but all I can think of is that Cal lied, or at least was economical with the truth about his trip to St Trenyan. He probably *did* go to St Trenyan on the way to or from Bosinney, although he was only out for a couple of hours max. Why wouldn't he say he'd been visiting Isla? Perhaps he didn't even know she'd be home from London?

I grimace as we reach the farmhouse. 'Let me get out of these clothes. I never thought I'd be so glad to be in my overalls again.'

After a good night's sleep, I've thrown myself into my important to-do list. I was just googling personalised dog outfits in the office when Eva calls me, exploding like a firework in my ear.

'Demi, darling! The photos are incredible. You look amazing.'

'Um. Great. I'm glad. I can't wait to see them.'

'Oh, I'll whizz them over now. Look, I have a proposition for you . . .'

'What?'

'I know you'd never leave Kilhallon but *if* you ever did think of moving on to even bigger and better things, I'd snap you up in a flash.'

I drop the towel on the chair. 'What?'

'Come and work for me in my cafe. You can have some training from one of my top patisserie chefs and we'll give you some coaching in the PR side of things. You're young, you're gorgeous and talented – I'm sure with my backing and your talents we could get a book deal. We could do a Cornish recipe book and a book of doggy treats. We could have a brand, "Proper Dog" or "Betty 'n' Mitch". It would be amazing.'

'That's fantastic but I don't know what to say. Would it mean moving to Brighton?'

'Well, yes, sweetheart, but you'd love it here. This is the seaside just like Kilhallon and the customers would adore you. I'd make sure you had lots of coverage.'

'But Brighton's not the same. I'm sure it's lovely but it's not Cornwall.'

'You'd get used to it in two wags of Mitch's tail, and Betty's if she had a proper one, the little love. I know this has come as a shock, darling, but why not think about it? Opportunities like this don't come along very often, do they?' Eva's tone hardens subtly. 'Unless, of course, there's something else tying you to Kilhallon. Or *someone* else?'

'I – well, not really. Thank you for thinking of me. I'm a bit overwhelmed at the moment. Can I think about it?'

'Of course, but don't take *too* long. Anyway, ciao! Love and woofs to Mitch.'

The phone goes dead and the silence in the study is a huge contrast to Eva's onslaught. She's mad as a box of frogs, I think, but clever too and famous and oh – *why* am I even hesitating to accept her offer? She's giving me the chance of a lifetime and I'd be crazy not to accept but it would mean leaving Kilhallon before it's even up and running, and leaving Cal too.

I lay my head on my hands on the desk, wishing the world would stop so I can get off. Things are moving so fast, with my job and Cal, I can hardly think straight. The phone buzzes again and it's a few seconds before I realise that it isn't mine, but Cal's.

Isla's name flashes up.

The phone buzzes and throbs, demanding his attention but he's down at the building site. Should I take it to him? Or take a message? Ignore it?

I press the green button.

'Cal! Thank God I got you!'

'Isla, it's Demi.'

'What?' she asks sharply.

'I'm sorry. Cal is out on site somewhere. He left his phone in the office and I didn't know whether to answer it or not.'

'Oh . . . Never mind, then.' Her voice has a brittle edge.

'D'you want me to give him a message?'

'No. Just tell him I called, please.'

'OK.'

'Thanks. Bye.' Click.

I stare at the phone. Before I have chance to tell Cal, an email from Eva arrives.

Wow. The photos from the shoot are amazing. Is that really me? I thank Eva, but reply without saying anything about her offer. I then print a couple of pictures and go out to find Cal.

He smiles when I arrive, near the field where he's labouring for the builders as they put the final touches to the shell of the cafe. The sound of hammering and shouts of the builders echo across the field. Cal lays down his wheelbarrow and walks over to meet me.

'How's it going?' I ask.

'Good. It's almost watertight now, so the following trades can start on the inside.' He looks proud and takes a swig of his water bottle.

'Great. Eva sent the photos.'

He grimaces.

'Want a quick look?'

'Do I have to?' He takes the print out and his grimace softens to surprise and something resembling pleasure.

'Well?'

'I suppose they're not bad.'

'They'll be great for business.'

'Yes.' He hands them back.

'And while I was in the office printing them, Isla called your mobile. I saw her name and so I answered it. I hope that was OK?'

His brow furrows. 'What did she want?'

'Nothing urgent.' Am I lying? Isla sounded upset. 'She asked me to tell you she'd phoned.'

He pauses then nods. 'Thanks. And thanks for bringing the photos. I'm glad you forced me into doing them now.' He catches my hand and brushes my mouth with his lips while the builders' backs are turned. 'You look gorgeous in those clothes, but even better out of them.'

His sexy words and the tingle of his lips on mine, make me long to drag him off to bed right this moment, still dusty and hot in his work clothes. For a moment, I feel as if I could fly back to the house. I should drink in the smouldering looks he gives me, and the kisses when no one is around. I should be enjoying Cal sneaking over to the cottage at night to make love to me.

Instead I keep wondering about Cal's 'secret' visit to Bosinney and now what to do about Eva's offer. I've lost count of the reasons there are to grab it with both hands. I can't think of a single one in favour of staying – except, of course, I'm in love with Cal Penwith.

And *that* is the biggest reason of all to leave.

I'm worse than Mitch with his bone, gnawing at the questions, and 'ifs' and 'buts' until I feel ragged. I should ask him why he went to Bosinney and lied about it. I *must* ask him. I have to for my own peace of mind because I'm blowing that one little lie – not even a proper lie – out of all proportion and I'm sure there's an explanation. I have to hold on to my instinct. Tomorrow, I'll ask him.

Despite all my doubts and uncertainties, I stayed over at the farmhouse again last night. Polly has gone to see her new grandson and won't be back for a week. I woke up to a breeze rattling the new window and the realisation that I need to talk to Cal about his visit to Isla or I'll go mad. While I'm getting dressed, I hear voices downstairs. It sounds as if there are people talking in the kitchen but the words aren't clear. The kitchen door creaks open and voices are more distinct. Cal's deep tones and a woman's, low and not quite steady.

Hastily pulling my T-shirt over my head, I tiptoe to the top of the stairs, cursing every creak of the ancient floorboards, listening.

'Cal, I'm so sorry to do this but I didn't know who else to turn to.'

'It's fine. Look, sit down, you don't look well,' he says. 'Can I get you a drink? Tea? Coffee? A glass of water?'

'No. No, I couldn't drink anything. I feel sick.'

'You're not pregnant, are you?'

'No! That would be a disaster. I mean, a disaster at this stage. We're not married yet, not that I care about being married before

I start a family, but I'm so busy with my work and having a baby would be terrible timing with Luke working so hard too.'

I hold my breath and will my heart to stop thumping so loudly though they couldn't possibly hear it from up here. By creeping down a few more steps I can hear what they're saying but every creak of the stairs makes me wince. Then again, I doubt if Cal can hear me any more because Isla is crying.

'Sweetheart. What's the matter?'

'Oh Cal, I have to tell you though he'd go mad if he knew I was pouring out my heart you. Luke's in trouble.'

'What kind of trouble?' he asks, more sharply than I'd expect.

The kitchen door gently swings with each gust of wind, cutting off parts of the conversation like the dodgy radio signal in the Land Rover.

'He's been working late a lot and spending a lot of time at the country club.' There's a long gap and then I hear a sob. 'I'm worried he's having an affair with Mawgan.'

'Then he's out of his mind. I could kill him!' Cal's voice is savage and I clamp my hand over my mouth to stifle a gasp.

'No. Don't say that. You can't say that . . .' Isla pleads.

'I can't help it. He'd have to be blind to do that to you. What the hell makes you think he's seeing her?'

'It's not one thing; he's spent so many nights away from home since we came back from holiday. He told me he was at the country club with the boys at an all-night drinking session but there's been some gossip around St Trenyan. He's been seen coming out of Mawgan's place. I can't be sure but she's had her claws into him in every other way so I can't help but think the worst.'

Isla sobs and Cal makes soothing noises, the kind he's never made to me, perhaps because he's never *had* to, or he thinks I've never needed him to. It's true that I don't want his pity and comfort.

'What will you do?' His voice is taut with anger, I can almost feel the tension in his body even though I can't see him.

'I don't know. Like you say, I could be wrong about Mawgan.'

'I'm so sorry, sweetheart. I wish I could help you though I don't know how. Why didn't you tell me all of this before?'

'Because you have enough troubles of your own. Because this is my mess and I'll have to sort it out. Because you have other things and people to worry about. Besides, you are helping, just by being here. By being you. Oh, Cal, I've missed you so much.'

I grip the banister, my heart in my mouth. I hate Isla at that moment. I hate myself for the jealousy that keeps me here, terrified of hearing something that will break my heart. I hate feeling this vulnerable. Now, when I thought I was stronger than ever, I'm weaker. I was better off on the streets: me and Mitch, with no one to care for us or anyone to care about.

'Right now, I'm only worried about you. Here, dry your eyes.' Cal sounds tense. Maybe I missed part of his reply to her. I just don't know.

There's a pause and I hear Isla saying. 'I shouldn't have come here.' Her voice is firmer but tinged with regret.

'Yes, you should. I'll always be here for you, Isla. Whatever happens. You know I'll always care for you. More than care . . .'

'You can't say that to me and I've said enough too.'

A window rattles upstairs and the kitchen door slams shut. My heart almost jumps out of my chest. Damn. I'll never hear them now! I've no choice but to creep down the rest of the stairs and stand at the bottom, ready to dash back up again if there's any sign of them coming into the corridor. I listen until I think my ears will bleed.

Isla's voice is stronger now and falsely bright like she's putting on a brave face for Cal's sake.

'Where's Demi?'

Cal hesitates. 'Asleep, I think.'

'Oh, is she having a lie-in?'

'She might be. I don't really know. She's in her cottage.'

I grip the banister tighter. So Cal couldn't bring himself to tell Isla that he slept with me last night and that I'm in his bed – supposed to be in his bed – at this moment?

'She works hard,' Isla says. 'You're lucky to have her.'

Whatever Cal says in reply, sounds like a grunt to me.

'I'm glad she can't see me like this. I'll go now. Thanks for listening to what I had to say.'

'You can always talk to me.' There's a gap and Isla sniffs loudly then blows her nose again. 'I'll take you home,' he goes on. 'And maybe you should tell Luke about your suspicions. It might shock him out of whatever's going on in his head. For what it's worth, I think you're wrong about Mawgan and Luke having an affair.'

'You can't swear to that.'

'No, I meant what I said. Luke may be stupid and reckless, but he's not completely barking mad. He can't be, to be marrying you.' Cal's voice lightens, jollying her along. 'I'll always be here if you need me, at Kilhallon. For any reason.'

There's a pause, during which I'm pretty sure Cal is holding Isla and comforting her. He may be kissing her. I just don't know but my imagination is working overtime.

'I shouldn't say this . . .' she starts again. 'I hope I haven't made a mistake with Luke.'

I hold my breath.

'No. You haven't. You think that now because you're so worried about this affair, which is probably nothing, but I'll help you all I can,' he answers.

'I know you're right but it's hard not to have doubts.'

There's an agonising silence again, when my imagination works overtime then I hear Cal saying gently. 'Isla, sweetheart, let me take you home.'

The sound of the back door opening jolts me into life. I run back upstairs, jump into bed and drag the pillow over my head, hoping the world will go away.

*

'Well, aren't you going to say something?'

We're in Cal's study when I tell him about the job offer the next morning. Nowhere seemed the ideal place so I just went for it after he'd come in from working on the new buildings.

'I don't know what to say, other than, congratulations.' He sits down at his desk, leaving me standing like I've been called into the boss's office for an interview. Yet he doesn't know that I'm testing him, gambling on his reaction and I already know that I have just lost.

I force a smile. 'I haven't accepted the job yet.'

'But you're going to?' He shakes his head at me. 'You *have* to, Demi. You can't possibly pass up an opportunity like this.'

'No, I suppose not, but it's a big decision.'

'What? Leaving a half-built Cornish holiday site that may or may not succeed – to train with a celebrity food guru? Leave the bright lights of Kilhallon for the back end of beyond that is Brighton?' He smiles. 'I'm surprised you aren't already on your way.'

'Well, I only found out a couple of days ago but I needed time to take it in. Consult Mitch and ask you. But if you really think I should go. I thought you might want me to stay, need me to stay. Who'll run the cafe?' I try to sound cheery but every word makes me sick. I picture Polly's face too.

'What I really think doesn't matter. This is amazing for you, Demi. I can't stand in your way.' He gets up. 'Congratulations again.'

'So that's it, then?'

'What's what? You don't think I'm going to ruin the rest of your life by asking you to stay? I care for you too much to do that.'

'Do you?'

'What?'

'Nothing,' I mutter, fighting back tears.

'Will you come over for dinner with me tonight? Polly's away . . .'

'No. No, I can't. I have a lot to do, a lot to think about. Goodbye, Cal.'

His hand is on my arm but I shake it off. 'Wait. I'll cook. We'll open some more champagne. Treat ourselves.'

'Sorry. I've lost my appetite.'

'Wait! Demi!'

'So now I know,' I tell Mitch when I'm back in the cottage. 'If he'd wanted me to stay, he would have asked me. Instead he literally breaks out the champagne.'

Mitch licks a tear from my face and stares curiously at my snotty nose and red eyes. 'In fact me leaving Kilhallon must be the answer to Cal's dreams because he can go to Isla now. She's free, she loves him, and I'm off the scene – not that I was ever on it – and yet . . .' Mitch barks, worried now, and I bury my face in his fur, knowing that it's too late. Kilhallon has become part of me.

CHAPTER THIRTY-SIX

For the final time, I take Mitch's lead from the peg by the cottage door. Though he was dozing in his basket, his ears prick up at the rattle of the chain. He looks at me, hopefully, asking:

'Are we going somewhere?'

'Yes, boy. We are.'

He nudges the backpack on the door mat. His tail thumps against it and he gazes up at me. I can tell what he's thinking: this will be a long walk with lots of rabbit holes to explore and trails to sniff and other dogs to meet and greet and boss. I clip the lead to his collar and sling the backpack on my back. It's heavy, much heavier than I remember but I am going soft now. I've spent too long in one bed.

'Are you ready?'

He jumps off his bed. I pick it up and he tilts his head on one side: where would he be walking that needs a dog bed?

'You'll get used to it. We both will.'

If I don't get out of the cottage this second, I may never have the courage to do it and the misery and uncertainty will grind on and on until I'm forced to leave. Not that I think Cal will catch me and try to stop me: I saw him leave this morning and I know he's gone to Bosinney. Polly told me he'd left without even having any breakfast although she had no idea the effect it would have on me. I haven't even told her I'm going, and that stabs at my heart. I'm a coward but I just can't face the pain of any more goodbyes.

Lugging a rucksack and a dog bed, while trying to control a confused and excited hound, is harder than I thought. Even harder when you can barely see because tears are streaming down your face. Closing the door on the cottage that's been my home for these past few months was one of the hardest things I've ever had to do. Almost as hard as letting my mum go; even harder than walking out on Dad.

I reach the old milestone on the moor and know I only have a mile to the main road and the bus stop. From there it's half an hour to the station and six more hours to Brighton. I kept the mobile Cal gave me: I'll call Eva on the train and tell her I'm on my way. She said I could have a flat there too.

Mitch marks the milestone as usual and roots around the brambles as I readjust the dog bed under my arm. He starts barking at another couple who have two lively Labradors in tow.

'Shh, boy! Come on. We need to catch the next bus or we'll be here until tomorrow.'

Mitch scampers off back the way we've come, barking madly.

'Mitch!'

He streaks right past the Labradors.

'Mitch! Come back!'

I drop the dog bed by the milestone and run after him, the pack banging on my back, and then I see him.

Cal running towards me, Mitch dancing round him, barking wildly.

I turn around, running away from them both towards the milestone, to the road and to freedom. Freedom from having to witness Cal loving Isla.

'Demi! Wait!'

His voice is louder.

I turn round. 'Mitch!'

Cal stops. Mitch stops too, the traitor.

'Come on, you stupid *stupid* dog!'

I walk off, glancing behind, tears of frustration in my eyes.

'Demi, come back.'

Mitch stands in the middle of the path, getting further away by the second so I stop too.

I feel rather than hear them catching me up. I become aware of the skylarks singing and the coconut scent of the gorse and the waves pounding the base of the cliff.

Mitch trots up, squeezes past me and sits at my feet.

'Do you want to tell me what all this is about?' Cal says gently.

'You know what it's about. I'm leaving.'

'What? You're taking Eva's job?'

'*You* told me to take it. You said I'd be mad not to go.'

He can't argue with that and my faint hope that he'd come to make me stay, disappears again.

'But . . . but . . . you might have told me first, not just stormed off like this!' He's angry and I don't blame him.

'I know I should have worked my notice. I ought to have given you time to find someone to replace me.'

He gasps. 'How could I ever find someone to replace you?'

'There are loads of people who could do my job. Hundreds.'

'Not someone as bloody rude and awkward and argumentative as you. Not someone who'll put up with my moods and my frankly lunatic schemes. Not someone with a dog who can charm the pants off hardened businesspeople. I need you, Demi, and no one else will do.'

'Eva's business needs me more. She told me.'

'She could never need you in the way I do.'

He reaches for me and no matter how much I try to damp it down, my heart starts beating harder and my hopes soar.

'I heard Isla tell you how much she needed you and I know you went to see her this morning. I saw you go out.'

301

He throws up his hands in frustration. 'Is that what's upset you? You're right. I have been to see her but my visit was partly business. She told me that she wants to use Kilhallon as a location for some of the scenes in the new costume drama she's shooting.'

'Oh, right. That's nice . . .'

'*Nice*? It'll be fantastic PR and very good income to tide us over the early days. There's more too. Some actor friends of hers want to hold their hand-fasting ceremony at Kilhallon.'

'Hand fasting? Who?'

'It's top secret for now but it's . . .' He names them and my gob is well and truly smacked.

'Those two are engaged? You *are* kidding!'

'Nope. They're going to rent the entire site for a weekend next spring but they're happy for us to announce it well before then. They wanted something completely wild and natural and they're going to donate the rights from the gossip magazine coverage to an eco-charity. You can imagine what the publicity will do for Kilhallon's street cred.'

'It will be incredible. We can get bookings from that for years to come.'

He smiles. 'I'll need someone to manage the catering, of course, and look after the celebs.'

'Wow. I'd love to . . . I can't wait to meet them . . .' He grins at me.

Realising what I said, I'm furious with myself. 'But I'm not staying.' And if his visit to Isla was 'partly business', I need to know what the other part was too.

'Of course not. You've had this amazing job offer that's way too good to turn down. And you can be a celeb if you go to Brighton.'

'Yes.'

'Even if I tried to persuade you to stay which, of course, would be wholly selfish of me and even if I was selfish enough to try to persuade you that Kilhallon was a better prospect than Spero's.

If I did that unforgiveable thing of destroying this opportunity, the way I've messed up other people's lives, you still wouldn't stay, would you?'

He looks at me, and I can't look away. 'No.'

'Because?'

'Because you went to see Isla at Bosinney after we had sex and lied about it to me. Because, after we'd spent the night together in your room, I could hear you and Isla talking in the kitchen.'

His brow creases. 'You heard our conversation from upstairs?'

'I have very good hearing,' I say, too embarrassed to admit I crept downstairs to eavesdrop on them.

'You must have.' The way his eyes crinkle at the corners lets me know he's teasing me just a little but I don't care how sexy and kind he's being, I still want to hear the truth.

'You were afraid to tell Isla about us after we slept together,' I go on, because there's no point in holding back now. 'I heard you lie to her about me being in your bedroom and you lied to me about taking her home and you want me to go to Brighton because it's easier for you if I leave.'

He groans. 'I'm not proud of lying about sleeping with you but considering the circumstances and the state Isla was in, I decided it wasn't the best time to announce it. The only reason I wanted you to leave Kilhallon was because it would be easier for *you*, not me. It wouldn't be easy for me to let you go. It would be agony, if you must know!'

'I can't stay here, knowing that. I heard her tell you she'd made a mistake.'

He shakes his head sadly. 'We all make mistakes, bloody great big ones, but that can't be changed. I can't just *un*love someone I've been so close to all my life but that doesn't mean I'm *in* love with her or because she might suddenly become available, I'd go running.'

'I'd understand if you did get back together. I *do* understand. I'd hate it but I'd accept it. That's why I'm leaving.'

He groans. 'Why the hell didn't you tell me you'd hate to leave? We're both stubborn, proud, stupid idiots, too afraid of admitting what we really want. Because what we *really* want rarely makes any kind of logical sense, it's a gut instinct and it may all go wrong. I've taken so many risks in my life, and some have got me into trouble, some have lost me everything but I – you – we're not the kind of people to live by rules and do the sensible thing. Are we?'

'No,' I say croakily.

He holds me. 'I have my pride. I'm not going to beg. But you know now. Read my lips. Even if Isla was leaving Luke, and she isn't, we're not getting back together. There was a time and a place when I wanted her more than anything in the world but that time is behind me.'

Do you know, I almost believe him? I want to believe him so much.

'Is it?' I can hardly hear the words myself.

'Too many things have happened and too many people have come into both our lives since. Too much has changed for her – and me.' He touches my cheek and I'm ashamed to say it's wet. 'Like you and Mitch.'

'Mitch?'

'Yes. You must know I've fallen for him.'

'No way. He wouldn't fall for you. He's a one person dog.'

'He's made an exception for me.'

'What makes you think that?'

'Just a feeling. The way he looks at me, the way he sniffs my crotch. A man can tell. You said it yourself, I'm hot.'

I start laughing and immediately hate myself for wavering. There's still too much I don't know about Cal; so much I want to believe in but can't quite bring myself to.

'So why did you go and see Isla this morning?'

'She asked to see me. She wanted to tell me about the actors and the shoot and to tell me she and Luke are going to try to make a fresh start in London, away from Bosinney, and Mawgan and her tribe.'

'I didn't realise.'

'It's for the best. Uncle Rory is selling the business and, more importantly, I can't imagine Kilhallon without you. I might fall apart again if you leave now. If that's selfish, then so be it, but please don't leave me.'

Mitch barks, nudges my jeans. I glance down, almost dizzy with the U-turn of emotions from misery to happiness. Cal pushes my hair away from my neck and kisses me. Mitch yips.

'Mitch. Can you *please* be quiet? This is important.' Embarrassed by my tears, I turn away to my backpack. 'I'll get him a chew.'

'Demi.' Cal grabs my arm. 'I wanted to show you something. I had it made ages ago and I was going to show you the other morning but then you told me about the job offer and I didn't dare.'

'Show me what?'

'You'll have to come back to Kilhallon to see it.'

He opens his hand, his palm waiting for mine. I only have to take it. My fingertips connect with his, because I have to trust someone sometime. I have to take a risk, we both do, no matter how crazy or mad or stupid. With my rucksack over his shoulder, he leads the way past the engine house, and the restored cottages. Mitch gallops through the heather and brambles. We stop by the side of the building that will be the cafe. It has walls and a roof now, and windows covered in blue plastic protectors. It's waiting for someone to give it life.

'Shut your eyes and no peeping.' Cal insists.

With my hands over my eyes, I hardly dare to breathe but I can hear the waves crashing against the cliffs and the gulls crying and I feel my heart thumping hard.

'OK. You can open them now.'

Cal whips a tarpaulin off a sign that was propped up against the wall of the cafe. It's blue and white and it carries the logo of the tin mine and the dog. And in big, bold, bright letters it reads, simply:

Demelza's.

'Remember I once told you that all the best ideas about Kilhallon were yours?' he says, softly. 'That was a lie because *everything* that's good about Kilhallon comes from you. It's taken me this long to finally admit it . . . and I have the right to admit it and no right to keep you here. But even if you leave, the sign stays. The name stays. You've made your mark on this place and on me.'

His voice drifts away and there's doubt in his eyes. He isn't sure what I'll do, he really *does* need my approval. 'I know we discussed names for this cafe. Many names but I've come to realise that there can only be one.'

If I could speak, I might, but I can't because my throat has developed a mysterious lump.

'Well, aren't you going to say something?'

'It's . . . it's perfect.'

'The sign may be, the name is, but I can't promise that our lives will be. The next few months will be tough, the next few years even harder, but if you can take that and stick with me, I'll be more than happy.'

Mitch sniffs at the sign and for a moment, I think he might, then my shoulders slump as he skitters off in search of more interesting places to pee.

Cal bursts out laughing and so do I. He pulls me into his arms.

'So will you?' he whispers. 'Be sticking around?'

I put my arms around his back and hold him like I might never let him go. He's right. This isn't perfect but it's a start. A very good start.

'You know, I think I just might consider it.'

ACKNOWLEDGEMENTS

Before I wrote my first novel in 2005, I had no idea how much of a team effort it takes to get the raw manuscript of a story to a bookshop shelf or e-reader. Now, I do! So, first of all, I want to thank my amazing editor at Avon Maze, Natasha Harding, who has been so insightful and sensitive in all her editorial suggestions from the moment she rang to say she loved *Summer at the Cornish Cafe*. A huge thanks to the lovely Eloise Wood too, who has steered this book through to publication, and to Joanne Gledhill, my keen-eyed copyeditor. I've felt in safe hands with the editorial team from the get go and any author will tell you how precious that is.

The Avon social media and marketing guys are officially awesome. Thanks to their fun and creative ideas, I've had to visit Cornwall to eat pasties and surf all in the name of work.

Even before Natasha saw the book, my agent, Broo Doherty, encouraged and supported me in writing it. We've been partners in this business for eleven years now, though it may seem like 111 to Broo at times, and I owe her a huge amount. You'll notice I include her in the same line as my husband, John, and my daughter, Charlotte, and my parents, as sometimes they have to put up with the same levels of writerly angst from me. I hope they also enjoy the very happy times this book has delivered – especially the 'research' trips to gorgeous Cornwall!

Thanks also go to Nell Dixon, Elizabeth Hanbury, Wendy Dixon, Janice Hume, Anne Cooper, Kim Nash and all my 'superstars' for their suggestions, the laughs, the coffee and cakes. Also to Lynsey of Debenhams Cafe, Lichfield, and Marie from Mim's Cafe, Bridgtown, for their cafe advice, and to the Budget Food Mummy blog for her recipes.

I'd like to mention the Cornish actor Rory Wilton (of *Poldark* and *Doc Martin* fame among others) for letting me use his name *only* for Uncle Rory and being a source of fun and actorly gossip on Twitter. I also owe my author friend, Bernardine Kennedy, and her daughter Kate, a doggy cake for letting me put their adorable Pug, Betty, in this book.

Finally, I send a huge hug and much love to Rowena Kincaid of the BBC TV documentary series *Before I Kick the Bucket* for reminding me through her courage and humour to get on with loving, living and doing what makes us happy – including writing *Summer at the Cornish Cafe*.

Demi's Recipe Notebook

I thought it would be fun to include some of the recipes which Demi, Sheila, Cal and even Polly might serve up at Kilhallon Farm and Demelza's. They're simple recipes that I hope you can try at home, and on a budget (just like Demi). One or two are from our own family recipes and some come from the fantastic Cornish food blogger Budget Food Mummy.

Cheese and Bacon 'Cornish' Pasty

(Recipe and introduction reproduced by kind permission of the Budget Food Mummy blog https://budgetfoodmummy.wordpress. com)

OK, so it's not officially a Cornish pasty because it doesn't have beef in it but it's a pasty made in Cornwall by a Cornish person, so that will do! Pasties were a staple diet for tin miners. Eating pasties is as normal to me as eating a sandwich so I eat a lot of them. However, I don't eat beef so this recipe is a great alternative. I don't actually make them that often but since I live in the town which was once famous for tin mining, I thought I should include the recipe. No pressure.

Makes 6 medium pasties.

For the pastry:
450g strong white flour (large pinch of salt optional)
100g butter
100g lard
175ml water

1. Put the flour and salt (if used) into a bowl. Cut off a quarter of the lard and rub into the flour. Grate or slice the rest of the lard and butter into the mixture and stir with a knife. Pour all the water in and stir until absorbed. Knead a little and leave for at least 30 minutes in the fridge before using.
2. Flour your work surface. Split the pastry dough into six equal balls. Gently roll them out into a circle about the size of a side plate/small plate.

For the filling:
200g cheddar cheese, grated
4 medium potatoes, cut into small cubes
1 small turnip, cut into small cubes
1 onion, finely sliced
10 rashers of bacon, cut into squares
salt and pepper

1. Place a mix of potato and turnip in a line on the centre of the pastry. Place the bacon, onion, cheese and salt and pepper on top. Be careful not to over fill the pasty or else it will all come out.
2. Fold the pastry over, making a semi-circle. Pinch the end and roll and pinch all the way round the edge until you get to the other end. If you can't get the hang of crimping (it takes practice) you can always use a fork to press the edges together.
3. With a fork, poke some holes in the top to let air escape. Brush

the top with either milk, egg or even water. Cook at 200C for 30–35 minutes.
4. Recipe for a veggie alternative filling can be found on the Budget Food Mummy blog.

Fish and Cornish Seaweed Pie

(Recipe and introduction reproduced by kind permission of the Budget Food Mummy blog https://budgetfoodmummy.wordpress.com)

Sea salad seaweed is very nutritious and it's optional to use the seaweed but I do recommend it!

Ingredients:
350g mixed fish (I used smoked haddock, cod and salmon)
2 leeks, chopped
1 carrot, chopped
zest of half a lemon
2 large potatoes, cubed
25g unsalted butter
25g plain flour
600ml milk
1 tbsp tarragon
1 tbsp sea salad seaweed

1. Preheat oven to 200C. Cook the potatoes in a pan of water until soft. Drain and return to pan. Add the seaweed and thoroughly mash together. Set to one side.
2. For the sauce, melt the butter in a saucepan. Stir in the flour and cook for 1–2 minutes. Take off the heat, gradually whisk in the milk and add the tarragon. Return back to the heat and bring to the boil, stirring occasionally.
3. Place the fish, leek, carrot and zest in an ovenproof dish. Pour over the sauce and top with the mashed potato. Cook in a preheated oven for 30–35 minutes.

Demi's Nan's Fly Pastry

This is an old family recipe from my husband's late grandmother who was actually called Elsie.

Ingredients
1 block of ready-made short-crust pastry, i.e. Jus Rol (unless you want to make your own as Demi and Nan did, naturally)
currants or raisins or a mix of both
butter
sugar

1. Preheat the oven to 450F, 230C or gas mark 8.
2. Divide up your pastry block into two equal-sized pieces and roll each out thinly to the same size.
3. Carefully lay one of the pastry pieces on a greased baking tray.
4. Spread the pastry with your choice of dried fruit.
5. Dot the fruit topping with tiny pieces of butter and sprinkle it with sugar.
6. Damp the edges of one piece of pastry with water. Lay the second pastry piece on top.
7. Seal the edges well and trim off any excess pastry.
8. Bake in the oven for approximately 20 minutes.
9. Dredge the cooked pastry with caster sugar and cut into squares or slices.
10. Be sure to keep the fly pastry out of Mitch's reach.

Cornish Potato Cakes

(Recipe and introduction reproduced by kind permission of the Budget Food Mummy blog https://budgetfoodmummy.wordpress.com)

I usually make these with any leftover mashed potato or a few potatoes I have left that I have no use for. It is a traditional Cornish recipe, although I have never found anywhere in Cornwall that makes them so let me know if there is anywhere!

Makes 12
Costs 7p per potato cake

Ingredients
4 medium potatoes, peeled and cubed
100g plain flour
50g butter, soft
2 tbsp milk
1 tbsp parsley
black pepper

1. Boil the potatoes until soft, mash and leave to cool.
2. Meanwhile, rub the butter into the flour until it turns into crumbs.
3. Add the mashed potato, milk, parsley and black pepper to taste. Stir together until well mixed. Divide into small patties.
4. In a large frying pan, fry the potato cakes in a little butter. Cook for 5 minutes on each side or until golden brown.

Demi and Cal's story continues . . .

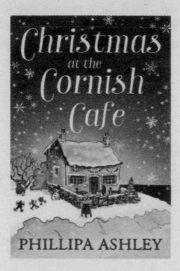

As snow settles on the Cornish Cafe's roof,
romance simmers inside . . .
Ebook available now

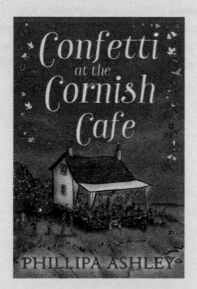

This is no ordinary wedding . . .
Ebook coming May 2017